W9-BQX-490

"If you don't drop that bloody Kraut pistol, I'll blow your head off."

Trotter stood at the top of the stairs. On the far side of the gallery was another figure. He stood stock-still, both hands raised gripping a revolver pointing straight at the main door.

Arthur pulled the trigger twice, and Ebenskrumm went tottering backward, in funny little steps, his hands thrown up, his automatic pistol spinning through the air.

By this time, Dobson had also moved, locking his right arm around Hackstead's throat. His hand clutched his own left triceps and the left hand pushed hard onto the back of Hackstead's head.

"Drop that gun," he muttered, "or I'll break your neck."

The Luger fell to the floor with a dull clunk and SS Oberführer Bernhard Hackensteiner's cap slewed from his head.

"There's no way," he croaked. "No way that disaster can be averted now."

THE DANCING DODO

John Gardner

BANTAM BOOKS
TORONTO · NEW YORK · LONDON · SYDNEY · AUCKLAND

*This low-priced Bantam Book
has been completely reset in a type face
designed for easy reading, and was printed
from new plates. It contains the complete
text of the original hard-cover edition.*
NOT ONE WORD HAS BEEN OMITTED.

THE DANCING DODO

A Bantam Book / published by arrangement with
Doubleday & Company, Inc.

PRINTING HISTORY

Doubleday edition published May 1978

Bantam edition / August 1980
2nd printing . . . July 1985

All of the characters in this book are fictitious, and any resemblance
to actual persons, living or dead, is purely coincidental.

All rights reserved.
Copyright © 1978 by John Gardner.
Cover art copyright © 1985 by Robert Cuevas.
*This book may not be reproduced in whole or in part, by
mimeograph or any other means, without permission.
For information address: Doubleday & Company, Inc.,
245 Park Avenue, New York, New York 10167.*

ISBN 0-553-25135-X

*Bantam Books are published by Bantam Books, Inc. Its trademark,
consisting of the words "Bantam Books" and the portrayal of a
rooster, is Registered in U.S. Patent and Trademark Office and in
other countries. Marca Registrada. Bantam Books, Inc., 666 Fifth
Avenue, New York, New York 10103.*

PRINTED IN THE UNITED STATES OF AMERICA

H   11 10 9 8 7 6 5 4 3 2

Author's Note

A full list of acknowledgments for assistance with this book would run to many pages. For technical assistance I must mention in particular the Ashford & Tenterden Recovery Group, especially Mr. David Buchanan and Mr. R. C. Freeman. Others who have given me time and facilities include Ted Hine, Denis Bateman, Ted Mercer DFC, Philip Reed and Mr. J. E. Stretch of Air Data Publications. If I have wrongly interpreted any of their technical knowledge—other than parts which I have knowingly "bent" under the unwritten license of an author of fiction—the fault lies with me and not them.

There are others, two of whom I cannot in all conscience pass by: my old friends Fred Nolan and Simon Wood. The latter has now worked with and for me as part-time and mainly unpaid researcher for over ten years.

Also, a deep debt of love and gratitude goes to my wife, Margaret, who, while in pain, and against medical advice, checked, rechecked and typed the bulk of the manuscript.

This is a work of fiction and sometimes the fiction crosses and merges with fact. As far as I am aware, the finding of the *Dancing Dodo*'s wreckage and the investigation and events which followed have not happened...yet. Some other events described in these pages have taken place.

Finally, the greatest gratitude of all goes to the one whose name appears on the next page. He gave up the bulk of his summer holiday in 1976 in order to act as general dogsbody around our home, ran important errands and assisted with both the manuscript and incidental graphics. He did this without any thought of self, and there were many times when I could not have remained cool and concentrated without his good humor and sharp wit. This book is dedicated...

To
My Son
SIMON
Without whom . . .

The dodo never had a chance. He seems to have been invented for the sole purpose of becoming extinct and that was all he was good for.

WILL CUPPY
How to Become Extinct

1

Children found it, though the birds and animals of Romney Marsh must have known of its presence for a long time.

It lay toward the southwesterly extremity of the marsh, but away from the main thoroughfares, burrowed into the soft earth which yielded to it, the reeds parting for its passage, swallowing it as though welcoming the metal shell and its occupants back to their natural state.

Then it settled into the silt, not quite submerged. Slowly the plants and grasses, the lichen of time, crept over its broken shape. No human came by or spotted it from the air.

Eventually it became just another irregular lump, slight on the flat landscape, and, when men did pass by that way again, it was accepted as part of the natural topography.

Though nobody had actually seen it happen, there must have been some—older people—who had an inkling, never mentioned openly, that it was there. Perhaps a noise in the night, a minute change in view; for within a decade the place became known as Dead Clump. Younger folk, interested in the locality years later, wondered how it got that name yet was not so marked on any map. Those who had a feel for such things knew that there was something not quite right.

Then, one Sunday afternoon early in the June of 1976, four boys on an aimless bicycle ride pulled off the rough track which ran near, piled their machines against the forward part of the hump, squatted down to drink a bottle of fizzy lemonade and then began to poke around, climbing onto the long mound, transforming it in their imaginations into whatever took their fancy.

It became their slave galley; then an armored vehicle patrolling the dangerous streets of Belfast; their castle keep; and, lastly, the treasure island of their fantasy.

Robert, tow-haired, brawny, at twelve years old their natural leader, was Long John Silver. The others became his pirate crew searching for Flint's treasure.

They measured imaginary lines by the sun, pacing out an arbitrary number of steps through the uneven roots and growths until they found a chosen spot.

"Look, there's already a hollow here," shouted young Robert, wrapped in his appointed role. The sun was hot and high, dredging what moisture it could from the ready land, and only a mild breeze fluttered in from the direction of the Channel, moving the few galleon clouds slowly against an endless depth of sky. "Dig here, men. It's here you'll find Flint's gold."

They scrabbled with their hands, the smallest boy wielding a short piece of stick, pulling aside clods of earth and weeds, enlarging the hollow. Presently it was wide enough for the bold Robert to insert an arm almost to the elbow. They were engrossed in the game, transported into a world of their own, more believable than that of home, school or television.

"There's something down here." Robert's fingers encountered an object which seemed to be caught, tight and out of view. He stretched farther downward, exploring the shape, pushing to get his fingers fastened around whatever it was.

"Pull it up then, Cap'n," urged another boy.

"Flint's gold," muttered a third.

The smallest boy waved his stick and chanted tunelessly, *Fifteen men on a dead man's chest . . .*

"I think it's a root." Red-faced, Robert tugged, panting, for a moment coming out of the fantasy.

He twisted the hard lump and there was the sound of wrenching, like the cracking of dry wood splintering at a turn. Pulling back, he withdrew what appeared to be a hard-packed clod of earth. The others gathered around, peering and pushing as though this was treasure indeed.

They crumbled and brushed away the caked earth.

"It's an old glove."

"Falling to bits. Old glove. Old leather glove."

"Full of earth and twigs though." Robert turned the shredding glove, shaking it, holding the worn leather by the finger ends.

It fell out at their feet: a partially preserved human hand, the bones plain and splintered where Robert had wrenched it from the arm.

MINISTRY OF DEFENCE
WHITEHALL

FROM: The Director of Security Coordination
TO: Group Captain R. C. Waterford DFC RAF
Director
13 (AIR)
DATE: Tuesday 29 June 1976

Following our brief telephone conversation I am
sending, by hand, our file on the subject concerning
wreckage of a B-26 Martin Marauder discovered in
Romney Marsh on 6 June 1976. Owing to the
information recently to hand, and the fact that one of
the bodies discovered in the wreckage was initially
identified as a former member of the Royal Air
Force, you are instructed to appoint a suitable
officer to work closely with the Investigating Officer
appointed by the U. S. Military Air Attaché's
Office—Colonel Bernard Hackstead USAF.

You will be aware that the circumstances concerning
these discoveries have already been subject to
speculation and some sensational stories in the press:
I refer in particular to those newspapers which have

4

made it their business to dig into local stories of apparitions and other paranormal phenomena claimed to have been experienced in the area over the past thirty years. I must therefore make it clear that the evidence contained in the enclosed file must remain classified for the time being and the whole, or part, can only be made available to non-subscribers at the discretion of the U. S. Military Air Attaché's Office, U. S. Embassy, Grosvenor Square.

2

They called Dobson back off leave, his first since the posting from the squadron to the Ministry of Defence. He got into London late in the afternoon of a hot July Thursday, feeling frustrated, sticky and overdressed. Everyone seemed to be on his way home, and as his taxi jerked up from Paddington Station into Praed Street, the accumulated heat and smell of the city wrapped itself around him like a solid envelope, even though the cab windows were open.

The West End simmered and boiled, caldron-hot, traffic barely moving and the stink of exhaust fumes rising to choke the throat. Aggravations spilled irrationally into Dobson's head. Couples moving, or greeting one another, on the early evening sidewalks carried with them small hints of illicit pleasure. Dobson reflected that a bit of illicit pleasure would not come amiss. Every bar they passed became a mirage oasis. It was all quite unreasonable, for Wing Commander Dobson was not a man to give himself lightly to the sins of the flesh.

He leaned back and angled his face toward the inflow of air, running a glistening finger around his tight collar, loosening his tie a fraction. It was like being strapped into a strait jacket after the freedom of the last ten days, but the telegram had said

6

he was to report immediately, and nobody would take kindly to his arriving at I3 (Air) in jeans and a T-shirt.

Not that Intelligence 3 (Air) was any big deal. It was not even part of the Ministry of Defence's Whitehall complex, and Dobson had never—in the two years he had served with this outfit—been under any illusion regarding its lack of importance.

I3 (Air) was a backwater, a kind of hospice for Royal Air Force officers whose careers were either dead or under sentence. He had no doubts about that. Even though the court of inquiry had not specifically blamed him for what had occurred, Dobson knew well enough that it was doubtful if he would ever fly operationally again; and certain that he would never again have his own squadron. They had attached more blame to the station commander, and he, being a very senior group captain, had been retired early. One officer had come out into the open and said that while it was the station commander's duty to monitor mess bills, the squadron commander—in this case, Dobson—should have drawn the group captain's attention to young Pole's heavy drinking.

The cross which Dobson carried was the stark fact that he had never allowed himself to recognize that Brian Pole was on the bottle. In moments of bleak despair he was certain that the whole business had been his fault. Two lives and two jet aircraft were the negotiable price paid for his own executive weakness.

I3 (Air) was housed in Clapham, above a grocery store on St. John's Hill. It was not marked as a Ministry of Defence office, which, Dobson supposed, allowed some people to unleash their fantasies about being an underworld cohort of the nation's security services.

There was no lift, only a steep flight of stairs which at this time of day was alive with secretarial people on their way down.

A young porter inhabited a glass-fronted box at the top of the North Col—as they jokingly called the staircase.

"Enjoy your leave, sir?" He was always far too bright, and inclined to take liberties regarding rank.

Wing Commander Sugden sprawled at his desk in the main office, in shirt sleeves, but looking worn and irritable. Makepiece leaned against the wall behind him. When Dobson came in they stopped talking. A pair of conspirators planning a palace revolution.

"You took your time," said Sugden, his face even more malevolent than usual. They did not like each other. Sugden had been an intelligence officer on a squadron for the early part of his career, and with I3 for nearly six years: a fixture. Dobson suspected that he had made a terrible error somewhere and now spent his time attempting to make I3 into a viable, useful department. Sugden was very thick with a lot of people from DI5 and 6. Dobson thought that spoke for itself.

"The wire didn't reach me until noon."

Sugden shrugged as if to say that it was not his fault.

"Must be a bore traveling British Rail after all those hours on jets." He never left it alone.

Makepiece asked if he had enjoyed his leave.

"Could've done with the rest of it." He had the beginnings of a headache just above the eyes. "What's the flap?"

"Not for me to say." Sugden enjoyed small mysteries. "The old man wants to see you. Snooping job, I gather."

Dobson raised his eyebrows in query, nodding his head toward the door of the group captain's outer office.

Makepiece signaled an affirmative. "Said he'd wait until you arrived. Ann of a thousand days and nights is still there as well. Perhaps that'll make up for being recalled."

Ann was a civilian: a civil servant, thirtyish, cool, efficient, with dark hair which she usually wore in a severe style, pulled back and tied at the nape of the neck. She had a friendly manner, though this often seemed to be at least partially obliterated by her businesslike approach to work. As though she wished to call attention away from some imagined deficiency in her features, Ann West wore large-framed, almost goggle-like, spectacles. She also had a penchant for black stockings and boots, which Makepiece read as an outward sign of deep inner sexual passion. Typical of Makepiece.

She was typing as Dobson went in.

"Thank God," switching off the machine. "He was hoping you'd be back before this."

"The wire didn't reach me until noon." Dobson felt he should have been able to rephrase it: the words seemed to come out like an excuse, learned by heart yet not entirely believed.

"I don't suppose it matters, only he's dining with the U. S. Air Attaché and madam keeps phoning to make sure he's not going to be late."

Dobson had never really considered Ann in any light other than being Waterford's P.A. Now, looking at her closely, he could see that she was an attraction he had noticed as little as the coat rack in the outer office.

Behind the large glasses there were bright and amused

gray eyes. Maybe her nose was a shade angular, but the skin was clear and the lips inviting—the face oval. She should, literally, let her hair down.

The thoughts slid in and out of his mind like a blink of neon. He put it down to the heat, and before he could ponder further, she had buzzed through to Waterford.

Rivers Crenham Waterford was within a few years of retirement. Big, gray, aesthetic and earnest, he had been a photographic-reconnaissance wizard in World War II, both on the ground and in the air. I3 was a bit of grazing pasture for his last few years, but he took it seriously and never seemed to grasp the essential truth that his department was entrusted with only routine or obvious work.

"Come in, David, sorry to drag you back. Needs must, I'm afraid, needs must. Thought you might have been here before this."

Waterford spoke in a kind of sharp military shorthand, never using two words when one sufficed, yet often repeating the ones he used, therefore canceling out the desired effect.

"The wire didn't reach me until noon." Dobson let the sentence trail off this time. Though it was the exact truth, he had wholly ceased to believe it.

Waterford waved him into a chair. "Not much time, I'm afraid. Dinner with the U. S. Air Attaché. We've a puzzle on our hands. Called you back because the Americans want a liaison man. Bit of detective work really." He gave a snort which might possibly indicate humor, then leaned across to pick a buff file from his "in" tray. He pushed it forward toward Dobson, lining it up with the edge of the desk. "Need to assimilate that. Classified, but you can sign for it, take it home, out of the building. Not missile sites or high-fly penetration. Mystery from the past, David. Great secrets of the war. The reason we called you back. Special interest in air history '39-'45, I recall."

"I did a paper on it, yes. Yes, I've read a lot ..."

"Good. A B-26. Marauder. Wreckage discovered in Romney Marsh, four, five weeks ago."

"Oh yes, sir, I read ..."

"Fine. All news clippings're in there, and the confidential stuff. Local amateur group dug it out with the police. Our people took over a couple of weeks ago. Probably have to go down there, take a look for yourself. Recovered six bodies, what's left of the poor devils. Five U. S. aircrew—dog tags check. One Royal Air Force officer. He checks as well. Aircraft number checks with squadron, and they've lifted one engine. That number checks. Identified the squadron and crew. Even started tracing relatives." He paused, as though embarrassed by the information he was about to communicate. "Probably some executive foul-up. It's a long time. Over thirty years. Fact is, David, there's no record of that particular aircraft ever going missing, and it would seem that some of the identified dead, including the Royal Air Force officer, are still alive."

3

Later, Dobson could not recall feeling any apprehension. Only a slight irritation at having been hauled back from leave to inquire into what could only be a wild paper chase. Files and records would have to be checked and rechecked, located, sorted. That could be the only answer.

Waterford was still speaking. "You'll be working with a Colonel Hackstead. USAF, of course. Spoken to him on the phone; haven't met him. He's got the additional information, and you'll stay with him until the investigation reaches a conclusion. You'll both render a full report—to the Ministry, through me, and to the Americans."

Dobson found himself nodding. A telephone rang in the outer office.

"Fixed up a first meeting with Hackstead at ten tomorrow morning. Grosvenor Square. Room 552. Suggest you read through that thing before you meet him." He reached out and laid his hand, palm down, fingers outstretched, on the file. "Questions?"

"You talk about identifcation, sir. I presume it's not visual identification of bodies." As he spoke, Dobson realized the stupidity of the question.

"Identification disks. Dog tags. After thirty years in the ground you can't—but it's all in the file." Waterford sighed. "Some of the remains are well preserved, though. Extraordinary."

"Sounds as though it's a matter of sifting documents."

"Imagine so."

"I'm to report progress to you, sir?" This time he felt it was the right kind of question.

Waterford rose, leaning forward, hands on his desk. "Only when it's over. Let Sugden handle everything else. You'll need extra subsistence, I suppose, keeping up with the Yanks while the pound sterling bounces around. Use your head."

"Sugden's briefed, sir?"

"I'll fill him in. Hope it's not too much of a chore. Must get on now. Must get on."

Dobson came out of the office clutching the file, smothered with the same sense of fatigue which had hit him at Paddington Station.

There was no sense of anxiety. No way of knowing about the darkness that lay ahead.

The flat near Charlotte Street was a Ministry letting. Even with flying pay Dobson could never have afforded the place otherwise. Someone, he considered, must be making a pretty penny out of the government.

It was hot and smelled musty after being closed up for ten days. He opened the windows, dumped his suitcase in the bedroom, locked the file in the old bureau, switched on the immersion heater so that he could have a bath and went down to the little supermarket in Great Titchfield Street, where he bought the bare essentials, calling in at the pub on the way back.

The telephone rang just as he started the bacon and sausage under the grill.

"Wing Commander Dobson?" The voice had a touch of humor embedded somewhere between the brain and larynx.

Dobson hesitated.

"It's Bud Hackstead," said the voice. "Just checking that our meeting is on for the morning."

Dobson said it was.

"Neat little problem, don't you think?" Hackstead had an almost British intonation. There was no aggressive sharp edge.

"I only have the bare bones as yet."

The chuckle at the other end of the line was almost

infectious. "Plenty of bare bones, Wing Commander. Say, I can't call you that all the time. Looks like we're going to be working together for a few weeks. I'm Bud."

"David."

"Okay, David. We meet in 552 at ten tomorrow, and I've taken the liberty of arranging a helicopter out to the site in the afternoon. If you've gone through the file you'll see they've only removed what's left of the engines. The fuselage is still there. We should really go see it before they take that away."

"Fine. To be quite honest I haven't been through the file yet. They've brought me back off leave for this."

"Join the club."

The bacon had shriveled to three tiny curled pieces and the sausages were burned black when he got back to the kitchen. It was after eleven o'clock before Dobson was bathed and in bed with the file resting across his knees.

On the preliminary page was the initialed list of subscribers—six names: amazingly few for a file coming over to I3 (Air). As a rule, files which arrived at Clapham had been read by half the Ministry, and the subscription lists usually looked like a petition to unseat the government.

The title page read:

Introductory Report on Wreckage of B-26 Aircraft Discovered Romney Marsh 6 June 1976.

4

The first pages contained the newspaper clippings. Then followed a whole sheaf of glossy photographs. The first in the pile showed a flat landscape with the long mound in the center and men in shirt sleeves examining the ground. Some carried spades.

It was that initial picture which, oddly, brought the first sense of dread, a sudden chilly crawling of the scalp. The photograph reminded him of something else, something already seen, though he could not place it immediately, a sense of being on the brink of unspeakable disclosures. The feeling was so strong that Dobson actually shuddered as he lay there in the hot bedroom, the familiar night sounds of the city floating in from over the roofs.

It was a strange sensation, for the worse photographs, which followed, produced in Dobson only a sense of curiosity. The first picture continued to play tricks with his imagination for a long time to come.

The next prints were of the wreckage: pieces of metal, twisted and marked; a series of shots building up the whole of what remained of the fuselage, with close-ups showing parts of the shell which still retained traces of markings and serial numbers. Then, separate photographs of individual pieces of the machine.

It began to get really unpleasant when the camera captured the interior of the fuselage. The flight deck, though crushed and smashed, was still recognizable, the instruments and controls identifiable, as was the pathetic bundle crammed between the starboard bucket seat and the bent longerons. The flying suit was shredded almost to rags, revealing bone and, perhaps, pieces of flesh.

There were three other shots taken within the aircraft, among the dirt, corroded metal, rusted wire and shattered aluminum. One body appeared to be propped up about a meter from the flight deck, on the port side. Only what was left of the top half was visible, and the legs seemed to have gone altogether. Another, on the starboard side, almost a third of the way back from what had been the nose of the airplane, was recognizable as human only by the half-disintegrated skull, together with one leg and foot, now clean bone sticking grotesquely from a concertina of rags and splinters.

The fourth was stretched out below what had been the deck turret. The clothes on this one were, incredibly, intact: the leather jacket and boots clearly visible, while the body itself looked like a strange shrunken tanned thing, the facial features quite clear though all pushed together in a mound of wrinkles, the bones showing through.

There were photographs of two other bodies, almost unrecognizable as such. One had been found toward where the tail and elevators should have been. It was now just a collection of bones. The other had been taken from the earth among the wreckage of the tail cone, almost three quarters of a mile from the fuselage—merely pieces of a human skeleton.

An aerial photograph showed the aircraft had been scattered widely. It was accompanied by a carefully plotted chart tabulating each large piece of wreckage. The chart was also marked with six dark crosses, indicating the position of the bodies. A line ran from each cross. At the end of the lines were names, carefully printed—Lieutenant Daniel Goldberg USAAF; Captain William E. Potts USAAF; 2/Lieutenant Herbert J. Flax USAAF; Flight Lieutenant Frederick Free RAF; Master Sergeant Wilcox Pride USAAF; Sergeant Edward B. Sailby USAAF.

The next section contained photostat copies of the statements made to the police by the four boys who had found the wrecked relic, then several police reports, and a number of pages given over to comments by members of the Aircraft Recovery Group.

Over thirty sheets listed identified parts of the wreckage and the exact position in which each piece had been found. After that came the preliminary identification of the type of aircraft.

A statement from the leader of the Recovery Group showed that by June 12 he had come to the conclusion, from visual evidence only, that the aircraft was a B-26 Martin Marauder. He noted that U.S. markings were still partially visible on the port side of the fuselage, together with traces of a squadron or individual code letter which could have been a C or an O. There were also indications of some form of insignia on the port side of the nose, directly below the cabin: yellow paint and what might have been the outline of a bird.

More positive identification came only after technicians from the Royal Aircraft Research Establishment at Farnborough arrived to examine, and start lifting, the remains of the big Pratt & Whitney R-2800-5 power plants. The port engine, they declared, would probably yield nothing, the metal being so seriously fused and blocked. The starboard engine was a different matter, and they were able to read off a serial number after only a cursory examination on site.

The serial was passed on to the Military Air Attaché's office at the U.S. Embassy in Grosvenor Square. In turn they sent it to Locator Information at Third Air Force Headquarters, American Forces (Europe), at Mildenhall. Mildenhall referred to Locator Information, United States Air Force Headquarters, Washington. Within twenty-four hours the computers in Washington identified the engine as having belonged to a B-26 Martin Marauder, last listed as being operational with 457th Bombardment Squadron, 323rd Group, stationed at Horham, Suffolk, in June 1943. The information also provided the aircraft's serial number, its squadron and group serials, its code letter—in this case C—and its nickname. The aircraft which now rested in the soft earth of Romney Marsh had been called *Dancing Dodo*.

Tired as he was, Dobson read on, the typescript blurring and swimming, as though a fine mesh screen kept coming between him and the file, the words running into each other as he plowed through the pages of technical data already collated.

There were three pages listing papers and personal effects which had remained intact and were little damaged: maps in perfect condition; a flight plan (Horham-Manston (Kent); Manston-Horham); two pay books and personal letters (indicating that *Dancing Dodo* had not been on a mission when it went in, for crews on operational flights checked in their personal documents before take-off); a metal case with six Lucky Strike cigarettes; two cigarette lighters; three rings; and, of course, six sets of identity dog tags—five of metal and one, belonging to the RAF officer, of some fibrous compound. The dog tags put names, serial numbers, ranks, religious affiliations and, in the case of the U.S. personnel, blood groups to the mortal remains.

The names and other details of the U.S. bodies went off to Locator Information, USAF HQ, Washington, with a query asking if these officers and enlisted men were serving with 457th Squadron, 323rd Group U.S. Eighth Army Air Force, Horham, in 1943. At the same time the available information on Flight Lieutenant Free was sent to the Ministry of Defence (Records). The details came back within twenty-four hours (seventy-two in the case of Free). All of the Americans were listed as having been on active service with 457th Squadron at Horham in June 1943.

Flight Lieutenant Free's record was still on file with the Ministry of Defence and showed that he had spent three months with 323rd Group 8th USAAF at Horham in 1943. It was here that the first note of warning sounded. While the computers in Washington had answered one specific question regarding the five names, an alert Ministry of Defence records clerk forwarded Flight Lieutenant Free's entire service record, which showed that he had been posted to a Royal Air Force operational squadron in July 1943, had been shot down over Germany in October 1943, spent the rest of the war as a POW and was repatriated and demobilized in 1945. They even had an address still current in 1960.

The U.S. Air Attaché's office made a notation, and further queries were passed back through Mildenhall to Washington.

It was as though everyone was anxiously awaiting the answers to these last queries, for the next six pages were taken up with preliminary medical notes. Dobson saw that the reasonably good condition of the bodies within the fuselage was attributed to a clear passage of air through what remained of the aluminum shell. He skimmed through the other details. As far as Dobson was concerned he did not really know his ischium from his humerus.

Then, on the final page:

**Department of Locator Information, USAF HQ,
Washington, D.C.**

Concerning B-26 aircraft, Serial 41-77659, *Dancing Dodo*. Records show this aircraft was left, together with two other aircraft, at Horham, Suffolk, when 323rd Group moved to Earls Colne, Essex, 14 June 1943. *Dancing Dodo* subsequently removed by road to 2 SAD, Neaton, and from there to Burtonwood, Lancs., for cannibalization.

Information as requested on the following personnel:

Captain William E. Potts DSC with Oak Leaf Cluster served with 323rd Group until October 1943 and transferred with Group to 9th AF IX BC through 1945. Returned U.S. December 1945 and continued to serve with USAAF until honorable discharge as Colonel in 1968. Current address held by this office.

Lieutenant Daniel Goldberg served with 323rd Group until October 1943 and transferred with Group to 9th AF IX BC through 1945. Returned U.S. January 1946 and honorably discharged. Current address held by this office.

Lieutenant Herbert J. Flax DFC served with 323rd Group until October 1943 and transferred with Group to 9th AF IX BC through 1945. Returned U.S. December 1945 and honorably discharged January 1946. Current address held by this office.

Master Sergeant Wilcox Pride transferred 350th Bombardment Squadron (H), Thorpe Abbots, June 1943. Missing in action May 1944. POW June 1944. Repatriated April 1945. Returned U.S. June 1945. Honorably discharged August 1946. Current address held by this office.

Sergeant Edward B. Sailby served with 323rd Group until October 1943 and transferred with Group to 9th AF IX BC through 1945. Returned U.S. January 1946. Honorably discharged. Current address held by this office.

The Appendix gave instructions for a joint investigation to be mounted by the Office of U.S. Air Attaché (Military) and Ministry of Defence Section I3 (Air).

Dobson closed the file, dropped it by the bed, stretched, finished the cigarette he was smoking, turned out the light and lay in the hot darkness.

On the precipice of sleep, the waking nightmare came once more to Dobson, his mind returning again to the few seconds of horror. He was airborne, with Pole and Black as his wingmen, bucketing at zero feet over the low flying area, along the calm Welsh valley. He heard his own voice, precise, with the orders.

"Echelon left. Echelon left. Go."

The two other aircraft slid into their stepped positions above him to the left.

Then—

"Turning right. Turning right. Go."

His hands and feet were firm on the controls and he felt the P1 Lightning respond as his head flicked up to check Pole and Black: watching incredulously as Pole slewed his aircraft left into Black. The buffeting from the shock waves, the tilting of his own aircraft as his ears picked up the grinding noise over the engine whine, and the scream coming through his headset.

Dobson awoke, drenched in sweat. It was seven in the morning and, outside, the sun still shone as the city shook itself in the new day.

5

Passing through the imposing entrance to the U.S. Embassy in Grosvenor Square, Dobson experienced an odd flash of *déjà vu*. The pair of security men were checking his credentials when, by some trick of the light or maybe a flaw in the plate glass of the doors, his reflection was distorted, elongated and troughed with waves, as if a series of curves had formed in flesh and bone.

Bizarre though the image was, Dobson recognized this contorted figure, and the thought process reached out quickly to pinpoint its identity: end of the pier mirrors (was it Brighton? Bournemouth?) only a few years ago, yet in the rush of events it seemed a lifetime. He even looked for the other reflection which should have been there, elasticated and blurred beside him. Then one of the security men was repeating a sentence, unheard the first time. "This lady will show you to 552, sir."

The most immediate thing about Bud Hackstead was his eyes; the clearness, grayness (like Ann, Dobson thought), and the humor within, overscored by the sunburst of lines around them. The coiled-spring vitality was the second, and more lasting, impression.

He must have been in his late fifties, but had probably changed little in the last decade, the vigor and energy husbanded

and nurtured in a manner which made Dobson feel insipid, a
weakling. He could foresee problems in the Atlantic Alliance.

There was no preliminary chat. Hackstead got straight
down to cases.

"Looks like it's going to be a long hard summer."
Hackstead flicked the file with a forefinger. "It's a jigsaw. We
haven't got all the pieces and we don't really know what the
picture is. But we have to remember this is about people. The
aircraft's *Dancing Dodo*, I don't think there's much doubt about
that. But the bodies, well, they're another matter. The bodies say
who they are. We know different."

"So we start with the crew? The crew and Flight
Lieutenant Free?"

"I already started." Hackstead stretched back in his chair,
arms loose, hands clenching and unclenching as though
performing an isometric exercise. "Last night I spoke long-
distance to Colonel William Edgar Potts, United States Air
Force, Retired. He told me some things that aren't in that file.

"I've known Potts on and off for some time. Not buddies,
you understand, but we'd nod in the street. He lives in Phoenix,
Arizona, now, with his wife Beryl, whom he met, in the true
tradition of all the romance magazines, when he was with 457th
Squadron at Horham. She's an English publican's daughter, and
to see her now you'd think she was a Daughter of the
Revolution."

"You told him about *Dancing Dodo?*"

"Nope. Not a word. Said I was doing some investigation
for the War Graves people. Asked him about Flight Lieutenant
Free." He chuckled, a low hollow growl. "That call must've cost a
fortune. It unleashed a flood. Old Bill Potts had to go and get out
his log books from way back. Didn't recall the name Free to start
with, but he found it, and remembered. There's a flight plan they
pulled out of the wreckage..."

"Horham-Manston: Manston-Horham."

"You got it. Now in Bill Potts' log book there's an entry
dated May 18, 1943. On that day he took *Dodo* on an air test. The
whole crew was on board, plus one passenger—Flight Lieutenant Free. They took Free down to Manston in Kent, dropped him
off and flew home to Horham." His eyes flashed with something
more than amusement. "So, David, *Dancing Dodo*, with those
identifiable personnel on board, really did make that trip shown
on the flight plan they fished out of the wreckage. Mind you,
they'd have had to be a shade off course to come down in

Romney Marsh. But those men made that trip. The only difference is that they got to Manston and returned to Horham. No sweat. So what've we got here, David? Are we seeing double? *Doppelgänger* aircraft? *Doppelgänger* bodies? Phantom corpses? You've heard the stories about men seen in flying suits walking around the roads down there: the old lady who regularly sees a guy in her garden 'dressed funny'?"

Dobson smiled.

"Nobody," Hackstead thumped the desk lightly with his fist, "nobody's going to convince me that the trip *Dancing Dodo* made with Free on board, on May 18, 1943, is just a coincidence. When I talked with Potts last night, I had spiders crawling up and down my spine. That guy's obsessive about *Dodo*."

"Perhaps we should start with the aircraft, then."

"Mmm," Hackstead gave a quick series of nods. "*Dancing Dodo* was left at Horham with a couple of other wrecks when the Group moved on to Earls Colne on June 14, 1943."

"And then taken by road to the knacker's yard at Burtonwood via Neaton. It did strike me that, possibly, an engine was removed and refitted to another aircraft."

Hackstead slowly moved his head from side to side. "No way. I called your people at the RAE, Farnborough. They're not shifting the fuselage until the day after tomorrow, but they have the airframe number. It's *Dodo*. No question about it. But how it got left at Horham, now that Bill Potts' other story, and he's paranoid about it. Leastways once he let it out of the bag. Sit back, brother Dobson, and let me tell it to you, warts and all, just like Potts told me last night."

Dobson realized, with some misgivings that he was becoming involved in the investigation. A few hours before, a few minutes even, the whole thing had presented itself as a dull chore. Now, Bud Hackstead's own and obvious enthusiasm changed all that. As the American talked on, it was as though the young Captain William Potts was there in the room with them. The years rolled back and the time returned when the air over East Anglia was never still.

6

The horizon tilted and then moved upward as Bill Potts throttled back and the aircraft began to lose height. They hit a patch of bumpy air and the great streamlined cigar-shaped fuselage vibrated violently.

"Watch out, Captain, I think we're on a C road," Wilcox Pride called through the intercom as he swung the deck turret guns to starboard.

"Okay, it's downhill all the way, fellas," Potts murmured. Then, to Dan Goldberg seated beside him in the cabin, "Let's have the gear down. Half flaps. She seems clean enough."

Goldberg nodded, selecting the undercarriage down. Potts advanced the throttles a fraction and increased the mixture to rich in order to compensate for the increased drag. Not as bad as yesterday when they all thought the big starboard Double-Wasp was going to pack up altogether on the approach to Horham. When you lost an engine on a B-26 there was little time to retrim before the torque pulled you right around and spun you through the sky like a pinwheel. The Marauder did not give you any second chances, and if something went wrong on the approach, like loss of power with the gear down, you had even less time to regain control.

Now, *Dodo* ceased her trembling, responding to flaps and power under Potts' and Goldberg's experienced hands, the altimeter gently unwinding as they slowly dropped toward the flat green and gold checkered landscape. Ahead, Potts could see the slash marks of gray runway scarring the gentle countryside of Suffolk.

Potts pushed gently on his right rudder pedal. He was aligned with the runway now and less than a hundred feet from the ground, the perimeter track racing below them as *Dodo* swept over the fence. Motoring in under power, Potts lifted her nose, chopping the throttles so that she drifted gently onto the concrete, her main wheels touching at precisely the same moment, the tires giving off their twin burns of rubber. Braking gently as the speed dropped away, he allowed the nosewheel to come down and make contact.

In the tunnel gun position in the tail cone, Ed Sailby grinned to himself as he called over the intercom, "Thank you, Captain Potts, sir; and my ma thanks you also for bringing us down safely." It was a ritual, and these men observed rituals as though their lives depended on them, whether they were returning from a mission or a routine air test like this one.

"*Dodo* brought you back," intoned Potts.

"Honor to the mighty *Dodo*," the four other crewmen completed the dialogue. Even Goldberg, who was never happy about that sort of thing, moved his lips.

Once back on the ground, both Potts and Goldberg tended to treat the aircraft in a cavalier fashion, revving the engines alternately as they fishtailed along the taxitrack toward their hardstanding.

Across the field, *Luscious Laura* came in, a shade too low so that Ernie Krabowitz had to open her up to gain height over the last few feet of the perimeter fence.

"Not a textbook landing, Krabowitz." Herbie Flax, now standing beside Potts, did a fair imitation of the brusque pedantic growl of 457th's CO, Colonel Lane.

The crew jeep came down the peri-track. Potts dragged heavily on his Lucky and gathered his gear together, walking toward the oncoming jeep, his crew moving and scuffling playfully around him. The dark serious Goldberg; little Wilcox Pride, his long-peaked flying cap pushed back; Ed Sailby, who reckoned he could get the pants off any woman in Suffolk (and Essex when they got there, Potts thought); and the ever-smiling Herbie Flax. Tonight, Potts thought, he would tell Beryl. Maybe he'd do more than that.

The Crew Room radio was switched to AFN and Glenn Miller played "String of Pearls." There were around fifteen or so aircrew stowing their gear and preparing to get over to their various mess halls, or to the newly opened Officers' Club. Work was over for the day. Tomorrow was a different matter.

"Captain Potts? Captain William Potts?" A young PFC, looking fresh out of high school, stood hesitating in the doorway, not daring to step over the hallowed threshold.

"Andy Hardy wants you, Bill," someone shouted.

"What is it?"

"Colonel Lane's compliments, sir. He'd like you to step over to his office for a moment. I have the jeep outside, Captain Potts, sir."

Colonel Lane stood with his back to the door, staring out of the window looking across the airfield. He had that erect, square-shouldered stance that one associated with long-serving career officers, as though the spine was encased in metal.

"You wanted me, Colonel?"

There was a pause, as though the colonel's mind was turning over an idea. "I saw you bring *Dodo* in just now."

"Sir?"

"Better landing than Krabowitz. Not a textbook landing. Not a textbook landing at all."

"Sir." Potts forced the smile from his face. Herbie would be amused by the accuracy of his mimicry.

"Air test okay?"

"Fine, sir."

"That engine?"

"I guess they picked all the flack out of it, sir."

"So she's operational?"

"Yes, Colonel."

Another pause. The sound of engines on an approach, but this time the colonel did not turn back toward the window. "The Group moves to Earls Colne on the fourteenth."

"Yes, sir, I know."

"You're going on a month's leave, Captain. You and your crew."

"Well, sir, that's . . ."

"Wait." He put out a hand so that it rested on Potts' sleeve. "You've got one job to do personally before you go. Just you." The aircraft had touched down. Potts saw it rolling to a halt at the far end of the runway. "I have two squadron airplanes totally unserviceable," Lane continued, not looking Potts in the eye. "*Bob's Baby* needs a complete new hydraulic system, and

Loadsa Pluck's a write-off since yesterday." Nobody had walked away from *Loadsa Pluck*'s belly-in after Abbeville yesterday afternoon. Two of the crew were in the hospital, the others had gone.

"Sir?" Potts waited.

"They'll be left here for transportation to Number Two Strategic Air Depot at Neaton. We'll eventually get replacements at Earls Colne. In about a month. When you come back off leave."

"Sir, if I may..."

"You may not." Quietly, but with absolute firmness. "Before we leave here there'll be one other aircraft marked up as totally u/s. *Dancing Dodo*."

"But she's in perfect..."

The colonel made placating movements with his hands. "I know, Bill. I know, she's the best B-26 you've ever flown; the rest of your crew'll mutiny; you won't fly a brand-new replacement, it's unlucky. I know it all. But this comes from the top—quiet, confidential, secret. We have to supply one operational aircraft in good order and without a crew, and we have to do it without knowing it ourselves. Some of those people at Daws Hill Lodge don't even want to know when they blow their own noses. Sorry, Bill, I drew lots, and it's a wonder that even I know 'cause I was supposed to do it without looking. You lost."

"But..."

"As far as you and your crew are concerned, *Dodo* has a permanent, and sudden, trim problem."

"The boys'll..."

"I've told you, they won't be any the wiser. Why do you think I've picked you, Bill? You can fly those bitches better'n most of us. So tomorrow morning you say you're not happy about something and you take *Dodo* up by yourself. You then scare the ass off everybody within sight of the field. You come down and report a serious trim problem. I send you all on leave. When you come back you report to Earls Colne, and *Dodo* just won't be there. No questions."

"He did just that," said Hackstead. "And it very nearly *did* cause a mutiny when his crew came off leave. One of them, Wilcox Pride, even got himself transferred on account of it. He ended up a POW. You know, David, that's bugged Bill Potts all these years, and I don't honestly believe that he'd told anyone about it until he talked to me last night. Then out it all came, like opening up a dam."

"And he told you with all that detail?" Dobson lit another cigarette.

"With every last bit of the detail, like he was remembering something that just happened. You can imagine what that was like on a telephone. And this is a guy who fought the whole war in airplanes and then went off and fought another one in Korea; then another from a desk—Vietnam. A guy who's spent hundreds of days flying and being shot at and watching men die. Yet he recalls that day in its entirety—all of it, David, as if that day was something special." He shrugged, hunching his shoulders and holding them, not relaxing, for a few seconds. "Well, I suppose it was special. He proposed to Beryl that night and married her on that leave. But it was strange, the way he told me. If you didn't know Bill Potts and his reputation you'd think he'd gone crazy."

"We only have his word for it..."

"And the tape I made during the call." The smile fast as a bullet.

"No, Bud. Recall is odd. Plays tricks. That day could be a composite thing. The clearest memories jammed into one sequence. We need some kind of corroboration."

"We'll get it." There was no arrogance: simply a statement flavored with a morsel of discontent. "Potts is sicking himself and his crew onto us anyway—in the flesh. That I could do both with and without, but he's got himself steamed up about some group charter visit to old wartime haunts. Tells me that he's getting his old crew together to make the trip. At some point we're going to be stuck with them, like it or not, so we might as well like it and make it work for us—to our advantage." He gave a little frown. "Potts told me something else, but I don't know if we can set any credence by it."

"Yes?"

"He said he saw *Dodo* again. August 1944. August 17, according to his log. With the Ninth Tactical Air Force by then, giving air support to ground forces. Same crew except Wilcox Pride..."

"And Free, of course."

"They were on a mission, bombing troop concentrations on the far side of the Seine. Somewhere up near Rouen. He got separated from the main force when he saw a Marauder heading east at speed, quite low. His idea was to home in on him; thought the pilot might be disorientated. Anyway, he didn't reach the aircraft, but he swore that it was *Dodo*."

"He identified positively?"

"No. He saw no markings."

"One Marauder looks like another."

"Right, that's why we don't set too much credence on it. The light was bad—it was dusk—but he swears that he knew it was *Dodo*. Says that Flax and Goldberg knew as well. He told me that in that light it looked as though it was painted gray-white. It looked like a ghost plane."

In spite of himself, Dobson smiled. Deep down he felt anxious. He would be glad of the opportunity to talk to Potts.

"So if *Dodo* was in operational order where did she go?" Dobson asked.

"I'd bet not to Burtonwood via Neaton."

"And Colonel Lane?"

"Killed, August '43."

"And there's nothing in writing?"

"Only what you've seen—*Dodo* left u/s at Horham and transported by road to Burtonwood."

"And we only have Potts' word that she wasn't u/s."

Hackstead nodded. "We're taking a helicopter ride at two-thirty," he said as though avoiding the question.

"Where would you put your money?" Dobson pressed.

"Where she went? I'd say they took it either to Tempsford or Harrington."

"SOE or OSS support?"

"That's it. The Racket, the Org, the Funnies, take your pick. They had a lot of nicknames, those outfits."

"The Heavies," Dobson stated.

Hackstead chuckled. "Yeah, the Heavies."

"And what would they want with a Marauder?"

"There were some weird things going on in 1943, David. The Moon Squadrons with their Lysanders dropping SOE people into Fortress Europe to—how did Churchill put it?—set Europe ablaze. The Office of Strategic Services coming up with all sorts of crazy notions. Left hands not knowing what right hands were doing."

"Crazy times. But why a Marauder?"

"There's only one answer to that. Why not?"

7

Romney Marsh has been called the eighth continent of the world. Its triangle is eleven miles deep, and its people are aware of its unique position: a place of sudden mists and a history of smuggling; an area which contains twenty-three parishes, with twenty-three churches and twenty-three lords of manors. The churches mostly have sturdy towers, for at the height of smuggling operations, the church towers were ideal places for stowing booty—mainly wool shipped to France. So the marsh has an instant romantic history, fed by fiction like the stories of Dr. Syn and the Marsh Riders. On the coast, the Dymchurch wall holds back the sea, while the Royal Military Canal makes the marsh almost an island.

There were no mists that afternoon, only the heat haze shimmering off toward the Channel. How many other corpses were lying deep in the soggy ground, Dobson wondered.

A young RAF regiment squadron leader, flanked by a sergeant and another man in civilian clothes, waited to greet them as the helicopter landed among the makeshift camp surrounding the shrouded remains of *Dancing Dodo*.

"Colonel Hackstead? Wing Commander Dobson?" he

asked in a pointless moment of verification. "My name's Follet. Only taken over this week, I'm afraid, so I missed all the early fun and games. This is Mr. Tyndle from the R.A.E., Farnborough. Our crash investigator."

Tyndle nodded, pleasantly but without enthusiasm, as though making it plain that he had a job to do and would get on with it better without intelligence people treading on his heels. He would be Board of Trade, Dobson knew: AIB—Accident Investigation Branch. Investigating officer, an expert who, with his team, lived in that specialized macabre world of dead aircraft, and the remains of those who flew or traveled in them. He was dressed in a white boiler suit. Other members of his team wore more drab, government-issue overalls.

"I'm at your disposal." The squadron leader had a plummy, hearty accent.

"I just want a quick look at the site, what wreckage is still left." It surprised Dobson that he was getting his word in first. "Nothing difficult."

"You got some transport we can use?" Hackstead sounded as though he was out for a pleasant afternoon and not particularly interested in wreckage.

"There's a jeep, yes."

"Okay." Hackstead turned brightly to the civilian. "You want to show us the mess that butterfingers pilot left you to clean up?"

Tyndle looked at him with extreme distaste, nodded and led the way to the largest of the tents—a marquee, with slatted board flooring. Three long trestle tables were placed down the center, and half a dozen men examined pieces of metal, ranging from thin slivers to large sections. A curved portion, which could have been part of the rubber framework, was propped against the table on the far left.

"These are the smaller items lifted during this past week." Tyndle had an odd, strangled voice, as though the words remained partially trapped within the larynx. "We try to get them into some kind of order here, mark them up and tabulate them before they go to Farnborough."

"Where you'll reassemble them?"

"Yes, we'll put her together again. Or almost together again."

"When you start doing the tests, Mr. Tyndle," Hackstead continued...

"Yes?"

"Could you include some of those sneaky little experiments that'll tell us how many times this baby was sprayed and resprayed?"

"I expect we could." He gave a patronizing laugh: the professional talking to an amateur.

"You do that, sir. Now let's go see the fuselage."

They took two steps toward the tent flap when Hackstead turned back. "Oh, and while you're at it, an analysis of the paint—country of origin and all that—would be a good idea." He smiled happily.

Slatted boards surrounded the remains of the fuselage, and padded metal retainers held the more fragile sections in place. They entered through the large hole torn out of the port side, crouching and following Tyndle's instructions about where to put their feet. The dark interior was illuminated by portable lights clamped to the undamaged longerons. A strong smell of disinfectant hung about the hulk like some slow-dispersing gas.

Dobson sniffed. "Problems in here?"

Tyndle held a handkerchief to his mouth. "There were bodies . . ."

"Yes, we've seen the photographs."

They climbed up to the cabin, squashed and battered. "The *Dodo* brought you back." The levity was gone from Hackstead's tone.

"Honor to the mighty *Dodo*." Dobson felt his neck tingle, a prickling sensation among the short hairs; a sudden feeling of cold. He shuddered.

Tyndle looked at them both, frowning, puzzled.

"Anything you want to tell us now, Mr. Tyndle? Anything we might need to know in advance of your report?" Hackstead did not look back at him, but peered at the shattered banks of instruments.

"Such as?"

"Such as what story the controls and instruments tell you."

Tyndle sighed. "We have a chart over in the tent. It plots an estimated picture of the impact."

"No, I mean the other stories. Was the gear up, for instance?"

"Yes, the gear was up. It's pretty certain that her flaps were extended to around a quarter, maybe a half."

"Fuel? I see the tanks all register empty. Is that just dispersal after impact or . . ."

"Two of the gauges are jammed a fraction above empty, but you can't rely on that. The engine fire extinguishers had been activated. I think while she was still airborne."

"No traces of fire?"

"None."

"Altimeter?"

"Was reading about fifty feet when it locked. Can't rely on that either. ASI jammed at around one hundred."

Hackstead nodded, narrowing eyes as he craned forward among the tangled instruments and controls. "Throttles right through the gate." He appeared to be soliloquizing. "Compass undamaged. Turn and bank to port..."

"The port wing hit the ground first, no doubt about that." It was as though Tyndle now realized that he was talking to someone who knew at least the rudiments of flying.

"Artificial horizon still working after first impact," Hackstead continued to ruminate. "That shows a bank to starboard. Nothing in the bomb bays? Not carrying anything special?"

"Nothing there as far as we can see. Won't be certain until we've got her out. One thing has struck us..."

"Mmm?"

"There's no trace of ammunition. Nothing on the trolleys or in the racks. We're told she was on an air test when she went in. She had most of the crew up, you'd think she'd have been armed."

They haven't been told, Dobson thought. Nobody's passed it on to the crash examiners. They don't know there are doubts. On an air test from Horham, that's all they've been told.

Hackstead frowned. "You're quite right. Interesting."

"Of course she was one crewman light," Tyndle said. "They carried seven operationally."

No mention of Flying Freddie Free of the RAF. They haven't even been told that, Dobson considered. As far as they're concerned, it's six American crewmen.

Hackstead raised his eyebrows, looking hard toward Dobson. Anything else? He appeared to be asking.

Dobson gave him a silent negative.

They retraced their unsteady way back through the battered fuselage. Apart from where great holes had been ripped in the side, the interior was relatively undamaged. Rust had crept into some places, and the aluminum skin had peeled back where it had been slit and opened, but the longerons, the bulkheads, junction boxes and protective casing for the wiring were all undamaged. Clusters of moss and lichen had grown and spotted large sections, but you could tell exactly where you were. Inside an aircraft.

Outside they stood silent for a moment. The RAF regiment sentries paced, bored, brassed off with the tedium of routine. Hackstead caught Dobson's eye and saw he was looking at one of the young sentries. The American started to plod over toward the guard. Dobson followed. Hackstead had that natural gift of command. He led like an experienced dance partner.

Hackstead stopped in front of the young man, and the squadron leader appeared beside him. As if by magic, Dobson reflected.

The sentry came to attention and looked speculatively at the squadron leader.

"They tell me it gets spooky up here at night." Hackstead raised his eyebrows.

"Some of the lads say so, sir. I'm not a great believer in that sort of thing meself."

"Some of the lads reckon they've seen anything?"

"Aye, sir. I think it's all moonlight meself. Trick of the moonlight."

"What do they reckon they've seen, then?"

"Figure, sir. Phantom figure, they say."

"Trick of the light I should think." Hackstead smiled and nodded. "We're going to see an old lady who thinks she sees this spook in her garden."

"Probably her compost heap," said Dobson.

"Sir," the airman acknowledged.

They let the squadron leader go on ahead. Tyndle had already disappeared.

"We goofed," muttered Hackstead.

"Seven to a crew?"

Hackstead gave a curt nod. "Should've spotted that. Potts only mentioned the ones I put names to. I led him. There must've been two more jokers in his crew at Horham. I'm going to roast Locator Information."

"You've done this sort of thing before, haven't you?"

"What sort of thing, for Chrissake?"

"Investigation. Interrogation. The soft technique, the hard technique, sneakies, dirty tricks."

"Now don't you go shouting CIA at me. Just don't start. Yes, of course I've done it before. Jesus, David, if it was just you the spooks would chew you up and spit you back."

"As long as I know."

"Okay, so let's go and see the kids who uncovered this mess."

"And the crazy lady?"

"Yeah, let's see where the phantom trampled all over her delphiniums."

Unsought, a vision of the interior of the fuselage crossed Dobson's mind, overlapped with the picture of Pole's and Black's aircraft twisting together and then being blown apart by a great red sun from the point of impact. For the second time that afternoon he shivered. The stink of disinfectant from the fuselage seemed to be sealed into his nostrils. It pervaded his clothing. He wanted a bath. When they got to the coast he would want to strip off and plunge into the salt water.

8

First they went to the address listed for Robert Mitchell, the twelve-year-old who had torn the hand out of Dead Clump. The squadron leader stayed in the jeep with his corporal, cautious of military people who never put on their uniforms. Dobson, standing at the front door next to Hackstead, knew how he felt.

The woman who answered the chiming doorbell looked harassed and untidy. She seemed uncertain when Hackstead told her who they were and what they wanted.

"You *are* Mrs. Mitchell? Robert's mother?" Dobson asked.

"Yes. Oh yes, I'm Robert's mother." She made no move to let them into the house.

"All we want is a few words with the lad." Dobson took half a pace forward. "It's quite important. We've got a job to do."

"Could be something in it for him," Hackstead lied. "I mean the United States Air Force is grateful he found the wreck. It may seem strange, but there're some relatives who'll rest easier in their beds knowing where their kin are buried."

"Yes, I understand." Mrs. Mitchell ran her fingers up into her hair, like a pitchfork going into straw. "It's just I'd rather his dad were here. The doctor said he wasn't to be excited. His temperature's down but he's still far from right yet."

"He's been ill?" Hackstead sounded genuinely concerned. "We didn't know."

"This wretched virus. Like the others. Like the men from up the camp. It's all the same thing. Doctor says you have to take care with bodies, and I mean he did touch the wretched thing."

"Men up at the camp?" queried Hackstead.

"You must know, surely. They've had a lot down with it."

"With what?" Dobson exchanged a fast furtive glance with Hackstead. The bodies in the fuselage had been in moderate repair. One at least still had most of its organs. He thought of the disinfectant in the aluminum hulk and asked himself what you could catch from dead bodies. Cholera? Typhoid? Disintegrating bodies had nasty habits. "I'm sorry," he said quickly. "Maybe we'd better come back some other time."

"I'll tell his father."

Hackstead was already down by the jeep, motioning the squadron leader out of earshot of the driver. He was talking rapidly when Dobson got to them.

"Nobody told us about a virus and some of your people being sick. Why in hell didn't you tell us? What's the medical opinion?"

"No need to get steamed up." The squadron leader was immediately on the defensive. "It's localized. Nothing serious. A virus, like flu. In fact they say it's a particular strain of flu, but it's been contained. There's absolutely no evidence that . . ."

"That it came from those bodies in the wreck? Who says so?"

"Our own medical people. They're keeping it very low profile. That's one of the reasons I've been posted here. We've only had ten cases. Local health people wanted it kept quiet. You know what a flu scare does these days—particularly in summer. Not the right time of the year for it."

"Like it's not the right time of the year to get food poisoning?" Hackstead looked furious. "Jesus Christ, man, we're investigating the circumstances of this wreck. You were duty-bound to tell us. No wonder they had the fuselage awash with antiseptic."

"Look, Colonel," the squadron leader had turned pink, "that was only a precaution. The medical people checked contacts. They think the wretched bug came from the continent. I think you'd better talk to them. They say it's contained."

Back in the jeep, Hackstead still fumed. "Contained?" he muttered. "What'd they mean by contained? You notice how Tyndle kept his handkerchief over his face when we were in that fuselage? They knew, but nobody bothered to tell us. We're only investigating the thing."

The cottage was off the main road. You went down a narrow track for about a quarter of a mile, and, suddenly, there it was. One gray stone cottage on its own. No visible sign of any other building, except a wooden privy at the back.

The garden was overgrown, with weeds twining and proliferating across a slab stone path and even up to the window ledges. There was a small porch where, once, honeysuckle had been trained up a rotting trellis. The door was open.

They knocked three times before the woman shuffled out to greet them.

"Mrs. Lambert?" Dobson asked, raising his voice.

"Yes." Her eyes moved lizard-like, constantly shifting, suspicious.

"We're from the Ministry of Defence. We've come to ask you about the man you saw in the garden."

"I told the newspapers all that. Told them all." She was very alert.

"Mrs. Lambert, we're sorry to bother you." Hackstead exuded charm from every pore. "Our superiors have asked us to talk to you about what you saw. They think it might be in your interest as well as ours. You smoke?" Offering a packet of squashed Chesterfields.

"No, no, can't abide them. My Jack got taken by them things, so the doctor said."

"I'm sorry." Hackstead put away the cigarettes. "Can you tell us what this man looked like?"

"Looked like? You mean looks like. I seen him plenty of times. Plenty."

"When did you first see him?" Dobson asked.

"That was in the war. I thought it was the 'Ome Guard up to their tricks again. Noises in the garden. This feller stood there. Just stood there staring at me, all dressed in white. If it 'ud been my Jack seen it, I'd 'ave told him straight, you've been at the parsnip wine again, Jack. Used to like his drop of parsnip wine. I reckon that played its part in seeing him off an' all."

"Has he been dead long, Mrs. Lambert?" Dobson heard himself sounding like some inexperienced curate.

"Eighty-six when the Lord took him. Eighty-six." The old woman grasped hold of the lintel with a brown wrinkled hand that looked more like an animal paw. "He were six years older than me and I shall be eighty-eight come Christmas."

"Eight years ago," Dobson said.

"About that, ah. Round about that when the Lord took him."

With the help of the cigarettes and the parsnip wine, Dobson thought. Aloud he asked, "And you first saw the man during the war? How often have you seen him since?"

"Hard to say. About once a month. Sometimes once every three months."

"When did you last see him?"

"Couple of nights ago," she said, firm and quite unshakable in her belief.

"You know who he is?" Hackstead reached for the cigarettes again, then thought better of it.

"I reckon we all know now." She gave a little wheezing laugh that, for some unaccountable reason, made Dobson shiver. "He come out of the plane they found over to Dead Clump. Only it weren't Dead Clump then. Not until the night that plane crashed. We heard that, you know, Jack and me. Plain as anything we heard it."

"And you didn't report it?"

"Didn't do to report everything. Not in the war. We kept ourselves to ourselves a lot. Tried not to get mixed up in the war. Jack didn't approve of it. But we heard that old plane come down, then that very night the man come, dressed funny, like he always is."

"How funny?"

"All in white. Head to foot with a glass thing in front of his face, only you can see his face quite plain in the moonlight when he comes."

"And he never speaks?"

"Never a word from him."

"Do you speak to him?"

"No, I just nods. Let him know that I'm here, and he shakes his head at me and walks off. Same every time."

"And he first came on the night the airplane crashed?" Hackstead was being amazingly patient.

"That's right."

"You're certain of that?"

"Positive." She grinned, like a child who knows it is telling some fantasy to adults, and wishes them to share in the game.

"And he still looks the same after all these years?"

"Well, of course he does. Shades don't get no older. Age shall not weary them, nor the years condemn; at the going down of the sun, and in the morning, we will remember them. We will remember them." She spoke it parrot fashion, but with care. "I always remembered him, though. My old friend he is."

"Yes," said Hackstead. "Well, we're most obliged to you, Mrs. Lambert. Maybe we'll come and see you again real soon."

The old woman nodded. Dobson thought she looked like a model made from cracked brown wax. Only the eyes glittered, alive in the wrinkled prune face. "If you like. I don't see many folk, not these days, except the lady that brings the meals on wheels." She gave a little cackle. "She looks like she ought to be on wheels, that one. And the doctor, of course, when he remembers. They don't bother much with Doris Lambert these days, but you're welcome."

Hackstead was three strides down the path when he turned. "Mrs. Lambert, where does he stand, the man from the airplane?"

She cackled again. Out in the jeep the squadron leader and his corporal turned at the sound.

"Just a bit to the left of where you are now." She raised a bent finger. "That's it, just about there, that's where I sees him."

Hackstead moved over and Dobson's eyes followed the American. Among the weeds and wild flowers, bordered by long grass, there was a clear patch of earth. It was roughly circular and looked as though it had been recently dug.

"Thank you, Mrs. Lambert." He picked a piece of stick out of the grass and pushed it into the earth several times, then tossed it back among the weeds.

"A loony?" Hackstead asked, back in the jeep.

"She seems alert, though. Old people get funny ideas."

"That story's been persistent for over thirty years—except for the crashed airplane bit: that's new."

"Obsession?"

"Don't know, but something's been in that garden. We'll bear it in mind, Br'er Dobson. As for now, I want to talk to the medicos. You fancy looking at some bodies?"

9

The head of the Pathology Department at the Royal Victoria Hospital, Folkestone, was away and not expected back for a couple of days.

The young assistant fully accepted Hackstead and Dobson's authority, but explained with patience that there was little he could do. The coroner had allowed the bodies to be released to Princess Mary's Royal Air Force Hospital at Halton. It seemed the sensible thing to do, what with the delay on identification and everything.

As to the influenza epidemic the young pathologist was firm. It was not an epidemic, he stressed. Yes, there was talk at one time of people having been infected because of contact with the remains of the aircraft's crew, but it was only talk. They had taken all the obvious precautions. Yes, it was a nasty and virulent strain, not really influenza in the accepted sense, but a virus which had been localized. It was now under control.

Could they see the pathologist's report on the remains? Well, they had the obvious authority, but it was not up to him. He suggested that they talk to Halton.

"Shit," said Hackstead.

They drove back to the site in silence and it was late when

Dobson returned to Charlotte Street. He went to bed uneasy in mind, and as he was entering that torpid state which comes just before sleep, there were vivid, nightmarish pictures of the corpses emerging from a jagged hole in the side of *Dancing Dodo*. They walked with purpose and one of them shimmered, distorted as though reflected in a convex mirror.

Dobson turned, restless, remembering his own reflection that morning in the Embassy glass doors, and the way he had looked for the other mirrored image. He wondered where she was and whom she was with. Certainly Karen Pole seemed one of the few who might have made the kind of wife . . . but it was no good thinking about it; exercises like that were for adolescents or people with highly dramatic imaginations. Then he drifted off into sleep during which there were no dreams of what was or what might have been. Just the black unknowing. A short course in death.

The telephone wakened him. It was almost nine-thirty.

"David, can you get over here? Charlie Sugden's going berserk." It took him several seconds to realize that Ann was talking from Clapham.

"What's wrong?"

"You seen the papers?"

"You woke me. Slept in. Long day." The day came back, vivid, unnerving: Bud Hackstead pursuing heaven knew what; the disinfectant inside the black hole of *Dodo*'s fuselage; aged Mrs. Lambert with her wrinkled paw on the lintel. "No. What about the papers?"

"All the classified stuff on the job you're doing. Sugden's wild."

"But Sugden's . . ."

"In charge as of this morning. The old man's been hoisted off to some conference. Very quick. I promised to track you down."

"You can't find me. Not for about an hour. Okay?"

"I'll try. Where'll you be?"

"Here. Unless I call in." He cradled the receiver as though it had horns and scales, and went, barefoot, to the door to pick up the mail and the paper. It crossed his mind that there was no need to tiptoe, but he did nothing about it.

It was on the front page of the *Telegraph*. Marauder aircraft, originally belonging to 323rd Bombardment Group, US 8th AAF, in 1943, found recently in Romney Marsh, was now the center of deep mystery. *Sources close to officers investigating the circumstances of the aircraft's crash* revealed that this particular machine was on the record as having been broken down for cannibalization in June 1943. Her original crew, who last flew her on a sortie to Abbeville on June 9, 1943, had all survived the war. The paper had all the relevant names and facts—*Dancing Dodo*, Potts, Flax, Goldberg, the lot.

He went through to the kitchen and dialed the U.S. Embassy, asking for 552. Hackstead was not in yet.

He was just about dressed when the telephone rang.

"You want to come talk with a newspaperman?" Bud Hackstead chuckled.

He had quite expected it to be Ann from Clapham. "Have you seen the papers?"

"Seen 'em, Dave. I wrote most of them."

"My boss is out for blood."

"Tell him to screw off. I have the franchise on this particular piece of demonology."

"Is that official?"

"As official as you're likely to get. Stick him on to me, I'll wrap him up in pieces of red tape and tie it so Houdini himself couldn't get out. Have you seen the *Express?*"

"Only the *Telegraph*."

"Great picture in the *Express*. I tell you that Potts was hung up about bringing his crew over here on some World War II shindig?"

"Yes. I'll remember you, in all the old familiar places."

"That's it. I've been figuring the best way to use that. Got more details on it now and I reckon that a newspaper like the *Express* could be a great help. I've talked with them, and we're lunching with one of their boys around one. You make it?"

"Your office?"

"Dave." He sounded hurt. "I thought we were a team. It's *our* office."

"I'll be there."

Carefully he dialed the Clapham number and got through to Ann. "You found me." He was actually smiling as he spoke. "I'm coming in to give myself up."

"Thank Christ for that; he's threatening the Official Secrets Act and Lord knows what else."

"Don't let him do anything stupid."

The photograph was on the front page of the *Express* and the story was their second lead. Seven young men grouped in front of the nose of a Marauder, or grouped around it to be exact, because they were posed in a way which left a clear view through to the painted symbol below the cabin—a cartoon-like dodo, strutting cheekily, a silk hat perched on the side of its head and a silver-knobbed cane under one wing. The legend, which ran one word above and one below, was clear.

Dancing Dodo, it said.

The men were all incredibly young, arrogant, jaunty; aggressive in leather jackets with sheepskin collars, some with the long-peaked baseball caps pushed back, two smoking oversized cigars.

He remembered old creaking Mrs. Lambert: Age shall not weary them, nor the years condemn. The parroted sentiment. The between-wars poem repeated annually to salve consciences. Then he realized that the line was not applicable to these figures. By now age *was* wearying them. Potts he could identify as the obvious leader wearing his dress cap, but he wondered which was Herbie Flax? Which Goldberg? Wilcox Pride? Sailby? Which the pair of jokers?

Dobson knew the photograph well by the time the taxi got him to St. John's Hill.

Ann looked at him hard as he came through the office door, a softening of the eyes, the mouth curling for a moment at one corner in a smile that linked them, as though in conspiracy. Then a quick, worried frown as she mouthed "Good luck." Confidently, with a grin, he winked at her. The returned look was one of pleasure.

Sugden and Makepiece were both there, in the group captain's office, sitting like a pair of recording angels on the day of judgment.

"What's the flap?" asked Dobson, trying not to sound too cocky.

Sugden's piggy little eyes scanned him with slow deliberation. Terry Makepiece looked embarrassed. He was, after all, very junior to both of them.

"I'd better be pushing off," said Makepiece.

"No, hang on, Terry." Sugden was blistering, you could hear it under the surface of his unpleasant, affected drawl. "This is part of a lesson in good internal security."

"I asked what the flap was." Dobson picked up a chair and drew it close to the desk. "I haven't time to come running up here, you know, Sugden, so what's all the panic?"

"I suppose you haven't seen the papers this morning?"

"Yes, I've seen a couple of them."

"Then you'll know there's been a security leak."

"What? *Dodo?*"

"Of course, *Dodo*, and I'm expecting a full explanation, Dobson. Who you've talked with, where you've been. Contacts on the telephone. Everything. You're under my control, you know. The group captain left explicit instructions."

"Did he now? I gathered the final reports were for him. You were to be used for assistance. Cash, passes, contacts, all that sort of thing. I don't think we have any actual control in this investigation, Charlie, it's very much an American show."

"While the group captain's away, I shall insist on reports—particularly when it concerns a blatant security leak like this." He thumped the little bundle of daily papers which lay on the desk.

"Controlled leak," Dobson said slowly.

"Controlled? Who says so?"

"Talk to Colonel Hackstead, Charlie. He's leading and I'm an observer. If you want to make a real fool of yourself, talk to Bud Hackstead, but don't expect me to come running over here every time you think something funny's going on. And I'd prefer it if you did not go prodding and probing around in this affair until Hackstead and I have got some of the ends tied up."

Sugden opened his mouth and then closed it again: like a netted salmon.

"I am your control," he spluttered.

"Have it your own way." Dobson began to enjoy himself. "As far as I'm concerned, if we have to play security games, you can be my servicing officer. And you can start work here and now."

"I warn you..."

"You'll warn nothing, Sugden. I'm telling you. Read your terms of reference."

"It's perfectly plain." Sugden's saliva burst from his lips in a fine spray. "This is a joint operation..."

"Investigation."

"By the U.S. Air Attaché's Office and ourselves."

"The accent is on the Office of the U.S. Air Attaché, Military. You try directing the investigation and see how far it gets you. You're here to service me, Sugden. Try coming on strong with Colonel Hackstead."

"I'll have you replaced. Terry can take over."

Dobson shrugged. "Try it. Pick up the phone and try it."

"Wait in the outer office." His eyes were wide, popping unhealthily. "You as well, Terry."

Dobson did not argue. He went, leaving the door open, and even walked past Ann without looking in her direction, half his mind rejoicing, the other half raging with fury. He had not felt so in control of events since before the Pole accident.

Terry Makepiece came through, looking nervous and apologetic. "You sure of yourself on this one?" he asked quietly, as though fearing the walls were sprouting electronic gear.

"Why? You scared he's really going to give you the job?" As he said it, Dobson knew it was unfair. Makepiece had done nothing to him.

Makepiece made a hopeless gesture. "I don't know the details. Except what's in the papers. Sugden's close."

Dobson gave a monosyllabic laugh. "Likes playing at being an intelligence man. Don't give it another thought, Terry. If I know Bud Hackstead he's already forgotten everything Sugden ever knew about security. The answer to your first question is yes. Yes, I am sure of myself. Sugden's role is one of support, and if he tries anything with Hackstead he'll get a mouthful of metaphorical knuckles."

One of the telephones gave a short, imperative ring. Makepiece answered it, then covered the mouthpiece. "For you," he said.

Hackstead was at the other end. "Who's that mother I've just been talking to?"

Ann stood in the doorway, mouthing that Sugden wanted him. Dobson asked Hackstead to hang on. "Tell him I'm on the phone. Be in as soon as I've finished." He knew the smile was more than a fraction cocky. "My chief's been called to a conference," he told Hackstead. "You spoke with the second man here."

"He oughta be running for your Parliament. He'd be good at it, he's a bigger idiot than most of them. You want him taken out altogether? It would be a pleasure."

"No, we need all the cretins we can get. See you at one o'clock. And thanks."

Sugden had almost recovered his sly composure by the time Dobson had waited to light a cigarette and go through to the old man's office.

"I've spoken with the U.S. Air Attaché's department," he began.

"I know." Dobson disciplined himself to one brief smile. "You believe me now?"

"What can we do to help?" There would be no hint of apology.

"You might do something personally. Two things. First I want to make contact with one or two people who were serving with the Moon Squadron at Tempsford in the summer of '43."

"Special Duties 161 Squadron, you mean." Sugden made a prissy face.

Pedantic sod, thought Dobson. Aloud he said, "yes."

"That shouldn't be too hard. And the second thing?"

"It might also be helpful if I could have contact with a former high-echelon SOE type likely to have been in and out of Tempsford round about the same time. A senior conducting officer perhaps."

Sugden nodded. "How soon do you want to make contact?" He was all efficiency. Dobson could almost hear him making calls to his cronies, using all the lingo—*I have an agent in place, needs some advice.*

"Soon as you like. Sooner the better. You might get me some details of Free's time as a POW. Camp number and that kind of thing. Also names and addresses of any other people who served in whatever camp he was in. People who would have known him."

Sugden gave a slow and understanding nod. "I'll get this to you as quickly as I can. Don't you worry about a thing."

Dobson did not even thank him. Outside the door he stood for a moment looking at Ann. She looked back at him, gray eyes bright with humor, unspoken congratulations on an obvious victory.

"Dinner?" he asked.

"Tonight?"

He nodded. "Pick you up about eight?"

"I'll come over to your place. Seven-thirty."

"Good."

His stomach did not start turning over until he began the descent down the North Col.

For some reason Dobson expected the man from the *Express* to be young and rather smart-assed. He was not prepared for the soberly dressed and obviously senior man sitting with Hackstead in the Embassy office. They used Christian names on Hackstead's insistence.

"Any names, any names at all, appearing in your newspaper and you'll end up thirty feet down in Romney Marsh yourself," Hackstead grinned. Dobson wondered if he meant it. He probably did. The *Express* man, whose name was Charles, looked as though he knew the score.

"You mean the use of *your* names, of course?" Charles asked in a voice which suggested endless patience.

"Of course." Hackstead winked broadly at Dobson, who asked if they would fill him in on the details. "Not now, Dave." Hackstead's eyes traversed the room swiftly, and the message was plain. "Let's just chat on about life, love and the pursuit of happiness."

"I'd rather have lunch," said Charles.

The sun had finally come through, so they walked over to Half Moon Street. At Flemings they allowed Hackstead to order. He did so without imagination: the seafood cocktail, steaks and salad.

"Okay," the American began once the seafood cocktail was on the table. "Here's the deal as I understand it. Your newspaper has got together information regarding a Down-Memory-Lane trip by U.S. aircrew who served with the American forces over here during World War II—they come complete with wives, mistresses, children, uncles, cousins and aunts."

Charles nodded. "The whole trip is being laid on in order to take about one hundred and fifty of these guys back to the sites of their old airfields, let them stand in the fields from where they used to fly; let them go back to their old haunts." He chuckled. "Within reason, of course."

"And I'm suggesting to you that it would be a great idea to do a special feature on one particular aircrew." Hackstead spooned the seafood into his mouth.

"An aircrew of your nomination, of course," Charles smirked.

"Naturally, that's what it's all about, isn't it? You single out one crew. We name the crew and give you one hell of a story. We even assist in paying extra freight for that particular crew. Nothing but the best."

Charles looked apologetic. "That might be tricky. My editor could advise that we should not be beholden to you."

"Try it."

Charles nodded again.

"What we're after," Hackstead continued, "is a feature—a series of features, with pictures—on this one crew: ending the thing by tying it all into the airplane they found in Romney Marsh."

"The Marauder? The *Dancing Dodo?*" Charles was smooth. Smooth as a polished apple. Dobson wondered if there were any maggots inside.

Hackstead was still talking. "In return for your co-operation, we provide all possible information when our bit of detective work is over. Before that, we give you names, addresses, telephone numbers. A 159 per cent cast-iron exclusive story that could blow the lid off Fleet Street." He held up a hand. "One proviso. Nothing to actually appear in your paper until we flash the green light."

Charles spread his hands. "Sorry." He looked embarrassed. "I doubt if my editor'll wear that one. We always need freedom of action. Nothing that smacks of a deal."

"Nothing that smacks of a deal? You hear that, Dave? I feed them exclusive information, merely ask them to cut out one set of people from a trip that's being made anyway, and they say we want nothing that smacks of a deal."

"Come on, Bud." Charles leaned over the table. "You've given us nothing exclusive so far. Everybody's got the leak you dripped out last night. Any features editor on the Street could come up with this series from what you've given them. For all I know they've already started."

"Charles, Charles." Hackstead's head moved from side to side, an expression of pain and disenchantment. "You forget that you, and only you, have the real information—that these guys are coming over with a tour and *nobody else gets the addresses and telephone numbers.*"

"Anyone can get addresses and telephone numbers. Any good investigative journalist ..."

"You have them now," the American snapped. "By tonight you can have the deal tied up. Nobody can get those addresses and numbers as fast as you. For that matter, I don't suppose anyone else knows they plan to come over. You can have them under exclusive contract."

Charles appeared to be thinking it over. "Okay. Let's just say that we'll play fair. No strings, but we understand one another. Right?"

"That's my boy."

"You have another couple of names for me?"

"Get your notebook. I'm giving you the last two names, addresses and numbers. Nobody else has these."

"Including me," Dobson observed.

Hackstead gave him a quick, broad and good-natured smile: a face of open innocence. "One," he said, "Wilson John Sharp. Two, Rudolph Jacob Klein." He followed up with the addresses and telephone numbers. Sharp lived in Alexandria,

Virginia. Klein had an apartment in lower Manhattan. "Now you have the set," Hackstead told him.

"So have we." Dobson raised an eyebrow. "Washington working overtime."

"While the city sleeps, Dave. I mean while this city sleeps."

Dobson felt cut off: a stranger at the feast, for as Hackstead and Charles talked, it became obvious that they knew each other well. They spoke of people and places from another private life, never once enlightening him with quick explanations or footnotes to the chat.

So he sat back, chewed at his steak, contributed little and observed a lot. By the time they reached the crème caramel it was clear that Hackstead had, for some period, been press officer for the U.S. Air Attaché and he knew Charles' world of editors, subs, journalists, feature writers and sources like a true member of the cognoscenti.

Charles left them a little after three, and they strolled back toward Hyde Park.

"Where did all the secrecy go?" asked Dobson.

"It didn't. Just changed direction slightly. If Potts is anxious to come over, then we have to use him and his crew. I'd have preferred to keep them at arm's length, but I can't do anything about it. I've got to use them and welcome the chance to talk with them."

"Even though they might get in the way?"

Hackstead nodded. "That's the problem. I don't like the idea of corpses treading on corpses; I do like the idea of questioning corpses. Paradox. But if they're set on coming, I want to control them, and their movements."

It was in the pedestrian underpass that Dobson became certain there was a tail on them.

10

Hackstead had marked him as well. He had shoulders like a mountain bear, was tall and black, and dressed in a white safari suit.

They waited halfway up the steps leading to the park while Dobson had trouble with his lighter. As the tail came round the corner from the tunnel they both saw him hesitate for a fraction of a second and then come on.

He passed them, going up. Hackstead let him go for about three steps and then called after him.

"Hey, buddy, you got a light?"

The man paused, looking back to see if the plea was directed at him. He stopped, grunted and produced a gold Dunhill. He did not move, but let them come up to him, waiting until Dobson's cigarette was level with the Dunhill before flicking it on.

"What's your name?" To Hackstead.

"Who's asking?"

"I like to know who I'm dealing with."

"If you're following us, buster, you'll know soon enough. You'll be inside so fast you'll think the Concorde's up your ass."

"You must be Colonel Hackstead." The large black face devoid of any emotion.

"I'm Hackstead."

"Figures. They said you were a sonofabitch."

"And 'they' was right. Who's 'they'?"

"I got a message for Dobson." He turned. "That you?"

Dobson sighed and nodded wordless confirmation.

"There'll be a guy waiting for you at six in the bar of the Mayfair Hotel. His name's Denis, and he'll be wearing a red rose in his buttonhole."

"Who sent you?" Dobson did not really need telling. A bar at six; cryptonym, Denis; red rose in the buttonhole. It all smelled highly of Sugden or the comic-opera security people with whom he consorted.

"I just carry messages."

"And what's *your* name?" Hackstead was unmistakably icy.

For the first time, the bear showed his teeth in a wide grin. "They call me Trotter; *Mr.* Trotter." Turning away he walked up the stairs with great dignity.

Above them, in the park, the sun burned down from a blue-hazed sky. The pollen count was high and the humidity rising.

"What the hell was that all about?" Hackstead scratched his head.

Dobson did not speak until they got to the top of the steps. Somewhere behind them in the tunnel a young man began to busk with a guitar. "I should imagine it's Sugden. He has a fantasy life based wholly on hard-core security fiction. He thinks he's a cog in the secret world. I'm sorry. Just some checking I wanted to do. He makes it into a production number."

Hackstead looked at him sharply and they paced together toward the park. Across in Park Lane a group of tramps was squatting on the grass waving cheerfully.

"What sort of checking?" Hackstead asked.

"Tempsford, 1943. He can get to some of that old crowd. A lot of them still live in the past. Go through the routines, imagine they're still in it. It's either a Moon Squadron pilot or one of the SOE conducting officers."

"And you were thinking?"

"That they might remember if a Marauder was nipping around Tempsford in the summer of '43. They might even recall what it was actually doing."

Hackstead grunted again. "Worth a try."

"Sharp and Klein?" Dobson asked.

"Both sergeants. One in Virginia, the other in New York.

They were members of Potts' crew until July '43, when they were suddenly moved. Just shifted. The record says they went to 381st Group at Ridgewell. Went missing quite quickly. End of July. Funny how everyone who stayed with Potts came through clean, while everyone who left him went missing. Free, who doesn't count. Wilcox Pride. Sharp and Klein."

"All ended up POWs."

"Every one. In the bag, as your people used to say. Anyway, we'll have a chance to talk to the whole lot if Charles does his stuff and gets them over here."

"Sly, very sly. What're we going to do, assemble them in some old mansion like the end of an Agatha Christie book?"

"I had considered it a possibility. You can play the Finney role—Hercule Poirot."

"In the meantime?"

"I think we should take a run down to Romney again. Have a word with the ghost watchers, then perhaps go and visit Free. He's the odd man, remember. See what his memory's got locked away."

"Then to Halton? To the hospital?"

"If they haven't replied to the signal I fired off this morning, yes." He eyed a young girl in a long summer dress hurrying by. "I wonder who this guy Denis is. The one with the red rose you're going to meet at six. That could be interesting."

"Want me to find out? Someone somewhere is expecting a telephone call from me."

"Why not."

They increased their pace. The clouds were coming back and the air was beginning to hang heavy. Maybe thunder about. They skirted the Serpentine and made for the restaurant and the telephone booths. The first one had been vandalized. In the second it took Dobson three tries before he got Ann on the line.

"You're not calling off tonight?" She sounded like a small girl about to have a treat denied.

"Not likely. I want Sugden."

Sugden was brisk and inclined to speak in riddles.

"You send that big spade after us?"

"A messenger was dispatched by friends."

"Friends" usually meant the security services. Dobson wondered if Sugden was talking of friends past or present. The line was open and the conversation difficult.

"Denis was a conducting officer for SOE," he told Hackstead when it was over. "Regularly at Tempsford in '43. I hope that's what Sugden meant, anyway. We had to talk in crossword clues."

Hackstead gave a gruff chuckle. "Okay. I'm going back to Grosvenor Square. Helicopter at ten o'clock tomorrow suit you?"

Dobson thought about Ann and wondered what sort of night was in store. "Ten o'clock," he repeated without much enthusiasm.

Back at Charlotte Street he washed and shaved again, smoothing his cheeks with some Aramis lotion—still left from Christmas—turning his face from side to side, viewing it, without vanity, in the mirror. It was an odd face, he considered critically: not bad to look at, but with blemishes of which he was aware—the little clump of pockmarks on the right cheek, low down in line with his lips. As for the lips? Not sensuous, but not thin either. Largish eyes; kind, sharp eyes, described as hazel-colored on his passport. It was a square face with a straight nose. He put on a hard look, then smiled back at himself, shaking his head so that the lightish brown hair moved, one lock falling, as it always did, down onto his brow. "Dobson: man of action," he said aloud, laughing.

He changed. Lightweight suit, cream shirt and sky-blue silk tie. If the timing was off, he would not have to rush things when he returned from the meeting with Denis.

The thunder had arrived, though not the rain, rumbling over the city in great waves, making the heat within the flat oppressive and airless. As he took a final look in his bedroom mirror, Dobson realized that the dark full clouds were giving the effect of nightfall. It was quarter past five and you really needed a light to see properly. The tiny worries erupted. Would he get over to the hotel on time? If the threatened downpour began it would be almost impossible to get a cab. Would Ann be held up? Would he have to keep her waiting on the small landing outside his front door?

He switched on the light, and for the second time that afternoon, dialed Ann in Clapham. He always kept a spare key in his desk drawer. She was to bring it with her and use it if he had not returned by the time she got to Charlotte Street. She seemed pleased at his thoughtfulness.

"I'll have to hang on to it," she said. "Catch you unaware some night."

He crossed the living room and took his raincoat from the closet, starting to think about Denis. For some strange reason he imagined that Denis was an old queen, who, in his youth, had made regular trips through the Bedfordshire countryside to Tempsford, soothing, reminding, calming the young men and women he shepherded into danger. What a bloody awful job, Dobson thought, being a dispatcher of agents, wondering if they were ready to go, sometimes knowing they were not but, because of the pressure of the times, letting them leave just the same.

He had read most of the official stuff on the work of Special Operations executive and knew there was much more left unwritten. Above all else he wondered if Denis had known of a Marauder. If it was there at all.

His mind alive with pictures, thoughts turned almost visible, Dobson opened his front door and the thing was standing there, directly in front of him in the brooding thunder-darkness of the tiny landing.

11

For a horrible moment he thought it was the apparition of Pole or Black, returned for retribution. Then, with that clear knowledge which comes irrationally, forcing its way through cold terror, he saw that the flying clothes dated back from long before Pole or Black ever climbed into an aircraft.

It wore light khaki trousers, slashed, ragged, the color just distinguishable in the unnatural light on the landing.

The thunder rolled again outside, and a second later one brilliant flare of lightning.

There was a leather jacket with sheepskin collar turned up, a flying helmet framing the ghastly charnel face, illuminated for the brief second of the cloud-to-cloud spark over London.

The face was half bone and half flesh, some of it separating from the bone, hanging loose. Its fraying lips were drawn back to display black gums and long skull teeth. The eye sockets glinted with dead jelly.

In the first instant Dobson cried out and the figure made a long hissing noise, like the expulsion of air from a ripped inflatable cushion. The stench of putrefaction hit his nostrils, its foulness causing his mouth to open wide in a retching yawn.

The thought of vagal inhibition went through his mind.

Dying from shock. It happened: and could happen to him, feet rooted just inside his own front door, the hair on his head risen and tingling as though electricity passed through his body. After the first cry he could not draw breath and knew that none of his muscles would act on the commands he might pass to them through the eye and brain.

The jaw moved, teeth grinding, and another hiss, then a gloved hand rose from somewhere near the bottom of the leather jacket. It held something like a small brass blunderbuss, the muzzle belling out.

Dobson recognized it. An old Very pistol. The picture in his head overlapped the reality he did not want to see, standing before him. He saw a B-17, a Fortress, coming in to land, the red Very lights curving up from the fuselage to warn of dead or wounded on board.

Then the thing groaned, the hand came back and the Very pistol crashed down onto Dobson's temple. Once. Twice. The arm raised for the third blow.

He realized that he was on his knees and through the daze, terror and blood he could already feel dripping from his head, Dobson saw the edge of the door and grabbed for it.

He heard the pistol strike the side of the door and knew somehow that he only had a little strength left. He dragged at the door, felt it resist, then pushed, falling against it. One final effort and the door swung closed, the lock, far away, snapping into place. Then the shuddering blows against the woodwork so that the shock waves traveled through his own body slumped against it.

He raised his head, vaguely aware of the blood on his hands and around him. Then the silence closed in, comforting and warding off the stench of decay which came from the far side of the door. He could hear it scrabbling at the woodwork, but he did not want to be conscious of its ultimate victory, so he withdrew further into the darkness, only dimly aware of the pushing and the continued scrabbling.

Then, through the floating darkness, a voice calling his name.

His head did not seem to belong to him. It felt twice its normal size. There were two people looking at him, and a smell of disinfectant.

"All right, Mr. Dobson. You're all right. Just lie easy."

"No," he heard himself say and the terror was on him again.

The disinfectant in his nostrils, cloying and clinging from *Dodo*'s fuselage.

He retched and was violently sick into the bowl the nurse held for him.

By the time the doctors came in he felt a good deal better, but for the disorientation and throbbing head. They looked into his eyes with pencil lights, tested his reactions, examined his ears.

"You'd better stay here overnight, just to make certain, Wing Commander," the older one told him. He looked very Harley Street, very London Clinic.

The younger doctor wore a white coat and had hair which reached to his shoulders. He asked Dobson if he had seen the man who attacked him, and Dobson had the good sense to say that he had not gotten a clear view; though the nightmare persisted. By now he could not decide what was truth. Whether the assailant had really been the thing uppermost in his mind, or whether that was a dream projection, summoned from darkest fantasy during the period when he had lain unconscious on his living room floor.

They told him he had been X-rayed and there were no fractures. As far as they could tell there was no concussion or damage.

"You've got a couple of nasty cuts and the head'll be tender and painful for a while," the elder doctor said as they left. "Get to your own doctor as quickly as you can if you do have any blackouts or severe loss of vision."

They also said that the police would be wanting a word with him, and would he like to see his young woman?

His young woman? Ann? His young woman. Even in the confusion Dobson felt suddenly elated, a flush of happiness which he could not explain.

She told him how she had found him.

"I thought you were dead." The look of concern gave Dobson intense pleasure. "There was blood everywhere." She swallowed as though the thought made her sick. "Did you see . . . ?"

"Yes." The horror again, the ragged flesh on the eaten lips, the teeth and the hissing groan. It had to be a projection of his worst subconscious fears. "I messed up your evening." He shook off the sense of cold terror.

"There'll be others. I'm just relieved you're okay. I had to tell the police. I hope that was right—I mean it couldn't have anything to do with work, could it, the job?"

He forced a smile, knowing that it was spread very thin

across his face, and told her no, but could she get Sugden in to see him as soon as possible. Also, would she call Hackstead.

"I've already called Colonel Hackstead." She laid a hand over his. She had long fingers, he noticed. No nail polish, and the nails cut very short. "He's waiting outside. I like him, David. Tremendously efficient. He's terribly concerned about you."

"Does that mean I'm having to give up the pleasure of your company to the more raucous pleasure of his?"

"I think he wants a word. Why don't I go and call Sugden and let him come in. They told us we weren't to stay long anyway." She paused. "They say you'll be okay tomorrow. Would you like me to come down and help you get back to the flat? Maybe I can cook lunch or something?"

"What about your own commitments? It would be very . . ."

"Then I'll do it. Don't worry."

He grinned. "I have to talk with Sugden."

"Tomorrow. They're not letting anyone else talk to you tonight except Colonel Hackstead. I'll find out what time they expect to let you out and I'll call Sugden. I'll be here to get you home. Just rest, eh?"

She laid the tips of two fingers on his forehead just below the bandages. "All right?"

He nodded, part of his mind telling him he had a chance here. Nobody had shown this much concern for him in a long time. Since? The distorting mirrors on the pier returned to mind; and his reflection in the glass doors at the U.S. Embassy. When he next looked up, Ann was gone, leaving a trace of something expensive and pleasant which overrode the pervading antiseptic smell.

Bud Hackstead entered, remarking on the nursing sister who was apparently on duty outside. "Her legs end just below the ear lobes. What happened, Dave, that guy Denis blow a fuse?"

"I didn't get as far as Denis. You're not going to believe this." And he described what happened to an incredulous Hackstead.

"Dreams, Dave. You got yourself mugged and maybe had a bad dream as you came around. When they letting you outa here?"

"In the morning. I don't know if . . ."

"Don't worry, if you're thinking about tomorrow. Take the day off. Rest up, read a good book. Or better still, a bad one. The schedule's been changed anyway. With all this happening, I'd forgotten it's Sunday tomorrow. Nobody will want us down at Romney Marsh. Monday is fine. Thank God the hospitals stay open. I'll run down to Halton. Fixed it anyway. We'll do some ghost hunting and look up friend Free on Monday. Maybe tomorrow night I'll give you a call. Let you know what Halton've come up with: what tales the dead men tell."

Dobson felt tired, fatigue hoisting itself into his body by way of the pain.

"Take care." Hackstead leaned forward and pressed a large hand onto his shoulder. Dobson nodded and managed the thin smile again.

The nurse came with the pills as Hackstead left. Dobson took them without complaint, closed his eyes and began to float slowly down the stream of consciousness into the backwater of dark unknowing.

His head felt more bruised than aching in the morning. He even had a little breakfast and they told him he could get up and dress. His clothes were in the locker. The reflection in the mirror showed a chalky face under a white turban of bandages.

Naturally his legs were shaky and his head felt tender, but vision was clear and he did not feel sick any more. At about ten o'clock the younger of the two doctors came in to see him.

"You feel okay to be let out?" he asked.

"I'd rather."

"Feel like talking to the coppers?"

"If I have to. They the regular brand or something special?"

The doctor looked down his nose. "I'm not sure. You've had a man outside all night. A rather large gentleman has just arrived: says he wants a word. He *is* rather different."

Sugden had run amok, Dobson thought. Gone all spymaster on him. He told the doctor to wheel in the police and get it over with.

"You sure?"

He signified by starting to nod, but the bruising reacted badly. "Yes," he said, keeping the head as steady as possible.

"Watch how you go." The young doctor opened the door, leaving it ajar while he carried on a short conversation with someone just out of Dobson's line of vision. "You can go in now," he heard the doctor say.

"Wing Commander Dobson, I was sorry to hear about your little accident."

The towering black bulk of Trotter loomed in the doorway.

"Oh, Christ," he moaned. "I thought you only delivered messages. What's the score?"

The somber Trotter grasped an upright chair in one large paw, lifted it and put it down gently in front of the armchair which Dobson occupied. Slowly he sat, leaning forward, hands resting on his knees.

"Denis didn't make it through the night," he said.

12

"Let's see the card then."

Trotter brought his right hand forward, fist clenched. He opened the hand and there was the warrant card nestling in his palm. It was like a flashy conjuring trick.

"Detective Inspector Trotter." Then he added, a shade apologetically, "Special Branch."

"And Denis?"

"Was retired DI5. SOE in the '39-'45 conflict. Specialist in matters clandestine."

"And where did you come in?"

"I'm supposed to be asking, but we'll let it pass. I simply had to deliver a message. I did it as a favor. Sugden got hold of someone up the scale and they put him on to Denis. The meet was fixed. All that lot play the security game. They even use cryptonyms when they want to take a crap. I just go along with them. So I delivered the message. Practiced a bit of tailing."

"You didn't do too well. Hackstead's a heavy. You might've been in trouble."

"Yeah, I figured you'd made me."

"You were telling me about Denis."

"That was a cryptonym."

"So I gathered."

"He waited for you, at the Mayfair. For about an hour I should think. What'd you want to talk about? With Denis?"

"Things covert."

"What things?"

"No, Inspector Trotter."

"Quite right, you shouldn't tell me what you wanted with Denis unless I've been cleared."

"And I doubt if you have."

"You doubt right. Was it dangerous, though? I mean something current?"

"There's something current: of course there is. You know I'm working with Hackstead, but it's hardly anything dangerous. Classified, yes, but routine. What happened to Denis?"

"What happened to you?"

"I got mugged," he said, his voice betraying him.

"You got mugged and some."

"Okay. So what happened to Denis—whoever he is?"

"Denis," said Trotter slowly, "stayed at the Mayfair until around seven o'clock, talking with some fella he met in the bar. He then took a taxi home to his cute little basement apartment in Hampstead. About ten o'clock a neighbor called the police. There'd been noises of a nasty and frightening nature. Denis got himself a gastrectomy. With a knife, and not on the National Health. He was dead when they broke in. A lovers' tiff is indicated. You get that with the gay fraternity, you know."

Dobson had no reason for believing that Denis was gay, yet he had thought it all along. No hints or clues: just instinct. It worried him. He had been thinking about just that when he opened the door at Charlotte Street and walked into the terror.

"How old would Denis be?" he asked.

"Mid-sixties."

"History of pick-ups? Boys? Regulars?"

"You talk like the regular pigs, Wing Commander Dobson. You know what 'pig' stands for?"

"Tell me."

"Pride; Integrity; Guts. Yes, Denis had a regular. They're out looking for him now. The neighbors are a nosy lot and they knew all about Denis and his habits. Didn't approve of him. He used to come home with young lads: different young lads, when the regular was away." Trotter shook his head. "Tcht-tcht, I'd say that we'll be able to map out a history of Denis' way of life without much of a problem: find out his favorite pick-up spots.

It's what often goes wrong with faggots. Beware the green-eyed monster."

It hurt the bruises when Dobson frowned. He tried moving his head and it felt as though his brain was slopping about inside. "It goes wrong with those of us who are called normal, for the same reason."

"I'm not denying it. Any pick-up's dangerous in a city. You never know who's on the other side of that door."

"Or on the far side of the eyes."

"Right. So tell me what happened to *you.*"

"Someone hit me. On the outside of my front door."

"You're sure it was *your* front door?"

"Where else?"

"Denis' front door. It was you he was meeting, remember?"

"Oh come on. I was found..."

"Miss West *says* she found you inside your own front door at around seven-thirty. Nobody's leaned on her yet, but they might."

"Trotter!" His genuine incredulity matched the tone of his voice.

"Okay. I believe you. But the CID could ask. You never know. You see the guy who hit you?"

"Not really."

"What kind of an answer's that?" Trotter leaned forward, on the verge of turning aggressive. "I only want to establish there's no connection between you getting assaulted and the demise of poor old Denis."

"I got a shade disorientated. The bang on the head. Dreams get mixed up with fact."

"Okay, tell me about the dreams."

"You a superstitious man, Trotter?"

Mentally, Dobson wanted to retreat—anywhere, into a shell, into himself. He understood why people lost their memories under stress.

"What are you getting at?"

Dobson swallowed. "It seems to me that I got attacked by a corpse wearing World War II flying gear."

Trotter showed his teeth: pearls cultured by the National Health Service. "What'd he hit you with?"

"A Very pistol. You know, one of those things they used..."

"I know what they're for. A corpse?"

"In the flesh."

"It tie in with what you're working on?"

"In a strange sort of way, yes it does."

"You're not on anything?"

"Of course not."

"Okay, you'd be surprised at some of the pillars of our establishment who are. You think you were hallucinating?"

"I suppose I could have been. Never have done before. The whole thing's very clear. There was a smell."

"There would be with a corpse. You told Hackstead?"

"I told him. He didn't believe me either."

"Who says I don't believe you? Would you personally discount the idea that there's a connection between Denis getting carved and you being clobbered?"

"I'd think it farfetched."

Trotter rocked to and fro on his chair, like a medium going into a trance. "Hard on the ass, these chairs." He did not smile. "Yet there is some kind of connection between the experience and the thing you're working on?"

"If I was having a nightmare about the thing I'm working on, it would be like the experience, yes."

"You haven't told the medics about the corpse, have you?"

"No."

"Why not?"

"Because I have no desire to be locked away in a padded room for the rest of my natural."

Trotter thought about that. "You're out of joint with the times, friend. I believe you got duffed up by a corpse. You'd be surprised at some of the folk who go round doing people. Donald Duck, the Frankenstein monster, the three little pigs. Some of these guys go in for the bizarre. Mind you, it usually attracts rapists more than muggers. Element of terror." He scowled and pulled nervously on an ear lobe. "I find it very interesting that you say the corpse image could tie up with the thing you're working on. That makes two coincidences. You and Denis; and the tie-in with your current work in progress. One I can take. Two I worry about. You've told me, anyway, so I'll leave you in peace. They letting you out of here?"

"This morning."

"Going home?"

"Yes." Uneasy for the first time. Home? The landing. The door. Face to face with the horror.

Trotter's head sagged down and then lifted slowly. At the door he paused and asked Dobson if he knew where Hackstead could be found. Dobson told him Princess Mary's RAF Hospital, Halton.

"It'll keep. Nice talking to you, Wing Commander. Leave it with me and keep taking the tablets."

Around midday they told Dobson that he could leave anytime he wanted, but the doctor did not advise any strenuous work for a few days. They gave him a small supply of little white pills and dosage instructions, but they did not offer to call a cab or provide any other kind of transport.

At twelve-fifteen Ann arrived. Initially, the process of walking, the soreness of his head and the effect of the tablets made Dobson detached from the surroundings. But as Ann helped him into the car her breast brushed for a second against his fingers. It was a momentary experience and she showed no sign of having even noticed it, but the effect upon him was startling. Almost an adolescent mixture of embarrassment and delight.

They pulled out of the hospital gates and into the traffic.

"Sugden's in a panic," said Ann.

"Sugden." He closed his eyes, the nerves in his fingers still aware of the scrape with her breast.

"He's in a panic. Wants to see you. I had to assure him that you were okay. He's behaving like something out of a TV series."

"Have I got to go and see him?" The last thing he wanted today was Sugden.

"Lord no. He's coming to see you."

"Oh Christ."

She parked proficiently, in a space Dobson would never have considered, helped him out and let him lean on her arm as they crossed the road. People stared at his bandaged head accusingly, as though he had been mixed up in some bar brawl.

When they got to the landing outside his door, he thought he was really going to throw up. The association was overpoweringly strong, as though he could even still smell the stench of putrefaction.

She settled him in the largest armchair, made tea and chatted to him, long-distance through the open kitchen door as she prepared the meal.

Slowly the pain returned, as though his head was a huge eye full of splintered glass. Through the increasing muzziness he watched her moving, a quick precise economy, like someone working automatically on a production line.

Eventually they ate and she refused to let him help with the washing up. When it was done she came through again with coffee, pausing for a moment with her hand touching the back of his head.

"Sorry I loused up last night." He shrugged an apology.

"There'll be other nights."

"I hope so." He was almost tongue-tied, like an inexperienced schoolboy.

They talked fitfully, the conversation following what seemed to be a rich vein and then petering out suddenly into embarrassed silence. Tactfully she stayed off the subject of work and politics. They had just settled into a mutual swapping of life histories when Sugden telephoned. It was three-thirty and as soon as Dobson heard his voice, the pain sprang back as though triggered by some Pavlovian training.

"I've got a man watching your back," said Sugden.

Dobson sighed and murmured something about playing cowboys and Indians.

"I want to come over," Sugden continued, grave as a crypt.

"Why not?"

"If that's all right by you."

"We'll put the kettle on." The ache subsided, like an ebb tide gently washing away.

Sugden looked dramatic dressed in a dark suit, unsuitable for the weather, and carrying a military-style raincoat. The sky outside was cloudless. Ann let him in and he made straight for the window, signaling furtively to someone in the street below.

When all that was done, he faced Dobson, the skin on his cheeks glowing unnaturally red. Maybe he had a heart condition, Dobson considered.

"You heard about Denis?" Sugden asked, his voice assuming a parsonical lilt. "Poor devil. They made a mess of you as well."

"I got mugged, and I gather that Denis was murdered by some closet queen pick-up. Don't go jumping at shadows, Sugden. The shadows aren't there."

"Just doing my job." He looked disgruntled. "It's the hell of a coincidence, you must admit. Special Branch talked to you yet?"

"This morning."

"Who?"

"Trotter."

"That insubordinate clown." The cheeks blossomed, piggy eyes glittering bright. "Man's an idiot. What did he say?"

"You know what Special Branch are like. Executive arm of DI5. You should be able to find out what they think. I can't."

"You want Terry to take over?"

"Not bloody likely. I'm going to get Ann to unwind this Sikh hat later and see if we can replace it with a couple of Band-Aids. I'll be back in the morning. Back in the field," he added with a secret smile.

Sugden grunted, staying close to the window, glancing down every few seconds, as though he expected an event of great importance to take place in the street below.

"You took a couple of nasty knocks, Dobson. You certain you can carry on?"

"Look, Sugden. The secret squirreling isn't necessary. It's a small routine job. A little puzzle: there's nothing that's going to affect the future."

Sugden made a puffing noise, his mouth slightly open, lips protruding. "There are ways of doing things," he spoke quietly, convinced of his own reasonableness. "There should be order. It's something that I3 lacks. The discipline of control. Order. People should learn to use the correct methods. There are prescribed ways. Like on the parade ground."

Dobson did not have the heart to stop him. "Who is it you want me to meet?"

"You missed the appointment with Denis and *he* did not observe the ground rules. There was a fallback." He shook his head. "If he'd stuck to the correct procedure, he wouldn't be dead now. But I did the thing properly, Dobson. You can tell Colonel Hackstead that. He'll appreciate it."

My God, he's frightened of Bud Hackstead. Dobson nodded.

"There was a back-up, I saw to that." Sugden glanced downward once more. "If you think this place is secure I'll have him brought in."

"The back-up?"

"Of course."

"Who is he?"

"Call him Arthur." Sugden dropped his voice and looked steadfastly into the street. "He was a senior pilot with 161 Special Duties at Tempsford in '43." Sugden bit at his lower lip.

"What part of '43?" Dobson asked, modulating his own voice to Sugden's level.

In the kitchen Ann clattered the cups. He called to her, saying that she might as well set an extra place.

"From early spring to late autumn. The exact period you wanted is covered."

"Get him up here." Dobson turned from the window, walking back to the chair, leaving Sugden to make his signals in peace.

Ann came in with a tray, looking at him, smiling. Dobson smiled back. Once the tray was on the table he put out a hand. She glanced toward Sugden, who was lost in his Machiavellian moves, took a step toward the chair and placed her hand into Dobson's outstretched palm. He pressed gently and she responded.

"Later," she whispered drawing free, her fingers sliding against his.

Then the bell rang twice and Sugden sprang to the door. There was a muted conversation, one-sided, and Arthur was ushered into the room.

"This is the officer who wants to talk with you, Arthur." Sugden moved his hands like a market trader selling a bargain.

"Hallo, Arthur."

Dobson looked up at a thin, seedy man wearing a crumpled gray suit, the lapels of which were stained and spotted. He wore heavy-rimmed glasses and his hair was untidy, sparse but in need of trimming. When he spoke the manner was apologetic, the kind of deference which was part of a stock in trade. A representative, thought Dobson, or floor manager in an exclusive store.

"I hope I can be of help, sir." Arthur stood patiently waiting, subservient, not ill at ease but waiting to be asked before he sat, one hand fingering his RAF tie.

Dobson waved him into a chair and looked at Sugden, hoping that he would leave them alone. Sugden glared back and Dobson hadn't the stomach to move him on. Ann disappeared into the kitchen and there was a small disquieting hiatus while they went through a polite ritual of pouring tea.

"I gather you were with 161 Special Duties at Tempsford in 1943?" Dobson opened.

Arthur nodded. "From March 4 until the end of September. I've brought my log books if they'll be any help."

"One-six-one. The pick-up artists, eh?"

He nodded again. "It was my second tour at Tempsford. I was there originally with 138."

"Doing the Carter Paterson runs?" He smiled. Arthur must

have been a very experienced Special Duties pilot. "Your job?"
he asked.

"During my tour with 161?"

"Yes."

"Same as always. I flew Lysanders. Drops and pick-ups."
He hesitated. "I'd also done a combined Allied Services liaison
and controller's course. During part of that tour at Tempsford I
worked as a controller."

"Rank?"

"I'd just been put up to squadron leader." Arthur looked
away, avoiding Dobson's eyes.

In 1943, Arthur would have been around twenty-four.
Young: probably dashing in his own way. A tall slim hero who
flew secret operations into occupied Europe, riding the
high-winged, great drum-nosed, heron-legged Lizzies. Operations he could not talk about or share with anyone else.

"It's a different world, isn't it?" Dobson was almost
thinking aloud.

"It's not the world I fought for. Not any more."

"But you'd do it again?"

For a short time Arthur's face became alive, youth
re-emerging from behind the flabby skin and tired eyes.

"Oh yes, sir. For the reasons we had then I'd do it again. I'd
do it again anytime." The forties had been the time of his life.

"So you took people in? Into France?"

"And out, yes. France, Holland, Belgium. Everywhere."

"You know who?"

"Not really. I think I know some of their names now. Only
some—from the books. We made it a point not to know. Not
even their work names. We simply called them Joes. A Joe was a
Joe was a Joe—male or female. It was better that way."

Dobson waited, hoping that more would come sponta-
neously from Arthur as his mind arrowed back to the forties. But
the man remained silent, sipping his tea as Sugden drummed the
fingers of one hand on the table in nervous irritation.

"I want you to think back to the summer of '43." Dobson's
head was clear now. Neither ache nor pain. If Arthur
remembered anything it would have to be teased out of him.
"You weren't the only squadron flying from Tempsford at that
time."

Arthur took another sip of tea and said nothing.

"I want you to think about types of aircraft flying from

there during your tour in '43. In the summer."

Arthur's smile was almost indulgent. "You never saw Tempsford, did you?"

"No. I've read a bit. But me, I was . . . Well, I was too young to be in the war."

"I'll tell you then," Arthur began. "Yes, I can reel off a list of aircraft types coming in and out of Tempsford, but it was never as straightforward as that. It wasn't a straightforward place. I'll tell you what it was like the first time I went there." He dabbed his lips nervously and then patted his pockets. "You wouldn't have a cigarette . . . ?" Apologetic: embarrassed.

When the cigarette was lit and he had expelled a long stream of smoke, he began to talk, almost casually. His voice even sounded younger.

"When I got posted to Tempsford the first time round, I'd never heard of the place," he started. "All I knew was it was Bedfordshire and not too far from London. The first thing everyone remembers about it is that bloody railway level crossing at the village. There always seemed to be a train coming just as you got to it. Then you arrived and found the people at the gates were sharper than at most stations. It was odd because the place didn't look like an airfield. The mess was good—warm, cheerful, lots of chaps. But nobody seemed to know why they were there. One just didn't let on to new boys. Come to that we didn't talk about it much in the mess anyway. The CO simply shook hands with me, bought me a drink and said he'd find me some work in a day or so." He paused for another drag at his cigarette.

"The airfield itself just didn't seem to exist. It was like living in the middle of a bloody farm. It took me twenty-four hours to realize that there were runways—they were carved out between these great fields of vegetables. Beetroot and turnips. It *was* a farm. Ducks, crops, everything except Land Army girls. A lot of guards but no Landgirls. There was this damned gloomy house over on the far side, complete with strange-looking cowsheds. That was Gibraltar Farm, and the cowsheds were disguised Nissen huts. It was a couple of months before I even knew the name was Gibraltar Farm. You know about that place?"

Dobson inclined his head in an affirmative. He had heard of Gibraltar Farm and its uses. The last stopping place of agents due out; their first port of call on return.

Arthur was still speaking. "It was three days before I

worked out where the hangars were. They really had the
camouflage bit worked out. I knew there were aircraft. You
could hear them in the early hours or at dawn. But I wasn't
allowed near the hangars until the CO told me the whole story.
The security was terrific, you know. On Ops nights, Moon nights,
they would padlock all the telephone boxes for a ten-mile radius
and it was impossible to make a call out. Jerry never cottoned on
to Tempsford."

"The summer of 1943?" asked Dobson, wanting to get
down to business.

Arthur sighed. "Types of aircraft? Well, that summer we
were split between Tempsford and Tangmere. But we had the
Lysanders and Hudsons, Dakotas, Whitleys and Halifaxes."

"I was thinking more of American aircraft," said Dobson.
"Not the Dakotas ..."

"There may have been a Liberator or two there at that
time." Arthur sounded distinctly cagey.

"I was thinking more in terms of a B-26. A Martin
Marauder."

Arthur crushed out the cigarette stub. "I wondered if that
was it," he said. There was almost relief in his voice. "I've often
dreamed that somebody would ask me about it. *Overshoot*, I
mean. It *is Overshoot* you want to talk about? I mean nobody's
ever mentioned it in the official, or the unofficial, books. No
references at all."

"*Overshoot*," Dobson repeated, feeling the surge of pain as
his head came up sharply, all his intuition telling him that this was
one of the keys and that Arthur had it in his memory.

"Have they finally got the answers?" asked Arthur, eyes
bright. "I mean, I wondered when that Marauder was found
down in Kent the other week. I've wondered and wondered. You
know about one half of an operation and then the truth never
comes out—it just fades away. Nobody's heard about it."

Wait, Dobson told himself. Wait, take care. He knows
about something that's been long buried. "Tell us about
Overshoot, Arthur," he said without a tremor in his voice. "I
mean your side of it. Just tell it as you remember it."

"You'll know already that ..." Arthur coughed, cleared his
throat and started again. "You'll know that *Overshoot* was just
about the most foolhardy Op that ever went out of Tempsford."

"We'll pretend we know nothing." Dobson's voice
dropped almost to a whisper, so he had to force out a higher
volume. "That way we'll be certain of getting everything."

Arthur shifted but did not start to speak immediately. Dobson, realizing a second later that his reaction was premature, tried to accelerate.

"Our job is mainly one of listening, you know. Every nuance..."

"I'm sure. Okay, from the beginning."

"From the top: from the first thing you heard, the first thing that happened."

13

Nobody had known the names of the four men who came into Tempsford in the second week of June 1943. "*We* didn't know, anyway," Arthur said. "I suppose some of the top brass, maybe the American controllers, knew. But with that lot you could never tell who knew what or why. I'm not even certain whose Op it really was. I recognized some people who were undoubtedly SOE, because they were permanent ghosts at the farm. I just presumed that the Americans were OSS. But that's hindsight. Was it a joint Special Ops Exec/Office of Special Services show?"

"Don't muddy the pool." Dobson acted as a circuit breaker.

"The four men who came with the Marauder were certainly Americans and they lived mainly in Gibraltar Farm, only occasionally coming into the mess. They wore a kind of mixture of battle dress and flying kit, no badges of rank, and even the mess waiters were instructed to address them by single phonetic alphabet names: Baker, Charlie, York and Oscar. I don't know what they wore when they took off for *Overshoot*. They were in unmarked flying gear at the final briefing, but their arrival was just about as spectacular as you can get."

"Go on."

Arthur bent down and lifted a brown paper package Dobson had not noticed from between his feet, where he must have placed it on arrival. Inside, meticulously bound in clear plastic, was a series of log books. Arthur sifted through them, found the one he wanted and flicked through it.

"June 12/13. There we are. I did a drop and pick-up job just north of Le Mans. The drop was okay but the Joe I was supposed to bring back hadn't turned up. I came back by myself. It was just light when I landed. A good morning for coming home, I remember it very clearly because of what happened afterward. Blue and clear up there, and when you got down onto the deck the light was just starting to turn itself up, like on a stage when they bring up the dimmers—or whatever they're called."

"Yes."

"Taxied to dispersal and let the ground handling crew put her away. The usual car buzzed me over to the farm so that I could make a quick report—important that morning because of the other Joe not turning up. I had some papers to take over, I remember. Did all that, and as I was coming out of the main farm building where they did all the Ops planning, the duty IO came scurrying out of his office with the senior Ops officer. There seemed to be a flap on and I followed them out. There was an aircraft in the circuit—must have been five or six miles off but she was in trouble: bloody great black plume of smoke coming out of one engine. Around eight or nine thousand and losing height very fast. If you've ever seen an air accident, or . . . I'm sorry . . ."

"I've had my moments," Dobson said quietly. Pole and Black. The scream and the sunburst. The great snake of smoke and flame and pieces falling from the locked aircraft. He shivered.

"That Marauder landing really frightened me. She had thick black smoke pouring, oily, out of the starboard engine, which was running rough as hell, as if it was going to explode any minute. Or fall off. She had her gear down. We all just stood there and watched. I felt like a ghoul. Just waiting for her to crash. There'd been a lot of talk about Marauders: about their instability at low level with one engine gone. I think we just expected it to happen. Stood there like spare whatsits. They put a flare up, but it wasn't necessary. It was pretty obvious that we had a drama. Then I realized that nobody was doing a bloody thing. The senior Ops officer had his hands in his pockets and there were no meat wagons or anything.

"She got down to about two hundred feet, just outside the

perimeter, and we could actually see pieces falling off the starboard wing. But she came in dead straight; touched down and ran nearly the whole length of the runway. I said the smoke was oily? Yes, well, it really was—black, heavy, sticky. This great cloud of muck just followed her right down the whole length of the runway, spread out all across the vegetable fields. Really blotted out the view of the rear—she was coming in toward us, if you follow me."

Dobson and Sugden both nodded.

"Then, suddenly, the engine note changed and the smoke stopped coming, just as though somebody had turned off a tap. Both engines were running steady and she stopped—right at the end of the runway: just sat there, very much alive, and began to swing from side to side, steady and controlled. She did that about three times, so that the nose moved through around one-eighty degrees." He moved his hand on the table to illustrate.

"I didn't know then what it was all in aid of, so it seemed pretty weird—eerie. This crippled kite, the stinking black pall of smoke which really screened off the airfield, then the normality and this traversing action."

He stopped, looking from Sugden to Dobson and back again. They said nothing, waiting until he continued.

"I suppose she was on the ground like that for—what?— four minutes?" A small grunting laugh. "A little longer than we used to stay down in Europe for a drop and pick-up job. Anyway, she stayed on the ground doing the swinging bit at the end of the runway for about four minutes. Then the engines opened up and she turned right round to face back up the runway. Full power, brakes off, and away she went. Took off like the proverbial bat out of hell, with the wind—wrong direction, which must have been dicey—and straight through all that sticky black smoke, which meant a good deal of her run would be blind for the pilots. She disappeared for a moment into the gunk, and then we saw her climbing away." His hand formed the classic airman's descriptive picture of an aircraft moving upward, describing a post-take-off attitude.

"I remember being absolutely bewildered. The SOO just said, 'Bloody good show. They really have been getting some hours in on that.' Then the intelligence officer took me to one side and told me not to discuss it—even with anyone else who had seen the whole business. I went back to the mess for my eggs and bacon. As we drove over, the Marauder came in again. This time without the dramatics. Normal landing."

"And she stayed?"

"Oh yes, they tucked her away in one of the hangars—quite near the farm. Even flew in her own ground crew. I believe they were Americans."

"Markings?"

"She had American markings. I know that for sure. I think she'd had one of those paintings on the front, by the nose. The Yanks were pretty fond of drawing on their kites—popsies, Jane types: liked nicknames. I think this one had all that but they'd blanked it out."

"And she stayed there until *Overshoot* got under way?"

"Of course. That was the object of the exercise, wasn't it? Going from Tempsford because it was so secure. She did one or two more practice runs. Always early, at half-light. Saw one more myself. Same procedure and very convincing. Nobody discussed it, though I suppose we all thought about it. Wondered."

"But you were in on it?"

"Oh Lord, yes, but that was just before they went. I did one more drop and pick-up. That is, one more after the twelfth-thirteenth job. I took a Joe out and finally brought back the chap I'd intended to pick up on the earlier run."

"Dates?" asked Dobson.

Arthur thumbed through his log book. "June 28. I got back early hours of the twenty-ninth and that afternoon the old man sent for me and said I'd been taken off Ops for something more important—well, for *Overshoot*. They told me I was to be liaison with an American chap called Hennessy. He arrived that evening. They all did: Hennessy, and a couple of civilians I hadn't seen before. One was definitely SOE and I'm pretty certain the other was OSS, like Hennessy. Oh yes, and there was a Pilot Officer Prune type as well, all moustache and no chin. I can't remember his name. They brought a whole batch of the usual specialists—Met officer, another RAF IO, a Photo Recce chap; and, when it was all on, the AOC was around and some U.S. top brass."

Dobson asked him the names. The AOC had been long in the tooth then, and it was improbable that the American brass was still alive. "What was your specific job?"

"Simply liaison between the U.S. Eighth Air Force and our people. You'll know the Op was run under cover of a series of raids along the Belgian coast. I co-ordinated all that, checking out through the American fellow—Hennessy—that everything went off as scheduled. The timing had to be perfect."

Dobson nodded as though he understood exactly. "Let's pretend," he grinned at Arthur. "Let's pretend we know nothing about *Overshoot*. In fact, Wing Commander Sugden may not know. Just give us a rundown: subject, operation, intention."

"We were building up to the round-the-clock bomber offensive about then." Arthur spoke like a textbook. "U.S. Eighth by day. RAF by night. In fact the big night Ops were really getting larger all the time. The Hamburg firestorm took place at the end of July, and the Eighth Air Force Ops increased almost daily. *Overshoot* was a small, contained operation, designed to take out a large section of the Luftwaffe senior officers concerned with the night defense of Germany."

"Jesus Christ," Sugden muttered. He stopped drumming his fingers on the table.

"How?"

"At the briefing it was described as an aerial commando raid carried out by specialized personnel; and it was to be done on the ground." Arthur fingered his RAF tie again, then took out his handkerchief and dabbed his lips. "All very hush-hush and based on information which seemed to be coming regularly from the other side. As early as May our people knew of a Luftwaffe plan to make drastic alterations to the night defensive system."

"The Kammhuber Line?" Dobson asked, dredging back into his memory. The Kammhuber Line—that great chain of radar zones running from Jutland to the Mediterranean, under the control of Joseph Kammhuber, General of Night Fighters: General Officer Commanding the XII Air Corps of the Luftwaffe.

Arthur wagged his head. "We were apparently aware of a high-level conference planned to take place toward the end of June or the beginning of July. You know the organization of the Kammhuber Line?"

"Refresh our memories."

"The air defense system worked theoretically along a broad front of interlocking radar zones: one every twenty miles."

"Himmelbett zones," said Sugden, airing his knowledge.

"The senior officers from Himmelbett zones were to be at the conference, with Kammhuber and his people, as I've said, and the Geschwader leaders—group leaders of the operational squadrons."

"Quite a gathering."

"It was quite an operation. If it had worked."

"The conference took place?"

Arthur's thin shoulders rose and fell against the shabby material of his suit. "Who can tell? When the signal came to go with *Overshoot* everyone seemed confident. Time and place: St. Trond airfield near Brussels. They were all elated by that news because everybody agreed it was the easiest of the four possible targets. I remember there were airmen carrying out the models of the other three sites when we went into the briefing."

There was silence for the best part of a minute. Early July 1943, Dobson thought, trying to remember dates like a schoolboy answering a simple history question. He had written a paper at the staff college on the strategic errors made by the Luftwaffe in the night air defense of the Third Reich. He should know the dates and personalities; they were somewhere within his memory bank. There was something else there as well. Some uncertainty about that particular time. Names tripped through his head. The Geschwader leaders—Falck, Streib, Schalk. He could not bring back all their names at will. Head of Luftwaffe Command Intelligence kept dodging in and out of his mind—Joseph Schmid. Why him? Why Schmid? It was Kammhuber who was head of night fighters.

June 1943. But they were talking about *Overshoot* taking place in July, so why was Dobson's mind going back to June? Something had happened then, if only he could put his finger on it. Damn it, this was his special subject. June 1943. Kammhuber, General of Night Fighters; GOC of XII Air Corps.

Then it came, an intuitive date flashing through his head. There, then gone. Then again. He held on to it. June 24, 1943. Kammhuber. On that day, General Joseph Kammhuber fell from grace in the eyes of the Führer.

Above anyone else, Kammhuber had contributed most to the night air defense. He had suffered many rebuffs, because defense, in the eyes of the High Command, was an unattractive subject. Even the chain of searchlight batteries had been taken from his defensive line, usurped by the Gauleiters and repositioned around their cities.

Dobson had some of it in focus now. "General Kammhuber went to Hitler's headquarters toward the end of June '43," he said. "To Rastenburg."

"The Wolfschanze," Sugden added.

"He had plans to improve the night defenses. Hitler turned him down. Told him he'd got it all wrong, replaced him as GOC XII Air Corps. Schmid got that job. 'Beppo' Schmid, Chief of Luftwaffe Command Intelligence." Dobson gazed absently at

Arthur. "And you say that there was a conference on the change of defensive strategy planned as early as May?"

"That's what we were told. *Overshoot* was put together on that information. They planned it in May. Rehearsed it in June. I gathered there was information coming in all the time."

"And *Overshoot* got the green light during the first week of July?"

"Yes."

"A couple of weeks *after* Kammhuber was refused permission to go ahead with his new organization. Intelligence pinpointed the time and place of Kammhuber's conference?"

"At St. Trond."

"Why not a straightforward low-level attack on the airfield? Target identification and all that kind of thing?"

Arthur shrugged again. "You know what the Org was like."

"I didn't serve in World War II, and I don't believe everything I read about SOE and OSS. The Org, as you call it."

"But you know."

"I suppose so. I know what you mean. I know about the stupidity and pigheadedness, yes."

"The logic was that a direct raid in the vicinity would simply drive all that brass into the shelters. Instead of that there was a series of raids planned far away, over France and along the Belgian coast."

"And *Overshoot?*"

"The lone Marauder coming in high with simulated damage; losing altitude and obviously looking for somewhere to put down. From the information we had about St. Trond, the conference was supposed to be taking place in the administrative buildings which lay about four hundred yards from the end of the main runway—diagonally to starboard as I remember it, from the model and recce photographs. There was a taxitrack to the right near the end of the runway: the buildings lay beyond that."

"The other possibles were more difficult?"

"Yes. One of them was very tricky indeed."

"Just fill in the more precise details of the operation as you remember them."

"*Overshoot* was to come in high over the coast under cover of the other attacks. She would then begin her let-down west of Brussels, and start up the smoke pots housed in the starboard nacelle. There were others within the undercarriage recess, together with some junk from her to jettison over the airfield perimeter. They could keep the smoke going for a good three quarters of an hour if need be. Providing she got through the flack and the fighters, she could be down to a couple of thousand feet some twelve miles out from St. Trond. Gear down: normal signal of surrender."

"They really expected to get away with that?" Sugden began to drum his fingers again.

"They were very confident." Arthur did not even bother to look at Sugden. "Personally I thought it was a do-or-die Op. I didn't think they had a chance in hell of getting back, and I was dubious about them even getting there."

"And dubious about the strength of the information?"

Arthur thought for a moment. "No." He sounded a little uncertain. "No, I think we all believed the information. There was no reason for us not to believe it."

"Okay." Dobson passed round the cigarettes again. "Let me get it right. They were confident that they would be accepted by St. Trond as a damaged, surrendering aircraft? As such, they were to approach and land. Then the job was to make a pinpoint all-out fireflow at the administrative buildings?"

"To blast them with everything they had. Which was a lot. The aircraft was modified. In all they could rake the place with four cannon firing incendiary, explosive and armor-piercing shells, plus four .50-caliber machine guns."

All firing flat out for three minutes or so, Dobson thought, at a range of three or four hundred yards. If it got that far the Marauder could have done a lot of damage. He smiled. The whole thing was typical of the half-cocked, death or glory Ops which proliferated in the planning offices of organizations like SOE and OSS. Aloud he said, "I can see its appeal, but only if they were certain of their information: absolutely 100 per cent sure that those senior officers would be in that place at that time."

Sugden made a rasping noise in the back of his throat. "Jerry would never let 'em down."

"Oh, he probably would." Dobson's head had started to throb again. "If they got that far. There's plenty of documented evidence of Allied aircraft landing at German-occupied airfields. Arthur, you positively have no names you can give me? Not even a hint?"

"Only Hennessy. I'm pretty certain he was an OSS planner, but God knows if that was a cover name."

"And the Op definitely took place?"

"Absolutely. I was there. I saw her take off."

"Did you get anything back?"

"Very little. There were two reports, from separate Fortresses. Both of them talked about seeing a Marauder losing height over Waterloo—that stuck in my mind. Smoke coming from the starboard engine. We plotted it. Everyone seemed to think that *Overshoot* was bang on schedule at that point."

"Anyone fly a recce afterward?"

"If they did, we weren't told."

"And General Kammhuber lived. There is no mention of such an operation, no documentation, on either side?"

"I'm not an expert. Far from it." Arthur spread his hands and the defeated look came back into his face. "I've come across no mention."

"*Overshoot?*" Dobson queried reflectively, turning to Sugden. "Will you do a sweep of the files?"

Sugden gave an affirmative movement of the head.

"I'll check the American end. Perhaps some controller at Baker Street, or Grosvenor Square, got carried away. I wonder. We'll see." He looked hard and unblinking at Arthur. "You in work?"

"Yes."

"Happy in it?"

"Not particularly, but . . ." He stopped short. Dobson knew he was going to say that beggars could not be choosers.

"Perhaps Wing Commander Sugden can find you something more amenable." He caught Sugden's eye and saw the cold gleam of irritation. "We can get hold of him if we want him again?"

Sugden said they could. He was quite curt about it. Dobson thanked them both and they went through a little liturgy of farewell.

As Sugden got to the door, Dobson spoke again. "Free. I need that information."

"I've got people working on it." The round face flushed deeper than ever.

"Colonel Hackstead's very insistent about it." Dobson wanted, needed, information on Frederick Free and his place of imprisonment.

When the door closed behind Sugden and Arthur, he yelled for the painkillers. Ann came through and told him that he was allowed no more for at least an hour, so he bore with the ache while she sat on the arm of the chair and soothed his head, her long fingers smoothing the space between his eyes and the bandage.

Gradually the pain withdrew. They did not speak much,

for Dobson retreated into the labyrinth of thoughts which sprang
from the whole notion of *Overshoot*. Occasionally he raised his
head and smiled at her. Once she took his hand, and twice kissed
him gently on the forehead.

If it was *Dodo*, perhaps they had aborted late, become lost,
turned and run for home, disorientated, ending up in the marsh.
But that did not fit. Arthur said there were only four men. Four
men on *Overshoot*. Six bodies in *Dodo*. Arthur could be
mistaken. If it was *Dodo*.Of course it was bloody *Dodo*.

He thought about the Luftwaffe General Staff. Kammhuber and his people: his group leaders. Joseph Kammhuber,
desperate to reorganize and re-equip before the onslaught
became too much for his defensive line to hold. The planning and
discussions. A full-scale conference arranged so that his orders
could be implemented as soon as they were cleared by the
buffoon Göring and the Führer.

Then the trip to the Wolf's Lair at Rastenburg. Heat rising
from the sinister pine forest, members of the Begleitkommando
burning off the mosquito swarms with petrol. The checkpoints in
the perimeter fences. The barbed wire. Kammhuber unworried,
thinking the meeting was only a formality. Then Hitler himself,
pacing the drab room with its oak paneling and the Anton Graff
portrait of Frederick the Great. The Führer screaming that
Kammhuber was wrong, that the great flood of aircraft would
not come, that he was being a defeatist. Göring stood and
listened in silence. Only later did he turn on the general,
reproaching him and his "idiotic requests." While at Tempsford
they were faking the damage to the Marauder, the planners
leading four men to certain death, aiming at shadows. Why a
Marauder? Why? With such a history of trouble at low altitudes,
particularly with the gear down? Why? Why not? Dobson had
learned about planners. They worked on the details and logistics.
They did not have to go off and do the job.

"You look better." Ann broke the silence.

"You're good medicine." He raised his face and she bent to
kiss him, gently on the mouth.

She pulled away, again gently, but he pressed with one
hand in the small of her back and she kissed him a second time.
After a while he lifted his hand and placed it against the films of
material. Her breast was unfettered beneath, firm, the nipple
hard.

"When you're quite better," she said, husky, putting a hand
over his, but not moving it.

She was right, he knew, and after a few minutes he asked if she would try to make his head more respectable. They went through to the bedroom, where she slowly unwound the bandages. There were bruised areas running from above the right ear to the middle of the forehead, and the skin had been broken in a pair of gashes hard with caked blood, blue-black from the bruising.

Ann cleaned the abrasions and was just able to cover them with sticking plaster that was at hand in the small medicine chest his mother had given him years ago. He told her about the gift and how his mother had said he should carry it in his aircraft all the time—"just in case."

He felt much recovered now that the bandages were off. There was no need for another painkiller and he went and stood by her in the kitchen while she skinned the tomatoes and washed the lettuce. They were carrying the plates through when the telephone rang.

"I'm back," Bud Hackstead growled in his ear. "There's a lot to tell. You up to it?"

"I have a playmate here." He hoped it might put Hackstead off. Arthur and Sugden had been enough for one day. *Dancing Dodo* could go hang as far as he was concerned.

"The one I met at the hospital?"

Dobson told him.

"She's secure, I understand. Can I come over?"

There was no way out.

"Playmate indeed," said Ann.

"Well," he shrugged, grinning.

Half an hour later Hackstead was at the door, a heavy file under one arm, the other hand clutching a bottle of wine.

"Thank God for sanity." He came into the room and smiled lopsidedly at Ann. "I've been down among the dead men all day, and I have news, David. None of those guys they pulled out of the aircraft would've passed a physical for a cripples' reunion—let alone for an aircrew."

14

"Rickets," Hackstead said. "Rickets, and possibly osteomalacia."

"What the hell's that?"

"Adult rickets."

"I was at school with a boy who had rickets. I thought it was a childhood disease." Dobson had touched none of the wine; Ann drank a small glass with her meal—which Hackstead had refused to share. The American had almost killed the rest of the bottle.

The file he had brought with him lay unopened on the table and a slight breeze funneled its way up Charlotte Street, cooling the room minimally, occasionally billowing the curtains. In the kitchen, Ann clattered around with the dishes. "I'm not your natural *Hausfrau*," she told them as she removed the plates, "but for once I'll make an exception."

"Rickets," repeated Dobson.

"The pathologists at Halton went through it all. It's in there." Hackstead waved his half-empty glass towards the file. "But it's in a language which only the medicos understand. They gave me the simplified version. You're right, rickets is usually a disease contracted in childhood. Produces bow legs and pigeon chests. The other one—osteomalacia—is the adult variety and is usually found in women. That does horrible things like curving your spine and other bones."

Dobson leaned forward and riffled the pages of the file. It contained a number of closely typed pages and some unpleasant photographs. He closed it. The photographs were obviously of some of the bones and pieces of bodies removed from *Dodo*.

"All the corpses in the wreck are undoubtedly male." Hackstead drained the last drops of the wine into his glass. "It would seem that every single one of them had bone deformities. They also suspect that, in a couple of cases, the bodies were of a reasonably advanced age when the aircraft went into the marsh. So the crew were not your normal, fit and active, intrepid aviators."

"Cripples?" Dobson's voice was bleak and the pain had started to tweak at the side of his head again.

"They had problems."

"The Halton people make any other suggestions?"

"Not really. Like all medical men they can only make assessments on the evidence presented. They said it wasn't likely that little group could have handled a Marauder with any degree of satisfaction."

"More mysteries." Dobson stretched his back. "An aircraft that never was, a crew that are still alive, yet they're dead. Now they're cripples. Does it make any sense to you?"

Hackstead thought for a full minute. "No," his smile bland as a shop assistant querying your check.

Dobson grinned. "Well, I have news for you. Remember our friend Trotter?"

"The deliverer of messages?"

Dobson told him about Trotter being Special Branch, and of Denis' death.

Hackstead rose slowly and walked to the window. "So we're no nearer on that score. Pity."

"Denis was gay. I gather it might be a jealous gay job."

"The case of the fighting fairies." Hackstead sounded callous. That made sense.

"I've made some slight progress," Dobson said quietly. For a moment he wondered if his voice had not been strong enough to reach Hackstead, standing with his back to him.

The American half-turned. "What?"

"You've got CIA contacts."

Hackstead's face relaxed. "Don't start that again, baby. I told you, the way I mix with those people's like kissing a rattlesnake: you do it gently and as little as possible."

"Well, can you check out ex-OSS people?"

Hackstead appeared to think for a moment. "Some."

"A man called Hennessy. Worked for a while, beginning of July '43, at Tempsford."

"Hennessy his real name?"

"No way of knowing. Could be a work name."

Hackstead walked back from the window and sat down again. "I can but try. Why?"

"Can you also try to check out an operation—possibly OSS, probably in conjunction with SOE—called *Overshoot?*"

"Don't tell me: they got at Hitler and sent him over Niagara Falls in a barrel."

"The tale is that they tried to get a large hunk of the Luftwaffe night defense people. Using a B-26. Our B-26." He told the whole story, slowly and with care, leaving nothing out including his own thoughts on the dates in relation to Kammhuber and his falling-out with Hitler. Hackstead listened quietly, sitting upright in his chair, face impassive.

When it was over he said, "We oughta comb out the existing German stuff."

"Luftwaffe documents?"

"I reckon."

"Where?"

"A lot of their stuff got itself conveniently destroyed. We'll put a research man into the Imperial War Museum, just to see. I'll fix that. But our best bet would be . . ."

"Koblenz?"

"Took it right out of my mouth."

The German Military Archives were in Koblenz.

"So we get to see a bit of the world."

Hackstead shook his head. "Someone else gets to see a bit of his own homeland. We send a Kraut there. The Germans have an aversion to people like us nosing around their files."

"Any ideas?"

The American chuckled. "Wish Trotter was German. I'll find one of our boys. Leave Koblenz and the War Museum Documents Department to me."

Ann appeared in the kitchen doorway. "Is it still all silent service stuff?"

"Come on in." Hackstead made an expansive gesture. He suddenly seemed quite pleased with himself. "Thanks for looking after my boy."

"My pleasure."

"How's the head?" It was the first time he had made any serious inquiry into the state of Dobson's health.

"Comes and goes, but I'll live."

"For one who took the kind of beating you did, you're remarkably active—what with *Overshoot*, the goings-on at Tempsford and all."

"That was Sugden's work."

"You feel up to visiting Kent tomorrow? Have a word with a couple of the people who've seen ghostly airmen walking the marshes, maybe another chat with the odd Mrs. Lambert, and a small ride to Canterbury to see the real Frederick Free?"

"You organized that?"

"Sort of. I've arranged transport. Thought we could stay the night at some ancient caravanserai. They got a Hilton in Canterbury?"

"I think not. Unless they've bought the cathedral."

"There's always the County Hotel. Hot and cold limping pilgrims in every room." Ann was sitting on the arm of Dobson's chair again.

"You feel like coming?" Hackstead looked at Dobson, sounding as though he might prefer to go alone.

"Yes." Dobson was not going to miss out if he could possibly help it. "What time do we leave?"

"Pick you up noon, at the latest. You be okay for that?" The eyebrows raised and a tiny twitch of his eyes passing between Ann and Dobson.

"Should be okay."

"Think about it."

Dobson was thinking about it when Ann came back from seeing Hackstead to the top of the stairs. The curtains billowed again, flapping right up toward the ceiling.

"You want another pill?" she asked, looking a shade worried, the hint of concern behind her eyes and in her expression.

"I'll manage. The muzziness has gone. It's tender to the touch, that's all."

"No violent headaches?"

"Nothing to speak of, no."

"You're sure? Don't take risks, David. If it gets bad again you'll have to phone the hospital."

"I'm fine. The patient is making an extraordinarily rapid recovery."

"You'll manage tomorrow?" As though she was trying to tell him something.

"Hackstead doesn't want me to go?"

"He wants you. But he wants you fit."

"I'll be fit." In the back of his mind the decision was made. Terry Makepiece was not going to take over on this. He would see it through himself.

There was a long pause.

"I want you fit as well." She spoke at last, the trace of a smile on her lips. "Listen, will you be okay tonight?"

"Tonight?"

"Tonight. Here in the flat. Here on your own."

It had not crossed his mind. A night alone in the flat with the memories still fresh and close. He closed his eyes and knew immediately what she meant: the idea of the thing dripping putrefied flesh, hovering outside on the landing, waiting to complete what it had started. Fear.

"It's nothing to be ashamed of," she said, coming over and resting a hand lightly on the top of his head—as though reading his thoughts.

He breathed in and it was a slight effort. Anxiety again. "I'll be okay. Why not?" Trying nonchalance and knowing it was not working.

"I'll stay." She was simple and relaxed. "David, I'll stay if you'd like that."

He stared at her, the query obvious.

"No." She shook her head. "I'll stay and I'll sleep here. On the couch. Just to make sure you're not alone. Nothing else. Not yet. I've already told you: later, when you're really better. When all this is over. I want that, you know it."

He was not certain what she meant by "all this," but not since that other time, he reflected once more, had any woman given so freely of herself.

Only once had there ever been anyone else with the kind of understanding that was starting to flow between them. The distorting mirrors at the end of the pier. He dragged his eyes from Ann, trying to force the recurring truth from his senses, but it came bubbling up, breaking through the already frayed skin of the subconscious, generating the guilt as always.

Pole. They were going to break it to Pole later that week, the week of the distorting mirrors and the walk along the pier. They had spent part of the day talking about little else. She was to tell Pole that it was all over between them, that she wanted her freedom.

After the accident—was it two or three days after?—
Dobson had seen her only the once, in the most harrowing
circumstances. Perhaps Pole had even meant to turn straight into
Dobson's aircraft and not Black's. That thought had lowered
over him time and again.

"Yes, I'd like you to stay," he said quietly. "I understand,
and you're right, of course. But why don't you let me sleep here
on the couch? You have my bed."

"You'll sleep in your own bed, David." The hand moving
on his shoulder. "Come on, I'll get you organized. You need sleep
now. Tomorrow you mustn't hesitate to tell Colonel Hackstead if
you're not up to going. Understand?"

Sugden telephoned soon after Dobson was settled in bed.
He had moved heaven and earth to get details on Frederick
Free's life as a POW, and would be sending the information
around in the morning, with Terry Makepiece.

It was a quiet night, apart from the revolving thoughts and
the odd conscious series of waking nightmares as he lay on the
margin of sleep. He woke twice, but on both occasions did not
think of the problems or the specters, only of the fact that Ann
was out in the living room, just a few feet from his own door,
lying on the couch, covered by sheets and probably unclothed in
the sticky night heat.

The idea was both comforting and erotic. Both times, sleep
came again quickly, and he knew no more until she was there,
gently shaking his shoulder and kissing his cheek, a cup of coffee
on the beside table.

"I have to get going. Clapham calls." She gave a small
single-syllable laugh. "You know what they say about the
definition of a bachelor? One who comes to work each morning
from a different direction."

He shifted onto his elbows. No head pains. "I hope it'll be
only from one direction in the future."

"That, David Dobson, can be taken two ways."

"I meant from this direction."

"I know." The same warm smile. "It'll be nice."

Terry Makepiece arrived just before eleven.

"Christ," he said, standing in the doorway, "Sugden didn't
tell me they'd done a lobotomy."

"Very droll." Dobson pulled the door wide open and
found himself squinting onto the landing, the tweak of fear
flicking through his stomach. "You've got something for me?"
Makepiece was inside and the door closed. He opened the
official-looking briefcase. It was amazing that Sugden had not

made him come with it chained to his wrist. One flimsy file changed hands.

It was a summary of Flight Lieutenant Frederick Free's career following his posting from the US 8th AFF until his release from POW status, the later part taken from the final repatriation debriefing.

In July 1943 he was posted to No. 88 "Hong Kong" Squadron, which by August was settled into Hartford Bridge as part of 137 Wing, Second Tactical Air Force. They were equipped with twin-engined Boston aircraft, the Mark IIIs.

On October 15, three months after he joined the squadron, they were engaged in a low-level operation against the targets around Cherbourg, when Free's aircraft was bounced by a pair of ME 109s. The gunner/wireless op was killed in the first burst of fire, which raked the rear of the fuselage and damaged the starboard engine, which immediately seized up.

Free, who was about to turn away toward the coast at the moment the fighters struck, continued to make his turn, intending to run for it, but he was already down to something like nine hundred feet.

In his own words: *The aircraft behaved well enough on one engine and there did not appear to be any damage to the controls, but the other 109 came in fast, almost head on. I gave him a quick burst with the forward Brownings, but we had used almost all the ammunition on the targets. It did not make any difference. I saw his tracer passing below the nose and then felt them hit forward. That must have got Tommy. The aircraft juddered and we began to lose height very rapidly. The controls were sloppy and I could not get her up. I remember seeing a road and a line of trees directly ahead and we were sinking so fast that I thought we would hit them. We just cleared. Over the trees there was a flattish field. I just chopped everything, banged flaps down—though that didn't make any difference—and lifted the nose to try and reduce speed on impact. Her attitude was good, but we crunched into the grass and skidded for what seemed a couple of miles—I suppose it was around fifteen hundred yards. I thought she was going to break up and at first couldn't believe it when I found myself out and running. There was no fire. No explosions.*

He had a few cuts and bruises, together with a wrenched shoulder, probably done as he was getting out of the escape hatch. A German patrol picked him up within the hour. They treated him quite reasonably and carted him off to the police station at Valognes, some twenty kilometers inland from Cherbourg. Things were not so good there but he stayed for only one night.

On the following morning he was moved, together with six other RAF and USAAF aircrew, under guard to a railway station and put aboard a train. For the next forty-eight hours the six men and four guards lived together in a locked compartment which was only opened up for food to be brought in, or for the relief of nature. At the end of this uncomfortable journey, the prisoners found themselves loaded into trucks and taken to a camp—the Dulag Luft, aircrew interrogation center, at Oberiusel near Frankfurt. There he stayed for nearly three months.

Three months in an interrogation center? Puzzling. Not unheard of, but not usual. There were a lot of aircrew passing through the POW system toward the end of '43, from memory of what he had read; Dobson thought they siphoned them off into the larger camps fairly quickly. Query, he noted.

Early in January, Free was finally passed on: Stalag Luft III at Sagan, a hundred or so miles east of Berlin, near the Polish border.

Stalag Luft III was all too well remembered. The great escape in—when?—February? March? 1944, with all the repercussions which were still being felt by some people even now in 1976. Fifty escaped POWs, out of the seventy-odd who made a mass tunneled breakout from Sagan, had been murdered by the Gestapo on the orders of Hitler, via his hatchet man Kaltenbrunner, chief of the RSHA—the Reich Central Security Department.

Another mental query.

Free remained at Sagan until the prisoners were all removed, sometime in January '45, and forced-marched away from the sweeping Russian offensive. He was among the exhausted POWs picked up near Lübeck by the advancing British First Army five days before Germany surrendered to the Allies.

One short appendix note remained. For a period of about one month (*it may have been nearer six weeks*, Free told the debriefing officer), he was removed from Sagan and taken back to the Dulag Luft, this time in Frankfurt itself. The dates were vague. Sometime in the early summer of 1944, or late spring—around May, June.

Dobson flicked back through the pages. What they had here was obviously an abstract which contained no details of the interrogations by the Germans. Just the bald facts that Free had been interrogated twice, at length—once after the mass escape from Sagan, to which he was returned. Questions, questions, questions. He closed the file.

"I'll be telling Sugden myself." Dobson passed back the file. "We'll need a copy of this—and more. I'll have to talk with Hackstead. Just take the precious documents back to El Supremo and be careful that the KGB don't pilfer them on the way."

Makepiece had the courtesy to grin.

Ann did not even try to linger on the phone when Dobson got through to Clapham, except to ask him if he could, perhaps, call her from Canterbury that evening. He said he'd move mountains to do so but did not have her home number. She gave it and put him through to Sugden almost before he had time to scribble the seven digits into the flyleaf of his diary.

"Makepiece got to you?" Sugden asked immediately, as though they had been engaged in a dead-letter drop.

"He got to me. I read it. He's on his way back."

"What you required?"

"Partially. You're servicing me, right?"

"Of course. They're my orders."

"What the Ministry's given you is an abstract. It's incomplete."

There was a noise at the other end of the line which sounded like an obscenity.

"The subject—" Better play his game, Dobson decided. "The subject spent a considerable amount of time at an interrogation center after going into the bag. More than usual. He then went to Stalag Luft III. For six weeks or so he was taken back to an interrogation center—around May–June '44. In the abstract you have, there are no details of the interrogations."

Silence, Sugden waiting for more.

"Stalag Luft III," said Dobson. "The mass breakout. There're still people around who were there—who weren't part of the great escape. Get to them, would you? See if any of them remember Free. Tactful, no heavy questioning. I also want confirmation of dates—dates of the breakout from Stalag Luft III—I'm only working from memory but I think February or March '44. And I want to know what Free told his debriefing officer about the two sets of German interrogations. I want to know that quite quickly. Tonight."

"Roger."

"I shall be at the County Hotel, Canterbury. Colonel Hackstead and I will be there, hopefully by early evening."

"I can't promise..."

"I know, but you'll do what you can."

"I'll telephone in any case."

The doorbell rang.

"I think Colonel Hackstead's here. Talk to you this evening. Oh, and Sugden...?"

"Yes?"

"Thank you."

"We're all in this operation together." Sugden sounded more pompous than usual. "You're the one in the field. You have my complete support. How's the head?"

"Fine."

As he opened the front door, Dobson experienced a sudden explosion of fear which made him step back, the door half open. He had expected Bud Hackstead. For a snapping second as he slipped the latch he thought it could be...

"Hi. Just a friendly call." The grinning bulk of Detective Inspector Trotter seemed to fill the landing.

15

It took Dobson several seconds before he realized that his hand was clamped to the door as though held by bonded adhesive; his body rigid with tension which brought the pain flowing back into his head. Fear; realization of what might have been there.

"Hey man, you okay?"

The petrified muscles slowly relaxed.

"You okay?" repeated Trotter.

Dobson nodded, opened the door a little and allowed Trotter into the room. Involuntarily he glanced at his watch. "Colonel Hackstead's picking me up at noon."

"No problem."

Trotter lowered himself into a chair. "You working again already?"

"You know what it's like. Keeps you off the streets."

"What is work? and what is not work? are questions that perplex the wisest of men."

Dobson gave a puzzled tilt of the head. Unsuspected depths in Trotter.

"The Gospel of Krishna," the big policeman said by way of explanation.

"I wouldn't have put you down as ..."

Trotter raised a hand, palm outward as though warding off a blow. "Work keeps me *on* the streets not off them. We get all kinds and they quote a lot; specially the idealists, the religious and politicos. I can quote you in forty-three religions and about the same number of political theories. Marx is the favorite these days."

Dobson gave a wicked little smile.

"I've worked myself up from nothing to a state of extreme poverty?" he quoted.

The melon quarter grin again. "No, friend, Karl, not Groucho Marx. More like—let me see—From each according to his abilities, to each according to his needs."

"If you don't want to work, then the state has to keep you?"

"Well?" Trotter thought about it. "Well, we established that you're working today in spite of your bloodied brow. I came to talk about Richard Martin Lewis."

"Lewis?"

"Spelled like the gun. Tell me about Richard Martin Lewis, Dobson."

Dobson's mind clouded, confused. "I don't think I know him."

"You met him."

"When?"

"Yesterday afternoon."

"Yesterday?"

"Sugden brought him here."

Dobson considered the implications. "You've got markers out. Watchers."

"If you want to put it that way. Just keeping an eye on you. All part of the service. But we got very interested when Mr. Lewis turned up with Sugden and his boy scouts. Jeez, it was like a game of hide and seek out there in Charlotte Street yesterday afternoon."

"As bad as that, huh?"

"Dobson, I don't know how much experience you've had, but Sugden had guys loitering on the corners reading day-old newspapers." Trotter looked tired, Dobson thought: a man who was forced to work long hours and played hard with whatever time was left. "Then he brought in Richard Martin Lewis."

"He brought a man here, yes. But I wasn't given his name."

"You don't recognize the name I'm laying on you?"

"Sorry," he said, making a vague gesture of apology.

Trotter looked fixedly at his hands. On the right index he

wore a gold Greek puzzle ring. "Those of us who have the honor to serve with Special Branch had dealings with Mr. Lewis some ten years ago. Not me, Dobson. Ten years ago they were only just reconciling themselves to allowing people of my shade into the Met."

"Lewis?" Dobson reflected aloud.

"Formerly Squadron Leader Lewis. Wartime flying man. Civilian, working with the Ministry of Defence. A little problem over classified material being offered to an intelligence Officer of the Deutsche Demokratische Republik. East Germany to those who ain't had the benefit of education. Cold-war stuff. Only small in the newspapers. D notices were heavy stuff in those days, but I read the file. They put the lights out on the press."

"I remember nothing of that." Ten years ago. A lifetime.

"I thought you might not know," said Trotter. "At the same time I thought you *should* know. There was no case. No action. It was even rumored that poor old Richard Martin Lewis was being set up. Clean bill of health, but he resigned." He looked up from his hands, steady into Dobson's eyes. "Suppose there's no point in asking what you talked to him about?"

"None at all." Mentally he queried if he was being taken by Sugden, or if Sugden, in the role of super case officer, had been taken.

Trotter nodded. He looked sad, as though there was something he would like to say: personal, like woman trouble, or a family confidence he could share with nobody else. "If you were DI5 you'd probably fizz off and report me for exceeding my duty, but I think you know why I'm telling you."

"My boss?"

"Sugden does not inspire my confidence. No man without humor inspires my confidence."

"If it makes it any easier for you, he's my servicing officer on this one. I suppose Hackstead's my boss really."

Trotter did not smile, but began to heave himself from the chair. "Now Hackstead gives me confidence. So much confidence that he scares the eyes out of my head." The old smile returned. "I'd not tell that to anyone you know, Dobson. Hackstead is a recognizable figure in my profession: knows his job, experienced, and would sell his nearest and dearest if the mind took him, and if it meant carrying out his occupation correctly."

They got to the door.

"I don't suppose you've had any more thoughts about the dear departed who tried to scalp you?"

"Not a glimmer. They caught up with Denis' boy friend yet?"

"Mmm." Affirmative. "He's got one hell of a watertight alibi. No way he could have done it, so we're back to the other ideas."

Hackstead turned up a little after midday, in high spirits, dressed for the part of a touring American: fawn slacks and a jacket blinding in a busy check pattern. As they got into the car—a gleaming black Mercedes—Dobson noticed the colonel's shoes. All of sixty quids' worth, he decided with acknowledged envy. Security officers going about their secret work in a black, German-manufactured car laid on by the American Embassy. He thought of Arthur again and of the "Joes" he had carried into Fortress Europe with their heavy radios, forged papers; dropping down into dim-lit fields to trembling uncertainty. *It's not the world I fought for.*

"Charles has done the trick," Hackstead said, as though the fate of mankind depended upon it.

At first Dobson thought he was talking about Charlie Sugden, then he remembered Charles the journalist, and the deal: Potts' old crew returning to the sites of their former acts of valor.

"Yep, right down the line. They won't print a word until they've had 'em here for a week."

"They all coming?"

"Except one," the American smirked. "One of your ghosts. Klein can't make it."

"Oh?"

"On account of the fact that he's doing a ten-year stretch in San Quentin for armed robbery."

"Pity. It would've been better to have had the lot."

"Don't worry about Klein. You look better today," Hackstead grinned.

"I told you I'd make it."

"Slept like a top, I'll be bound. You ready to talk to the ghost sighters?"

Dobson had forgotten that before they were to see Free the day would be spent with those who had stories of specters on the marsh.

As they cleared the main snarl-up of the West End, heading toward Northolt and the helicopter, Dobson asked about progress.

"Hennessy?" he queried.

"Takes time." A chuckle like a gambler with a stacked deck. "Patience. Doubt if we'll get an ID on him though. So much went on in the time between the OSS being disbanded and the setting up of the CIA. There were things people were anxious to forget—names as well. A lot of cremations, paper funerals. But I've got a man working on it, and another at the Imperial War Museum sorting through all the Luftwaffe stuff with a magnifying glass."

"And Koblenz?"

"The jolly old Bundesarchiv? Yes, somebody'll be on his way tonight. Deutsche, like we agreed." He gave a sideways look at Dobson. "Covert, I'm afraid, but it's safest. They're our good friends now in Koblenz, but it's better they shouldn't know we're sniffing—even at shadows. Anyway, they'll be more co-operative with Herr Blenkinsop."

"Blenkinsop?"

"We call him that in the office. Real name's Kursbuch, which, if you're not up on your Kraut, means 'timetable.' Mr. Timetable. Old Peter Kursbuch used to run an excellent timetable for us once. Set your watch by him. Used to come over that damn Wall like a stone from a slingshot." He smiled, bland, seraphic. "I'm a Kraut, you know, David. American Kraut. My grandfather came right out of Nuremberg—name of Hackensteiner. I changed that. My old man stayed Ernst Hackensteiner until the day of his death." He closed his mouth, lips tight. "I ain't got nothing against religion, but a name like Hackensteiner sounds Jewish and my family were 195 per cent Lutheran. Nothing racist, but I took on an all-American name."

"Like Schwartz or Goldberg, or even Kissinger?"

Hackstead's shoulders lifted and fell in a small puff of laughter. "Or Wernher von Braun?" he said. "Anyway, Peter the Timetable will be winnowing his way through whatever they've filed away in Koblenz. The Luftwaffe files got well shredded also, you know, so don't set too much store by it. Don't hang by your toes."

"I said it'd be a paper chase."

"Yep, but we're not chasing the paper. Our job is to look up a few gibbering goblins."

Around Dead Clump, the remains of the fuselage had been lifted, leaving only a strangely symmetrical oblong grave. Dead Clump was dead at last.

The marquee, where the Farnborough people were collating the fragmentary sections of wreckage, remained, and

there were several RAF trucks parked on a roll-up mesh
hardstanding just off the small track which led past the site.

Squadron Leader Follet waited for them, a sergeant
standing nearby. There were one or two other RAF regiment
airmen around, and Dobson noticed the boy Hackstead had
spoken to on their last visit. He was with a small squad lined up
receiving instructions from an NCO. They looked like a guard of
honor. The jeep was parked up by the trucks; next to it stood an
imposing staff car with a WRAF corporal trying to look
interested in polishing the windshield.

"Almost through here now." Follet saluted, smiling the
satisfied smirk of a man glad to be rid of a problem. "Nice to see
you again, sir." He made the "sir" a plural by looking from
Hackstead to Dobson and back again. It was all very insincere.
"Laid on a car for you this time. Not so drafty as the jeep, eh?"

Hackstead took no notice, looking around him and noting
the changes. "How are the people who got sick?" he asked.

Follet showed surprise. "Doing fine, sir. I think. Doing
well."

He doesn't bloody know how they're doing, thought
Dobson. Not a clue. "No more cases of this flu thing?" He did not
make it sound friendly.

"None at all." The happy look returned to Follet's face. "Fit
as fleas, all of them."

"And the Farnborough lot?"

"All but wrapped up. Crating the final bits and pieces. May
be a few nuts and bolts left in the ground, but they've been pretty
thorough."

"Their Mr. Tyndle still with you?" Hackstead asked.

Follet nodded toward the large tent. "Over in the museum.
We call it the museum." A half laugh.

"We'll have a brief word and then get on our way."

Follet led them over to the tent, the sergeant in tow, like a
dutiful dog. As they passed, the small group of RAF regiment
airmen came to attention. Hackstead paused, spotted the young
Sentry again and wandered over.

"We talked before."

"Sir."

"Last time we were here, Colonel Hackstead asked you
about some of the men being unhappy," Dobson cut in. "Strange
things in the night. You didn't think much of that. I recall you
thought it was a trick of the moonlight."

"Sir."

"Any more of it gone on?"

A long pause. Dobson heard either the sergeant or Follet shifting. It was an unhappy sound in the still air. A fidgety, unnecessary movement.

"Well?"

"Why—aye, sir. Aye, there's been some more of it. Some of the local people around here talk about there being...well, ghosts, sir."

"I think Tyndle'll be wanting to get on," Follet said.

The hell with Tyndle, Dobson wanted to shout.

"You don't go much on those sort of things though, do you?" Hackstead joined in. "You said to me you're not a great believer in that kind of thing yourself. I've got a good memory."

The boy—because that was all he was really, a big, tough, trained, likable boy—looked uncomfortable. "Well..." He moved from the rigid position of attention, his eyes sliding away behind Dobson's shoulder, pleading, asking for help from Follet or his sergeant.

"You've changed your mind," Dobson said quickly, before anyone could come to the boy's aid.

"Well..." he began again. "Well, there's some strange things around this area all right. Strange."

"Not the moonlight playing tricks after all then?" From Hackstead.

"I don't know, sir, something funny though. Maybe locals playing jokes—but some of the lads have seen it. I've seen it."

Behind them came an irritated sigh from Follet. "Out here on the marsh, at night, it can be a bit eerie."

"Seen what?" persisted Dobson.

"Like a figure, a shape, gray shape. There one minute, then gone. Silent."

"Frightening?"

"Not exactly, sir. More, well, more puzzling."

"Souvenir hunters. Poachers." Hackstead sounded unimpressed, turning away as he spoke. Dobson could have imagined it, but he thought there were signs of relief on the faces of Follet and the sergeant.

A gray shape. Dobson clearly saw the shape he had encountered on the landing in Charlotte Street, the face peeling off flesh and the hissing noise coming from bared ragged gums; the gap where the mouth should have been. It terrified him again, even at its brief crossing of the mind: haunted him, like the gray shape that was supposed to haunt the area around the now dead Dead Clump. For the first time that day, his legs felt unsteady as they crossed the few yards to the flapped entrance of the wreckage-sorting marquee. They had almost reached it when there was a sudden breath of wind: chill, momentary.

The long trestle tables, inside what Follet called the museum, had been all but cleared of the debris. Now the pieces, large and small, were mostly packed in neatly labeled boxes. At the far end, crates and flat wooden cases awaited the small amount which still remained.

Tyndle spotted them as they entered. He was probably on the lookout and had heard the helicopter landing. He spoke briefly to one of his assistants, then came across smiling.

"You've come back to see us again, then." He addressed Hackstead.

"You got the fuselage out?" Hackstead, easy, relaxed.

"Quite incredible considering age and the time it has been there." Tyndle's eyes glowed, his face bright with professional enthusiasm. "All this stuff'll be packed and en route to Farnborough by the morning."

"Then what?"

"A long job." It was not exactly a sigh. "Long, but very interesting. We'll try to piece her together and make whatever deductions we can. What went wrong. A good few years since she went in, but that only makes it more of a challenge."

"How long'll it take you?"

Tyndle made a small gesture with his hands, like a salesman telling you it was impossible to promise delivery by a certain date. "We have to be patient, Colonel. She's been buried here for some thirty-three, thirty-four years. You'll come down to Farnborough and see us going through the motions, yes?"

"We shall be doing that, never fear; and you'll let my office have any developments as quickly as you get them? Anything you may feel is significant? Even if it turns out to be a false trail."

"Of course."

They had six addresses of people with strange stories to tell, but the only interesting contact was an elderly man who was a poor sleeper. He claimed that quite regularly he would get up in the middle of the night and wander around, make himself a cup of tea or a sandwich. Often he had seen a figure standing in the lane which ran past his cottage; or moving about, as if searching for something. Sometimes he seemed to be bathed in light, as though using a flashlight.

Could he distinguish any color?—color of the figure, or what it was wearing? Oh yes, his eyesight was still keen. The thing he saw was always dressed the same; from head to foot—white, gray-white. Very spectral it looked.

He was the only one on their list who even bothered to offer them a cup of tea. He lived exactly two miles from the remote cottage inhabited by the aged Mrs. Lambert.

With the six interviews done, by around quarter to seven in the evening they had only one decision to make. Bearing the last old man's story in mind there was no contest. The description was too like that of Mrs. Lambert's friend who visited her regularly, *dressed funny*.

"Okay," said Hackstead. "One more call, then we'll go on to Canterbury."

They drove down the same bumpy track, saw the same overgrown jungle of a garden, the cottage, gray and somehow stark against the overcast sky, for the heavy cloud was now really beginning to pile in. There would be a lot of rain before the night was through.

Only one thing was different. The cottage door was open, and parked close to the low broken fencing skirting the garden was a police car.

A young uniformed constable came out of the front door as Hackstead and Dobson came up the stone path. He had his cap in one hand and looked as though he was coming to the end of his turn of duty and wanted to be off home to the wife.

"Can I help you gentlemen?" He was courteous yet conscious that his uniform gave him an edge over a lot of people.

"Mrs. Lambert," Hackstead began.

"We want a word with her," added Dobson.

"Anything in particular?"

Hackstead's hand went into his pocket for his identification. In quiet, precise and simple language he told the constable exactly who they were, adding no details except the fact that Mrs. Lambert had claimed to have known about the crashed aircraft for years but had offered a report to nobody.

"She'll offer none to anybody now, sir." The policeman's face took on the familiar, often hypocritical, look people assume when talking of severe illness or worse. "Mrs. Lambert is dead."

16

The lady from Meals-on-Wheels had arrived at her usual time, around one-thirty, as she always did on Mondays, Wednesdays and Fridays. Old Mrs. Lambert was stubborn and even resented having hot meals brought in to her three times a week.

When the lady got out of her van she saw Mrs. Lambert lying in the doorway. She had been dead for some time.

Whatever the cause of the old lady's death, she had fallen and struck her head, hard enough to split it badly, on the doorpost. The doctor, who got to the scene within half an hour—about ten minutes after the police—was of the opinion that Mrs. Lambert had either died from a stroke or been killed by the blow to her head as she fell. Only a post-mortem would provide the answer.

The body had long been removed to the Royal Victoria Hospital, in Folkestone, and the constable was there to make certain the property had been secured, and that there were no domestic pets around. His instructions were to remove all keys into safekeeping.

"Natural causes then?" Hackstead was not really asking: stating.

"Not much doubt about that, sir. Our car came out, of

course, but the house hasn't been messed about—not more than it was already: not a particularly hygienic old duck, Mrs. Lambert."

Dobson tapped his head. "A bit ...?"

The constable grunted an affirmative. "Had some strange ideas. The kids around here say she was a witch."

"Doesn't surprise me." Bud Hackstead's attention appeared to be wandering, his eyes shifting around the overgrown garden.

"Who's your boss?" Dobson asked.

The policeman gave him the name of the inspector at Romney, and added, "Would you mind if I finished locking up?"

"Go right ahead. There's no point in us hanging around. Thanks for your help."

The constable gave a little salute and began to move round to the rear of the cottage. Dobson followed Hackstead down the path toward the car. Once the policeman was out of sight, Hackstead stopped and moved quickly back into the long grass to the left of the path.

"Here, over here." He spoke low and urgently, standing among the grass, weeds and wild flowers where, on their last visit, they had seen the circle of what looked like freshly dug earth.

The earth, dug clean, standing out from the surrounding overgrowth, was now more clear than before. Instead of just a circular patch there was a hole, the earth piled, almost neatly, around its perimeter.

"The late lamented Mrs. Lambert's regular visitor's been digging for gold," Hackstead observed, still speaking softly. "Away quick, we don't want to draw attention to that. Let the coppers do their own investigation."

The hole was around two feet deep and there was a circular indentation at the bottom, as though somebody had buried a biscuit tin, dug down as far as the lid and pulled the whole thing out, dragging it up from the soil. You could see the marks where a pair of hands had scooped out the earth on either side to get a grip on whatever had been extricated.

"Hidden gold?" Dobson asked, once they were back in the car.

"Definitely Canterbury, sir?" The pretty WRAF driver half-turned, a tincture of sarcasm in her voice, as though the long series of drives from point to point was at last wearing her down.

Hackstead grinned. "Definitely Canterbury, Corporal."

"Hidden gold?" Dobson repeated.

"Folding money in the mattress," said Hackstead, still keeping his voice down. "A pile of loot in an old cashbox buried in the garden?"

"Just a thought."

"Did she fall or was she pushed? That's my query."

"Coronary, stroke, or stroke to the head with a blunt instrument, as the official language has it."

"A blunt instrument like a Very pistol?"

"It had crossed my mind." It had more than crossed it; the thought, and the same horrific picture, had lingered. "A Very pistol, or more likely the trowel, or whatever he was using to dig with."

They sat in silence for a minute or so. "Police matter," Hackstead finally announced. "Leave it to them."

"You sure? Absolutely sure?"

"Why not?"

"If she got clobbered by . . ."

"You're still obsessed by spooks. Shadows from that bloody aircraft." He was not irritated, but firm. "You think because some idiot freak dressed in scary fancy dress tried to mug you it's got something to do with this investigation."

"At least talk to the lads in blue, Bud. Have a word; and with the doctor. See if she could have been attacked. It's happened before, you know: old folk found dead, cause of death heart attack, stroke, call it what you will. They fall, smash their heads open and the doctor says, yes they were due to go like that someday—old age. Cuts, gashes, broken skulls, all secondary injuries. In fact, when they look a little closer, some bastard's come in and smashed them. Cause of death blow to the head. At least ask."

Hackstead sat upright—Dobson thought of old Group Captain Rivers Crenham Waterford, the real chief of I3 (Air), now at a NATO conference, leaving Sugden in charge. Hackstead was sitting to attention, just like the groupie. They traveled about half a mile while the American made up his mind. "Okay," a curt nod, unusually curt for him. "As a special favor I'll talk to the inspector and to Mrs. Lambert's quack. Satisfied?" His hand reached out and tapped Dobson lightly on the knee.

"Satisfied."

They came into Canterbury on the A28 and it was nearly nine-thirty before they walked off the High Street into the splendidly timbered, beautifully maintained County Hotel.

"What time'll you require me in the morning?" the WRAF corporal driver asked as she negotiated the traffic and pedestrians, which, even at this time in the evening, clogged the High Street.

"Make it here at five tomorrow afternoon." Hackstead winked broadly. "But as far as your boss is concerned I want you here at midday. Take some time off for yourself."

There were messages at reception for Dobson. A Wing Commander Sugden had been calling urgently since about six. Would Mr. Dobson call him back as soon as he arrived. He had even left a private number.

17

Sugden sounded anxious. "I have the information for you. Thought you'd have been there sooner."

"We had a little holdup. No problem."

"You wanted more information regarding the pilot from 88 Squadron. About the interrogations—there's nothing on file. Just a note to say they asked standard questions and kept him hanging around. He went into the bag on October 15, '43. A few days later moved into the Dulag Luft at Oberiusel, and then to Stalag Luft III in January '44."

"We've got all that. This is just a repeat. What I want are definite dates."

"About eighth or ninth. No precision."

"The bloody man has one hell of an inaccurate memory. Okay, the second interrogation?"

"Dates?"

"Of course dates: I'm not talking about science fiction."

"Same as the abstract. He couldn't recall the exact dates; just knew it was sometime in late May or early June."

Dobson sighed. "The breakout dates from Stalag Luft III. You'll recall I didn't have them at hand. Remember? You were going to check."

"The Great Escape—as they call it—took place on the night of March 24/25, 1944." God, he sounded smug: Sugden had got this one right, you could tell it in the resurrected change of tone.

"Then he was there. Free was at Sagan when they all went through that tunnel." But Frederick Free, Dobson was certain, took no part in the escape.

"You still with me?" asked Sugden.

"Yes, I'm here. Our subject's second interrogation? Anything to do with the escape?"

"There are a few notes on that interrogation, and, yes, the escape was mentioned *en passant*. Threats apparently. The Gestapo were there as well as the usual Luftwaffe interrogators: reminded him a number of officers had been shot from Sagan and it wouldn't be difficult for them to organize the same thing for him. Apart from that, just routine stuff: squadron strengths, invasion preparations. It must have been fairly close to D-day. They'd be pulling in all the extra intelligence they could get."

"Yes, but why him? Why Free?"

"Who knows? If we combed the files I expect we'd find he wasn't the only RAF man hauled back to the interrogation centers."

"Comb the files. Go ahead, comb them."

"Will do."

"What about contacts? People who knew and saw Free at Sagan?"

"Couple of names. I'll put you on to them when you're back in town. Any idea how long you'll be down there?"

"Not long. Give me the names."

"Now?"

"The names."

"They won't mean anything to you."

"You're servicing me."

"Call them Partridge and Peartree."

"Like Arthur?"

"Better be safe..."

"Than sorry? I know. I want to ask you about Arthur and the strength of his information anyway."

"Oh?"

"At least I want to ask you about Richard Martin Lewis—Arthur, as you prefer to call him."

"For heaven's sake, Dobson, this is a private phone. It's not secure."

"We are not investigating the Russian Med Fleet nor their nuclear strategy. Sugden, I wish to heaven you'd stop playing World War II cowboys. We haven't got an office in Baker Street and we don't run people over to Fortress Europe in Lizzies any more. The cloak and bleeding dagger business went out with the electronic satellites. Friend Arthur was suspected of being a naughty boy."

"Wheels within wheels."

Dobson had a mental picture of Sugden running a finger along the side of his nose. "He's okay then?"

"Straight. Absolutely. By the way—*Oversh*—the Op we talked about."

"Say it, Sugden, nobody's listening. Say it aloud. *Overshoot*. What about it?"

"I've pulled some pictures—Photo Recce stuff: well, one picture really. It all looked feasible. I mean the airfield layout. The way Arthur described the Op. Things were in the right places, if you see what I mean."

"I'll come in and look at it."

"Maintain contact."

"If you mean will I ring in? Affirmative, but don't hang by your toes."

Hackstead was not in the bar when Dobson came down. He filled in the waiting time with a lager and recce in depth on the local and tourist talent. There was nothing to make you do cartwheels.

When the colonel arrived he looked spruce, fresh, bathed and clean-jowled. He was also wearing a different pair of slacks, which clashed with the same dazzling check jacket.

"Been talking to our mutual friend Flight Lieutenant Frederick Free, onetime Royal Air Force," he said squeezing himself onto the bar stool next to Dobson, and ordered a stinger.

"How is he in death?" he asked Hackstead.

"Free?" The barman did some kind of Cuban rhythm with a silver cocktail shaker. "Free sounds happy and very much alive in death." Hackstead sipped at the stinger and nodded approval.

"You tell him he bought it three decades ago?"

"My dear Dave, a brash American Kraut I may be, but I'm sophisticated enough to know you don't lay that kind of news on a dead man at the other end of a horn. We'll drop him a hint tomorrow. We have a date. Ten-thirty in the morning. He's got a bungalow less than ten miles away."

"So we drop in for social chats." Dobson realized the

problems. They were entering Sugden territory. "Who are we, Bud?"

"Air historians working on a book about World War II aviators. All very official. Government backing, here and in the States. Living memories of men dicing with death, life in the POW camps, Ops—the whole thing."

"Free give you the impression he'd talk?"

"Like the back of a record jacket."

"Line shoot?"

"Don't try that forties chat with me. I was there, baby, I used it. Yes, he'll shoot lines by the column inch. What did the boys used to say? *There I was, upside down in a cloud, on fire, nothing on the clock but the maker's name.* By the way, I've also talked to Potts' former navigator—Herbert J. Flax: retired tycoon immigrant, now residing in his English country house near Folkestone. *You're* going to see him tomorrow afternoon. I've hired a VW for that purpose. Hertz."

"Me? No us?"

"You." The flashing red light smile, fast as the second change on a digital watch. "I'm doing the tourist bit, remember? Soak up the far past, walk the Roman pavements."

"So I get to talk to Flax while you go swanning around with your Pentax?"

"Something like that."

"Flax," Dobson nodded. "Am I still an air historian?"

"Naturally. As far as he's concerned I'm the official American publisher. Flax came on very heavy when I called him. Thought I was some kind of journalist. Said his personal war story was sold exclusively to the *Daily Express.* I convinced him that this was very much a government-backed project, and he finally agreed to see you."

"The *Express*'ve got cracking fast, then."

"Went as quick as a fiver in a pub. Which is good news for us."

Dobson nodded. "Only one thing. Credentials? What if he asks for ID?"

Hackstead took a sip of his stinger, savoring the bite. "Give me credit for doing my job, Dave. I just talked with the office. Your new credentials—and mine, come to that—will be ready by midnight: coming down by fast car. We got more news from Washington, by the way. The pair of missing members of Potts' crew. The sergeants—Sharp and friend Klein who languishes in San Quentin."

"Well?"

"Just a few details of when and where they went down. Dates. Operations they were on. That kind of stuff. They also have some details about where they spent their time as POWs."

"Yes?"

A tiger smile. "They were together." He drained the stinger. "They were together for most of the time in the American compound—the South Compound—at Stalag Luft III, Sagan. Ain't coincidence a strange, long-armed beast?"

"Free in one half, Sharp and Klein in the other. I don't suppose Master Sergeant Wilcox Pride ended up there with them?"

Hackstead stroked the stem of his glass in a vaguely erotic manner. "No, they sent him to Stalag Luft I at Barth. Let's go eat."

Dobson half rose, then remembered Hackstead's further promises. "You haven't told me how you got on with the law and the medical profession yet."

"Ah." Hackstead dropped back onto the stool. "In a nutshell, the law are interested and the doc isn't. Professional etiquette, you know. Hippocratic oath."

"No joy then?"

"The law'll have a go at the quack. At least they'll press to make sure of the cause of death. Same quack who looked after those kids during the influenza scare that wasn't influenza."

"The virus?"

"Some virus."

They looked at one another, aware of the chatter going on around them: the high-pitched forced laugh of some woman in the corner, a graying executive type ordering three gins and a vodka, two newly arrived couples meeting up. Kisses all round.

In Hackstead's eyes there was a signal. Information not passed on: doubt looming over the horizon. For a second the contact broke as the barman materialized and asked the gentlemen if they would like another drink. Hackstead shook his head and the barman sidled away reluctantly.

"When I called the office," Hackstead began, "there was another message waiting for me. Would I call Wing Commander Charlie Farnsbarnes, or whatever his name is, over at the RAF Hospital at Halton."

"Where you saw the pathologists?"

"Yeah. While I was there I mentioned there'd been some strange influenza-type infection around Romney—kids who found the aircraft, some of the RAF regiment people. They knew all about the RAF regiment boys because they had them there: checking out the strain. The quack at Halton wanted to let me know they'd separated the virus; knew what it was; identified it."

Dobson gave a facial query.

"The RAF regiment people—and the boys, for all I know—got themselves a dose of Rift Valley fever."

"Rift Valley fever." He felt like an idiot just repeating it.

"Rift Valley fever is not a virus disease known in this part of the world, that's all." This time Hackstead stood, intent on getting in to dinner.

"Symptoms?" Dobson asked. He felt as though he was trotting along to keep up with the American.

"High fever, chills, headaches, sickness, pains in the limbs. Usually transmitted to humans by cattle, sheep, other animals: and usually in Asia. I think we'd have known about it if the local farms had been subjected to bouts of something like Rift Valley fever. The RAF people had very mild attacks, but that's what it was."

They reached the dining room, were shown to a table and went through the ritual with the napkins, menus, wine list. Waiters hovered. The place was half full. It was all smooth and pleasant, gleaming silver, clean linen, good, efficient service.

"Your deductions?" Dobson asked when they had ordered.

Hackstead shrugged. "None, Sherlock. Except it worries me. You know about Fort Detrick?"

"Your chemical-biological warfare center?"

"Right."

"I thought it wasn't used as such any more."

"Officially, no. Unofficially, I wouldn't know. All I'm saying is that Rift Valley fever was one of the things the biological boys worked on there. It's even said that it was used in Vietnam. What they call a dry agent, particularly suitable against Asians. Not deadly, but the madmen who think up these things might classify RVF as an incapacitating weapon. There were plenty of tests done, including delivery systems via aircraft."

"But all that's been going on since the late fifties. We're dealing with the forties."

"I know. Just worries me, that's all. Before I go to sleep I'm going to call that kid's parents—the one who found the wreckage: make sure he's okay."

"Mitchell," Dobson said, almost to himself.

"Yes."

"Robert Mitchell."

The seafood cocktail arrived, and for the remainder of the meal, they went through the interrogation routine, and Hackstead ended up by doing a quick briefing for Dobson's meeting with Flax.

Bathed, comfortable in his room ready for bed, Dobson let his mind travel in circles around the sinister oddities connected with *Dodo*. The aircraft itself, the crew and the pathologist's report on them; the horror on his own landing in Charlotte Street; the appearance and the reappearance of Trotter; Denis—dead Denis—Arthur and *Overshoot*. Now Mrs. Lambert, dying, possibly of old age, in her doorway; the hole in her garden and the figures seen by her and the old man. Now he had Hackstead getting steamed up because an expert had decided some of the men helping with the wreckage did not have flu but Rift Valley fever; unheard of in England. Over all of it, two things lapped and dissolved in his thoughts: the same old haunting picture of the mound and the men ready to dig, and the sight of that stench-ridden, putrefied thing going for him with the Very pistol, with the darkness and thunder raging over London like a ghost blitz.

His Trimphone rang: discreet, not the clamor which usually assaulted him in the offices at Clapham.

"Are you okay? I thought you said you'd ring me?" Ann's voice fringed with worry. He thought of her sitting waiting for him to call. Perhaps killing time. Waiting. Wanting to hear his voice.

"Oh Christ," he said. "Darling, I've been tied up all day. No excuse but work." He really did not know what to say. "We were sidetracked. Bud got onto some weird ideas: and there's been a bit of a tragedy—old lady we had to interview just died."

"Oh, David, I'm sorry, but it's you I'm worried about. How's the head?"

As the day wore on he had adjusted to the bruising. No headaches and, except for one moment out at the crash site, no signs of weakness.

"I'm fine. Really I'm okay."

"I thought you should've had another day or two off."

"The sooner we get this job tied up, the sooner we might get down to some overdue living."

"You promised to call me. When you didn't, I got concerned. You did promise." For the first time there was a hint of pique.

"I know, but . . . Well, the job."

"You didn't mind me calling you?" Dobson wondered if there was a shade of sarcasm in the question.

"It's the best thing that's happened all day." He heard the weariness in his own voice. "Yes, I promised to call you. I'm sorry, it's been a bitch."

"You've got a lot on your mind"—the conciliatory gambit.

"Still no excuse."

The pause felt as if she was trying to make up her mind. "None needed," she said at last, "as long as you're not ill."

"Truly, I'm all right." A crackle on the line. Dobson wondered if some operator was listening in. Perhaps Sugden's attitude was getting to him.

"When'll you be back?"

He felt the flurry in his abdomen, the teen-age flutter of excitement when a girl smiled, or a day went well, Christmas Eve, some unexpected longed-for surprise. It was her voice, the question, simple, yet loaded with vibrations, things unsaid.

"By tomorrow night with luck."

"Call me. Even if it's late." Silence, then—"Or perhaps I'll call you."

"Either way would be good. How're things at the waxworks?"

She giggled. "This is not a secure line," deepening the voice, giving it a shade of Sugden's preposterous pomposity. "The boss is acting like it's a fully run operation."

They talked for another fifteen minutes. The good night was long and almost adolescent in its reluctance.

As he lay smoking his last cigarette of the day, Dobson thought about her: the way she moved, the manner her hair swung with her head, the smile; the eyes, changeable as the sky. Then came the erotica. He pushed it away, banishing it, for that was to come and time would put all things to rights.

When the light was out and he settled, on the brink of sleep, *Dodo* came back into his head.

From childhood he remembered the American aircraft, the huge B-17s straining upward, formating, droves of them heading out toward the coast. The skies, as people often said of that time, were never still. He could have seen Potts' Marauder, Free's Boston—even on that last operation. He thought of what it must have been like to leave the golden or green fields—with those wonderful patchwork shades of color you only get in England—to fly into that special hell with 190s hammering down from all sides and the flack rising like Guy Fawkes Day rockets;

slowly, then fast, furious, rocking shattering aircraft, the shouting inside stricken planes, the moments of absolute panic; fire; explosion; blood; the screams; the living trapped, unable to do a thing, inside the last long fairground ride to earth in a section of falling aircraft.

Inevitably he turned circle and as sleep came the only image in mind was the two locked jets and the ball of flame all mixed up with the distorted mirror images at the end of the pier.

18

The man who greeted them at the door of the neat little bungalow just off the Dover Road could only be in his mid-fifties, yet looked older. Dobson could not equate him with the person whose file he had studied only twenty-four hours earlier.

He was tall; gray hair, in good condition with no signs of thinning on top. He looked exceptionally fit even though one would take him for nearer sixty-five than the decade younger which he must have been.

In the couple of hours which followed, Dobson concluded that Frederick Free was a man who had grown old, as far as looks were concerned, long before this. The experiences of war did that to some people. He had probably looked forty at thirty.

Viewing him now, in the flesh for the first time, Free seemed soft-spoken, an unflappable character one would have thought, not the kind of person born to failure, a survivor. The bungalow itself proved that there had been at least modest success—six rooms, a more than adequate garden, beautifully kept in spite of the summer drought of this present year. Inside, the furniture was a clever mix of good modern with one or two antiques, well chosen.

Free was exceptionally courteous, settling them in his main living room, then excusing himself to get the coffee from the kitchen—obviously pleased to see them, anxious to assist.

During the short time Free was absent, Dobson watched Hackstead with professional pleasure, for the American swept the room with his eyes, taking in every small detail, tracking around the walls, entrances, exits, decor, furniture, the eyes themselves like remote-controlled surveillance lenses.

The only link with their investigation was almost hidden from view, low on the wall diagonally opposite the drum table: a framed set of two drawings—technical sectional drawings of aircraft. The top one was of a Boston; below it hung a Messerschmitt 109. Dobson squinted, straining forward—they were quite small reproductions. He thought it was possibly an ME 109G-5. The vanquished and the victor? An ME 109G-5? he thought. Christ, I'm getting a pedantic specialist in my old age.

Free brought the coffee in, and they made small talk for a while before Dobson broke in.

"You're retired then, Mr. Free?" They had arranged it so that Hackstead would come on with the heavy questions, leaving asides like this to Dobson.

Free smiled, a little self-satisfied, settling back into his chair, coffee cup poised in one hand, the other patting the leather arm. "Retired early," he said. "Sold out while the price was right. Bought this. Suits me, but I'm thinking of getting a little place in the sun. Anyway, this damned country ... Well, I don't mean that, but it's getting so expensive here." His speech was precise with frozen undertones beneath the relaxed friendliness.

They let him drift on. "I've been lucky. Very lucky when I think of what's happened to some of the boys. Well, you read it in the papers, don't you?"

"It was a long time ago, the war. People change."

Free paused. He had a slight tic, a twitch, in his left eye. "Sometimes it seems like yesterday. Other times a million years ago. So much has happened in between."

"The pub?"

"Lucky there. Bought it for a song with the old gratuity, the back pay, and a little help from the bank. Extended. Put in a restaurant. You probably know the place, The Crossings ..."

"Yeah, I know it," interjected Hackstead, fast, as though he wanted to get on.

They sipped their coffee, primly, and Hackstead raised a minimally quizzical eyebrow. The coffee tasted as though it had come straight from Imperial Chemicals—Research. He built up a business with a restaurant using coffee like this? Dobson was amazed.

"Well." Free rubbed his hands together, between the knees: an anxious gesture. "I expect you want to ask questions."

"If we could." Hackstead glanced at his watch. "We've got plenty of time, but my partner has another appointment this afternoon."

"Okay, shoot. Old 88 Squadron, is it?"

"You weren't with them for very long, were you?" Dobson tried to give it as little strain as possible.

"No." The tic in the eye moving about once to the second. "No, 'fraid not. Bit of bother with a couple of 109s."

"Near Cherbourg. We read the report you made after it was all over."

"Yes." Free looked uncomfortable, shifted slightly in his chair, reached for the coffee again. "A Circus Op. Piece of cake as a rule. I didn't see the bastards."

Still talks the lingo, thought Dobson. Sounds as though he's still there. "You did quite a few Circus Ops in the short time you were with 88?"

"About ten. Not much of a record really. Not what I'd have liked. We spent a lot of time practicing smoke-laying for D-day. I missed that."

"You're nostalgic about it, though—the time with 88?"

"Fairly. The comradeship and all that. Sounds a bit sentimental nowadays. People who weren't in it don't seem to understand. Funny, isn't it?"

"Some prefer to forget."

"How was it when they got you in the bag?" Hackstead starting the build-up.

"Odd," Free answered without even stopping to think. "The troops were okay, but things weren't so good until they got us to the interrogation center. It was okay there. Not like you see in those old films. It wasn't all tough and pressing. They had Luftwaffe interrogators; some bastards, of course, but for the most part they were reasonable."

"We went through your record." Hackstead again. "They kept you at the interrogation center for a long time. Same man do all the questioning?"

"Two of them."

"The old routine? One hard and one soft?"

He thought about that one. "No, they were both quite reasonable chaps."

"What kind of questions?"

He thought about that as well. "It wasn't just a matter of questions. Oh, to start with, yes. We went through the name, rank and number bit. Then they got on to the actual Op. Targets, general tactics. Didn't seem to expect answers. Didn't get any either." The self-satisfied smile again; not smug, just an indication that, as he would probably have put it, he kept his end up.

"Then they began to tell *me* things. That was what struck me most: how much they knew. They knew one hell of a lot. Who'd been posted, names of blokes' popsies: and the Ops. They knew a great deal about the Ops. We're still told they didn't have much of an intelligence network in England, but they were bloody well-informed. It was either the old espionage or some of the chaps talked their heads off—and I don't believe they did that."

"They named names?" Hackstead, leaning forward.

"Names, aircraft serials, nicknames, people's records."

"Did they know about you? I mean your previous postings?"

"Yes. Yes, they knew about me all right." He scowled. "At least I think it was then. Gets a bit jumbled. They gave me a second going-over, you know about that?"

"After the business at Sagan, yes."

"Yes, after the escape. The Great Escape. I can't recall whether they told me about my previous career on the first or the second go."

"You mean your period with the Eighth Air Force, 323rd Group?"

Free laughed. "You're as bad as they were. You know it all."

"We know you did liaison work with 457th Squadron at Horham, yes."

"The Luftwaffe interrogators knew that as well. Yes, they knew that at the first center. I know because they talked a lot about aircraft types—Blenheims, Bostons and the Marauders at Horham."

"They ask you much about the Americans?" Hackstead's offhand probe.

"As I told you, it wasn't so much a case of them asking. They knew, that's all there was to it. They were more like friendly chats than interrogations."

Just like this, thought Dobson. It was working well with Hackstead's method. The gentle chat. Just the three of them. The best and most effective form of interrogation known to man.

"And what did you think of Stalag Luft III when you got there?"

"Not much. Good spirit among the chaps, but pretty bleak. Those bloody trees all around. No views. Bloody awful trees."

"Just some establishing queries." The American was at his most charming. "Just to check your memory."

He asked all the important ones fast—what was the Kommandant's name? Von Lindeiner. There was a ferret (they called the guards whose job was to sniff out possible escape plans ferrets) known as "Rubberneck." Did Free remember his real name? He was a corporal called Glemnitz—no, Glemnitz was the other one: Rubberneck's name was Griese.

Ten out of ten, Dobson marked him.

"You were aware of Harry?"

The code name for the big escape tunnel.

"We were all aware of it, of course."

"You were taken in on it?"

"I did some stooging—keeping cave, you know. I was a late comer."

"You weren't offered a place in the breakout?"

The embarrassment once again. "Well, near the time they did ask me, yes."

"But you didn't go?"

"No."

"You turned it down?"

"We weren't all built in the same mold." He gave a grunt of a laugh. "For me der Var was over."

"I see." Hackstead curt, but not unsympathetic. "It became unpleasant after the breakout?"

"You must know all about that. They brought the Gestapo in, and the civilian police. Some people played the fool with them. To be honest they scared the hell out of me." His face went very solemn. "Then, in April we got the news."

"The shootings?"

"The shootings," he repeated.

"And soon after that they took you back to the interrogation center."

"Quite soon afterward, yes."

"When exactly?"

"May, June. One loses track . . ."

"If it was soon after the news of the shooting of those who had escaped, it would be nearer May than June."

"I suppose so."

"Before or after D-day?" Hackstead was starting to pile it on now.

"I don't know. Before. I'm pretty certain it was before."

"May then. Call it May when they took you back to Oberiusel."

A pause in which Dobson was conscious of a jet, high but audible, passing over the bungalow.

"They didn't take me back to Oberiusel, and you bloody well know that as well. They took me to the main center in Frankfurt itself. Look, this is getting to be like a clip from a TV thriller. What's it all about anyway?"

"I'm sorry." Hackstead flicked on the charm as easily as a con man doing the three-card trick. "It's just that you're an unusual case, Mr. Free. We think you might even make a whole chapter in the book. Two lots of interrogations and you didn't have anything big to do with the escape from Sagan. It's interesting."

"Okay." The unflappable man back on form. "Yes, they took me to Frankfurt. I honestly don't have any idea of the date, but by your logic I would say sometime in early May, mid-May."

"And they kept you there?"

"A month," a shrug, "six weeks."

"Or two months? Had the Allied invasion started by the time they got you back to Sagan? To Stalag Luft III?"

"God, yes. Had it not?"

"When they took you out to Frankfurt, what did you think?"

"I was a bit frightened if you want the truth. There were so many stories going around. I thought, this is it, I'm for the chop."

"But they moved you out by yourself."

"No. I was the only one they took to Frankfurt, but they took out some of the Polish officers, and a few Dutch. But I was the only one that went to Frankfurt. I saw none of the others again."

"Did you have much contact with the Americans while you were in the camp?" Disarmingly offhanded.

"By the time I landed up there they'd been separated—segregated—for some time. I didn't personally if that's what you're after."

"Okay, now to this lengthy second interrogation. What was it all about?"

"Would you like more coffee?" His hand swinging

between them. Negative from both. Free nodded. "The second interrogation? It was strange. At first I thought it was to do with the escape. It seemed like it. The Luftwaffe interrogators were okay, but they were very nervous. The place was full of chaps who'd come down from the heavies—Lancs, Halifaxes: Americans from the Fortresses and Libs. But the Gestapo were around. I had a dose of them for the first three days."

"Threats?"

"Quite open threats—tell us all about other possible escape plans at Sagan or we'll do to you what we did to your friends. Very heavy gentlemen."

"And what did you tell them?"

"The truth. I didn't know of any other plans."

"Violence? Torture?"

Free shook his head. "Only threats. Three days of them. On the fourth day they went away and I was told they'd be taking me back to Sagan. Only they didn't."

"Instead?"

"Instead they put a pair of Luftwaffe officers on to me. Same techniques as before—telling me what they knew."

"They concentrate on anything in particular?"

"It's not easy to recall it all, but, yes, they seemed very interested in my time with the Yanks."

"In what way?"

"They gave me a lot of names—Yanks who'd been with 323rd Group and the 457th Bombardment Squadron. Asked me if I knew certain people."

"And did you?"

"Some."

"You tell them?"

"When I recognized a name I told them. They usually told me what had happened to the individuals. Names came back, but not the faces."

"Faces?"

"They showed me photographs."

"And you identified some?"

"Yes, there was no harm in that. I didn't get the point of the exercise."

"They concentrated on people, individuals?"

"And aircraft."

"Oh?"

"They kept asking if I remembered the nicknames of any of the old 457 kites—the Marauders."

"And did you?"

"Some."

"You flew with some of the American crews from Horham."

"Not on Ops. But, yes, I got some hours in on Marauders."

"And they asked which ones?"

Free's brow wrinkled. "Yes." As though something had just made sense. "Yes, they did, and that was odd, because *they* told me about a trip I did—the last one in fact."

"A flight test." Hackstead was leaning fully forward now, ready for the Sunday punch. "Flight test which was used as a ferry trip to drop you off at Manston."

Free's face went blank. You could not tell what he was thinking, whether it was surprise or sudden recall, the memories flooding back as if something important had clicked in his head.

"Jesus," he said. "That's what they were after. I didn't catch on at the time, and a lot of water's gone under the bridge since then—a lot of ale as well. They kept going back to that. What the hell was the name of the bloody thing? Hang on, I'll get it in a minute. *Luscious Laura?* No, no, that wasn't it."

"Try *Dancing Dodo* for size," Dobson said, pitched low.

"That's it." His face lit with pleasure. "My God, after all these years I've got it. They kept going back to old *Dancing Dodo*— the captain was a particular mate. The memory." He banged his head with a balled fist as though trying to force names and images into his brain.

"Potts," said Hackstead.

"Bill Potts." He whacked a thigh with the palm of his hand. "I wonder what happened to him? They didn't tell me. They went on and on about all sorts of crates that flew from Horham but, yes, they talked a lot about *Dancing Dodo*. My last night at Horham we had a party and the CO suggested that Bill Potts should fly me down to Manston. Bill Potts, my God. Old *Dancing Dodo*. There was another chap I remember from his crew— Jewish—Goldstone; no, Goldberg..."

"And Herbie Flax and Wilcox Pride..." Hackstead continued.

"Wilcox Pride, yes."

"Sharp and Klein."

"Yes, and a fellow called Sail-something. Sailby. Last trip I ever did in a Marauder; mind you, I wasn't sorry about that. Bitches they were. You don't happen to know what became of that lot, hell of a good crew."

Hackstead stretched right back in his armchair, not even a hint of a smile on his face. "Did you know, ex-Flight Lieutenant Frederick Free, that Potts, Goldberg, Flax, Wilcox Pride, Sailby and yourself were pulled out of Romney Marsh among the wreckage of a Martin Marauder the serial numbers of which correspond to those of the aircraft you call good old *Dancing Dodo?* In many respects we—that is, my colleague and I—are talking to a ghost. You're a dead man, Mr. Free. Dead and in small pieces in the mortuary of the RAF Hopsital, Halton."

Free's face went gray.

19

Meeting Herbert J. Flax was quite a different experience than that of the morning talk with Frederick Free.

Free had been successful in a quiet way. Herbie Flax's success was more apparent, glittering and dangling like Christmas baubles.

Dobson took the VW and drove out on the A2, turning off toward the village of Wootton. About a mile farther on he came to a pair of iron gates set into a wall. The stone columns on either side were surmounted with great guarding eagles. Not worn and beautiful old eagles, weathered with time; but modern, badly carved eagles. They could have been made of plastic and there was no denying their cost would be exorbitant, but the workmanship told the truth—really skilled stonemasons are in short supply.

It had probably been quite a pleasant old house when Flax bought it. Now, flat oblong pieces jutted from it, a wide crazy-paved patio surrounded the place, and the swimming pool fronted the property—there was little that was discreet about Herbert J.—"call me Herbie"—Flax.

It was just after two o'clock and the Flax family had finished lunch and were sitting around the pool. The sun had come out again: yesterday's low front superseded by another warm spell.

Introductions all around—Herbie, his wife Laura, Joe and Little Herbie—teen-age boys who certainly were not Laura's children, for she was probably herself only a year or two older than Little Herbie.

They ended up—Dobson and Flax—lying on pool loungers, Dobson feeling overdressed, Flax happy with a brandy and a cigar. He droned on about how great it was to see him and about how great he was and didn't Dobson think the house was great? Dobson said yes he thought it was great. Then:

"Can we talk? Please, Herbie. It's quite important."

He took it well, drew in on the cigar, waved it in Dobson's direction. "You're short on time, I'm sorry."

"*Dancing Dodo?*" queried Dobson.

There was a pause, a deep drawing on the cigar again followed by a long exhalation. "Old *Dancing Dodo*." Dobson could have sworn there was a sentimental catch in Flax's voice. "You know, until the other day I hadn't thought about *Dodo* in years. Come to that I hadn't thought about the war in years. As far as I was concerned it was the future that counted. Now I got the future." The cigar waved in a motion encircling the pool, house and grounds.

"Everyone I've talked to who flew in Marauders gives the impression that she was a bitch aircraft. Yet the people who flew *Dodo* all seemed happy with her."

"With *Dodo*, yes. None of us were keen on the airplane as a type. Tell you the truth some of the boys got themselves posted when we lost *Dodo*. They said it was because of *Dodo*—she was kinda special—but I think they'd had enough of the machine. Yes, she was a bitch airplane if you didn't get to know her well, and a lot of the guys who came over didn't have the time to get on intimate terms with her. We loved *Dodo*, but what I really believe is that most of us loved her because Bill Potts and Dan Goldberg were the two best Marauder pilots in the business. Well, the best bar one."

"Bar one?"

"A guy out at MacDill Field, Florida, where we did our first training on the B-26. I guess he stayed there through the war. Potts and Goldberg were trained by him. What in hell was his name? No, memory's gone for names. Potts'll tell you when he gets over. Now this guy could do anything with that airplane. The only man I ever met who really liked the Marauder. Mind you, Dave, I liked *Dodo* because Bill Potts was so good, but even with Bill on the stick later, when we went to the Ninth TAF, I didn't like the aircraft."

Dobson nodded, waiting for around a count of ten before asking, "The members of the crew who left after you lost *Dodo?*"

"Yes?"

"Did you miss them as much as *Dodo?* I mean, you were a happy crew until the split."

"Two of them were okay. Great—old Pride, Wilcox Pride, was a great guy to have around; and Sharp—Wilson Sharp—he was regular. The other one was okay, but the least liked. Nervous little guy, quick-tempered. Klein. Rudy Klein. Funny, he used to get on well with Sharp. They left together."

"They ended up in the same POW camp as well."

"I'll be darned. No, Klein was okay, young little bastard, cocky, but the only one out of place. Wasn't quite as close to us as the others. That's a funny thing—I just recalled, you know Sharp and Klein were the only members of that crew who never came up on air tests unless it was absolutely necessary. Only the pilots had to go—regulations—but we all usually went, except for those two."

"At the reunion . . ." Dobson slowed down. "At the reunion of *Dodo's* crew, Klein will be the only absentee."

"Rudy Klein? He's not . . . ?"

"He's in jail."

"Doesn't surprise me," Flax grinned. He seemed almost happy that Klein was in jail. "Where?" he asked.

"San Quentin."

"Serious?"

"Ten for armed robbery. I'd call that serious."

"That's serious." The noise from the back of his throat could have been a laugh. An arid sound. "Sure I can't get you a nip of brandy?"

Dobson felt gravely tempted. He had the start of a headache and slight sickness—whether because of this particular job, or a reaction to the events at Charlotte Street, he could not tell. In the end he refused.

"Herbie, I want to talk to you about one incident that might just stick in your memory."

"Anything, Dave."

"We talked with Bill Potts long-distance the other day: went through a lot of things . . ."

"Who is 'we,' Dave?"

"I don't understand."

"You said 'we talked with Bill Potts'..."

"Figure of speech. The royal 'we' if you like."

"Okay."

"Bill Potts says that you all saw *Dodo* once more—once more after Horham, I mean."

"Huh?"

"He even gave us—me—a date. August 17, 1944. You were shooting up troop concentrations around Rouen. Turning to go home he saw another Marauder on an easterly course, quite low. He thought the crew might have got disorientated, so you went down and tried to formate on him. He turned and went away fast."

"Jesus, yes. Yes, I remember that. Yes, I saw that aircraft. We all did."

"Potts says that you couldn't see any ID markings but the camouflage was odd for a Marauder. He said it looked as though it was colored a gray-white. Looked like a ghost plane."

"It was weird." Quite suddenly the bounce had gone out of Flax. He lay very still and quiet, as though the confidence was knocked from him by the recall. "I think that was one of the things I'd rather forget—I had forgotten. Spooked us all for a while. Well, spooked Bill and Dan, and me." He sighed, his chest rising as though he found it difficult to get his breath back. "One airplane's very much like another, but at the time, even though it looked funny—no ID and this strange color—we could have sworn it was *Dodo*.

"There's a short story by someone," Flax continued, as though speaking thoughts without any particular audience. "That writer Roald Dahl, I think. I read this story once and it reminds me now of what it felt like seeing an airplane all gray-white that we thought was *Dodo*. In this story a guy goes on a recce, supposed to take him an hour. He goes missing and then turns up a couple of days later. Thinks he's only been away an hour. Then it comes back to him. He's formated on this huge assembly of airplanes—all types of crates mixed up together in a huge group, British, German, American, Italian; and they're all heading in for a landing on this huge green belt above the clouds. The dead aircrews making their last trip. That's how it was seeing that Marauder. Yes, I remember it clearly now. Really spooked us."

"I know the Dahl story," Dobson nodded. He even knew

the title—"They Shall Not Grow Old." He thought of dead Mrs. Lambert and the friend in white, *dressed funny*, the hole in her garden and the old lady standing by the cottage door, her hand like a withered paw, quoting, *We will remember them*.

Aloud, and for no particular reason—certainly not with any sentiment—he muttered the whole passage:

"*They shall not grow old as we that are left grow old: Age shall not weary them, nor the years condemn; at the going down of the sun, and in the morning, we will remember them.*"

"That's the one." Flax still had not resumed his old buoyant manner. "'They Shall Not Grow Old.' That some poem? No good on poems myself."

"Yes." Dobson heard the bitterness, could even taste it at the back of his throat. "And who does remember them, Herbie?"

"Hey, Dave. You okay?" Flax raised himself on his elbows.

Dobson relaxed. He wanted to cry and his head hurt. He took a deep breath. Then another. "Sorry, Herbie. I get riled about it sometimes. I wasn't old enough to be in it, but it riles me. I . . . I lose my sense of proportion. You've been very kind to me. Sorry if I stirred unwanted memories."

"They're gonna be stirred anyway, with the guys coming an' all." He swung his legs over the side of the lounger. "Dave?"

"Yes?" He felt a little better now.

"What is it all about? The questions? Talking about that spook airplane, the mystic Marauder? You a spook? I don't mean a ghost, spirit spook. You know what I mean."

"Not really. I know what you mean. But I'm not a spook the way you think. Let's just say I'm in the business of Air Historical Records. Sometimes records get warped and have to be straightened. I'm in the straightening department—part time."

He felt Flax relax again after that. The goodbyes had to be said. Laura; Joe; Little Herbie.

"Nice to meet you, Dave. Will we be seeing anything of you at these shindigs the *Express* is arranging for the boys?"

"More than likely."

They stood by the Hertz VW, parked below the patio. Farther up the drive, Dobson caught sight of a couple of cars. He was not good on cars but one looked like a fast and furious Ferrari. The other was more obvious—a Rolls Corniche. It had to be with Herbie Flax really. Only the best.

"About those eagles, Herbie." He could not resist it.

"Aren't they great? Local craftsman knocked them up for me."

"Splendid, but you should get them aged. Put a little time on them."

"Yeah? How do I go about that, Dave? You know about that kind of thing?"

"I know one trick, Herbie. Old stonemason's trick. I know because my old man was a clergyman, and clergymen have a lot of business with stonemasons. You wash them. You wash the stone eagles."

"Wash them?"

Dobson nodded. "You wash them with cowshit."

"You look terrible," Hackstead said when he walked into the main lounge of the County.

Hackstead was drinking tea and eating little sandwiches—cucumber and tomato and smoked salmon. Triangular and very proper.

"The head played up a bit. Maybe I should've stayed in town and not done this jaunt after all."

A waiter appeared. There were fifteen minutes to go before the car was due. He ordered tea—providing they could make it fast. All Dobson wanted now was to be back in Charlotte Street, mugging corpses or not, preferably in bed with Ann soothing his brow—or something.

"What'd Flax have to tell us?"

"Klein was the odd man out in the crew: got on, but not as close as the others—close with Sharp, though. He also confirmed Potts' story about seeing *Dodo* again in August '44."

"Really?"

"Said it was a weird experience. Got quite sober about it." The tea arrived.

"What have we got, Bud? What have we really got?"

He was starting to feel confused by the labyrinth of information—the realities and doubts. The ghosts and the tangible items.

Hackstead finished his last sandwich and saw the WRAF driver standing in the doorway. He mouthed that they would be out in a minute.

"Don't know, David, don't know. I need some time to collate. Can you do me a written report on the Flax interview and your own notes on our session with Free?"

"Not tonight I can't."

"At your leisure. Tomorrow. I'll be away all day."

"Where this time? To Bath or Stratford-on-Avon with your Pentax and tourist guides?"

Bud Hackstead gave him an unnervingly severe look, then smiled. "No. I had an afternoon to remember. Got some good film. Had some time off in the dim and distant, but that's it." He leaned forward, a hand hovering over Dobson's small plate of sandwiches.

"Naughty." Dobson slapped the hand away.

"I'm going over to Halton again tomorrow," Hackstead announced. "See the path. people. Maybe go have a look at Tyndle and his boys at Farnborough. I doubt it, though, I think it'll be Halton all day."

"The Rift Valley fever scare?"

"Yep." He reached forward. Dobson was not quick enough. The last smoked salmon sandwich was in Hackstead's mouth before he could get to it.

By eight-thirty Dobson was back at Charlotte Street, his head splitting again. At eight thirty-two he dialed Ann.

"You sound beat up."

"Tired. Headache. Shouldn't have gone." The headache came in waves. When it was bad it was rotten, then it would slide away and return just as he thought it had disappeared altogether.

"I'll be at your front door in half an hour," said Ann.

"You look dreadful." She walked straight in, her hands on his shoulders, guiding him back from the door. *You look terrible*, Hackstead had said.

"I feel rough." The nausea had returned.

For a moment she cradled him in her arms, stroking the side of his head—the bruised side.

"You were right; I was wrong. Should have listened; should have rested."

"Symptoms?" she asked, like a nurse, very efficient.

"Headaches. They come and go," he told her.

"Bad?"

"Bad, then decreasing—almost normal twenty minutes ago. Terrible now; and I keep feeling sick."

"Into bed," she said. "Go and lie down." A pause as she held him very close, the tips of her fingers resting on his head. "Lie down, my darling, please. I'm going to get a doctor."

"No. We both know the trouble. I went back too soon."

"Nevertheless. Duty quack. Through the Department. Bed." She steered him toward the bedroom door and, thankfully, he slumped onto the bed, stretched out and closed his eyes. Vaguely, he heard the extension telephone ping.

There seemed to be a lot of comings and goings. Then a

doctor arrived. He said his name was Marsh and that he was the Ministry duty quack.

"I'm going to give you an injection to remove the pain and give you a good night's rest; and some pills—three a day. No dashing around, though. At least, not tomorrow. It's nothing serious but bangs on heads can make you feel groggy. The sooner you relax and get rest the sooner you'll be back to normal." Marsh was filling a syringe.

Ann sat close, leaning over him.

"I'll be in the other room. All night," she said flatly, "if you need anything. If you wake, I'll be there."

"I doubt if he'll wake." The doctor had overheard. "Get Charlie Sugden up here as soon as you can in the morning."

He had to talk with Sugden, though really he had forgotten what about. Arthur? Richard Martin Lewis? The photographs of St. Trond? Something else bugging away at the far back of his head, out of reach.

Then the drifting began. Like a huge, long pull-back on a zoom lens everything diminished: the room, Ann's face, far, far away, and he knew nothing, just the great peaceful silent tunnel of sleep.

20

The door opened. He saw the handle turning, gently at first, and then watched, fascinated, as the hinges swung back.

Ann peered around the space between door and jamb. "Oh, you're awake." She spoke very quietly as though not quite certain, even though his eyes were open and looking straight at her.

She came over quickly and sat on the bed, hand to his head. "How do you feel?"

"Fighting fit."

She pushed him gently on the chest. "Well, you're going to do as Dr. Marsh instructed: no whizzing around."

"I've got to see Sugden."

"He'll come here. Leave that to me."

"And I must do the reports. Hackstead'll need them."

"We'll work something out, but you're not leaving this flat. Not today, not if I have to stay here myself and strap you down."

"I heard bells."

"The telephone. I took it on the extension: hoped it hadn't wakened you."

"Trouble?"

"Just Hackstead's office confirming that he would be at

Halton all day, and probably until much later this evening. Left instructions that you were to be called if anything urgent cropped up."

"I told you..."

"I didn't argue with them. We just hope nothing urgent comes out of the blue."

"What's the time?"

"Nine-thirty."

"Christ, you ought to be at..."

"Clapham knows I'm here." She looked him straight in the eyes, almost a challenge. "I told them I dropped in to make sure you were okay. They had to know—or they'd have found out. I called in the duty MO, remember?"

With surprise he realized that he was hungry. "You really doing the cherishing bit?"

"The slave."

"Bacon, eggs, fried bread, toast, coffee."

"That's a very good sign. One English breakfast coming up."

"Ann?"

"Yes?"

"I'm not fooling around, you know. I'm not that kind of fella."

"Go with it. I'm not that kind of girl either, even in this day and age."

"Good." She was at the door. "You couldn't give Sugden a call?"

"Such romance. Yes, I'll call him."

"Get him over here, Annie."

"Ann," she said firmly. "Without the *e*, and never Annie."

Sugden arrived on the dot of eleven. Dobson was propped up with pillows and leaning back trying to look weary. Whatever it was the doctor had put into him—both in the injection and the pills which Ann had started him on after breakfast—was doing a power of good. He felt in just the mood to deal with Sugden. The weary look might just put the wily Sugden at a disadvantage.

"Well, well, how's the patient?" Sugden rubbed his hands together as though washing them—the Pontius Pilate syndrome. He carried a briefcase.

"Progessing. I'll be up later, but the quack demanded a day of rest."

"Sure it's wise? Getting up, I mean. Terry'd fill in, it'd be perfectly secure."

"Nobody's going to do any filling in. With a little help from my servicing officer I'll be fine."

"Good, good. Just want to be careful, that's all. The groupie'll be back on Monday." He looked unhappy at the thought. He wants it all neatly bundled up and himself well-covered by the time Group Captain Rivers Crenham Waterford gets back in the driver's seat, Dobson thought.

"I just did too much too soon."

"Yes, I know." Then, the old pomposity returning in a flood, like someone turning on a garden hose: "I saw the medical report first thing this morning."

"Then you know it all. I need a day's rest, but there're things to be done."

"Yes, yes, down to it, eh?"

He opened his briefcase, producing from it a single folder which he placed in front of Dobson. It contained an aerial photograph—recce picture—taken from around nine or ten thousand feet. It showed an airfield—the familiar triangulated crisscross of runways, peritracks, dispersals, hangars and buildings; only it looked as though someone had gone over it with explosive darts. There was a caption attached to the bottom and Sugden had got the thing marked up with arrows, dots and circles—a very professional job.

He read the caption slowly:

IWM Photograph C.4560, it said at the top.
British Official Photograph (Air Ministry)
Picture issued 1944. There was no exact date of issue.

"It's the only photograph on file of St. Trond." Sugden puffed out his fat little chest. He had really done them all a favor. It had probably taken one telephone call—two at the most. "You'll see," he went on, "that I've marked up the conditions for *Overshoot*. The airfield was clean then—no bloody great craters all over it in '43."

Dobson examined the minutiae of the photograph, noting the position of the buildings in relation to the runways and taxitrack, equating them with the way Sugden had marked it up to show how *Overshoot* could have been accomplished.

"Okay," he nodded. "Technically it was possible, but I want to talk about our informant."

"Arthur." Sugden looked away. "Yes, you mentioned that."

"Arthur." He dropped the name heavily. "Richard Martin Lewis. Onetime squadron leader Royal Air Force. Had a good job with the Min. of Defence until—when?—1966?"

"I know all about that." Sugden snapped it out as though Dobson was treading on hallowed ground.

"Well, you may, but I don't. First, I'm asking you, as my servicing officer, is the man you cryptoed Arthur in reality Richard Martin Lewis?"

"He is."

"The Richard Martin Lewis who worked for the Ministry and became involved in a scandal concerning the offering of classified material to an intelligence officer of the East German government in 1966?"

"Yes, and if you know that you should also know that he was cleared of any involvement."

"Nevertheless he resigned and he's looking pretty far gone."

Sugden puffed a bit. "Look, David, there are some things one doesn't have to explain. I got to Arthur through the right connections."

"You mean D15 or 6?"

"If you want to be pedantic."

"You would agree that Special Branch are the executive arm, the legal power, behind D15?"

"Yes."

"Then why are they still interested in Richard Martin Lewis?"

"It's that bloody spade Trotter, isn't it?"

"It's a member of Special Branch."

The pause was quite long. "Do I have to spell it out to you, man?" Sugden asked eventually. He was holding a fair head of steaming anger.

"Some of it."

"As your servicing officer I guarantee that Arthur's clean." Another pause. "All right, without going into long-winded details, it was a setup. It's still a setup. Arthur's under cover."

"Then you took one hell of a risk bringing him to this flat."

"I had it watched. I followed all the practical safeguards."

"It was still spotted. I'm not happy about it."

"He's as clean as you'll get."

"Okay. Now what about these characters who were in the bag with Free—what did you call them? Partridge and Peartree?"

"What about them?"

"I shall want to talk. I shall also want a written guarantee regarding Arthur, and written guarantees concerning these other two."

"You won't take my word?" He was on the red-faced point of bluster.

"No."

"Then I suppose I'll have to comply." It was like watching a slow puncture in a bicycle tire. "When do you want to talk to them?"

"Not today. Tomorrow probably, I'll let you know. Today, Wing Commander Sugden, I want to borrow Miss West."

"Borrow . . . ?"

"I've been ordered to rest today. Instructed not to do any rushing around. I fancy I'll be doing some more rushing as of tomorrow morning. By that time I have to have two confidential reports on Colonel Hackstead's desk. I can't do it all alone. Miss West's security clearance is good enough. I wish to dictate the reports to her here. Then she can type them: I have my own portable. After that—which might take the whole day—my mind will be ready to deal with other matters, like having a word with the two Free contacts."

"Well, I suppose . . . We've got a lot on at the . . ."

"You've got nothing on except this and a couple of never never jobs. You can spare her for the day. If I finish early I'll send her back to you."

"Well?" Uncertain. "Well, I suppose if she's willing. I'll have to ask her personally."

"She's willing, but ask away. One more point. Free's relatives, living and/or dead. If dead, when? Okay?"

The reports took about three hours: a complete résumé of all Dobson's views on the Free interview, and a detailed—almost question and answer—précis of the time he had spent with Herbie Flax.

Ann typed and sealed them, then took them off to Grosvenor Square, while Dobson finally got himself out of bed, bathed, shaved and dressed. He felt better than he had since the business on the landing.

She cooked dinner and, afterward, they sat close sipping coffee and talking.

Dobson wondered if this was the moment. If the time and place were right. Just after nine o'clock he made the first tentative move, the first kiss—they had kissed often during the day but this was the first real thing since the aborted beginning that morning.

As she turned her body toward him, sliding a thigh over his, the telephone rang.

The voice at the other end had a foreign accent he could

not place. "Mr. Dobson?" the voice asked.

"Dobson," he confirmed, uncomfortable, wanting to be off the instrument as quickly as possible.

"Wing Commander Dobson?"

"Yes."

"Blenkinsop."

Blenkinsop? Who in the name of...? Blenkinsop? Yes, Blenkinsop. Kursbuch—Timetable—the man Hackstead had sent over to research the Bundesarchiv in Koblenz.

"Timetable?" he asked to be certain.

The voice laughed. A happy pleasant laugh. A man with a sense of humor. "You have me. Colonel Hackstead's office put me on to you. The colonel is out of town and I have just got back from Koblenz. I have with me a document which might be of some help. I've been through a great deal of material, but I think this is most important, and as the colonel's office tells me you are working on the case with him, I felt I should bring it to you."

"Where are you?"

"At Heathrow. I have telephoned the Embassy but they say the colonel will be late. I do not want the responsibility of this document overnight. Could I bring it, perhaps, to you? Or would you like to come to me?"

"What is it exactly?"

"I don't know if it's wise to..."

"What is it? We're not in Berlin, it's not the bloody Russians. We're time travelers. It's old history."

"Old history that's never come to light. It may be nothing."

"Bring it to me then." He gave the address. Then: "The document, Blenkinsop. A clue?"

"A letter. A personal instruction from Göring to Field Marshal Sperrle, who commanded the Luftwaffe's Third Air Force. It's an order concerning an operation."

"Dated?"

"Yes."

"When?"

"May 18, 1944."

"The operation?"

"You must see the document."

"The operation?"

"I will come now. It's here in my briefcase."

"The name of the Op, Timetable?"

"It is concerned with some operation called *Rattengift*."

"My German's not too hot. What's *Rattengift*?"

"I'm coming to you now."

"Okay, but what's it mean in English? *Rattengift?*"

"It means *Ratpoison*, Mr. Dobson. *Ratbane*. Operation *Ratpoison*. I come now."

21

"Herr Kursbuch?" Dobson queried, opening the door.

"Oberstleutnant Dobson?" he replied with that same amusing vocal connotation Dobson had picked up over the telephone. "I can come in? No secret passes? No code words?"

Kursbuch could have been a retired docker or a miner. Past his prime, worn out in service one presumed, but the frame still large, the muscles waning a little now, but still there and effective. He had one of those faces they call craggy when a man is young or approaching middle age. Now Kursbuch had leaped over the sixties, the face was like seasoned granite, carved and weathered by years of struggle: a big tough resilient face. In the eyes, which were bright with humor, there was also another reflection which said, "Do not screw me or I'll break you like a twig."

Kursbuch seemed surprised there was someone else in the flat.

"Ann West," Dobson explained, then realized that it needed clarification.

"Miss West." Very correct.

"It's all right. She's with my department. She's cleared and knows most things."

"Good," Kursbuch responded. "I am sorry about the cloak-and-dagger conversation from Heathrow. It's the open phone booths they have these days. They give me the willies. I have been used to taking great care."

"I understand." Dobson waved him toward a chair, and the German sat down, again very correctly, a briefcase placed like a tray on his knees. He must have been a hell of a man at one time, Dobson considered. What was it Bud Hackstead had said about him? *Mr. Timetable. Old Peter Kursbuch used to run an excellent timetable for us once. Set your watch by him. Used to come over that damn Wall like a stone from a slingshot.* That would have taken a lot of doing—still did for that matter—coming over the Berlin Wall on a regular basis.

"Drink?" Dobson asked.

"I would like coffee, maybe. If it is not too much..."

"It's no trouble at all," said Ann, meaning it and turning straight toward the kitchen.

When they were alone Dobson asked, "You've turned up something?"

"Maybe. Just a possible. I'll go back tomorrow, on the morning flight, and see if there's anything else, but I thought Colonel Hackstead could be checking out some things here in your own archives—Imperial War Museum, maybe the Weiner Library even, and Ministry files. It's the code name which strikes me. One I've never heard of and never read about. Besides, this little missive was tucked away in a whole pile of stuff put aside before the Nuremberg trials of blessed memory. It was never used."

"Can I see?"

"That's why I'm here." He opened the briefcase and drew out a single photostat, preserved carefully between two thin sheets of card.

The letterhead was flamboyant—the Luftwaffe flying eagle crest, the talons clutching at a black swastika. Hermann Göring's name figured largely, together with his formal title of Supreme Commander—*Oberbefehlshaber*—of the Luftwaffe. The only address was *Fuhrerhauptquartier*, Hitler's headquarters, which could have been anywhere from the Reich Chancellery to the Wolf's Lair, the Eagle's Nest or the "Führer Special," as the headquarters' railway train was known.

Dobson understood enough. The *Führerhauptquartier* meant wherever the Führer happened to be, and wherever that was you would find the court, for Hitler, like the Tudor monarchs, went on his royal progresses with the whole machinery of advisers, generals and sycophants.

He also knew the meaning of the other words which showed clear at the top left-hand side—*Geheime Reichsfache*—Secret Reich Affairs. It meant an A plus classified document.

After that his knowledge faltered. He made a despairing gesture. "My German's not..."

"...too hot. You said so on the telephone. You wish for me to make a translation?"

"If you would. There's a typewriter..."

Peter Kursbuch, old Timetable, had already spotted it. He rose and began to tread toward it. For a big man he trod softly, walked with great stealth, even here in this room in London—as though no movement should call attention to him, so that he always presented a picture of composed, quiet calm.

"Miss West can..."

"I'll do it. No problem. I've handled most machines in my time, Wing Commander..."

"David."

"David. Good. Peter." He made a mocking, Tarzan-like movement of communication establishment. "Most machines, from typewriters to bazookas, motorcars to Steyr-Solothurn machine pistols."

Dobson cocked an eyebrow.

"Not standard German Army equipment, no," shrugged Kursbuch. "Kripo and SS." The big face changed as if for a moment life had ceased. "Bud Hackstead will tell you that for a time, and for my sins, I was with the SS. I was a Nazi, that's why I hate the Communists. However, I was not a good Nazi. As a member of the SS I disobeyed an order. I refused a posting to Auschwitz."

"And?"

The laugh exploded, almost joyfully. "And I spent a lot of time on the eastern front. I was a lucky boy. They flew me out from Stalingrad with six bullets in my flesh: flew me out in a clapped-out Junkers 52 with one dodgy engine. Now your people take me on trust—and for my specialized knowledge. The translation... He sat down at the typewriter and slid a piece of paper into the rollers.

As he worked, Ann brought in a big tray with a large jug of coffee and two cups. "It's your day of rest," she whispered. "He came to hand over a document and go. For your own sake don't keep him long. Come to bed as soon as you get rid of him. I'm going now. I'll be waiting so don't be too long." Her eyes calm and beckoning. She said loudly, "I'm going to bed, Herr Kursbuch, if you'll excuse me."

He stopped typing. "It has been a pleasure, Miss West. You are kind and also discreet. I trust we meet again." A bow which, in old war movies, would have been accompanied by a click of the heels.

He made no comment to Dobson, just sat down again at the typewriter and carried on working. Five minutes later he handed over the completed translation and the original.

"I go now?"

Dobson hesitated. This was Hackstead's territory, but he should at least check. "Could you stay a moment? After all there's the coffee..."

"I thought you'd never ask. The coffee on the airplanes these days. Ugh. Like ersatz—in the war we Germans had..."

"I know, acorn coffee—substitute. I believe we had powdered milk, which was as bad."

"Ah, but you also had the Americans with their rations and their PXs."

They both laughed and Dobson poured the coffee, sitting opposite the solidly upstanding Peter Kursbuch, who had not hesitated to tell him that he was once a member of the SS.

The typewritten translation had been executed without a single X-out or error. It was from Göring himself to Generalfeldmarschall Hugo Sperrle commanding Luftflotte III—the Third Air Force. The text was austere:

> Following the Führer Directive 55 of May 16, 1944, you are instructed to proceed with RATTENGIFT as previously arranged in conference. All other parties have now been notified and your instructions for the date of this operation will now come to you directly from Chef OKW.
>
> Heil Hitler!
>
> Göring
> Der Reichsmarschall
> des Grossdeutschen Reiches

"He liked pulling rank." Dobson smiled.

"Fat Hermann was above the common herd of generals. He was anxious that people should appreciate that. It was a fine point. Subtle as the sting of a scorpion."

"Führer Directive 55?" queried Dobson.

"May 16, 1944? I wouldn't know. There were many. You will have to check."

"Chef OKW?"

"Keitel. Chief of the High Command."

"What makes you so interested in this one?"

"My brief was to go through as much Luftwaffe stuff as possible in connection with some possible covert operation concerning the use of a British or American—most likely American—aircraft. I found none. This I found. The tenor of the text strikes me. The secrecy of the orders. Its direct link with one of Hitler's well-known orders; and, most of all, the coding of the operation. I have never seen an operational code of any importance titled *Rattengift—Ratbane*. I know most of them— *Weiss, Taifun, Merkur, Seelöwe, Fischreiher*, of course."

Dobson looked bewildered. He knew and understood *Seelöwe—Sealion*, the invasion of Britain. The others were just words at which he could only make guesses.

"I had forgotten. Your German. *Fischreiher, Heron*, the attack on Stalingrad; *Seelöwe...*"

"I know that one."

"You make progress. What about *Weiss, Taifun, Merkur?*"

"I'd guess *Mercury* for the last one."

"Good. Operation against Crete. *Weiss—White*—attack on Poland; *Taifun...*"

"*Typhoon.*"

"So. Attack on Moscow. You want to try more?"

"I think we can leave it."

"They were some of the big ones. I know most of the others also. They're in the books. *Rattengift* I have not heard of. It rings bells of suspicion. I have instinct, Bud Hackstead tells me."

He drained his cup. "The coffee is good. I'll go now. Tomorrow back to Koblenz and look to see if there is more on *Ratbane*. You and Bud will doubtless do your own pieces of research."

Dobson continued to look at the original document. Apart from the official file number from the Bundesarchiv there was a small notation in ink below Göring's signature.

"That contemporary?" he asked, pointing.

Kursbuch looked over his shoulder. After a long pause, "I would say yes."

The notation said *Ampt VI*.

"*Ampt VI* was . . . ?" Dobson knew he had been trying too hard, trying to remember too much. He was a specialist in the air war '39 – '45. Incidentals escaped him. He should know what *Ampt VI* was. SS—he was aware of that.

Kursbuch's face went dead again. "*Ampt VI—The Ausland SD.* Schellenberg's lot. SS Foreign Intelligence modeled, to start with, on the much vaunted British Secret Service—your SIS."

"I thought Admiral Canaris . . ."

"The Military Intelligence, David. You'll have to mug up on your Nazi chain of command. Canaris—until his downfall—was in charge of the Abwehr. They worked together, of course, after a fashion. Loved each other after a fashion. Working with the SS was like working with unstable explosive, or being a male spider who will be consumed by its mate as the natural physical end. Schellenberg won. Canaris went to the wall. But you know all that."

Dobson nodded. "Of course." Literally Canaris did not go to the wall. They hanged him for indirect involvement in the July 20 Hitler bomb plot. "If this was some kind of a covert Op . . . ?"

"The *Ampt VI* notation means that it probably was. One of those many things which happened—the SS and Abwehr working in harness. SS/Military Intelligence operation; clandestine; target . . . ? Look up the *Führerweisungen 55*. Clues, clues. It could really be quite elementary, my dear Dobson. What your great Sherlock Holmes called the three-pipe problem."

They shook hands gravely and Dobson saw him out, went back into the living room, glanced at the bedroom door and felt suddenly tired and anxious. He picked up the document and translation, went to the old, almost crippled bureau, extracted a heavy card-backed Ministry envelope from the top drawer, inserted the papers, sealed them and placed the package into the largest pigeonhole within the desk, closed up, locked it and put the key in his pocket.

He was halfway to the bedroom door when something else passed through his mind. The Führer directives. He hesitated, like some old man uncertain in crossing the street, the decision too much to make. It would only take a moment, so why not?

Between the pair of windows which looked down onto Charlotte Street was his long, low bookcase containing what he called his traveling library—most of the technical stuff that really interested him, together with the few novels he thought worth retaining in this day and age of computerized fiction.

He kneeled down and begun to run his fingers along the titles, moving to *Hitler's War Directives 1933–1945*.

He took it out, lit a cigarette and flicked through the pages, fast, exasperated, Directive 49...52...54...55: *Führer Order of May 16, 1944.* Drawing in on the cigarette he read quickly through the directive, its subject...*The Führer has ordered*...He went cold, actually shivering as he read on, right to the end. It was signed by KEITEL himself:

5. The Orders laid down for secrecy in paragraph 7 of the order of December 25, 1943, No. 663082/43 for Senior Commanders will apply.

The Chief of the High Command of the Armed Forces.
signed: *Keitel.*

He now knew at least the relationship between the so-called *Rattengift* operation and the directive. If they were both linked, and if the connection was made with *Dodo?* It could be a million things, but what with the name of the Op, and what was already happening, the pointers were starting to take direction.

He sat there for a few moments more, very much aware that Ann was in the other room. Waiting. Perhaps too tired to wait—tired like himself. But he needed to clear his head; to make decisions on action now.

At last he picked up the telephone and dialed the U.S. Embassy. Hackstead was not yet logged back in London. He dialed Hackstead's private number and let it ring twenty times. Right. Technically Hackstead was in charge, but he would cover himself. Maybe not even tell Hackstead some of what he was doing—was that childish? The magician producing the rabbit, the clever fictional detective bringing in the right deductions on the last page, Perry Mason asking to be allowed to present new evidence which had just come to light. Childish? No, he would cover himself.

He dialed Sugden's home number.

"Hope I'm not disturbing you," he began, a shade tentative, then—nuts to that—"Dobson here..."

"I was just going..."

"Forget it. First, I'll see Partridge and Peartree tomorrow afternoon. Both of them. You let me know where: first thing in the morning. Second, who's the best archivist researcher you know?"

"Well...?" Deliberating.

"Come on, Sugden, this is important. You're the man with all the secret boys on call, the one who can whistle up the wind. Whistle it now, break it if you have to. Who's the best?"

"Dowl," the uncertainty gone. "Montague Dowl."

"Get him at first light."

"Dowl? I don't know ..."

"You're the wonder boy. Get him."

"He might be ..."

"If he's in audience with the Pope or the PM—which amounts to the same thing—get him. Whatever."

"I'll do my best."

"Not enough."

"All right. What's this about? You sound excited."

"It's tremendously important if I'm right. I'm going to give you one word. I want Dowl to check out every archive in sight over there for that one word—Imperial War, the Ministries, Weiner Library—everywhere including the House of Commons loo."

"The word?" Good old, bad old, efficient old Sugden again. For the flicker of a second he thought of Trotter and wondered if Special Branch had the line wired.

"The word is *Rattengift*. I spell. R-A-T-T-E-N-G-I-F-T."

"Got it."

"Right. Third, you recall I asked for a record check on Free's relatives?"

"I have a note ..."

"Double the speed. I want it yesterday morning."

"Right."

"Fourth and last."

"Go ahead."

"I want a really top-grade surveillance man."

"Simple."

"A man who can never be seen. Get the invisible man if you have to."

"Top grade," Sugden repeated.

"And he's got to know about focal lengths. I want him down in Canterbury tomorrow. Frederick Free. Pictures. Full face. Profiles. In close. It's too much to expect him to get them by the time I see your Partridge and Peartree, but I want them fast."

"I could set the right man off tonight."

"Go to then, Sugden, go to."

"Wilco."

That was bloody typical of Sugden, Dobson thought:

Wilco. Bloody wilco, roger and out. Bandits twelve o'clock high. Angels one five. Wilco.

He crushed the butt of his cigarette, took a deep breath, rose, turned out the lights and made for the bedroom.

Ann understood. She expected nothing. "Just lie close, darling David. All things eventually sort themselves out."

She fell asleep quite quickly, but Dobson lay there, Ann's naked body against him, his head trying to compute the odds, make the right kind of connections, draw at the straws in the wind. *Rattengift. Ratpoison. Dodo.* The crew with rickets. Rift Valley fever. *Führerweisungen 55.*

Number 55 was the directive dealing with—to quote, *Ref: Employment of Long-Range Weapons Against England.* The V-weapons. The V-1s, doodlebugs they had called them, those little stubby-winged unmanned aircraft which began to assault London after D-day; and the more dreaded V-2s, the monster rockets (child's toys in today's arsenal of death) which packed a punch of almost two thousand pounds of high explosive in their warheads.

He also pondered on all he could remember about Hitler's boasting and bragging concerning the "miracle weapons"—his secrets which would, as he so often claimed, "banish London from the map." Everyone—historians, military experts—had assumed, reasonably, that all these many references concerned the V-1s and V-2s, the jet aircraft, the huge torpedoes and such. Even when defeat was absolutely certain, Hitler, in that claustrophobic, mad, unreal atmosphere of the bunker in Berlin, still claimed that his miracle weapons would do the trick in the end. He was far gone then, but...? How? What? Why? A clapped-out Marauder and Hitler's miracle weapons?

Eventually, Dobson dropped off into a peaceful sleep. Dreamless. His only memories were of half-waking twice to feel the comforting warmth of Ann beside him.

They both awoke around seven, intertwined and looking, profiled on the pillow, into each other's morning eyes.

They made love then for the first time: slow and long; gently at first, a testing of each other's ways, then growing and entering not a ruttish frenzy but something which took them beyond all previous memories.

There was passion and wildness—abandonment, Dobson supposed old-fashioned people might call it. After that they were easy with each other; free. There was a lot of joy, pleasure, fun.

For Dobson it erased the past forever and they both drew strength from it.

Then came the laughs, the extra enjoyment. Lying naked and close, Ann leaned over and took her spectacles, the big round lenses, placing them carefully on his limpness.

"Can't it see that I'm ready again?" she giggled.

So it all began once more, something as near to a pact, a physical commitment, as any two people could wish for.

22

Ann had been gone only ten minutes when the telephone started ringing.

First Sugden.

The photographs were organized and should be back in London by the afternoon. Partridge and Peartree would meet him in Clapham at three if that was okay, and he had got Dowl at the Imperial War Museum. Dowl, the best archivist in the business.

Hackstead called ten minutes later.

"I tried to get you last night." Dobson made it sound ominous but Hackstead appeared indifferent.

"Last night? Oh boy. I hate to tell you this, Dave, but you see I didn't get back into town until about an hour ago. That corporal... the WRAF corporal: the one who drove us to Canterbury."

"What about her?"

"She took me down to Halton. I fixed it, and did I fix it?"

"Don't tell me. I don't want to know. What about the Rift Valley fever?"

"They say it's 80 per cent certain that's the virus, though they admit there could be error. I think they're a mite worried that it's a strain of flu that has some relationship with the good old Rift Valley type of fever—similar symptoms."

"Even Pasteur made mistakes."

"Last night?" For the first time Hackstead sounded interested. "What'd you try and call me for?"

"Blenkinsop."

"What about Blenkinsop?" Wide awake, the alertness explicit in his voice.

"He came in from Koblenz: with a document for you."

"Where's he now?"

Out of habit, Dobson glanced at his watch. "Probably on the way back to Koblenz. He just brought the paper over for you to see. Photostat. He had a feeling about it."

"Nobody told me. Where'd he stash the stat, in the duty night safe here—at the Embassy?"

"No. I've got it. It's quite interesting."

"You've got it—seen it? What's it about? He had no business . . . He was told to report directly to me with anything." For a moment there, Hackstead sounded almost feisty. Then, controlled, even with a light laugh. "But I wasn't here, was I?"

"You were cavorting."

"True, Br'er Dobson; and what a cavort."

"And you left orders that anything should be passed on to me—anything urgent that came up."

"Quite right. Come on then, what's this paper?"

"It's a classified order, tucked away in the archives, never even saw the light of day before the Nuremberg trials. Big Hermann to General Sperrle about some clandestine Op."

"Oh? Who was Sperrle? I should know."

"In command of the Third Air Force—Luftflotte III."

"Oh, that Sperrle? I thought it might've been Milton Sperrle from Hoboken." Chuckle. "What's Blenkinsop's real interest? What's the gimmick?"

"Blenkinsop says you reckon he's got intuition. He told me that little lights started to flash."

"Timetable has intuition okay. If there're flashing lights it means something."

"Whether or not it has anything to do with *Dodo* is another matter."

"What is it?"

"You'd better see it yourself."

"Coy coy coy."

"No, just careful." He thought of how he had pressed

Timetable on the call from Heathrow last night. This was different. He was talking on a direct line to the American Embassy. Direct lines to any embassy were notoriously insecure.

"Okay. You want me to send around for it, or can you make it over here? How are you, by the way, Dave? I forgot to ask. Sorry."

"I've had some very special R&R myself."

"Hope it was as good as mine."

"I am, as they say, in the peak of physical condition—except for the bruised head."

"So you can make it over here?"

"Delighted."

"Lunch? Lunch with our friend Charles from the *Express*? He wants to go over the schedule they've fixed with *Dodo*'s old crew."

"More than delighted. Only I've got to be in Clapham by three. The Big White Chief comes back on Monday and I think Sugden wants all the outstanding paper work finished—not just this. All the crossword puzzles: In, Out and Too Difficult. Sugden runs a tidy department."

"Noon?" asked Hackstead. "We meet Charles at twelve-thirty."

"I shall be with you at the noon hour."

Hackstead looked as though he had been up all night—which, in fairness, he probably had.

"I know," said the American. "But you should see the other fellow."

"I can believe it." Dobson unlocked his briefcase and handed over the envelope with the Göring-Sperrle photostat and translation.

Hackstead began to look at the contents of the envelope. He was examining the photostat first.

"*Rattengift*," almost to himself. "See how my Kraut ancestry holds up. *Rattengift*? *Rattengift* means—rats, rattraps? No...?" He peeked under the photostat at the translation. "*Rattengift. Ratpoison.* Well, I was pretty close. Not bad for a clean-living American boy with Kraut parentage. Never heard of an Op coded *Rattengift*."

"Neither had Timetable, and he says he's an expert."

"Oh, he is. What the heck was the *Führerweisungen* 55? Führer directive?"

"Yes."

"There you go. Which one of Mad Adolf's commands was that? You checked?"

"I checked. Number 55 was signed by Keitel. It concerned the employment of long-range weapons against England."

"Jesus H. Christ. The V-1s and -2s."

"Uh-huh."

"Rockets. The doodlebugs, buzz bombs and rockets. How in tarnation do you equate that with *Dodo*?"

"Don't ask me. Blenkinsop didn't know either. He just said he was doing his job, had never heard of such a code name for an Op, thought it smelled and brought it over."

"He does have intuition, that I'll admit, but . . . ? Another fine mess he's gotten us into. *Rattengift*. Long-range weapons against England. *Dodo*? I don't see it. He's gone back, you say?"

"Blenkinsop? Timetable?"

"Yes."

Dobson nodded.

"I have to hand it to him, he's got some kind of ESP as a rule, but I don't see this one. We'll wait. Maybe he'll sort something else out."

Charles, from the *Daily Express*, met them on time at the place where Dobson had first lunched with Hackstead, near the Embassy.

They had the schedule all set up. Potts, plus wife; Goldberg, by himself; Sailby, plus wife; Wilcox Pride, by himself; and Sharp, plus wife, would be arriving at Heathrow around noon on Monday. They would be met by Charles, a couple of cameramen, the features editor and their old buddy Herbie Flax—plus Laura, of course.

"We're doing it all first class," Charles told them. "Bloody Hilton, it'll cost a fortune. We pay accommodation and normal meals, but no extras."

The first night—the Monday—would be spent in London. In fact they would be given the first two days in London—conducted tours; time off to visit any old haunts left standing; old friends.

"On Thursday we are taking them out early: American Military Cemetery, Cambridge. Then down to the site of the old Horham airfield, and on to Earls Colne. Friday, Norwich and back to London. Friday evening we tie up the interviews. All Saturday, interviews and TV—we've got an agreement with ITV that they'll release nothing until we start doing the series on the Monday. On Sunday we take them down to the site of the *Dodo* wreck . . ."

"There's nothing there, you know," Hackstead mused. "It's all being gone over at Farnborough—and they can't go see it."

Charles nodded.

He's a smooth bastard, Dobson thought, smooth as ice and twice as slippery, sitting there, confident with his smart Seiko digital on one wrist and a gold ID bracelet on the other, all done up in the lightweight gray suit that looked new and handmade to match the varnished personality.

"We'll explain that to them. Saturday night we're giving a special dinner at the Hilton. You want to be there?"

"Maybe." Hackstead's thoughts were momentarily elsewhere. "Let's see how we can set it up. Sunday down at the site? Morning?"

"Just before lunch. They can have the afternoon looking around New Romney, Dymchurch. We thought some of them might like to take in Canterbury Cathedral. What time do you want them?" Charles brayed.

"I've just about fixed it all. Cocktail party and dinner in a setting they'll adore. Place called Fenwell Manor. Inland from St. Mary's Bay. I have connections and the owners'll be away. We have the run of the place and there's enough room to sleep the lot if necessary—I don't know about your boys, though."

"We'd like one camera at least."

"I'll check it out. Dave here, and myself; possibly a couple more security guys. Got to keep this one tight, Charles. After all, you talk about it costing a fortune but we're putting up some things, you know."

"I haven't been told about the Fenwell Manor thing." Dobson knew he should not show pique.

"In good time, Dave. It's not settled and you and I have a small briefing to go over. The other guest is going to be Flight Lieutenant Frederick Free."

"Oh."

"What time do you want them there?" Charles asked again.

"I should imagine between six and seven. I'll check with you." He turned swiftly to Dobson. "And you do know about the Fenwell Manor bit. Hercule Poirot? Remember?"

"The butler did it," said Dobson, priding himself on a good exit line as he left for his interview with Partridge and Peartree at Clapham.

It was just before seven when he finally got back to Charlotte Street, disturbed by what he had learned from the interrogation. Trotter's car stood outside the house and its owner loitered with intent in the hallway.

23

"You work odd hours and go to odd places, Dobson." He gave his melon segment smile. "I have a word?"

"Depends. I've got a date."

"It's serious. We really do have to talk. I mean, death follows you around like nobody I've ever met."

"What d'you mean?"

"Let's go up to your place. I mean your recent visit to Kent—to the marsh, Canterbury and places adjacent."

"Old Mrs. Lambert?"

"Among others."

"Others?"

"You haven't seen tonight's papers?" Trotter handed him a copy of the *Evening Standard*.

"No."

"You made a special visit when you were down in Kent."

"You really have had the tabs on me, haven't you?"

"No. It came out in the local investigation this afternoon."

"What local investigation?"

They were in the building now, climbing the stairs, almost at the landing.

"You went to see a wealthy American. A Mr. Herbert Flax."

"Yes. Part of our investigation."

Trotter nodded and then stood still, looking straight into Dobson's eyes.

He knew, as he fumbled for his key and said, "What about Herbie Flax?"

"Wealthy American businessman Herbert J. Flax got himself shot sometime in the last couple of days. They didn't find him until this afternoon. He was sitting in his nice highly polished Ferrari motorcar in a layby. Someone put two bullets into his guts and another, at close range, through his throat. The local doc says it could have happened any time in the last forty-eight hours, and Mr. Flax left his home a couple of hours after you visited him—that is according to his widow."

Dobson opened the door of his flat and ushered Trotter inside.

"After you," said Trotter. "Please, Dobson, after you. I come in peace, but there are some things you have to understand."

"Such as?"

Dobson closed the door, keeping his body toward Trotter; that wide smile was too pleasant—all the smart chat, the far-out Special Branch man who lived as though he had just walked out of a TV series. Behind it all, danger smelled like a sewer, or the stench of putrefaction from the attacking corpse on the landing.

"We are now involved up to our neatly tied navels. I sit down?"

Dobson nodded. Trotter sat, hands on his knees, not relaxed, but in a position from which he could move at speed, one hand gripping the chair arm to give himself leverage if it became necessary.

"Come on then, how involved?"

"Think about it. We know about you, your involvement's obvious. There is CIA involvement. You can't deny that."

"I wouldn't know."

"Well, I'm telling you: you're part of a Ministry tributary intelligence outfit which usually takes care of things way down the line. First..." He raised one hand, fingers extended in a Greek curse, and began to count off the list. "First, your acting boss is a mate of some of the heavies at the Ministry. He puts in an application for a contact with some guy we called Denis. I deliver the message. Denis gets killed. Second, you get beaten and could've been killed. Third, we know what you're working on and realize that it's old history, but—whatever it is—that old history is dangerous. Fourth, one old lady you've talked to in Kent dies..."

"That was supposed to be a heart attack."

"Maybe. I'm told they're not too sure any more. Might have been zonked. She fractured her skull when she hit that door."

"For a Special Branch messenger you know more than I do."

Trotter paid little attention. "Fifth..." he went on without a pause, "you visit two people down in the same area, a retired guy called Free and an American multi-millionaire. Within a couple of hours of you—and it was you, alone—talking to Herbert J. Flax, the dude goes out of his front door like a pack of hounds are after him. Almost forty-eight hours later they find him, still in his beautiful expensive motor, with three 9 mm bullets in uncomfortable places. You, Mr. Dobson, and your American buddy are investigating the wreck of an aircraft which went into Romney Marsh over thirty years ago. The bodies inside do not tally with those they are supposed to be. We get murder and mayhem. Now I've got the funnies breathing down my neck asking questions. I should imagine Sugden's going through the same process on a slightly higher level."

"You think Bud Hackstead or myself...?"

"Come on, Dobson. Don't be stupid. You and Hackstead are like Snow White and the Snow Goose. You're professionals. But now with Herbert Flax taking the short cut to oblivion, my people're concerned. So, I might add, are the police."

Trotter fumbled around inside his jacket and brought out a tattered copy of the *Evening Standard*. "It's on the front page, small but full of fun. Read it."

Dobson opened up the newspaper and saw the piece immediately—low down, across three columns, WEALTHY AMERICAN SHOT DEAD. He looked around, trying to make a decision about either a drink or a cigarette. He settled for the story. As Trotter had said, short but fun. Terse and a lot between the lines.

Retired millionaire industrialist Herbert J. Flax (55), who for the past three years has lived in a £100,000 luxury mansion near Wootton in Kent, was found shot dead this afternoon in his red Ferrari Boxer in a layby in Lyminge Forest.

The Kent police are taking advice from Scotland Yard and this afternoon it was revealed that this could be an American criminal killing.

"This has all the hallmarks of the kind of gangland killing

we so often read about," said a Metropolitan Police officer this
afternoon.

"Sixth," said Trotter, apparently out of nowhere. "You've
had contact with Richard Martin Lewis—I forgot to mention that
episode."

Dobson's head was spinning with ideas. *Rattengift?* Now
the criminal fraternity. Drugs? Just supposing they had been
doing a drug run...? Ridiculous, the aircraft had been in the
ground for a long time—the papers and charts on board; the
bodies.

The telephone rang.

"You seen the papers?" asked Hackstead, cool as a menthol
cigarette.

"Seen them? Yes, I've seen one of them. That nice Mr.
Trotter of the SB brought me a copy and he is, at this moment,
quietly doing me to a turn under a microwave grill."

"Okay, I'll get him off your back."

"It's that easy?"

"It's the least of our problems. Special Branch I can
handle."

"D15 and 6?"

"Like putty. Our problem's Charles."

"Charles?"

"Naturally, with Flax gone they want to start running the
Dodo crew visit early. I've talked with him and I'm speaking to
the features editor in ten minutes. I'll try to get them to give it a
low profile. You know: Flax was to have joined members of the
aircrew with which he served during World War II who will be
on a visit to England next week."

"He'll do it?"

"I live in hope."

"Listen, Bud, I've got Trotter here but I'll say it just the
same. Look out for Free, he's the tinted one in the pile of logs.
Watch your back. Nazis and the Luftwaffe I can take, they've
been removed. The underworld connection makes me unhappy." Dobson felt very much in command of the situation.

"You and me both."

"Okay."

"Hennessy."

"Still looking into it."

"And do what you promised—these guys off my back."

"Two minutes flat and they'll be running away, groveling."

Trotter still grinned. "Your mate Bud Hackstead?"

"He says you're getting your marching orders."

"That'll come as no surprise."

He looked like a man who wanted to say something else. It was an expression Dobson had seen in Trotter's face before.

"Dobson, I like you." The big policeman unbuttoned his safari jacket. "I wouldn't want to see anything happen to you. Just want you to know that I'm around. Whatever anyone tells you, I'll be watching out for you. No sentiment. Right?"

"Right."

A bell. This time the front door. Ann held her arms out to greet him, then saw Trotter.

"It's okay," Trotter was already near the door. "I've got the gift of prophecy," I'll lay odds that one of those guys I left downstairs'll be coming up here like a member of the Olympic uphill running team."

As he said it, they heard the footsteps heavy and fast two floors below.

"Freddie, or Joe, whichever, I'm on my way down," Trotter shouted.

"Claud, they want you urgent on the radio. You and you only."

"Claud?" Dobson felt his facial muscles collapse.

Trotter, already at the top of the stairs, turned. "So the name's Claud Trotter. Ha ha."

"Painful for you," Dobson shouted after him.

"Trouble?" Ann collapsed into a chair.

"As well as a sense of humor, a high IQ and a great body, you're gifted with second sight." He went over and kissed her. "Our dear acting boss was closeted with a couple of gray faceless wonders when I left. It stank of discomfort. Was our black friend part of that?"

"I should imagine so. One of our aircrew got himself murdered. The American I went down to see near Folkestone."

"Oh Christ."

"I was his last visitor—except for the man who put in the bullets. Let's have dinner out, I'm starting to get claustrophobic."

"Give me time—as they say in the best Hollywood tradition—to freshen up. I'm all in favor of a night on the town."

"I said dinner."

"You missed something?"

"What?"

"I was carrying when I came in—at least when I arrived. I left them on the landing."

Dobson went to the door. Outside, neatly standing side by side, were a pair of suitcases. He brought them in.

"It means?" Eyebrows raised in query.

"That I have not given up my flat yet, but, if you'll have me, I'm coming to stay here—for a while: and if you'll have me."

There was nothing he could say except to burble about could they talk of some kind of permanent basis. She put two fingers softly on his lips.

"Time." She smiled, her eyes, far back, reflecting some pain from the past—like Trotter's look, he had seen it all before. "Give it time. I'm making you an offer. Hurl me into the street if you want."

He held her very close.

"The nearest you're going to get to being hurled into the street will be as far as L'Étoile. It takes three minutes from this door. Go and get ready."

As he waited, with his usual patience, for Ann to dress, the doorbell rang.

He had his hand on the knob when the warning light flashed in that part of him which was fast developing instinct. The horror of the decomposing airman flickered, vividly, through his consciousness.

"Who's there?"

"It's okay, Dobson. Me, Trotter."

"Oh Christ, not now."

"Please. For your own good. Take a minute and you might save years. Please."

He opened up and Trotter came in quickly. He carried a cardboard box.

"I don't really like doing this," he said, as though the place was riddled with mikes. "For your personal safety. I think it's important."

Inside the cardboard box was a standard shoulder holster, a box of .38 ammunition and a Smith & Wesson—the .38 Bodyguard model with all the extras.

"Don't like them." Dobson did not smile.

"Like them or not, I'm asking you—my chief is asking you—to carry it."

Dobson picked the revolver from the box and hefted it in his hand. It had been a long time since he had even fired on a service range—and that was with the old standard-issue .38, not anything like this fast-draw job with the cut-down two-inch barrel.

"You *really* think it's essential?"

"All the time."

"*All.*"

"Have it near your pillow at those times. You do know . . . ?"

"Yes, I know how to use one."

"Get it on now then; load it and get it on under that set of executive threads."

Dobson sided the chamber, loaded the weapon—working fast in case Ann walked in on them—balanced it on a chair arm while he slipped off his coat and fitted the holster, pulling hard on the straps. Once his jacket was on again he slid the revolver into the holster and shrugged himself comfortable. It felt strange, lumpy and unwieldy.

"Could've been tailor-made," was Trotter's comment as he left.

You could not see the bulge from the holster or revolver.

At last they were ready—Ann in something flowing, light, fine, gray and elegant. They actually had the door open when the telephone started to ring.

"We're out," Dobson said firmly.

She shook her head. "You're on a job. It may be nothing."

It was Sugden.

"It's Dowl. He's turned up a reference to the word you gave me."

The evening was going to be ruined, Dobson knew it. If Dowl had unearthed something that quickly, then he would at least have to look at it.

"Where?" he asked.

"Imperial War Museum. This afternoon."

"You look at it?"

"Not really."

Liar, bloody liar.

"Consists of ?"

"Classified letter. Order—instruction. German. There's a photostat and translation. You ought to come over and pick them up."

"Send Terry Makepiece with it—on the wings of Mercury."

They had to wait for twenty minutes and when the bell rang, Ann retired into the bedroom. As he went to the door, Dobson reflected that her scent was there and Terry Makepiece had a shrewd sense of smell.

The large envelope changed hands without a word. Then:

"He wants you to sign for it," Makepiece said. "Can't I come in?"

"I'm on my way out. I'll sign here and then be very rude and ask you to leave quietly and quickly."

Makepiece gave a knowing grimace. "That's how it is, eh?"

Ann came through and sat quietly while he opened the envelope. The photostat was on top, stapled to the translation. Clipped to the whole lot was a small "With Compliments" Ministry of Defence slip. Scrawled in longhand were the words, *I think I'll try the Weiner Library next—Dowl.*

The letterhead was simple, plain and sparse compared to the Göring-Sperrle document. On the right-hand side was printed *Führerhauptquartier*—the Nazi court again: Hitler's traveling circus. On the left the heading sent a fast cold slide running down Dobson's spine, as though someone had dropped an ice cube into the back of his shirt. It read: *Der Sekretär des Führers: Reichsleiter Martin Bormann.*

The page was signed—a scrawl with the name typed below it: *M. Bormann.*

It was addressed to SS Obergruppenführer Ernst Kaltenbrunner.

"Jesus," Dobson said aloud, his eyes running down the page. He took in the opening—*Mein lieber Kaltenbrunner . . .* and the word *Rattengift.*

Quickly he turned the page to read the translation. Ernst Kaltenbrunner, successor to the looming deadly Heydrich. Chief of the RSHA—the SS Security Department under whom the whole of the most dreaded sections operated: the "Spheres of Life"; the Ausland SD about which Blenkinsop/Timetable had spoken; the Kripo; the Gestapo. Bormann to Kaltenbrunner. A power duet of ultimate evil.

The translation read:

My dear Kaltenbrunner,

You will have now received the Führer-Directive No. 55, May 16, 1944, and the further instructions. RATTENGIFT is to take place after all. I know that your specialists will have chosen wisely, and I believe that this together with the use of the Führer's other Vergeltüngswaffe, will quickly bring an end to the war and victory for our glorious Reich.

Heil Hitler!
M. Bormann

There it was again—*Vergeltungswaffe*: the reprisal weapons, the terror weapons, the miracle weapons, about which he had been thinking as he fell asleep the night before. The V-1s and V-2s. Again the Directive 55; and *RATTENGIFT*—*Ratpoison*: the code word nobody had ever heard about; and Dowl's scribbled note—the Weiner Library. That would have significance, there would be a lot of Kaltenbrunner's work in the Weiner Library because it contained a great deal on the concentration camps—concentration, experimental and extermination.

"You've gone pale." Ann reached forward and touched his hand.

Dobson shook himself from the diabolical thoughts which had begun to teem into his head. No, this was work, but it could wait. Tonight celebration was in the air. Ann had taken a decisive step in his direction—a fast decisive step.

"Okay. It's an interesting piece of paper. But work will still be there tomorrow."

He locked the documents away in the bureau and slipped the key into his pocket, thinking how easy it would be to break the desk open. You could do it with a penknife. As they walked toward the door he suddenly became more conscious of the weight over his left breast and the slight drag on his shoulder where the holster straps rubbed. He was determined to forget it and enjoy his night out.

It was almost midnight when they returned; few people in the streets; cars parked as usual. It struck Dobson that he should start noting and counting the cars which were parked regularly near his building. People in Security always did that in the best novels: part of the stock in trade.

He leaned toward Ann, kissing her as they got to the doors of the building; then, pushing one arm forward, he swung the right half inward so that she could enter.

Dobson followed her in, and smelled the stench the moment the door rocked back. There were a million horror pictures in his head, the fragments of that other incident. The stench was of rotting flesh, and this time there were two of them—the same repellent decomposing faces, the U.S. aircrew jackets—one even had an officer's cap, moldy and green, cocked on the raddled skull. They came fast, one of them hissing through the hole where its mouth had been. In the claw bones of the hands they clutched what appeared to be metal bars, raised, wielded to crush and batter.

Ann shrieked, then shrieked again with a paralyzing echo of terror which seemed to fill Dobson's head.

Then he remembered, and reacted. He pushed Ann, hard, with his left hand, conscious that she was falling away to the left of the small vestibule. At the same moment he jumped right as his other hand moved—it seemed to him in slow motion—inside his jacket. He felt the hard butt of the revolver, felt it coming out, saw the metal bar raised above his head, and the other scarecrow figure of death wheeling toward the falling Ann. His hand came up, and then the shots, like blasts of high explosive in the enclosed space, his wrist jerking as the weapon kicked back in the one-handed grip.

24

The twin explosions. Ann's piercing shrieks.

One bullet smashed into the wall—he saw the plaster fly. The other must have hit something—though how do you shoot an apparition?—because the thing coming at him with the metal bar let out a scream: inhuman, echoing above the shock waves of the shots, a kind of bleating tormented sobbing as the creature lost balance and tried to claw its way toward the swing doors, making this whimpering awful vocal cacophony.

Whatever anyone tells you, I'll be watching out for you. No sentiment. Right? Trotter's words in his head. Well, where the fuck was Trotter now? Watching out for him at some safe distance?

Dobson turned from the sight of the thing squirming toward the door, the revolver now in the two-handed grip, leveling it, facing the other bestial decomposing form.

Ann was on the ground, her screaming silenced. That terrified him more than anything. The thing had already hit her once and was raising the weapon to strike down again—the hand, half clear bone, gripping it hard, the sweep-down starting with enormous power.

The shot was impossible, the angles all wrong—Ann too

close, himself positioned badly: so Dobson lifted the barrel, both eyes over the small sight, wide open, the aim well clear of both victim and assailant. He prayed there would be no serious ricochet, and fired in quick succession. Two shots.

Brick and plaster sharded from the wall above the creature's dripping torn and shredded head. Dobson felt something slice over his cheek like a razor and saw the thing turn from Ann toward him, hearing the familiar hissing noise redolent with malevolence.

He leveled the revolver directly at it, and watched as it shrank back, the claw bones opening, allowing the metal bar to fall against the polished floor. His finger tightened on the trigger—but how could he kill something like this?

For a moment his attention drifted, flickering toward the still form of Ann huddled on the ground, and he was aware that the hissing half-faced thing had turned and was running, grabbing at the bare dry wristbone of its companion, heaving, pulling and dragging its fellow specter through the doors.

The thing being dragged was still whimpering, sounds which had the form of distorted human speech: "Ep-ee . . . ep-ee go-erg . . . ahhhhh . . . ep-ep-ep . . . eyssake . . . ep-ee . . . go-erg . . . go-erg . . . da . . . da . . . dan . . . ick-ick . . . ickee . . . ahhh . . . oh . . . ep . . ."

They were gone and the doors swung to and fro, brushing together, the rubber seals kissing with a soft pneumatic sound.

Dobson did not try to follow, to break through the doors and rush into the street, though half of his senses cried out for some kind of revenge against this revolting and violent intrusion.

He went straight over to Ann.

There were shouts from somewhere and the sound of a car. Then another. Brakes. Doors. The swing doors being roughed open and the noise—seemed very far away—of a police siren.

A young constable was kneeling beside him, turning Ann onto her back. Her eyes were closed, but she was breathing and moaning. Then the eyes opened. She tried to move, winced horribly, then focused on Dobson, smiling through pain you could almost touch.

"Did you get the number of the truck?" she whispered.

"Just stay quiet, love." It sounded such a stupid, inadequate thing to say, and he put out his hand, brushing her hair with his palm. Beside him, the young constable was speaking softly into his personal radio, asking for an ambulance.

"You okay, Dobson?"

Dobson turned still kneeling. Trotter and a pair of men in civilian clothes had come through the doors. Outside there were bright lights, movement, cars, activity, faces close to the glass, uniforms.

Dobson heard himself shouting, spitting out words. "You were supposed to be watching out for me, you black bastard. You stinking shit. What's it all about, soul brother? This time they got Ann: two of them ... two of the ... damn corpses again. You were so concerned about me, and now look," his finger, his whole hand, stabbing down violently in Ann's direction. "Look what the bastards have done and where *were* you?"

"Hey, Dobson..." The big man made a quieting conciliatory gesture. "We'll get them. The car was spotted. We're giving chase. They can't get away, not in the traffic around here."

"They shouldn't have got in. Giving chase? ... Now perhaps someone'll believe me. They were corpses, Trotter— Christ, you can still smell them."

He glared, watching as Trotter's head inclined. "Yes, it stinks in here, but're you okay? You got blood on your cheek."

Dobson put his hand up and felt the wet patch and the soreness. He looked at his hand and the blood on it, remembering feeling something slicing at his cheek when he fired the last two shots—a piece of flying brickwork maybe?

Trotter was speaking quietly to the constable, his bulk hunched over Ann. "As for corpses," he straightened up, "they're bleeding corpses—rotting or not—one leaked," pointing to the swing doors, where a trail of blood spattered in smears and droplets across the polished stone floor. "Must've winged one with the cannon. Best present you ever had, the cannon." He tried to put a hand on Dobson's shoulder, but Dobson twisted away.

"You reckon she's okay?" Trotter asked the young constable who had Ann's wrist between his fingers, feeling the pulse.

"Shoulder's smashed up badly, sir. Very badly; and she's in a lot of pain."

Then, out of nowhere, there were ambulance men and a pain-killing injection to put Ann away from the noise and inevitable confusion going on around them. One of the men wanted to clean up Dobson's face, but he brushed him aside. He wanted to stay with Ann, it was all his mind could center on. Then there was Trotter beside him again, wanting the whole story.

"Fuck you, mate. That's my girl and she comes before anything else. You know the full story—two rotting corpses jumped us with metal bars. That's all you need. Go chase your villains and my ghosts. Catch the bastards and we'll talk later. One thing, though, when you've got them, I want to see those two raddled suppurating killer corpses. When you catch up with them, I want first go."

The Special Branch man knew when not to push, so he allowed Dobson to go off in the ambulance with Ann.

At the hospital they would not let him go with her when she was finally wheeled away, through the Casualty Department, but left him sitting there until a nurse came and took him to a cubicle and a doctor had another look at the graze on his cheek.

"Bartley," the white-coated doctor introduced himself. Through the curtains Dobson saw Trotter loitering, looking out of place among the medical paraphernalia. "You know Dr. Marsh."

"How are you, Wing Commander?" Marsh laid a friendly hand on his shoulder.

"How's Miss West?" He felt more furious than hurt, more angry than in any kind of shock."

"Miss West's undergoing surgery," Marsh began bluntly. "In many ways she's been very lucky. An inch or so to the right and she would probably be dead. She received one very powerful blow on her left shoulder with, I gather, some metal object. You're familiar with anatomy?"

"Enough."

"The clavicle is shattered, crushed down onto the scapula, which has also sustained fractures. Naturally, with a blow of that force, at that point, there's been some damage to the shoulder joint. The trapezius muscle's been affected and, of course, there's damage to the nerves." It was the language of *Medicine for the Ordinary Man*.

"*En clair* she's got a severely crushed shoulder," grinned Marsh.

"Permanent damage?" Dobson asked.

Bartley shook his head. "It'll take time. She's in a bit of shock. Once the shoulder's plastered up, she won't feel that much pain. Be able to move around quite well within twenty-four hours. Even discharged in a day or so. As for the rest, we just have to wait. When it's all knitted and settled—when the plaster comes off—then it's going to be a case of physiotherapy. Getting the muscles working again." He stopped short, glancing at Marsh.

"That will probably take time and patience." Marsh looked Dobson straight in the eyes—you could never tell with people who did that, Dobson thought. "She'll need help, persuasion. Love?" A query.

"She's got it." He was satisfied. "When can I see her?"

"Tomorrow."

"I might be tied up. Can't I see her as soon as she comes round from surgery?"

"That could be in the early hours—four, five in the morning."

"I'll wait."

"Wing Commander, I..."

"Is there a rule against it?"

Marsh looked, pleading, at Bartley.

"No," said Bartley. "I just think you should try to go and get some rest when you've finished with the police. We can always call you. She'll be dopey when she comes round and..."

"Tomorrow I might just not be able to make it."

Bartley took a step back. "I'll try and have a room prepared for you near the ward. I understand."

"Phone," Dobson heard himself speaking like some curt heavy. Maybe it was the revolver—or the anger and frustration.

"Of course."

He dialed Hackstead's home number—the flat in Ebury Street.

"Hi," came the tired voice.

"I hope this isn't bloody inconvenient..." began Dobson and Hackstead's tone altered immediately to one of instant vigilance.

"What's up, Dave?"

"Plenty. You awake?"

"Just dozing off. You sound strung out."

"I got hit again. Me and Ann. It was Ann who caught it."

"What d'ya mean, hit?"

"Coshed. The same guy and he brought a little friend with him."

"The walking corpse?"

Dobson almost said, "in the flesh." "Horrible, Bud. Reeking and horrible suppurating disintegrating corpses in U.S. uniforms. One was even wearing a moldy cap—an officer's cap."

"Ann?" Even over the telephone Dobson could hear movement, as though Hackstead was hauling himself up from bed and starting to get organized.

"She's okay but they've smashed up her shoulder. Badly." He went on to give the details as briefly as possible. Hackstead asked where he was, and said he would be over within the half hour.

"Good. I've got Trotter outside flatfooting all over the Casualty Department."

"For Chrissake."

"And I'm not nuts, Bud. I got one of the bastards."

"The police got him, you mean?"

"No, I wounded him."

"I didn't know you carried."

"Winged him, but I hope Trotter's here with the news they picked up the pair. Someone's trying to freak me out, Bud. Freak me and kill me and/or both."

"I'll be over."

The nurse came in to tell him they had a room ready for him upstairs, that Miss West was still in surgery and Mr. Trotter was most anxious to talk with him.

Trotter was docile. They did not speak going up in the lift with the pretty blond nurse who had dark rings around her eyes and looked ready to drop. The corridors were like polished glass and people moved with that sense of purpose you find among anyone who can, and has to, move around a hospital at night.

The room was a small private ward: a bed with a locker which had earphones and a push-button radio installation on one side. A rail went around the bed and the plastic curtains were pulled back. In one corner there was a hospital trolley and a large cylinder. There were also two uncomfortable-looking tubular chairs packed on top of one another.

The nurse asked if there was anything she could get them and Dobson said more tea would be nice but only when she had time. Trotter shook his head and the nurse went away.

"Okay, I'm sorry I blew up at you back there." Dobson put out a hand as a peace gesture.

"My fault," the big policeman shrugged. "Yes, I was doing it like I promised. We knew you were settled in the restaurant, so I took my team off and we went for a bite. Left a young copper—kid law—there on watch. We were driving back when he yelled in on the radio about the shots."

"Did you get them?" He knew the answer from Trotter's face.

"Again, my error of judgment. I'm sorry. We came straight for you. The kid law shouted a description of the car—it turned out to be a rented black Cortina and two guys coming out of the building. We came straight to you. There was an area car in the

Tottenham Court Road. We knew the direction they were headed, no number, but there was obvious panic. I had no doubt they'd be picked up fast. We came to you. I should have gone on straight after them in our car." He lifted and dropped his hands in a gesture of helplessness. "These things happen, but thank God you had the gun, man. You did some damage to one of them."

"I saw that myself. They were funnies again, Claud. The weirdos; corpses, rotting and stinking."

He nodded, picked up one tubular chair from on top of the other—using one hand—and set it down. Dobson stretched back on the bed.

"The whole thing's a funny. My chief'll have my ass come the dawn. The world's gone mad. I hear your girl's going to be okay."

"She's alive. Whether she'll ever be able to move her shoulder again's another matter."

Trotter remained wrapped in thought. After a while: "There is one thing. They found the car."

"Great." Without enthusiasm.

"Abandoned, as you'd imagine."

"Where?"

"Near Victoria Station."

"So?"

"So the usual production number—scene of crime people, the loops and whorls brigade. You winged him somewhere fleshy, Dobson. A lot of blood."

"Nothing else?"

"Not when I last heard."

The nurse came back with tea, and word that a Colonel Hackstead wanted to see them.

"Time I was making for an away day." Trotter's grin was gone. "I'm sorry, Dobson. Truly. I meant what I said earlier. That's why I've been hanging around here. To apologize."

Hackstead looked tousled but calm. "I met friend Trotter in the hallway. He seemed broody."

"He screwed it. They had me under surveillance and he blew it."

"That I do not like." Bud Hackstead paced the room, long regular strides, heavy, but his body carried in a compact manner: the walk of a man who could turn and kill or maim in a second if necessary. "Why the action from that lot? We were handling it."

"We were, Bud, but it's gone rotten somewhere."

"Yes," irritated. "I can't link it in. What happened?"

Dobson told him, using all the detail he could bring himself to recall. "Don't laugh it off this time, Bud. This wasn't random—not just a weirdo mugger getting his kicks by dressing up, this is the *Dodo* connection, and then there's Herbie Flax."

"I know, I know, and I can't figure it." He stopped at the end of a pace and turned, looking toward the bed. "When we spoke, earlier on the phone..."

"When I asked you to get Trotter off my back?"

"Yeah, when the news came about Herbie Flax."

"Yes?"

"You said something about Free. You said he was the odd man out—the one to watch out for. What were you talking about?"

Dobson told him. All of it: from arranging the covert photographs of Free to the interviews he'd had that afternoon with the two ex-POWs from Stalag Luft III at Sagan—Partridge and Peartree, who had been prisoners with Free.

Their reactions had worried him ever since. Both had been positive and he was convinced that they were genuine articles. Even accounting for age and change of circumstances, the man down in Kent was not—from the photographs—the Free they both remembered (one better than the other) from Sagan. Neither did this pair of witnesses have any recollection of Free during the last days. Their memory was that he had been removed from the camp never to return. Both were certain that neither this man in the photograph, nor the Free they recalled, was on the final great march out of Stalag Luft III—away from the Russian advance—early in 1945.

Hackstead turned away and stood by the window, looking out across the glow of the city.

"You've been doing a good job, Dave. I got to admit I thought Free was clean. I have antennae like most people who've been doing this job for a long time."

Another long silence. From where he lay, Dobson could see the little finger of Hackstead's right hand, resting on the window ledge, tapping with a regular beat. He straightened up and turned, a movement of decision.

"I'll go down first thing in the morning." Hackstead's face was set tight, as though some unseen surgeon had performed a very fast lift of the skin. "Our Mr. Free needs some vocal sorting."

"I'll come with you."

"You've had enough, what with tonight..."

"We're performing the same dance, Bud."

"True, baby." The old Hackstead with the slow tough grin. "Very true, but sometimes you have to do it as a formation team. I have work for you here in town now. Check, check and doublecheck your sources. What I really mean is you've got to sieve those witnesses—what d'you call them?"

"I didn't; Sugden did. Partridge and Peartree. They're straight up, Bud, clean as they come."

"They're Sugden's." He pulled a wry look. "I would've thought that was enough for you to double check." It was typical of Hackstead on form; Hackstead's thoroughness. "The way surprises have been dropping on us from a great height, I'd say we couldn't be too careful."

"But . . ."

"No buts, Dave. Let me talk to him."

"Okay. What about Charles and his features editor?"

Hackstead snapped his fingers and thumb—about three times, raising his arm as he did so. "They're going to play it down. Got to use it, of course, but it'll be low-profile stuff in tomorrow's paper."

"What're your real plans, Bud? What d'you really think?"

"I have plans. Fenwell Manor plans. What I really think depends on two things. What Timetable turns up—if anything— on this present Koblenz outing: and what Mr. Free has to say for himself." The grin again and another snap of the fingers. "Whatever the whole picture is, once we've finally got the jigsaw together, you'll be fully briefed. I have to get my head straight on certain matters. By the way . . ."

Dobson shifted on the bed, raising his eyebrows.

"When you get in to see Ann, give her my love."

"Of course."

"And put your jacket on. That artillery must be scaring the pants off the nurses."

Alone, Dobson eventually dozed off until a nurse shook his shoulder. The room was gray with dawn and he was awake immediately, turning fast, one hand reaching under his left shoulder. Then he relaxed.

"Miss West's awake, Mr. Dobson," the nurse said quietly, her uniform rustling in the half-light. "We've told her you're here and she wants to see you." She gave a little smile. "She was even worried about how her hair looked."

He nodded, ran his fingers through his own hair and swung his legs over the side of the bed.

"She's still very sleepy—the anesthetic—and we'll have her on pain-killers today."

They went through the door and along the passage. It felt like dawn, hardly any noise or movement in the vast building around them. He glanced at his watch and it said four-thirty. For some odd reason he recalled that someone had once told him more people were born and more people died around this hour than at any other time of day.

They had her in a very small private room leading off a main passage to a larger ward. She looked terribly small, her face tiny on the pillow, still white, but the eyes alive and bright, not dead with dope as he had dreaded.

"Hallo," she said in almost a whisper. "Thanks for coming."

"I didn't go away."

"They told me."

"How d'you feel?"

"Numb. Sleepy. But glad to see you." Her right arm slid from under the bedclothes, though it seemed to be detached from the rest of her, as though she was willing it to move without having proper control. He grasped her hand and squeezed it.

"I had a terrible nightmare, David. Two...two..."

"I know. Don't worry yourself. We got attacked by a couple of men dressed in funny suits and masks, that's all. You came off worst."

Her head moved in an affirmative nod. Just the once, then the eyes closed and she had to struggle to open them again. "Am I...?" she began.

"You'll be up and around in a couple of days. They've promised me that."

"Truth?"

"Truth, Ann. Just rest. I'm here."

She gripped his hand and closed her eyes. A few minutes later the nurse appeared again.

"She's asleep," she whispered the obvious. "Best to leave her."

"I'll stay if it's okay by you."

"There's no danger. She'll be out of bed this afternoon. Won't feel anything but the discomfort of the plaster cast." Her face told him that she felt he was being overdramatic about it all.

"Has nobody told you this is a security matter?" This time he did overdramatize, turning so that his jacket fell open, revealing the holstered revolver.

The nurse did not come back until it was time to get the ward going onto a morning routine.

Dobson hung around while they were washing her and getting her settled.

"You stayed," she said when he went in again.

"Feel better?"

"Less dreamy. You need a shave." She winced, trying to move the left arm. "I keep forgetting. They've got me walled up solid down this side."

"I told you in the night—you'll be up and about in..."

"A few hours. Today. The nurses told me."

"There you go."

The door swung open and a nurse hurried in. Hackstead was outside and had to see him urgently. He mouthed "sorry" to Ann, and she gave a little grimace using her eyes and nose, telling him she understood.

Hackstead looked frantic; there was no other description.

"I thought you were off to see friend Free..." Dobson began, automatically looking at his watch. It was almost twenty minutes to nine.

"*We* are off to Farnborough." Bud Hackstead spoke fast: a man in an edgy hurry.

"We?"

"I've just had a call from Tyndle. They knew last night but left it until this morning."

"What?"

"There're two pieces from the *Dodo* wreckage that've got nothing to do with Martin Marauders or any other kind of airplane I've ever heard of."

"You sound frightened, Bud." Dobson felt his own guts churn. He was tired, as though last night's events had just caught up with him. Hackstead's face showed, if not anxiety, then a kind of concern that might give even the most courageous man cause to consider what fate had waiting around the corner.

"I *am* frightened, Dave. From the description Tyndle gave me on the phone, I'm terrified—and I have my reasons. Let's go."

He turned back. "I'll tell Ann. Give me sixty seconds."

For a moment Hackstead relaxed. "I'll give you fifty-five," he said.

25

What goes on within the huge complex of buildings, hangars, offices and laboratories that surround the large airfield which is the focal point of the Royal Aircraft Establishment at Farnborough is nobody's business. It is also everybody's business.

Every few years, thousands of enthusiasts and sightseers flock to Farnborough and are herded into enclosures, or group themselves on the hillside overlooking the broad flat sweep of green Hampshire plateau, to see the latest in both military and civil aviation put through their paces. These visitors do not see the other side—the areas where the real research into faster, higher, safer and—from a military point of view more lethal aviation goes on, all day and every day. Sometimes all night.

Hackstead and Dobson went down by official car.

"What gives?" Dobson asked, once they were really settled and driving.

Hackstead inclined his head, in the ghost of a nod toward the driver.

"I still want to talk about one thing," Dobson said quietly.

Hackstead nodded, looking straight ahead. He liked to drive—even from the rear.

"The pair of freaks: last night . . . It only came back when I was coming through the vestibule at Charlotte Street just now." Hackstead had allowed him ten minutes to wash and change.

Hackstead waited, moving a little closer, cocking his ear so that Dobson would not have to speak louder than necessary. They had reached the turn through Roehampton and were now on the highway, picking up speed.

"In the middle of it all, when I let go with the gun . . ."

Hackstead grunted.

"I got one of them. It stopped the other from finishing off Ann. The wounded one was trying to speak—as the other was dragging him to the door."

"Yes?"

"We *are* both agreed now that these attacks—the first one on me, and last night have *Dodo* connections?"

Hackstead shrugged. "From the descriptions . . ."

"Quite: the rotting body make-up, the tattered Air Force gear."

"Okay. Something—someone warning you off. But why not me as well?"

"Perhaps they don't think you scare so easily. Whoever it is has gone to a lot of trouble. Those things are bloody realistic—the stench of the grave; everything. They also stay in character under pressure."

"Meaning?"

"Meaning that when that ghoul came for me on the landing at Charlotte Street, he hissed at me. I tell you, Bud, terrifying."

"Uh-huh. I believe it."

"Well, last night, the character I winged—and I got him badly, Trotter's seen the inside of the car: a lot of blood."

Hackstead made a noise to demonstrate he did not approve of Trotter and the interference they were now getting from the heavies of D15 and the SB.

"The thing—that's all I can call it—must have been suffering pain, but he stayed in character. He was yelling for help, but it came out like a cry from something that had rotting vocal cords. It was only as I came through that hallway just now that I cottoned on to what he was saying."

"Which was?"

"He was crying out something that sounded like: 'Ep-ep . . . ep-ee . . . go-erg . . . ep-ee . . . go-erg . . . da . . . dan . . . ick-ick . . . ickeee . . .'"

"Ickee." The creased grin. "Ickee indeed."

"I just heard the words right." Dobson had them in his brain, the translation clear. "What that thing was trying to say was, 'Help me, Goldberg...Dan...quick...quick.'"

"Character actors we've got?"

"I *know* that's what the thing was saying. The one having a shot at crushing Ann's skull was Dan Goldberg—or his dead double. 'Help me, Goldberg...Dan...quick...quick.' I know that's what he was saying," he repeated with emphasis. "And if it was a guy playing at being a corpse, and shot up at that, it was a remarkable performance."

"Perhaps they got him from the Actors Studio, or the Royal Academy."

Dobson looked hard at Hackstead to see if he was being flippant.

He was, and realized fast that it was offensive to his partner. "Sorry, Dave, you may be right. You've said it all. I don't know what we're dealing with here. I just don't know, damn it." Hackstead leaned back. "All I can say is that Tyndle's got me worried."

They sat in silence as the driver overtook several slow-moving trucks.

"You seen the *Express*?" Hackstead asked.

"How can I have seen the *Express*?"

Hackstead rummaged in his briefcase and passed a copy over.

Herbie Flax's murder had got fair space on the front page. There were no photographs and little more than had been in the newspapers on the previous evening. The kicker was in the final paragraph:

> *During the Second World War, Mr. Flax flew as a navigator in Martin Marauder squadrons, both with the Eighth United States Army Air Force and the Ninth Tactical Air Force—in Britain and Europe. Ironically he was to have attended a reunion of his old aircrew who arrive in London on Monday, under the auspices of the* Express, *to participate in a series of features giving the crew's reactions to life in Britain which will start next week.*

"They're going to begin running on Thursday," Hackstead said.

"That cock up our thing at Fenwell Manor?"

"No, they've promised not to disclose their aircraft was *Dodo* until the Monday—though Christ knows what we'll get by then."

"And He ain't going to tell us unless D15've got a bug up in the attic."

Hackstead did not smile. "I did hear your Home Secretary's authorized a wiretap on the pearly gates."

They were expected at Farnborough. The security people kept them waiting for only five minutes or so before an open yellow truck pulled up. It had an RAF driver; a civilian sat beside him. On the rear of the truck was a *Follow Me* sign, used for leading aircraft off the taxitracks.

As they skirted the perimeter a four-engine Hercules took off, smooth and steady, making it look the easiest thing in the world. The nose of the Hercules did not look normal: a flying testbed for some device, Dobson presumed.

They slowed and came to a halt beside a set of buildings dominated by a massive hangar. Through the spaces between the buildings and hangar, you could see what looked like a junkyard of aircraft pieces—a tail plane towered, lonely, from a pile of scrap, and there was the whole nose and flight deck of a BAC 111 held straight on wooden chocks. Tyndle stood with a couple of other men just outside the hangar doors, which were half open on their massive rollers.

As they got out of the car, a P-i Lightning came down, out of nowhere, onto the main runway about two miles away.

After Hackstead's general worried preoccupation, Dobson expected to find Tyndle looking grave and concerned. He appeared relaxed, more friendly than ever, and very much at ease on his home ground.

"Welcome to AIB and AID," he said, hand outstretched. "You know the setup, don't you? This is really the RAE's Accident Investigation Division. The Accident Investigation Branch works hand in glove here, so to speak."

Hackstead nodded and Dobson said hello. Tyndle's colleagues were introduced merely as Frank and John.

"You'd like to see how we're progressing?" Tyndle put out his hands, shepherding them into the hangar.

"I want to see the boxes," said Hackstead. "That's what we're here for."

"In good time. We're not going to have a crack at the blue

one until this afternoon—I should say our specialists from the labs and explosive sections aren't going to have a crack at it until then. Let's show you what else we've come up with." He did not seem unduly concerned.

Somehow, Dobson felt deflated. He also picked up a new tension in Hackstead's bearing, a stiffness in the way he walked, as though pressures and anxiety were getting to his muscles.

It was hot in the hangar, with the lights on, even though the air-conditioning plant pumped away at full strength.

Dobson had never imagined anything like it. The vast space—he had been in plenty of hangars but this seemed larger than most—was subdivided into roped-off areas, each containing parts of aircraft wrecks.

In the space nearest them, the wreckage of *Dodo* lay, spread out in sequence, the ripped and tangled fuselage held up by large wooden stanchions, the interior obviously strengthened, and chicken wire now filling the gaping holes. The skeleton of the tail plane was being rebuilt, and parts of the nose had already been pieced together and stood, forward of the fuselage, but unattached. Men were busy laying out sections of metal on the ground, attempting to put together at least the shape of the wings; while the two engines—one seemingly merely a block of fused metal—were on chocks, positioned correctly in relationship to the fuselage.

"Progress, eh?" Tyndle swept his arm toward *Dodo*.

"It wouldn't surprise me if you got her airborne again as well," grinned Dobson. For the first time he really began to take to Tyndle.

"It's quite a place you have here." Even Hackstead was starting to show he was impressed.

Tyndle smiled. "You haven't seen anything yet."

"Yes, but what about these boxes, that's what the panic's about, isn't it?"

"We try not to panic, Colonel. Patience. We don't want to have to go over it a dozen times. We're waiting for Professor Reeves from Porton Down. He's bringing the cultures back with him. Anyway, he can explain it far better than I. Also we want him here when we open the blue. Come over to the aircraft. We've had some good luck already."

"Luck?"

"We know something about the crash. Something—not all. There're some mysteries, but we now know pretty well what the condition of the aircraft was when it hit the ground. Very hard to understand, but we have all the ingredients of a great detective story."

"Fast," said Dobson.

"Facts." Hackstead's face granite. He had been put out by Tyndle's reluctance to get on with the main proceedings. Dobson still wondered what the main proceedings, in fact, were.

"Okay." Tyndle led them over to the forward section of the fuselage and the remains of the cockpit. "You remember when we went into the cabin down at the crash site, you asked me if there were any immediate signs from the instruments?"

"I remember exactly."

"There are six immediate things. First, there are signs that the auxiliary fuel tanks had been removed. There's no trace at all. I would say that she had hardly any fuel left at all when she hit. Maybe a little, and it's damned hard to tell after this length of time, but it would seem she had a very small amount of fuel left at the moment of impact."

"Second?" Dobson asked.

"Second, and most strange, the fuel had been turned off."

"Off?"

"There were two sets of fuel cocks on the Marauder. A pair up front, pilot-operated, and another pair—one on either side of the bulkhead between the navigator's compartment and the bomb bays. We've located both sets. They were intact, and, while there is rusting, which helps to some extent, there's no doubt whatsoever that when that aircraft hit the ground all four cocks had been turned to fully closed."

"Jesus," said Hackstead without any feeling.

"Three, I was right about the extinguishers being operated. The extinguisher controls are under a small flap in the cockpit floor. There is a directional device—so that you can select the whole contents to either engine, or both. It was pulled up, in fact it's jammed up, and not because of impact. It was also directed at both engines."

They stood, silent but for the noise around them in the hangar. Someone working at the rear of *Dodo* was whistling.

"Okay." Hackstead broke the silence. "They had the throttles right through the gate, on full power, and the fuel cocks were off and fire extinguishers operating. It doesn't make sense."

"Neither will point number four." Tyndle looked from one to the other. "The propeller feathering switches were on. That didn't happen on impact either. Both airscrews were fully feathered."

In other words the big four-bladed propellers were spinning free from the airflow and not being driven by the engines.

"Five?" asked Hackstead.

"There *was* fire. I was wrong about that. There was, we think, in-flight fire in the port engine."

"The one that's just a hunk of metal?"

Tyndle inclined his head. "We haven't tried to take it apart yet, but traces of metal belonging to the port nacelle were found a long way back down the crash path. They've been carefully split open and some are very well preserved. The indications are that there was some kind of in-flight fire in the port engine shortly before she went in . . ."

"Like the proverbial lead balloon." Hackstead was a picture of incredulity. "It sounds like they set her nose down, cut everything off and just let her go in."

"With the airscrews feathered and the trim right, she might possibly have made a gentle glide in. Even with the reputation of the B-26 it could have happened."

"And the crew all sat there and waited for the impact. They had no power; fuel cut off; props feathered. How was she trimmed, by the way?"

"Can't say. Trim controls are all mushed up."

"What's your last point, then?"

"It's possible someone did get out."

"Santa Claus? Leaping onto his passing sleigh?"

"The escape hatch at the rear—the camera hatch—is missing. It was not torn off on impact. We think it was taken out, dropped for a quick exit. Also parts of the pilot's escape hatch have been found—a long way back, two miles or so. That would indicate that it was opened in flight. It's located on the starboard top of the cockpit canopy."

Hackstead ran his fingers through his hair and walked slowly up to the aircraft, held together in such a fragile condition. He placed his hand gently on the fuselage, where the paintwork showed slight signs of change—the vaguest outline of the original cartoon *Dodo*.

"What in the name of all the saints happened to you, baby?" he said. "You're some dumb airplane." Then, turning to Tyndle, "Nothing more? I mean, you didn't find any fairy rings or anything?" He seemed to finish the question abruptly, as though he had said something in bad taste, or something that brought back a painful memory.

There was a shout from across the hangar. "Sid? Sid Tyndle?"

"Coming," Tyndle called back, excusing himself and walking rapidly in the direction of the voice.

Hackstead looked at Dobson, his smile a little crumpled, but the good nature, his normal self, back there on lips and in eyes.

"From now on," he said, "Mr. Tyndle will be known between us as El Sid." Then he raised his voice. "What the fuck happened in this airplane, Dave? What ghastly thing happened?" His finger pointed toward Dobson like a pistol: "And you haven't heard the nasty side yet. I haven't told you what they've found among the wreckage."

"Rift Valley fever." Dobson made it sound like a wild guess. "They found a bottle of germs."

"Two. Not bottles, but two. Two boxes. Metal boxes. One opened and one still sealed. That's why we're here and that's why the great panjamdrum from Porton Down is here, and why they've got the whole one in a little sealed bunker, because Christ knows what's in that. And just to complete your happiness, Dave, there's probably a third floating about somewhere. They found some kind of container, lead-lined, which has had something odd in it. The first two are oblong. The other is circular. Like a big cookie tin. Ring any bells?"

The bells rang. Dobson was standing there in Mrs. Lambert's garden looking down at the hole freshly dug in the earth with the imprint where someone had recently pulled out a circular object.

Across the hangar, Tyndle was calling to them that the people from Porton Down had arrived and would they come over.

"You bet your sweet ass we're coming over," muttered Hackstead.

26

The office—if you could really call it an office—stretched almost the entire length of the shorter side of the hangar. It was light and very airy: one wall a huge window, a massive sheet of glass which allowed you to look down, right across the hangar. At a glance from the window, a man could oversee almost everything going on below.

There were four metal-framed casement windows, spaced and in line, along the opposite wall, part of which was occupied by a workbench—tools, microscopic instruments, some radio parts. In one corner a pile of boxes and chests took up a lot of room looking as though they were there for constant use, to be pulled out, their contents sorted through, used and returned (probably to different or wrong crates).

Only one end of this large oblong room bore any resemblance to an office. There was a large desk, incredibly tidy; swivel chairs and a few service-issue chairs. A long beige bulletin board, almost entirely covering the wall behind the desk, carried a Sasco Year Planner and up to around a hundred photographs, some grisly, of aircraft, wrecks, details. Between these were pinned holiday postcards, cartoons and odd scraps of paper bearing notations and messages.

The room was filling up with people. Hackstead stood with Tyndle, talking earnestly with a gaunt, wispy-haired man in sporting tweeds (in this weather?) with leather patches on the elbows of the jacket, and a younger man, bronzed and sharp as a commando knife. There were some military around also—three incredibly young-looking officers, in shirt-sleeve order, a couple of RAF types and several civilians, one of whom was setting up a blackboard onto which was pinned a blowup of the original chart of the *Dodo* wreckage, the one they had seen in the tent at the crash site on their first visit.

Hackstead detached himself from the group and came over to Dobson.

"Well, he seems to know what he's talking about, but it makes me very twitchy."

"Who? You haven't filled me in on the damn picture yet."

"Old Prof Reeves from the bio department at Porton Down."

"Leather patches?"

"You got him."

"Who's the Barber of Seville with him?"

Hackstead allowed a smile. "Drimgollen." His eyes narrowed, boring in at Dobson as though they were trying to make a photocopy of his brain. "Dr. Drimgollen is a specialist in bacteriology."

Tyndle was hovering, trying to shepherd people into chairs. Hackstead grabbed at a comfortable swivel and held on to another for Dobson. The Army and RAF people had to make do with standard hardbacks. Tyndle and one of his men—the one he had introduced simply as John—were organizing the top brass into a semicircle around the desk, paying particular attention to the seating of Professor Reeves and Drimgollen. Everyone showed great deference to them. Biological warfare research carries a lot of clout, Dobson thought, even if it's not supposed to be going on at Porton Down.

Hackstead nudged him, leaning across. "Don't look now, but we've got company."

Dobson queried with his eyes.

"By the door," whispered Hackstead, sitting back again and staring aimlessly at the high ceiling, lips pursed in a soundless whistle.

After a slight proprietary pause, Dobson shifted, taking in the whole room and its occupants. He left the door until last.

Leaning beside it were two men, both with tired eyes and alert bodies. It seemed a paradox but the moment you saw them you became conscious of that as a fact—the faces, well tanned and fit, the eyes looking as though they had been awake for several nights in a row, but the bodies, even in the leaning postures against the wall, ready for anything—a fight, first aid, women.

"SIS?" mouthed Dobson.

Hackstead put on a big, straight-lipped grin. It was not a look of amusement. "Betcha a quid to a punch in the balls." He spoke through clenched teeth. "SIS, DI6 or 5 or whatever they call themselves these days. It means that my people can't keep them off any more, baby. We're among all the delicate byways—most of which come to a dead end in a great big fancy weave of red tape."

Tyndle was trying for silence. On the third go he got it.

"I want to make sure everyone here is in the picture," he began. "The job we're doing today is really not the business of either the AIB or the AID. However, as certain matters have come to light following our own investigation of a crashed aircraft, we are heavily involved."

He stopped to move around to the blackboard and wreckage chart. "Over the past weeks we have been collecting and gathering the wreckage of a B-26 Martin Marauder which, it appears, went down in Romney Marsh sometime in the forties. We can't be exact. John here," he indicated his colleague, "is a specialist in cleaning and rejuvenating documents from crashed aircraft . . ."

"He means I usually sponge oil off cockpit papers," John said with a certain amount of sarcasm. "With the ones from this airplane I need help."

A subdued buzz of humor passed across the room, subsiding fast.

"As he says," continued Tyndle, "he needs help. There's a certain amount of authentication to be done, so we can't give an exact date of the crash."

"Nicely covered," muttered Hackstead.

"However," the AIB man went on, "to get down to the matter in hand, we started to piece the aircraft together. Most of you have seen the result so far. Very early on—in fact on site itself—there was at least one piece of wreckage which we thought had probably not come from the aircraft at all." He gave a little spluttering, nervous laugh. "In fact one of the boys wanted to leave it where it was. But we brought it back just the same. On our first run-through, sorting the bits and pieces, we realized that we had three suspect items. I have one here."

He stretched behind the blackboard and brought out a metal drum some ten inches deep and a couple of feet in diameter. Tyndle turned it around all ways, so that everybody could see. Originally it had been colored in a matt black and the paintwork had stood up well. There was little rusting. The interior was obviously lead.

"There's no doubt in any of our minds that it is a container of some kind, that the lid section is missing and that it was originally tightly sealed. There are small particles of rubber still intact around the rim, and a serial number stamped into the metal on the outside."

He made a signal to someone near Dobson's left, and a screen to the right of the desk was suddenly illuminated with a close-up picture of the metal, near to the rim of the drum. Quite clearly, stamped into the casing was a serial for all to read: SS/4042/A1/KZS.

Tyndle shrugged. "It means nothing to any of us. All that can be said is that it does seem to be an object of military origin. It came out of this aircraft." He waved his hand at the wreckage chart, a finger slowly moving in toward the plan. "We found it here." He indicated a point slightly to the left of where most of the tail assembly and cone had been dug out. It was almost directly in line with the cross, to the right, which marked the position of Sergeant Edward B. Sailby's body.

"On its own, that find would not have worried us overmuch. The other two do. One is here, in this room. I am assured that it is now perfectly harmless. The second is in a protective chamber over on the firing range. It is intact, locked in, and the reasons for this will become obvious to those who do not know about it already."

His hand moved behind the blackboard again. He needed to turn his body completely and use both hands to bring the object out. It was, like the drum, a metal container; this time oblong in shape, some ten inches high, roughly two feet long, and about ten inches across. Tyndle tipped it forward. It contained what appeared to be five cylindrical objects with smooth rounded tops, from each of which projected a small nozzle, no more than a quarter of an inch high. The empty space in what was to Dobson, the top left-hand corner had obviously held a sixth cylinder.

Tyndle set the box down gently on the desk and turned back to the wreckage chart. "This gray metal box was taken out of the earth here." His finger moved upward from where the drum was located, to a point slightly to the left and just behind the main portion of the fuselage. "Its significance is startling, and, I think you'll all probably agree, somewhat worrying."

Once more he reached behind the blackboard and produced the missing sixth cylinder. It was in two halves, having been carefully sawn through about three inches from the base.

He took the two pieces and held them together as one. "Most of you use these in your homes every day. They're more sophisticated now, I'll grant you that, but you use them. This is an early example. Probably one of the first ever made and used. This, gentlemen, is an aerosol can."

Dobson and Hackstead exchanged glances.

"The man who invented it called it an *aérosol vecteur*. His name was Professor L. Dautrebande. His address, in the nineteen forties, was in Chaussée de la Grande Espinette in the Rhode St. Genève district of Brussels, and his work throughout the latter part of the thirties was almost wholly concerned with perfecting the aerosol spray. He wrote several papers on it and when Belgium fell into the hands of the Nazis, they took over his factory and his research. There was talk—no, I'm underestimating the talk—there was grave concern regarding what use the Germans would make of Professor Dautrebande's *aérosols vecteurs*."

"So," continued Tyndle. "We had found a container with six blown aerosols. The next problem was to discover if they had, in fact, ever been loaded aerosols, and if so, with what were they loaded? I took the decision myself and called in Porton Down. Professor Reeves has kindly consented to come up today and give us his opinion."

Reeves was a shy man, and they had to strain forward in order to hear him. He appeared almost diffident, self-effacing, as he picked up the cutaway aerosol cylinder. His language was that of a layman: simple, straightforward, explaining matters without recourse to the more specialized speech of his profession.

He was also brief. It was clear, he told them, that the cylinders had at some point contained a substance, but, as they had been in the ground for at least thirty years, it could be well-nigh impossible to tell exactly what that substance was. At Porton Down they had opened up the cylinder he was now holding, taken samples from the rusting deposits left on the inside, and grown cultures from them. He continually referred to his colleague, Dr. Matthew Drimgollen, who he said had done most of the work. The cultures were grown much as you would grow cultures from urine samples in an attempt to diagnose a virus infection.

"And we got results. Not positive, but definite results," he said. "The cultures produced the viral bacteria which are normally associated with a particular type of fever that usually affects cattle, sheep and similar animals—known generally as Rift Valley fever, though it is similar in many ways to certain species of influenza. The disease produced through this virus is transmittable to humans and not normally found in this part of the globe. The remains in the aerosols are very weak strains; probably dormant; inactive—that is, until we started messing about with them."

He looked toward Tyndle, as though asking if that was enough. Tyndle nodded and rose.

"So you see, gentlemen, we have a problem. At some point—and it isn't our job here to discover the whys and the wherefores—a container with six aerosols, presumably filled with a highly infectious virus substance, was activated, either in the aircraft or after it crashed."

He ran his tongue across dry lips. "Our real difficulty is the third item. We have a box, exactly like this one, but sealed and with what appears to be some type of timing device in the lid. Presumably it also contains aerosols similar to these. We have no way of knowing what those aerosols contain, or if what they contain is, after such a long period, active."

His next pause was for effect. "That is the situation. We, in conjunction with Professor Reeves and his colleague, Dr. Drimgollen, have come to certain decisions. I think they are practical. There is a small danger, but we have, I believe, minimized this. The box—which differs from this one only in color—has been X-rayed and examined by Captain Hume and Lieutenants Hawthorn and Little. They are all experienced bomb disposal experts and their analysis is that they can get the lid off the box—the blue box—without activating the aerosols."

He turned toward the chart again. "The blue box, incidentally, was found among the wreckage here"—slightly to the right of the main remnants of the fuselage, about midway along. "Now I'm going to let Captain Hume tell you exactly how they are going to go about this operation. If it is successful, which I've no doubt it will be, Professor Reeves and Dr. Drimgollen can remove the aerosols in safety and examine whatever the contents at their leisure."

"What about the black drum?" Hackstead spoke loudly; a hard, pressing query.

"I know what you're thinking, Colonel." Tyndle made a half-appealing gesture. "The drum could well have contained yet a third device which is missing."

"I mean just that; and if it did exist—this third device—then it would be the largest. Logically the largest would be the most lethal."

Tyndle nodded. "It's the right thinking. Jock MacDonald, one of our most experienced men, went down to the crash site at five o'clock this morning with a team. They've even taken the dogs."

"The dogs?" Dobson asked aloud.

"We have dogs." Tyndle looked puzzled, as though Dobson should know of these things. "Dogs trained to sniff out metals, fabrics. Better than electronic detectors, some of them. We didn't use them before, but now . . . well . . ."

The whispers around the room were growing to full chatter. Tyndle knocked on his desk. Like a headmaster who's worried about keeping order on parents' day, thought Dobson.

"I think Captain Hume . . . " Tyndle started, but Hume was already striding up to the desk.

Christ, Dobson realized how young he looked. *Experienced bomb disposal expert*, Tyndle had said. He looked young enough to be simply head of school. A kind of updated Raleigh from *Journey's End*. Only the uniform was that of the seventies, and there was an MC ribbon sewn onto his shirt pocket. Wonder where he got that? Belfast? Or defusing a tricky one in Derry?

He even spoke like head of school. "First I think I'd better explain the 'gubbins' with the aid of photographs and the X rays . . ."

The box was exactly like the gray one they had already seen, with the exception of the top and the bolts—eight of them, big screw bolts, one on each corner and one in the center of each side. On the top was a circular piece of apparatus.

Hume told them that the bolts were rusted in solid, as was the clockwork timing and firing device. The bolts were explosive; when the timing device was activated, the bolts should, in theory, blow, and the outer lid would spring off.

"The aerosols apparently work in exactly the opposite way to those we're used to using these days," he said. "The little titties you can see sticking out of the ends of the ones in the gray box are fully extended. They're activated when they pop out."

The nozzles were held down by an inner plate, on top of which were six springs to give the necessary downward tension. Then the lid, bolted on top of that, kept the whole thing tidy and safe. Once the lid blew, the springs lost their tension and the inner plate would leap off, so releasing what Hume called "the titties" on the aerosols.

Dobson did not like to think what might be in those damned cans. He positively dragged his mind away from it and concentrated on what the boy captain was saying.

"... very difficult to know its stability after so long. May be quite harmless. But even if it isn't, we won't be that close, and we'll have the protective garb on. One thing's for sure. None of us in the chamber is going to get hurt by the explosive bolts."

The idea was to lock the device to the floor of the stressed-concrete shelter in which it lay at present. They were then going to bore through the lid—crosswise between the bolts—removing two strips of the outer lid which would reveal the holding plate beneath: strips about three quarters of an inch wide, cut to avoid the springs.

They would then clamp the holding plate down—there had been men working already in the shelter, drilling and setting bolt holes into the floor in the correct places. A U-shaped piece of metal, bent to the correct measurements, and with bracketed ends, would slip tightly over the inner plate and the little brackets could then be bolted to the floor.

"After that's done we'll get to work with the long tools," Hume grinned. The complete schoolboy down to the jokes, Dobson marveled.

By the long tools Hume meant pliers, hacksaws and cutters with four- or five-foot handles. With these they would get the timing device away, cutting the connecting wires. Then unscrew the bolts. Once the main lid was off and the inner plate bolted down, they could, as Hume put it, "sneak inside and plug up the titties."

The schoolboy wit was harmless, Dobson decided. The lad really did seem to know his stuff.

The audience began shuffling once Hume finished.

"There's no need to tell you," Tyndle called out, "that the three officers will be wearing protective clothing and masks as well as their normal anti-blast gear. A directive has already been issued that from fourteen-fifteen hours until further notice, nobody will be allowed within a mile of the range shelter."

"Are the entrances adequately sealed?" It was the first time the sharp Dr. Drimgollen had spoken. He had a voice like he looked, you could have cut out a piece of toughened glass with it.

"Extra seals have been fitted this morning."

"And what happens if the box blows? I mean, what happens to the young officers inside?"

"We get them out fast, of course."

"Thus releasing at least a little of what's inside the aerosols."

"We can't just leave them in there, Doctor." Reeves raised his voice above its normal quiet level.

"If it's something—providing there is anything still active—if it's something lethal, we'll be exposing a very large area to high risk."

"We can't very well just take the thing off Beachy Head and drop it into the sea." Reeves' voice dropped a shade at the end of the sentence, as though he had suddenly come to the conclusion that this might, after all, be the best thing to do.

"There's a risk either way." Drimgollen gave a quick sardonic smile. "I suppose we're all in the risk business."

The conference began to break up.

"Apparently we're lunching with the VIPs," Hackstead gave Dobson the nod.

"You look dead worried." He did: Hackstead appeared to have aged ten years since the conference started.

"Aren't you?"

"I've got confidence in those boys."

"Great."

"Rift Valley fever rarely kills."

"Ha." Hackstead turned and faced him. "That was in the gray one, sonny. I'm not concerned about Rift Valley fever. You don't know your history."

"The war in the air, 1939-45, that's my specialty."

"Well, hear this. Those bloody *aérosols vecteurs*. Do you know anything about them? Do you know the plan the German High Command had for those nice little squirters?"

"It's not my department. Tell me what they were going to do with them, Bud, and stop looking so anxious."

"Okay. This is documented and for real. They were going to sail along the Channel and release a spray from the aerosols, a spray that would be carried by the prevailing wind across Britain."

"Deodorant?"

"*Clostridium botulinum*. It's the toxic botulin which is produced as a waste product from *Clostridium botulinum* that's the killer. Theoretically, eight ounces could wipe out the world. That's really why they called that trick off, I suppose, but it had the Allied command worried stupid. They actually isolated the toxin at Fort Detrick during the war. What if some idiot Nazi decided it was the real end game? What if it's that stuff in the blue box and the lads cock it up?"

"Even mad Nazis..." Dobson began.

"It's not science fiction," Hackstead was saying close to his ear. "The botulinus toxin can be made as easy as you make cookies. It's thoughts like that which worry me—dealing with things over which you have no control. If they had sprays of RVF on that airplane, why not the real zinger as well?"

"You're out of your tree," said Dobson.

27

The sense of *déjà vu* was so incisive that Dobson continually felt he was in the midst of a dream: the images were all there, clear and decisive. It was only when he put his mind to it that he realized he had seen it all before, on the newscasts from Northern Ireland and in old war movies.

Now here he was, David Dobson, sitting in a Land-Rover with two other people, walkie-talkie crackling in the front, and a radio receiver hissing behind them. Two other Land-Rovers and a small truck were also pulled up nearby, their sight lines straight over the flat dry green of Hampshire, looking toward the big mounds of sand against concrete bunkers, where they normally tested the lighter types of weaponry—the medium-caliber machine guns.

Forward of the big sand bunkers there was the little concrete hut: square, windowless, and with one small metal door in the side, locked tight and sealed once the three young officers were inside. They looked like spacemen in their protective gear over the armored jackets; the big visored helmets on, and breathing apparatus hanging down in front, to be donned when they started work. It would be bad enough with the blast-protective visors, how much worse with the masks on underneath?

Yet they had seemed jaunty enough as their Land-Rover took them away, cool and calm.

The three men had disappeared into the small concrete shelter, the door was closed and the Land-Rover which had taken them down was now parked with the set of vehicles waiting, full of patient, tense men, some with binoculars, most with their ears stretched toward the radio links—their contacts with the officers who would be, at this moment, sizing up the situation inside the shelter.

At lunch Dobson had been depressed to find himself seated, low down the table, next to the sardonic Drimgollen.

The bacteriologist addressed nobody. He simply applied himself to his meal, drinking the soup as though it needed straining first, and cutting his meat with careful, incision-like strokes of the knife. He's not a surgeon, though, Dobson told himself, he's a bug specialist. Halfway through the main course he decided that, if Drimgollen was not going to talk, he would.

"This Rift Valley fever virus..."

"Yes?" Drimgollen turned his head, the expression quite pleasant.

"Well, what I mean... There's no doubt about it? You're certain?"

"What's your interest?" The query put easily, yet still like a knife driving right for the brain.

"I'm the Royal Air Force investigating officer."

"Oh." Completely disinterested.

What the hell? Dobson thought of Sugden. Why not? "Ahm, I don't think you follow me, Doctor?" He tried to do the blank face. "Security aspect."

"Ahhh." Drimgollen moved his head in a conspiratorial downward motion.

"What about Rift Valley fever?"

Drimgollen gave the gentlest of shrugs. "It was there at some time. Pretty potent, I should imagine, and possibly mixed up with the odd epidemic influenza virus."

"What d'you make of it?"

The doctor sighed. "Not my job."

"If it was?"

"Someone had a Martin Marauder with at least a case of aerosols on board packed with a nasty virus, unlikely in Europe, but calculated to cause sickness to cattle and humans. Possibly of epidemic proportions."

"Someone?"

Drimgollen smiled. "Us or them? I'd put cash on the Yanks—some private scheme that went wrong. I reckon that aircraft of yours was heading out, not in. After all, the Yanks did a lot of pioneer work in the field of biological warfare; used it in Vietnam."

"And what of Porton Down?"

"Got to keep abreast of the times."

"What you're saying is that there's no doubt that aircraft was a biological warfare delivery system."

"I've no doubt about it. It's perfectly obvious what it was."

"If it was the Yanks the rest of the Allied High Command would have known. The crate went in. There'd be one hell of a panic."

Drimgollen cocked an eyebrow. "How long have you worked in the cape and stiletto business?"

"Long enough."

"Then you know about turning over stones and keeping quiet about what's found under them. In any case, perhaps nobody knew for sure—and the Allied chiefs of staff need not have known at all. From what I can make out, the secret boys had a lot of it their own way during the '39–'45 mess."

"You mean something really hush-hush: really minimal knowledge? The Op takes place, the aircraft never returns, they wait for results: none—write it off as a failure?"

"Could be."

"What about the aerosols being positively identified?"

"You mean Dautrebande? He'd got most of his conclusions on paper before the war started. There's no solid proof, as yet, that those aerosols came out of his Brussels factory. You'd need really conclusive metalurgy tests to prove it."

"And the other box?"

"The one they're having a crack at after lunch?"

Dobson nodded.

"Anybody's guess. RVF, swine fever, really nasty flu virus. Maybe some of the other stuff the Yanks concocted—maybe anthrax. I'd probably have gone for anthrax or brucellosis with a touch of bad flu. Enough time before D-day to let them get into a convalescent period, just as the epidemics were dying down. Set the Nazis back a treat."

It had Dobson concerned now. He thought of himself and I3 (Air), the deadbeats. If the thing was an unearthed American operation there might be a few left who wanted it kept under the stone. Put a low-grade intelligence outfit in with the Americans and let the CIA, or whatever, bury it. They would be covered—I3 (Air) would see to that: Dobson, stupid Dobson, would see to it. He remembered Hackstead's violent reaction at the first news of people investigating the wreck being taken ill.

"I think I'd better say something in confidence if you have very strong feelings about this being a possible American biological Op."

"Yes?" The cocked eyebrow again.

"I'm only the stringer on this. It's an American aircraft; there are complications. I'm under the control of Colonel Hackstead—ostensibly from the U.S. Military Attaché's Department, United States Embassy."

"Mmmm?"

"He's in an anxiety state. I know it, simply because I've worked with him from the start."

"So?"

Guilt began to trickle into Dobson's head. A sellout on such slim evidence? Observation? Bud Hackstead sometimes got excitable. Did he really have anything to go on?

"Well . . ." Even now he could hear the uncertainty in his own voice. "Okay." Mind make up. "After the conference just now, he looked more anxious than ever and he started talking about *Clostridium botulinum*—is that the right name?"

Drimgollen nodded. He said nothing for a moment. Then: "Botulinum toxin. Terrifying." Only he did not sound terrified.

"He told me the German High Command had a plan to float it in from the Channel using aerosols."

"Not quite correct." Drimgollen still showed no signs of fear. "They had a plan to float various things across England using the prevailing wind and the aerosols. I really think the German High Command put a stopper on the manufacture of *Clostridium botulinum* at a pretty early stage. The Americans isolated it at their little fun palace, mind you. In the forties."

"And did they put a stopper on it?"

"Without any doubt. You know that technically . . . ?"

"Eight ounces can wipe out all life on this planet, yes."

"Technically. But just think about what happens if the prevailing wind changes, or they get the dosage wrong. I think your colonel's being a shade dramatic."

"Hiroshima was dramatic and they didn't really know about the fall-out effects."

"No, but they did know—do know—about the effects of botulinus toxin. Only a madman . . ." He stopped as a waiter took away his plate. "If you're really concerned, ask your colonel straight. Then come and see me before we let the daredevil disposal men into the act." He shook his head. "Anthrax, brucellosis, even psittacosis, I can believe; but not the other. Far too dangerous to one's own side."

"What if it was a German biological operation?"

"Using an American aircraft as cover?"

Dobson, strangely, suddenly realized that Drimgollen had no way of knowing about the bodies in *Dodo* that were not the claimed bodies; *Overshoot*, or any of it. "Yes, using a Marauder."

"It's the only alternative, and the German High Command weren't that stupid."

"The V-1s and V-2s?"

"War. Good weapons when they finally got them off the ground. The German High Command did some stupid things on behalf of their beloved Führer, but late in the war they wouldn't have let him have a sniff of the botulinus toxin. No way, I promise you. But if you're worried about your American boss, and the possibility of it being a Yank Op, then you go and ask him fast."

"We didn't have this conversation." Dobson surprised himself at times; or was it Sugden's influence again?

He did ask Hackstead, directly after lunch, taking him to one side as they waited for the transport.

"Bud," a hand on his arm, "listen, it's a way-out thought, and maybe I'm speaking out of turn, but do you know something that I don't about that bloody blue box down there?"

"Such as?" Hackstead was inclined to be belligerent.

"Such as it came out of an American aircraft? Such as it could have been an OSS job that went wrong? Such as you might just know what's in those aerosols. You got steamed up before lunch—a touch of the botulinus toxins."

Hackstead held him steady, the eyes unblinking. "Yes, Dave, I got steamed up. Let's not quibble, we both know what this is all about. There was a biological operation using *Dodo*, it's got to be that, either way. If it was us—the Yanks as you might so delightfully put it—then it's hidden and buried and I can't dig it out. If it was a German job, then there's no way except patience and examination. If it was one of ours, which I doubt, I swear to you I know no details. But I have to admit that I got carried away back there. I have a particular loathing for disease."

He wiped sweat off his brow with the back of his hand. "It terrifies me, and, like people who are scared of flying, the more I read, the more I worry. I read about *Clostridium botulinum* and the botulinus toxin only the other day. When this blew up—particularly when they were all talking about the aerosols this morning—I got the horrors." The crooked grin and the little laughter wrinkles around his eyes. "I had a good talk with Prof Reeves during lunch. No, Dave, I have no idea what's in that box, but Reeves tells me the most unlikely occupant is the one I was worried about."

It was enough for Dobson. Walking across to the Land-Rover he even felt a mild disgust with himself for thinking that Bud Hackstead was using him as a fall guy—a prune. Bud had already proved their partnership.

Now they waited, in the Land-Rovers and trucks, looking out toward the shelter.

The Hercules they had seen take off earlier appeared to be doing a series of roller landings, touching down and then opening up and taking off again.

Both Hackstead and Tyndle had their binoculars trained on the shelter. Dobson looked around, the people from the AIB sat, impassive, in their vehicle; the two security men stood, leaning against the truck which contained all the military communications gear. He turned, and for the first time saw there was an ambulance discreetly parked out of sight behind the row of vehicles. As he turned, he saw Professor Reeves and Drimgollen, close together in the front of a plain Dormobile to the right. The back of the Dormobile seemed to be crammed with equipment, among which sat two men, whom Dobson had noticed at the morning conference. The men wore protective silver coveralls, unzipped and with the hoods down.

Then the radio began to crackle and Hume's voice came over, like a man talking to his maiden aunt about a day trip into the country.

"It's damn hot in here," Hume said. "They appear to have put everything in the right places. The bolt holes look to be well aligned—Tony, can you check that clamp, is it going to be okay? All right, Refuse Control, we're going to work. As quickly as possible because of the heat and discomfort. If we find it's going to be too long a job, I shall ask for a rest and you can come down and bring us out. Acknowledge."

Refuse Control; Dobson thought it a sick code.

The controller in the truck was responding. "Okay, Dragon One. Refuse Control. We read you full strength. Acknowledge that we'll pull you out for a rest as long as the device is left safe."

"Dragon One—I'm not that damn stupid. We're about to anchor the box and start cutting..."

So it began, the radio exchanges, terse, calm, each step from inside the shelter explained in simple language and acknowledged quietly.

"Okay, she's anchored; nobody'll move this lot. Refuse Control, Dragon One, we will start cutting the first strip in exactly thirty seconds, acknowledge. Dragon One."

"Dragon One, Refuse Control acknowledge."

They could hear the heavy breathing and, as time passed, the minutes dragged. A cliché, Dobson thought, glancing at his watch; minutes into hours. They had only been inside for twenty minutes, yet in the voices you could feel the heat, discomfort and effort.

"Dragon One, Refuse Control, we are just going down the far side and we'll have the first strip off. I'm going to clamp and bolt it, then we want out for a rest. Too hot and stuffy in this gear. Will you give us half an hour breather? Dragon One."

"Refuse Control; Dragon One. Roger. Clamp off and then call us. We'll be down to pick you up. Refuse Control."

"Dragon One."

Hackstead and Tyndle said nothing; they just sat there, sweating.

"Dragon One, strip's off, clear of the springs. We're putting on the clamp."

"Refuse Control. How long, Dragon One?"

"Two, three minutes."

At the end of the line a Land-Rover started its engine and began to ease forward. To the far left the Hercules came down for another roller landing; she touched, ran half the runway distance, then lifted her nose and climbed away, retracting her gear on the turn.

"Dragon One, Refuse Control. First clamp on and secure. Bolted down, nothing'll move it, safe as Maggie's drawers. Can we come out?"

"Refuse Control, we're on our way."

The Land-Rover picked up speed heading toward the shelter. Before it got there the metal door opened and the three astronaut figures emerged. You could tell they were exhausted simply by the way they moved and held themselves. They closed the metal door, and plodded wearily toward the oncoming Land-Rover.

A Jaguar fighter came out of nowhere—probably in from Boscombe Down—dropping with beautiful precision onto the runway, losing height and touching down like a feather. The reverse blast of the engines took a second or so to reach them as the aircraft ran, slowing, down the runway.

"Okay, everyone." The controller from the Army truck. "I'm giving them half an hour to dry off."

The Land-Rover with the disposal men was driving off in the direction of the main buildings over to the far right.

"Stand down for half an hour. Refuse Control out."

"Take thirty," said Hackstead. "This is the life, eh, Dave? No sweaty offices. Everyone else working but you."

"I've got a couple of jobs to do," Tyndle grunted. "I'm going to run my boys back to our department. Be here again in time for the finale, okay?" He hoisted himself from the driving seat and walked away to the vehicle containing his team. The engine started and they moved off.

"You going to have a little wager on what's in those cans?" Hackstead asked.

"Give you ten to one on anthrax or brucellosis."

"You been talking with Drimgollen. I saw you. No bet, that's what Reeves reckons. You ever had anthrax or brucellosis shots?"

"Didn't know you could get them."

"I don't know if you can."

"I'm up-to-date on everything else."

"You wanta bet?"

Dobson considered. Remembering the doom warnings and the talk about botulinus toxin, he decided that Hackstead was really right. "All bets are off," he said.

After a while he asked if Hackstead thought he had time to call the hospital.

"Leave it be till this is over. You'll see her tonight; or tomorrow if we're too late back."

"I would've thought tomorrow would be our day with Free. You were going down to him today, remember."

"I remember. I'm going to sort Free once and for all."

"You still adamant?"

"Meaning?"

"Last night you said I had enough on my plate with Ann. You wouldn't let me consider coming with you. If you go tomorrow, I am coming."

"Nope."

"Why?"

"Because I've had more experience, and I can tell you it's a one-man job. If I pick up anything you'll be the first to know. I promise you, Dave, if Free's our baby you'll know and you'll be in at the kill."

"He had no parents—no relatives alive at the end of the war; you know that?"

"I do now."

"The two of us worked him the first time, Bud, why not...?"

"Don't worry, I've got some big boys around, but I understand how you feel. If it's Free behind the freaks, you'll have your go—and before our friends from Special Branch or that pair of hot potatoes over there have a chance to get to him."

At the same moment they both felt the presence of a third party. Drimgollen had drifted over from the Porton Down Dormobile and was about to lean through the window on Dobson's side.

"Going well, eh?" He really had quite a pleasant manner when one got over the sharp look.

"Seems okay. You met Colonel Hackstead?"

"I had that pleasure before the conference. Pity they didn't have time to install the cameras." Drimgollen smoothed one cheek, as if checking his shave.

"We all rather thought it was a matter of some urgency." Hackstead had begun to rub his cheek in unison with Drimgollen, as though it was some secret sign.

"I understand you managed to get some kind of filter pump into the wall, though," said Hackstead.

"Just in case." The doctor spoke as if he really did expect things to work out badly.

"In case of what?"

"If one, or all, of the aerosols blow, we can draw off some of the air inside the shelter and do an analysis."

"You think of everything, don't you?"

"Professor Reeves thought of it. I wanted TV cameras. The Prof took preference, it's in the natural order of things, and I'm a great believer in the natural order."

It was all on again in around fifteen minutes. The Land-Rover came across the skyline to their right, where the main buildings lay, and deposited the trio of explosives experts.

They stayed outside the shelter for a few moments, adjusting their gear as the Land-Rover drove quickly back to the huddle of vehicles.

Finally the young officers put on their masks and helmets, pulled down the visors and opened the shelter door. Over the radio system Hume's voice came on again, strong: "Dragon One, we're going in. Refuse Control acknowledge."

"Refuse Control."

It began all over again: the terse, laconic exchanges with the occasional background noise from inside the shelter. After half an hour they had removed the second strip of outer casing and clamped down.

"Refuse Control. You want another rest now she's secure, Dragon One?"

"Dragon One, no, we'll finish it now."

"Refuse Control."

"I'm going to start sawing through the timer," they heard Hume say. "The whole thing's rusted in so tight I doubt if any of the explosive charge is viable. The connecting wires are probably rusted right through. We're moving to the corner of the shelter—that is, the far left-hand corner from you, the one farthest from the door. Using the long hacksaw."

"Refuse Control," came the acknowledgment.

"Dragon One. Tony Hawthorn's using the saw with me, and Brian's to our left, watching for any changes in attitude."

"Refuse Control."

"Starting the saw now. Cutting. She's going through like the proverbial cheese wire. The thing's falling to bits with rust. Almost through the timer. She's just about to..."

They heard the small explosion through the speakers a second before it drifted up from the hut. Not a big bang, more like a series of popping sounds. Then Hume's voice:

"The fucking thing's blown. Christ, all the bolts have gone...and the outer casing—it's taken away one of our straps, blown clean off. Two of the aerosols operating...fine mist ...fine spray—like mist...just like most...vapor."

"Refuse Control. Get out of there, Dragon One. All of you, out as fast as you can and then seal off the door."

Already the Porton Down Dormobile was screeching away, giving a nasty tail-shake as the tires bit the hard earth. As it roared off, Dobson caught a glimpse of the two men in the rear zipping their silver-colored protective suits and pulling the hoods up over their heads. The ambulance followed a second later, and as the two vehicles streaked toward the shelter they saw the metal door swing back a fraction and the three officers pile out, almost falling over one another to get out and seal off the door.

Through it all came a soft, unexcited voice on the general intercom. "I want instructions, immediate to the station commander and the director of the Establishment. No aircraft to land or leave. For the time being no person, repeat *no* person, to enter or leave the Establishment. Any queries, tell them I can have the Minister of Defence or the Prime Minister's personal authority within fifteen minutes." It was Professor Reeves.

Tyndle's voice sounded more choked and strangled than usual. Probably it gets worse under stress, Dobson thought, hardly hearing the words.

"That lad carries a lot of clout. No doubt about that; a lot of clout," Tyndle said.

28

The time of the explosion inside the shelter was exactly sixteen fifty-six—four minutes to five. Dobson had glanced at his watch at the precise moment the bolts blew.

He reached forward for a pair of binoculars—Tyndle and Hackstead already had theirs to their eyes, getting close in on the shelter and what was happening around it.

The door was well sealed off, and the three young officers were either flat out or on their haunches, some ten feet from the little blockhouse.

The Porton Down Dormobile slewed around to within a few paces of them, the rear doors opening before it came to a halt. The pair of men leaped from the back of the van, and one started to run toward the trio of explosives officers. He was yelling something. One young officer had reached up to open his visor and the man from Porton Down was telling him to keep the visor closed down.

The other of Reeves' technicians began to drag what looked like a hose from the open end of the van. Both the Porton Down men were fully encased in silver protective coveralls, complete with hoods, over which they wore visored helmets. Through the glasses, Dobson could see that Reeves and Drimgollen were firmly sealed off in the front of the Dormobile, windows closed and a glass screen down behind them, enclosing the scientists in a fully airtight compartment.

The explosives men were being grouped together, standing, facing the technician with the hose. A second later a fine spray emerged, the Porton Down man directing the nozzle to saturate the trio who had come out of the shelter. The other technician was giving orders for them to turn so that each would be fully sprayed with what could only be some form of powerful liquid anti-toxin.

The whole thing took around a minute, then the spray was aimed at the shelter itself, high above to start with, then down the walls, starting around the now sealed door. The men from Porton Down covered the entire shelter and an area all around it, constantly lifting the nozzle so that the cloud of spray rose some thirty or forty feet into the air, almost making the stone and concrete invisible through the glasses.

In the meantime the three disposal officers were being shepherded toward the ambulance, and for the first time, Dobson saw that the ambulance crew were also dressed in protective clothing similar to that worn by the Porton Down men.

The radio link began to hiss again. "Refuse Control is signing out. Professor Reeves has now taken charge and will speak on this frequency in a few moments."

Nobody said anything, and there appeared to be no movement from the other vehicles. The only thing different was that the two security men had walked back to their car, parked a fair way behind the line of official transport. Dobson noticed they were inside, with the windows up.

The radio crackled again. A few seconds later the quiet, unassuming voice of Professor Reeves came through. He was painfully correct, economic and simple, as he had been at the morning conference.

He described what had happened as "a slight setback." The three young officers were unhurt, if shaken, and had been removed to isolation.

Before the operation, it had been agreed that, in the event of any possible serious biological risk, Reeves was to assume overall control answerable to nobody. The shelter had been well doused with a powerful anti-toxin and he felt that there was no immediate danger, so some of his initial instructions were being relaxed. Aircraft were still prohibited from landing or leaving, but the bulk of the work force could go—apart from those who had been within a mile radius of the shelter. This, naturally, meant all the observers. They were to go immediately to the AIB and AID offices and await instructions.

Air was being drawn out of the shelter for analysis. Once this was done they would know if the situation was serious.

Anyone, Reeves said, who needed to get in touch with families or friends could do so by telephone, though he reminded them all of the Official Secrets Act.

"Shit," said Hackstead with feeling.

Half an hour later they were lounging around in the AIB office, feeling not really worried, but more intensely frustrated

About seven o'clock, there was a telephone message to say that packages of sandwiches, flasks of coffee and drinks were to be left for them down in the hangar.

Tyndle seemed to be constantly on the telephone, and Dobson thought it was about time to call the hospital. It would be near visiting hours now, and most of the others seemed to have made calls out to families.

Out of deference, he approached Tyndle. "Okay if I make a call to London? To a hospital? My girl friend had an accident."

Tyndle gave him a curt nod. "They've had no luck with the dogs," he said. "I've just had Jock on from Kent. A few nuts and bolts but nothing big."

"So there's another joker lying around somewhere."

"It would seem so."

They took about five minutes to get him transferred to Ann's ward when he got through to the hospital, and the sister who answered sounded rushed, harassed or just plainly out of sorts. It was a surprise, then, when she asked if Dobson would like to speak with Miss West.

She sounded very bright until he told her he would not be able to get in to see her that evening.

"Tomorrow I'll make it for sure," he said, crossing his fingers like a schoolboy, hoping that by tomorrow night the whole lot of them would not be sitting around in some hospital isolation ward.

"They say I can come out on Sunday. Your turn to pick me up."

"I'll bring you home, don't worry."

She said that, apart from the difficulties of being walled in with plaster down one side—and the problems of learning to balance because of it—she felt fine. No pain. "It just itches like hell. You know, under the plaster."

They talked for about ten minutes. The telephone parting was prolonged, neither wanting to let the other go. For Dobson it was worse, speaking with his head turned away from the main body of the room. There were between twenty and thirty people hanging around in the place; telephone privacy was impossible.

People were breaking up into little groups. The military and RAF types started a couple of bridge games, while the AIB and AID boys caught up with some of their paper work. The DI6 men sat apart, going through notebooks, their heads close together. Hackstead had found himself a comfortable swivel chair and appeared to be dozing off.

Dobson decided it was the best course of action. He threaded his way through the packed room, finally got himself a comfortable chair, placed it near to one of the outside windows, looking across all the junk of wrecked aircraft, and eventually fell asleep.

There was a sudden blaze of light, and the sound of voices; stirring all around, muttered grumbles.

He shook himself awake, looking automatically at his watch. It was four-thirty in the morning and people were rising. Tyndle stood by his desk talking to Reeves and Drimgollen. Both of the scientists looked haggard, red-eyed and pale.

"Gentlemen," Tyndle called in his odd strangulated voice, "Professor Reeves has some news for you. Can you get yourselves together. Come up around the desk. These two gentlemen have been doing laboratory tests all night—well, since just after five yesterday afternoon—and I think they're anxious to get some sleep."

Everybody started to move up, dragging chairs, or just walking over to lean against the walls.

Reeves made a gesture toward Drimgollen, who took a place directly behind the desk. He started to speak almost at once, his voice strong, the same sharp confidence there in spite of the fatigue. Perhaps superbacteriologists like Drimgollen had conquered the fatigue problem.

"We have answers for you, gentlemen," he began. "It could be much worse; the strain's very weak and the disease does not alarm us as much as it once did. The aerosols—at least the two that fired—contained active cholera vibrio. It has deteriorated over the years, but it *is* active and there's a fair amount locked away in that shelter. But that's not your problem. I think it unlikely that we're going to have an epidemic on our hands, but local hospitals and doctors will be alerted—without publicity or fuss, of course. We have decided we should take the utmost care with all those who were near the site. Some of you will not be up-to-date with cholera vaccinations and we intend to deal with those cases now. Can I have a show of hands from those who are, currently, protected?"

Dobson's hand shot up. Like the Accident Investigation people, I3 (Air) had a ruling about vaccinations being kept updated.

He glanced around. The United States Military Air Attaché's Office had a similar ruling, for Hackstead's hand was up. One or two people shuffled, looking sheepish: not covered. Those with up-to-date vaccinations were free to go.

"Sorry I wasn't very sociable last night." Hackstead was at Dobson's elbow. "I needed time to think."

"So did I."

"Bet you both ways against the middle that the circular joker contains at least a dozen aerosols and that it's in mint condition."

"You're going down to see Free?"

"You know that." The light came back into Hackstead's eyes. "And I'm still going alone, buddy. I'll go check Free—could take a day, two days. You check your source. What day is it?"

"Saturday. Saturday, July 17. *Dodo's* old crew arrive Monday morning. We've got to get our skates on, Bud. Where's our car and the driver?"

By six they were almost on the outskirts of Roehampton, and Hackstead needed cigarettes. They stopped at a news agent's shop and Hackstead emerged clutching a pile of papers and some cigarettes.

As they pulled away he tossed the *Express* in Dobson's direction, lit up and started to glance through the *Mail*.

"Nothing about Farnborough's hit the *Express*." Dobson began to run his eyes over the columns again to make certain he had missed nothing.

"Goddamn it!" Hackstead exploded.

"Who? What?"

"The fucking *Mail*. They've blown the story about an American aircrew's visiting Britain—look at this: *Do You Remember the War? Reunion.* Miss Lynda Lee-Potter. Look at that: *Stay home, Wilbur, there are some nasty shocks waiting down memory lane.*

Dobson laughed aloud. "She doesn't know how right she is."

29

Dobson's limbs ached as he climbed the stairs back at Charlotte Street, then his guts turned over as a sound floated down from the landing in front of his flat door. The gentle scrape of a foot. He felt for the revolver. Still there and out fast.

"Hey, man, it's only me. Watch that shooter, I don't want to end up in the pine box just yet." Claud Trotter stood, beaming, on the landing.

Dobson holstered the revolver, hanging onto the banister rail with one hand, breathing hard. "What can I do for you?" he asked. "I'm damn tired."

"Just watching out for you—like I said."

"I can believe it. Your gray faceless bosses were hanging around where I've just come from."

"Farnborough. Yep, I know. They asked me to see you got in safe and sound." The usual smile slid from his face like an unset Jell-O flopping out of a mold. "I'm on trial, Dobson. After the balls-up the other night I've been told to be a good boy, or else back to the slave market. I only wish they'd tell me what it was all about—*really* all about. I suppose you wouldn't like to . . . ?"

"You know more than is good for you already." Dobson leaned against the door, feeling for his keys. "Maybe you know more than I do. It takes a lot of figuring." He had his key in the latch now. "Just don't crowd me, Claud. Keep your distance. I don't like those you have to associate with. They give me the creeps."

"Can't say I'm too keen on them. You know, Dobson, with the wrong politicians at the top, those guys could become a regular Gestapo."

Dobson shook his head. "No, Trotter, your lot would be the Gestapo. Your bosses would be doing a nastier job altogether. May I bid you good night—or good morning?"

"Get your rest. I won't bother you, but I'll be watching out." Trotter turned away and Dobson stumbled into the flat.

The pillows smelled of Ann, delicious, animal, feminine. He asked for an alarm call—eleven o'clock.

When the telephone rang it was only nine-thirty.

He felt bleary, perhaps really aware of the meaning of the word for the first time.

"Oh, you're back, good show," Sugden wallowed into his ear through the instrument.

"I'm back, asleep and had an alarm call set for eleven."

Sugden was babbling on about something, puffing away on the phone. A talking head: all lip and no bottle, that was Sugden.

"Okay," Dobson cut him short. "I wanted to see you anyway, I have things to talk about. Things concerning Arthur."

"Not again?"

"Very definitely again." Dobson was thinking of his conversations with Drimgollen, and the last one with Hackstead.

"All right, we'll talk about Arthur again, but I have something for you. Eye-bulging. Dowl, he's turned up another *Rattengift* document."

Christ, Dobson just remembered: he had never even mentioned the Bormann-Kaltenbrunner letter to Hackstead.

"Another one?" Frantic to leap from his bed and check that the Bormann letter was still where he had left it.

"The Weiner Library."

"He said he'd try there—because of the last letter." Dowl had scrawled a note—*I think I'll try the Weiner Library next.*

"Well, I have it here. Sinister stuff, Dobson."

"Where's here?"

"Clapham, of course," as though he never took any time off.

"A document?"

"Like the others—document, letter, instruction. Sinister stuff this," Sugden repeated.

"Whose signature?"

"Himmler's right-hand thug. Ernst Kaltenbrunner."

Jesus. "I'd better come over." Dobson hung up and made for the living room to check that the Bormann-Kaltenbrunner letter was still there. It was, neat in the pigeonhole where he had put it on Thursday night.

Heading back into the bedroom he dialed the U.S. Embassy. They had him through to Hackstead's office in seconds.

A cheerless, flat female voice answered. Oh, it's Wing Commander Dobson. I had an instruction to call you. Did you now? Colonel Hackstead wanted a message passed on. He left for Kent about half an hour ago and said the wing commander should not be disturbed until later. Dobson could probably get hold of him at the County Hotel, Canterbury, this evening. But the colonel said he'd call anyway.

At least Hackstead was on the job—Free-chasing.

He stretched back on the bed. Sugden could cool his heels for a while. He, David Dobson, was going to have a bath and shave. Then whiz over to Clapham, take a look at whatever Dowl had turned up, assess its importance and then make another appointment with Arthur.

Drying off, he decided that, depending upon Dowl's latest contribution and anything Hackstead turned up, it was time to do a little more research of his own. He finished shaving, went back into the bedroom and dialed Clapham.

"I thought you'd be here ages ago." Sugden was annoyed.

"Held up. Sorry," as brightly as he could manage. "We never close, you should've learned that by now, old boy." He was very pleased with the "old boy" bit. Sugden's language.

"No need to come on heavy," said Sugden to Dobson's surprise. Maybe Charlie had teen-age children.

"Just a small chore."

"Yes?" Sugden sounded suspicious.

"I want some books out over the weekend. Anything you can lay your hands on concerning the V-weapon offensive—both sides; strategy, technical, anything you can get."

"Wilco," said Sugden, back on typical tack.

Dobson rang Farnborough. Tyndle, sounding exhausted, was still in his office. "What can I do for you?"

"Didn't ask yesterday," Dobson began. "The Marauder's

compass heading. I seem to recall you said the compass was intact."

"Right. I've a note here somewhere. The compass is still in working order. We read it off, but it'll only give you her track down the crash path..."

"Which might just roughly correspond to her flight path—unless she swung right around. Read away."

"Three-four-two degrees—magnetic, of course."

"Got it. Thanks. See you soon." He was off to dress and make a dash to Clapham.

Sugden was rubbing his hands. Hallo, he's got something taped—sewn up—Dobson thought.

"Got your pile of books coming over." Sugden made it sound rather as if he had managed to pull a clever trick on the stock market. Very bullish.

"Good." Dobson sank into a chair, aware in a surprised kind of way that he could feel the holster jerk heavy under his left shoulder. He had not remembered even putting it on.

"Sorry if I woke you, but it did seem urgent. Believe you were out of town all night. Anything up?"

Nobody had told Sugden about the Farnborough business, so Dobson was not going to talk about it.

"Just took longer than we expected—looking at the way they're piecing the aircraft together at the RAE."

"Ah yes. Good old Farnborough." Sugden held a large envelope out to him. "The stuff from Dowl," he explained.

Dobson took the papers from the envelope and his first thought was that you had to admit the Nazis were way ahead of their time with letterheads. But this was a nasty—the swastika within a laurel wreath topped by the eagle of the Fatherland. Underneath: *Sicherheitsdienst der Reichs: SD Hauptamt.* Kaltenbrunner's own little domain: no, his empire; the SS Security Service, headquarters of the SD. There was the same label—*Geheime Reichsfache:* most secret Reich document—and Dobson could see at a glance it was more than an ordinary nasty—Kaltenbrunner himself to the Kommandant of the concentration camp at Sachsenhausen: SS Obersturmbannführer Anton Kaindl.

Sachsenhausen. Dobson's brow creased in disgust. Sachsenhausen: death camp; extermination; medical experimentation—and something else? Something quite recent.

Forgery, that was it. They had picked up a former SS

officer—Schwend, was it? SS Sturmbannführer Friedrich Schwend? Wanted for atrocities at Sachsenhausen. Picked him up in Bonn because he could not pay his hotel bill. Schwend, the man who was in charge of the great bank note forgery: the plan to ruin the British economy by flooding the country with counterfeit cash. They had even paid an agent, the infamous Cicero, with some of the forged currency.

Dobson's eyes swilled along the German text picking up the odd word: *Rattengift* was there, and *Chef OKW*. He flicked the page over to read quickly through the translation:

SS Obergruppenführer Ernst Kaltenbrunner—the fanatical, treacherous, second-rate, chain-smoking Kaltenbrunner—to Anton Kaindl, Kommandant of KZ Sachsenhausen. The document read:

> RATTENGIFT is now in motion and you will proceed with my instructions 44/XK/5 regarding the chosen prisoner. The medical staff and officers who are to carry out the final phase of our part in this operation will, of course, accompany the prisoners and deal with the last things at the airfield designated.
>
> The date will be given to you within four days of the operation and will come directly from Chef OKW. You have my full authority as invested in me by the Führer to act on these orders from Chef OKW.
>
> Heil Hitler!
> KALTENBRUNNER

It had to be a German Op then. The whole tenor of the letter was the clincher. *Rattengift—Ratpoison*. The aerosols; Rift Valley fever; cholera; and whatever was still left buried or floating around in Romney Marsh. Drimgollen again, in his head, *It's perfectly obvious what it was*—a biological warfare delivery system. But why a Martin Marauder?

The circle in his head again. A German Op that went wrong? Why an old American aircraft when they had all that sophisticated gear, the rocketry, there and waiting to be used—and it was used to some success. The thing did not make sense.

He would need to speak with Arthur again about

Overshoot; and do his own reading on the V-weapon offensive.

As if on cue, there was a tap at the door and Price, the duty officer, came in with a load of books, not quite staggering under the weight, but red-faced and breathless. "I hope to God these'll do."

Dobson took a sneak preview. Lusar's *German Secret Weapons of the Second World War; Evidence in Camera*; Dornberger's *V-2*; von Braun's *History of Rocketry and Space Travel*.

"They'll do for a start."

"Well, well. Good, good." Sugden rubbed his hands together.

"We have to talk." Dobson gave Price the hard look.

"Ah." Price hovered, so Dobson walked firmly to the door and opened it.

"Thanks for picking up the books."

Disgruntled, Price made an exit, crab-wise and reluctant.

"I mustn't be too long myself . . ." Sugden still stood.

"Charlie," the patient voice. "We have Arthur to talk about."

Sugden looked at his feet. "Yes." There was an embarrassed and unhappy aura emanating from him.

"What d'you mean, yes?"

"Nobody got hold of you before you left Charlotte Street? After we last talked?"

"Who, for instance?"

"I thought perhaps that impossible man from Special Branch . . ."

Dobson felt trouble, it was in the air all around him, like static.

"Why should Trotter get hold of me?"

"I tried to get in touch with Arthur. After you rang; after you said you needed to talk."

"And?"

"And he's not available."

"Come on, Charlie. You found him; you assured me he was straight. Colonel Hackstead's given me a direct order to recheck him. Recheck Arthur—Richard Martin Lewis."

"Well, Colonel Hackstead'll have to pull him for you. I haven't got the necessary rank. I don't know if Colonel Hackstead has either."

"Don't say we need the Archangel Gabriel?" He was completely serious.

"Special Branch has him."

"Then perhaps my friend Trotter . . . ?"

Sugden shook his head. "Arthur's clean—or at least he was clean of that business with the East Germans in '66. It was a setup. Apparently there have been complications, though." He appeared to be lost for words. "Look, David, he hasn't had access for a long time. He's been working for one of the departments. Cover. But Special Branch picked him up early this morning, and D15've got him tucked away."

"You mean they've got him behind some wire, deep in the heart of Wiltshire or somewhere, with a hard bunch of confessors?"

"I believe that's what they call them these days. Yes, I think he's with a pair of confessors. Out of reach anyway."

"Christ." He had to get hold of Hackstead. The County Hotel, Canterbury—but not until later; or Hackstead would call him anyway.

"David." Sugden was being far too considerate. "I know Arthur's wartime background."

"So do I, mate. Make no mistake, I had him checked like you'd check a dodgy engine."

"He was with 138 Special Duties; and with 161 Squadron. Exactly as he said. I've seen his log books. I know people he was with. Know them personally. He was at Tempsford and Tangmere; he did it all. Of one thing I'm certain, as far as the info on that *Overshoot* is concerned he's clean as Ivory Snow. What he passed to us that Sunday afternoon in your flat's as clean as . . . as . . . " He searched for the right word.

"As a whistle." Dobson finished it—uninspired.

"That information is pure. I promise—swear."

"He seemed a disillusioned man, our Arthur."

"I have no details. I should leave it to Hackstead."

It was all he could do. He knew it. Start meddling with the kind of gray wonders who had been in the background during the Farnborough business and there would be more sweat. He nodded and went over to his personal locker to get the charts he would need—Europe and southern England.

Carrying the books down the steep stairs, Dobson knew he had no options. The weight of the books hung heavy between his arms. Then there was Ann. First priority—flowers for Ann and a visit to the hospital, arrangements for her coming home. Home? Charlotte Street was home for Ann now. The books seemed less weighty at that thought. Flowers. Lots of flowers. Chocolates as well. A big box of chocolates. With almost shocking surprise, Dobson realized that he did not know if Ann even liked chocolates.

30

Dobson took her things straight over to the hospital, then arranged to come back and pick her up at noon on the following day.

He took a taxi back to the corner of the Tottenham Court Road and walked through to Charlotte Street, dropping in at the takeout curry shop on his way.

As he entered the apartment building, he thought he spotted Trotter's car, down the road. *Don't crowd me*, he had told Trotter, but you couldn't really call a car parked a hundred and fifty yards or so from the front door crowding.

He reheated the meal, set out his small table and ate with the delicacy of a steam shovel, washing up and putting everything away once finished, just to square things off. It was going to be a long night, and possibly a pretty lengthy day tomorrow.

At nine-thirty he telephoned Hackstead at the County in Canterbury. Sorry, Colonel Hackstead was out. No, they did not know when he would be back, would he like to leave a message?

"Ask him to ring David urgently no matter what time he gets in."

The table cleared, he took out the European charts, his

navigational protractor, slide rule, ruler, pencils and the note he had made when Tyndle gave him *Dancing Dodo*'s compass heading.

From his notes he examined the Romney Marsh area on the chart, and made a small *x* at the exact point which had been known for so many years as Dead Clump. The fuselage had been pointing inland, and the compass course reading was three-four-two degrees magnetic. Supposing *Dodo* went in around the spring of 1944. Okay? He did a couple of small sums and arrived at the magnetic differential between 1944 and now. Then another sum to give him a true bearing. The true course would be three-three-four. If the aircraft had arrived at that point on a straight heading from the continent—from Hitler's Fortress Europe as it was then—where exactly could it have come from?

Dobson worked out the reverse track and drew a straight line from the *x* in the middle of Romney Marsh, out across the Channel and over the broad chart of the Continent.

If *Dodo* had come in from the other side of the water—taking her range as a maximum of just over five hundred and seventy miles, presuming that she wanted to do a round trip—and if she had held a course from which she did not deviate, the aircraft would have come in from occupied France—anywhere from the southwest of Lyons, right over the Bourgogne, and Nivernais, touching the edge of the Champagne district, flying to the east of Paris, then almost directly over Beauvais, after that west of Amiens and Abbeville, crossing the coast a shade west of St. Valéry, then the English coast somewhere between Dymchurch and New Romney. That was always supposing she was not flying out of some Belgian or Dutch airfield along the coast then turning in over the Dymchurch-New Romney area; and always presuming the crash path was almost a replica of the flight path.

All this was pure speculation, but the last document—from Kaltenbrunner to the Kommandant of Sachsenhausen—had explicitly spoken of an airfield and there were dozens along that particular route—along the line he had drawn across France.

Sachsenhausen kept coming back into his head. From what he recalled, they had done some pretty nasty biogical experiments there. Ask Drimgollen, he would know all that stuff—the poison gases and germ experiments; the when and where. Later, for there was still the alternative possibility. The American theory.

A biological warfare delivery system, that was what *Dodo*

had been; but not on that air test on May 28, 1943. Confusion. Suddenly, as so often happens when the mind has been worrying away at a problem, one thing became absolutely clear. The Marauder *Dancing Dodo* had been placed, accurately or inaccurately, in order to be found: bodies and all, flight plans, charts, documents, letters. That was what it was about. *Dodo* had been on a one-way delivery trip and people were meant to find her, even meant to see her go in. *Rattengift* was a German operation to place the canisters of Rift Valley fever, cholera and God knew what else with great accuracy into Britain's back yard. But *Dodo* was meant to be seen and approached then and there.

Again the question, why a Marauder? Why not one of the V-weapons? Whatever the reason, Dobson was crystal clear in his head that this was what it was about. *Dancing Dodo*, the flying biological bomb.

Free. Frederick Free, whom his old comrades from Stalag Luft III could not now recognize. The linchpin. He looked at his watch and wished Hackstead would call. He stopped, wondering if anything had gone seriously wrong; if Bud Hackstead was safe. Then his mind rolled back again to the eternal question—why not a more sophisticated delivery system?

He gathered the books together and went through to the bedroom. Working in the prone position was not the best way of going about things, but if he fell asleep while studying, there was always tomorrow—after Ann's return.

Dobson had just settled himself and was reaching out to pick up the first book when the telephone rang.

"Hi, Dave, what's new?" Hackstead sounded too bright for this time in the evening. There was even the suspicion of a slur in his voice.

"I finally got you." Dobson put down his book and reached for a cigarette. "I have news. Had some when we were at Farnborough, in fact, but forgot about it. Then some more turned up, but you'd already left."

"Shoot," Hackstead said softly.

Dobson shot—the Bormann-Kaltenbrunner letter, then the Kaltenbrunner-Kaindl instruction. Both concerned *Rattengift*. There was a long silence at the other end of the line. Then:

"It figures. Anything else?"

"Just that I'm coming to certain conclusions."

"Such as?"

"Such as *Dodo* was really meant to go in, and living people were meant to find her, take out the bodies, try some salvage and get well and truly infected with the RVF and cholera..."

"And whatever else was in that circular container." Hackstead sounded grim. "That's all good thinking, Dave, and it ties in with things here. The only point that worries me is—if we're right—what in hell's name was Jerry playing at? They had rockets, flying bombs..."

"It's the only fly I can find in the lubricant."

"Christ, they were even still launching the V-1s from Heinkel 111s when we were on the banks of the Rhine."

"Just now, when I read you the Bormann, Kaltenbrunner, Kaindl letters, you said it figured, as if it tied in with your work down there. What d'you mean? You making progress?"

"In a way, but I haven't put the pieces together yet."

"Want to tell me?"

The silence was so long that Dobson thought Hackstead had been cut off. "You still there?" he asked.

"Yep. Just trying to collect my thoughts. I've seen Free again. Hate to admit it, Dave, but I'm getting vibrations now. I'm with you. I do not think our friend Free, in his little bungalow, ever went near a Boston aircraft, or Stalag Luft III at Sagan."

"A phony?"

"That's how I'm starting to see it; so I'm calling in a couple of my people and we're going to start putting the pressure on. Tomorrow afternoon."

"For Chrissake, watch him. We don't want a runaway on our hands."

Hackstead gave a short chuckle, as if Dobson was being really witty. "No way. I've got him boxed in."

"If he isn't Free, any idea who he might be?"

"An educated guess?"

"Yes, an educated guess."

"The way I reckon it is that if Free isn't Free, then he's the sole survivor from *Dodo*'s last mission; and if that's the answer then I guess he knows where the other body's buried."

"The body shaped like a biscuit tin?"

"Right."

Dobson did not like the sound of it. Bud Hackstead was at high risk if any of their conclusions were in the slightest sense accurate.

"You want me to come down?"

No pause, "Not in a thousand years, Dave. I want you there in London. I might not make it back for the arrival of Potts' gang, and I've got to have someone there I can trust. How's the lady, by the way?"

"Coming out tomorrow. Heavily plastered in the wrong sense, but cheerful and willing."

"Glad to hear it. Potts' gang, Dave..."

"What about them?"

"I want you to take care and special note of one of those guys."

"Which?"

"Dan Goldberg, the co-pilot."

"You want to tell me why?"

"Just a tiny error in my last conversation with Free. Watch out for Goldberg; and I do mean watch. You might even find out what I mean before they arrive; certainly soon after."

"No more than that?"

"Not a hint more—not on this phone anyway. You'll see what I mean."

"Regular Sherlock stuff. We still going to do the Fenwell Manor thing—the butler did it?"

"Why not?"

"If you break Free, will we still need...?"

"We need Fenwell Manor and my little scheme there more than eggs for an omelet."

"Okay, if you want to play a big denouement scene..."

"You got it."

"Call me tomorrow. Or shall I call you?"

"I'll call you. Tomorrow evening, but you've forgotten something, Dave."

"Such as?"

"Such as your source for the detail on *Overshoot*."

Trying to keep it as cool as possible, Dobson told him about former squadron leader Richard Martin Lewis. "Anything you can do about it?" he concluded.

"What? Tunnel under the wire at that place they've got near Warminster, and pick him out from among the heavies and the confessors? You jest, Dave." Another pause, in which Dobson knew Hackstead's brain was doing a series of complicated aerobatics. "Are they still keeping an eye on you?" he asked at last.

"Trotter's around."

"If anything big breaks. If I want you fast—down here..."

"Yes?"

"Throw him. Throw him good. I want us with the credit, not that bunch. Can you do it?"

"Throw Trotter? I should imagine it's possible."

"May not be necessary, but just in case."

They talked for a little longer, then Dobson went back to his books. After five minutes he knew there was a distinct possibility that he might fall asleep while still working. He dialed the operator and asked for an alarm call at ten. If he did drop off, that would give him two hours in which to get organized for Ann.

He then began to read, making occasional notes on the pad he had used to work out *Dodo*'s last possible track. As he dipped into the pile of books and magazines, things began to fall into place.

31

It must have been well after five in the morning before Dobson dropped into an unwilling exhausted sleep. By then, he had waded through reams of material—revising his former knowledge of the final, desperate V-weapon assault on England during 1944 and the early part of '45.

Originally the rocket offensive had been planned as one gigantic operation—using the flying bombs, launched from the ground and from converted Heinkel bombers; the long-range artillery (which could hit little farther than the immediate British coastline); and the great A-4s which the British later knew as the V-2s.

The work and the plan, on paper, was one which might well strike terror into the hearts of the Allied troops preparing for the D-day invasion. Certainly it would terrify the civilian population. Rockets and pilotless aircraft loaded with explosives landing among them was Jules Verne stuff—or H. G. Wells' prophecy—the land of science fiction in the 1940s.

But the huge offensive did not work out the way it was planned. Fear at first, yes; but much confusion among those who directed the new terror assault from occupied Europe—foul-ups, communications difficulties, supply problems and weapons with only limited precision.

In the early hours, Dobson went back to two vital points. First, the *Führerdirective 55* dated May 16, 1944. Second, the three letters concerning *Rattengift* and mentioning Hitler's orders for the long-range attack to begin. His interest lay in the dating. Göring's letter to Sperrle, in charge of the Third Air Force, was dated May 18, 1944. The two other letters, still reposing in his desk—from Bormann to Kaltenbrunner and Kaltenbrunner to Kaindl at the Sachsenhausen concentration camp—were dated May 18 and 19 respectively. All three letters concerning *Rattengift* had gone out as instructions within four days of Hitler's orders for the long-range attack on Britain.

He picked up the text of Hitler's Directive 55 and read, for the twentieth time, the translation. The Führer ordered the attack to use the flying bombs—launched from land and air— operations by the Third Air Force; the long-range artillery and the A-4 rockets—the V-2s.

This last was pure fantasy, for those weapons were not even ready for limited use until nearly the end of 1944. Hitler planned his offensive, a counter to the known invasion preparations, to begin in June.

The bombardment—the directive read—*will open like a thunderclap by night*... The words crossed and recrossed Dobson's tired mind. There was no mention of *Rattengift* in Hitler's orders.

Then, through the maze, came the first signs of clarity. *It will open like a thunderclap.* A thunderclap was preceded by lightning. What if the launching of the V-weapons, in the early summer of 1944, was but the follow-up to something much more sinister? The inauguration of an epidemic disease on a vast scale in England before the Allies began their invasion of Europe?

An uncontrolled confusing epidemic, or series of epidemics, attacking cattle, sheep, livestock, men, women and children, followed by the thunderclap of the V-weapons.

It was only a theory, but there, on the verge of sleep, Dobson had a whole outline skeleton of the reasons and plan for *Rattengift*. A little checking, some specialist help, possibly from Drimgollen, and he might know why *Dancing Dodo* had come in over Romney Marsh with its crew that was not its crew.

The idea was still there, fixed solid in his head, when the bedside telephone rang and the operator told him it was his alarm call—ten o'clock.

Dobson looked at his watch. There was little more he could do today but check a few facts, and maybe talk to someone like Drimgollen. Today was the day of Ann's return. He now had ninety minutes to bathe, shave, dress, tidy the flat and get to the hospital, smiling and relaxed. The nightmare which painted itself, Boschian-like, in his mind, was not to be shared by anyone as precious as Ann: and the nightmare had to be exorcised fast, if only for the selfish reason that he had found Ann.

She walked haltingly, but with a paradoxical lightness of step.

Naturally, the climb to the flat tired her a little, but she smiled with pleasure on seeing he had taken time to lay the table ready for their meal. Dobson left her, sitting comfortably with a glass of lager, while he made a dash for the curry shop.

As Dobson approached the swing doors of his building, lugging the plastic bag of food, he glimpsed a familiar black Rover, parked some fifty yards up Charlotte Street. Trotter still wasn't crowding him, but he would like a word. Richard Martin Lewis stuck in his mind.

He could heat up the meal. It would not take a minute.

Trotter sat in the passenger seat, next to the driver; a thick-jowled marker sat in the back.

Trotter wound his window down. "You okay, man?"

"A word wouldn't come amiss."

"Your girl, she's out of the hospital then."

"A word."

"Doesn't look overnimble. Hope she's going to be ..."

"Trotter."

"Okay, okay." He opened the door and they walked to the pavement.

"Christ, Dobson, what you got in that bag? Indian food? I can smell it from here. Can't stand Indian food. Give me the good old Italian any time. Minestrone, and the scaloppina di vitello alla Bolognese. Mmmm." He kissed his fingers in an Italianate gesture.

"I asked you not to crowd me."

"Am I? Have I done anything ... ?"

Dobson smiled. "No, but please keep clear. Please."

"Do my best, but you know how it is. You know I'm in schtuck with my bosses. Got to play it safe. They're worried for you—and Miss ..."

"West."

"West."

"I hear there are subsidiary problems." Dobson slipped the button on his jacket, turning so that Trotter could still see he was being obedient—wearing the shooter.

"Subsidiary's a big word."

"Richard Martin Lewis."

"Oh, him."

"I just thought a word. After all, you warned me off in the first place. Made a special trip to let me know I was associating with him."

Trotter frowned. "So I did," the smile not as broad as usual. "Your big brothers've got him. What's the problem; the trouble?"

Trotter put a large black hand against Dobson's chest, fingers splayed. There was no pressure. "I wouldn't know."

"Come on."

"Only know one thing. He was stepping out of line and ran a dangerous private life."

Dobson thought of the seedy Arthur with the grease spots on his lapels. A dangerous private life?

"Meaning?" he asked.

"Leave it alone."

"Meaning?" He put his hands over Trotter's big paw, lifting it clear. "We're both in the same business."

Trotter thought for a moment, then shrugged. "I only know one thing. Richard Martin Lewis is like a subway train on the Central Line."

"Meaning?" Dobson repeated.

Trotter neither smiled, leered nor sneered. "Meaning he travels in both directions. That's always dangerous in this business. Leaves you open to temptation."

Dobson would get no more than that. It was enough to be going on with. "Herbie Flax?" he asked.

"Three nine-mill. bullets, ruined him and the beautiful upholstery of his motor. Local CID going frantic. I gather some of our people watch from a distance; keeping clear."

"Same as with me?"

"Sort of."

"Like I said before, Claud. Please keep clear. Give me some air."

"Carry that curried muck around with you and you'll get all the air you want from me." The old smile broadened. "Don't worry."

"And don't eat too much pasta. See you." Dobson turned away. Then, over his shoulder: "See you at a comfortable distance."

"Look after the lady." Trotter raised his hand and began to walk back toward the car.

Dobson quickened his step. Lunch would be a time for relaxation. He had to put the whole thing out of his head, clear his skull—until later. Not much later, though, because time could be running out. He had no way of telling when the sand in the hourglass would dribble to the finish, or the clockwork run down.

The meal was a great success and they laughed a lot.

"You really aren't in any pain, are you?" he asked, and she shook her head, like a solemn child, still and grave for a moment.

"Don't be gentle with me, David," she said at last. "I do know; they had the sense to tell me. Once they've got the concrete off it's going to be a long haul mending the muscles and getting the arm working again. But I'll do it." Her good hand moved across the table, fingers crawling like a small insect or sea creature, a scuttle between the now empty bowls of beef biriani and vegetable curry. "I'm not going to be proud, darling, but I will do it; though I don't know if I can manage it alone. Am I being a forward hussy?"

"Already," he smiled (right at the far reaches of his mind the antiseptic smell of *Dodo*'s interior combined with the thought of what might yet come). "Arriving on my doorstep with your cases like that. Hussy."

He held her one good hand in both of his and told her that he loved her—across the smeared plates and the dishes congealing with the dregs of curry, the spice in their mouths and bodies, and the scent around them, with a hint of the lager with which they had washed down the meal.

She knew he had work to do. He tried to persuade her to leave any attempt at clearing up the dishes.

"I have one strong right arm and one operative hand. I can move about. I've got to, they said so at the hospital. You go and get on with whatever it is. If I get tired I'll curl up with one of your books." She laughed. "Curl up? Concrete buildings only curl up in earthquakes."

He really needed to talk with Drimgollen; had to get his number. Sitting, then lying, on the bed, thumbing through a thousand books would not get him the right answers. He flicked through pages, looking at drawings of the V-2 warhead, checking, rechecking, the problems the German scientists and military had experienced with it.

It did deliver its explosive charge, but the difficulties in those late years of the war were immense. Nobody today would have considered it a stable weapon.

He called Clapham for the address and telephone number of Dr. Drimgollen, currently working for the Establishment at Porton Down, then dialed. A woman said hello, repeating the number back to him. He asked for Drimgollen.

Sorry, the woman said (she had been in the bath), but her husband was away for the weekend. "He had to be away at the end of the week and he's got a conference starting in London tomorrow for two days. I can give you his hotel if it's urgent."

"I'd be grateful."

Drimgollen was at the Russell. Dobson called him there and arranged to meet for tea. He *had* to find out more about delivery systems.

32

The grand lounge of the Russell Hotel is grand. There is no other suitable word. Accept no substitutes.

Drimgollen sat alone, on a high-backed chair with a great tea tray on the small table in front of him. He rose, greeting Dobson with a certain amount of charm, though the cutting edge of his personality was still well honed.

A waiter appeared, stealthily, as if his job demanded that he should, like a Victorian child, be seen as little as possible and only heard when absolutely necessary.

Another tray of tea arrived, almost as quickly and with the same circumspection as the waiter.

"So, you want to talk about delivery systems in bacteriological warfare?" Drimgollen played host, pouring from the large silver pot, passing the triangular sandwiches. "With an eye cocked in the direction of that bloody Marauder, I suppose?"

"Yes."

"Getting to the bottom of it?"

"Getting warm, I think."

"Well, you know what I think. Told you already. That airplane was a delivery system."

"We had no long-range rockets, unlike the enemy, at that time."

"Then you still believe it was a covert Yank job?"

"Unsophisticated."

"Most reasonable and logical answer. You come up with anything better?"

"What if I told you that aircraft was deliberately pulled out of an operational squadron and is supposed to have been used on a mad, harebrained clandestine in Belgium from which it failed to return?"

"I'd say it proved my point."

"And what if the bodies we pulled out are not the bodies of the people which their dog tags identify them as?"

"Again, I would think it supports my theory."

"And if one of them, still alive and living in England, turns out not to be the person he says he is?"

"What's your theory?"

"I think that aircraft went down on the Belgian operation and was then used by an SS clandestine outfit. There's other evidence. I believe those two loads of bugs were meant for our cattle and our people. The only thing that worries me is that, with the delivery systems they had available, why use a captured American aircraft? Tell me about delivery systems today, Dr. Drimgollen."

He told Dobson about ultrasonic dissemination—of rocket motors with deadly agents injected into the fuel to form supersonic invisible clouds of death from great altitudes; of bombs and shells and Honest John, Little John and Sergeant missile systems which had stockpiles of interchangeable warheads explosive or biological; of the Bigeye and Weteye bombs with their televisual guidance controls so that even if a pilot misjudged his aim, the bomb, loaded with its poison, would still hit the target, and by then the attacking aircraft would be miles away.

He continued to talk of things like the self-contained units, external tanks that had been fitted on F-100, F-105s and F-45 jets, in Vietnam, for defoliant spraying and, he hinted, worse; of the dry bacteriological agents being better than liquid because you could fit more of the foul stuff into warheads.

"As early as 1960 the Americans reckoned they could wipe out 30 per cent of the population of the United States with ten jet aircraft," he said. "Then there were the Bolt rockets, built for high explosive but also designed to take two hundred gallons of GB."

"GB?"

"Sarin. Odorless, colorless gas that kills in minutes,

paralyzing the nervous system. The United States arsenals have been holding supplies of sarin since the late forties. But all this is old-fashioned. God knows what they can do now." He sipped his tea and bit into a sandwich. "I'll tell you one thing, the old aerosol system's still in. Different, but there for overt and covert delivery—bloody great clouds of the stuff ..."

"Like the Nazis planned to do from boats along the Channel?"

"The idea's the same. The method more scientifically viable."

"How precise? How accurate has a delivery system got to be?"

"Depends on what you're posting. There are complexities in biological warfare that don't begin until you have the goods—very difficult meteorological and biochemical problems, if you want the germs to arrive in a set location at a definite time."

"This is my problem. If it was a German operation, why not just drop the stuff from Luftwaffe aircraft and get the hell out?"

"High risk of inaccuracy."

"Why not use the rockets—the doodlebugs or the V-2s?"

Drimgollen laughed. "They may have struck a bit of terror into people, but only someone quite mad would have allowed those things to be used with biochemical warheads. Particularly if they demanded some reasonable accuracy. No scientist worth his salt would sanction the military use of biological agents in the V-weapons; and make no mistake, the German scientists were not mad professors. Anyway, it's academic whether they used a German aircraft or a captured American one. The thing went wrong. But for my money, if they were mounting a bio delivery, they were doing it the right way—for the technology of the time. If they wanted accuracy, they needed men to ensure it. What they got was—if it was German-orientated—pilot error, or malfunction; if it was Allied-orientated, they probably had an abort and then silence. Until now."

"But you would honestly say that even desperate military scientists would not risk the V-weapons as delivery systems?"

"Frightening little jiggers at the time, as I've said. But unstable: Guy Fawkes, Fourth of July stuff. They'd have had to be really desperate not to have chosen some other means."

Ann was reading when he got back. "You've had a million telephone calls," she told him.

"Bud Hackstead?"

"No, that little German, the one who came with the documents, or whatever they were. Kursbuch." She put the book down, dropping it on the floor.

"What did he want?"

"Said he was checking. Couldn't get Colonel Hackstead—he's being a shade elusive, isn't he, Hackstead?"

"Kursbuch checking in from Koblenz?"

"From the Regent Palace. He says it would be nice if you'd ring him back."

"He's got more?"

"Documents? I don't know. He didn't say."

Dobson did not care about documents now. There were other facts which Peter Kursbuch—old Timetable—might have locked away. Things Peter Kursbuch may possibly wish to forget.

"Other calls?" he asked.

"One. Real smoothie. Journalist called Charles, something or other. He's after Hackstead. You're definitely playing second fiddle on this, Dave." She winked. "Assert yourself. What's for supper?"

"Canned stuff. I'll get it, don't worry. Charles? Did he leave a message?"

"No, but he left a number. Wants you to call him."

She had written the number on the message pad by the main telephone: a careful, rounded hand, a girls' grammar school hand.

"I'll get food in a minute, sweet." He crossed to the sofa and kissed her, a gentle loving pressing of the lips on her forehead. "Got to make the calls first."

Charles had news. The kind of news Dobson could have done without. Bud Hackstead had checked out of the County and was not back in London—nobody could find him. The paper was going ahead with the *Dodo* story straightaway, on Tuesday, and the first feature would cover a visit to the crash site in Kent tomorrow evening.

Dobson was shaking when he put down the receiver.

"Darling, what's wrong?" Ann hoisted herself from the sofa.

Hackstead missing put him, at least technically, in charge. His brain would not function. Guidance systems gone. Should he go down the street, run to Claud Trotter and tell him? Or call the pompous puffing Sugden?

His duty was to call Sugden. Just when he had most of it there, the jigsaw almost complete in his head. Sugden first.

As his hand reached out toward the phone it started ringing again. He looked at it blankly, feeling Ann's right arm around his shoulders.

"You okay, David? David?"

"Yes, I'm fine. I'm sorry. Problems."

He picked up the telephone and spoke his name, aware of the quaver in his voice.

"Hi, Dave, I've been trying to get you. Your line was engaged just now." Hackstead through the receiver straight into Dobson's ear.

"Thank Christ."

"Dave?"

"Where've you been, Bud? I've just gone through a nasty section of hell."

"You shoot any red lights on the way?"

"Several. We've got problems. People've been looking for you. You went missing, Bud. I only just heard; I was going to call my boss."

"What's wrong?" Grit in his voice, the flip fast-talking toughness transformed to a different hardness. Hackstead the professional.

"Where are you? Give me a number, a location, in case the line goes, or we get cut off. Where are you?"

He thought they had actually been cut off, for the silence seemed to drift on toward eternity.

"I guess I should've called in." The gravel and iron still there, but, more relaxed, the familiar Hackstead. "Just didn't want to worry you, what with Ann coming out of the hospital and all. Called you to let you know I'm at Fenwell Manor."

"Staying there?"

"Yes. My friends left yesterday. Most opportune as it turned out. I'll give you the number."

Dobson copied the number, dialing code, everything, and then read it back.

"Check," said Hackstead.

"Opportune, you said."

"Very. Our dear undead Mr. Free was a naughty boy and tried to run. Soon after we spoke last evening as it happened."

"*Tried* to run?"

"I told you I had him boxed in. I've got a couple of my people down here with me. We have Mr. Free with us, in what you might call safekeeping."

"What you mean is you've got a pair of CIA confessors going over him with the hot irons."

"Come on, Dave. It's very civilized nowadays. We all do it—maybe not personally, but it's part of the course. Always has been."

Dobson shivered. He considered Arthur—Richard Martin Lewis—in the house near Warminster.

As though echoing his thoughts, Hackstead said, "Your own people have a friend in their care at this moment. You told me about that."

"Is Free our man?"

"I haven't got it in writing yet, nor all the details, but I'd stake a year's pay on it—in real money: in dollars. We'll have it all, the whole shebang, before you get down here with Potts and the rest of the crew."

"I wouldn't put money on that, Bud. One of the people trying to get to you is Charles."

"The *Daily Express* Charles?"

"The same."

"Why?" Curt, gritty again.

Dobson told him. All the details, the rearrangement of the schedule.

"Holy Christ." Hackstead seemed to be spitting into the telephone. "Tomorrow night?"

"At the site late afternoon. Charles wants instructions. Are we in a position to do the denouement scene, the Agatha Christie last act?"

"If we work on Free all night maybe. This is going to be cut very fine. I've got most of it in my head, but I want the last pieces of the jigsaw ..."

"I think I've got some of them. I've not been wasting time, Bud."

"Well, I've got a lot more. Free could be—will be—a little more co-operative."

"Shall I tell you ... ?"

"What you know? Save it. Just do as you're told, Dave, and we'll have them, and whatever foulness there is left in this business. Can you get to Charles?"

"Easy."

"Okay. Set a schedule with him. Late afternoon at the site, you said?"

"Yes."

"Okay. Get the times as exact as you can make them. Tell Charles he can have one camera with the party coming to Fenwell. One camera, the whole aircrew, wives, sweethearts, plus Charles himself. Fix the time and then let me know."

"What if there's a delay at Heathrow? It happens."

"You let me know after the arrival, because I want to talk with you when you've met that crew—Daniel Goldberg in particular."

"You already told me to watch Goldberg."

"Take heed then. Make him your first objective. Just talk with him and you'll know what I mean. I'm saying no more, but ten minutes' talk with Goldberg and I think—I'm positive—you'll be beating track records to get to a phone and call me with information."

"No more clues?"

"You'll see, Dave—elementary, my dear Dobson—I want you to get to Goldberg cold, without any preconceived ideas."

"Right, I set an exact time for the Fenwell Manor arrival, and I talk with Dan Goldberg, then I speak with you."

"Make Charles understand the timing's got to be right. If it is, then he'll collar the biggest story his paper's had since Moses parted the Red Sea, and make damn certain that he knows they've all got to be there—including Goldberg."

"I'll bring Goldberg personally, if you assure me he's the missing link."

"No, Dave. No, you won't bring Goldberg, because you'll be here already. Don't forget you're playing the star role—Hercule Poirot—and I've got to coach you, as well as listen to what you've found under the stones. I want you here a good hour before the crew and the journalists arrive: and I mean a *good* hour."

"I'll be there."

"You'll be there without Trotter in tow as well. I've told you that once already. Now can you do that?"

"I'll fix Claud Trotter. Bud, you have no worries there. I know just how to fix him."

"As long as you do. I'm not sharing this with his crowd. *Dancing Dodo* is our pigeon. We're going to kill it."

"Forget Trotter, he can be fixed. I promise."

Dobson strained his ear. There was noise in the background, like someone shouting at Hackstead.

"What's the matter? Bud, you okay?"

Silence.

"Bud?"

Another muffled shout, then heavy breathing. "Sorry, Dave, we had a little problem with dead Mr. Free. It's over now. I'd better get back to him." He was breathing very heavily, as though still involved in physical exertion. "No other messages?"

"Peter Kursbuch's back from Koblenz."

"When?"

"Tonight, I think. I only just got the message."

"He pull anything else from the files?"

"I don't know. Haven't spoken to him."

"Okay, leave him to me. Where can I get him?"

"Regent Palace Hotel."

"I'll call him now; check him out. You get an early night, Dave. You're going to get a heavy day tomorrow." Hackstead's breathing appeared to have become normal again.

Ann had gone back to the sofa.

"Feel like a day out tomorrow?" he asked her.

"Where?"

Dobson explained as much as was necessary.

"You're on," she said. "If you have to wheel me, you're on. What about food, can I . . . ?"

"No, you can't. I'll do it as soon as I've set things up with our man from the *Express*. That should give Bud Hackstead time to talk with Kursbuch. Once he's off the line I want a word with that tough little ex-SS man myself. One small piece of brain-picking, then how about tinned soup, tinned ham, pickles and tinned Russian salad?"

"I didn't realize you were a gourmet," she said.

33

After telephoning Charles, Dobson had hesitated, hand hovering over the telephone. He felt stronger now that he knew Hackstead was safe and getting on with the job.

Yet he had to know more; and know quickly. At this time on a Sunday night there was only one person he could possibly approach. Peter Kursbuch, old Timetable.

He began to dial and then thought, better still, go round there and surprise him.

At the Regent Palace, Dobson pushed through the crowd, up to the reception desk. A tired, uniformed blonde with an Irish accent dragged herself away from a bald American who was trying to make a date.

"You have a Mr. Peter Kursbuch staying here," he said, suddenly realizing that Kursbuch might not be registered under his own name.

"You'll have to ask the porter. Over there," indicating the island of imitation marble and real plastic in the center of the foyer. It was under siege and understaffed.

Dobson did not feel like arguing. "His room, honey," one hand reaching into his inside pocket, fingers finding the little plastic wallet, drawing it out and flashing it under her nose. His I3

(Air) ID—photograph and all: though the photograph looked like it had come from a crime lab—directly after death. "You'll have his room number here, I'm sure. We would like to keep this as quiet as possible. You wouldn't want lots of uniformed men in helmets running around the hotel and frightening the guests, would you? I can be very soft. On the other hand, I can be a real bastard." He reflected he had probably been watching too much television during the slack period; before *Dodo*.

The Irish girl must also have been an addict of "Special Branch," "Kojak," "The Sweeney" and all the other cops and robbers soap operas.

"Holy Mother of God," she muttered, nodding, turning away to check through the big accounts ledger.

Dobson felt pleased with himself. If Trotter had one of his goons around, he would be slightly confused by now.

The girl came back. "He's in 502, sur. There won't be . . . ?"

"Is there a house phone?"

She nodded, pointing toward the end of the desk. Miraculously the phone was not in use.

Kursbuch answered immediately. He sounded sleepy grunting "Yes" in a voice suggesting he was irritable.

"Porter, sir. Just checking you're in. I have a special messenger here with a registered package. Can he bring it up?"

"What's he look like?" Not suspicious, just careful, Dobson thought.

"Just an ordinary government messenger. One moment . . ." He covered the mouthpiece and counted to twelve. "From the American Embassy, sir. Can I send him up? You have to sign for the package."

"Okay, but tell him to make it fast, I'm just going to have a bath."

"Less than a couple of minutes, sir."

At the door of 502, he slipped the button on his jacket and checked that he could unholster the revolver if necessary. He expected no trouble, but, like old Timetable himself, he was getting used to taking great care. He tapped at the door and waited.

It opened only a fraction—less than an inch—and from inside Kursbuch said, "Pass it through with the pad. I'll sign and push it back to you. I am naked."

Dobson put one hand on the revolver butt and hit the door with his left shoulder.

Kursbuch reeled back into the tiny passageway leading to the bedroom; Dobson got a glimpse of the open door to the bathroom. The bath taps were running.

Kursbuch *was* naked: a bizarre sight, for the craggy, tanned face and the big hands, so impressive when you saw him clothed, now looked out of place attached to the white, flabby body. Only the triceps and thigh muscles looked hard. The rest had gone over the hill, an unco-ordinated sprawl of fat and flab.

"I'm sorry," stuttered Dobson. "I thought you were being tricky."

"What?...What are you doing?...With my nakedness...You..." He did not finish the sentence. Dobson came forward and put out his hand to help the man up.

Kursbuch waved him away, rolled over and was on his feet very fast. Dobson remembered his stealth and way of moving. The flabby white flesh had deceived him, and Kursbuch was angry, angry enough to take violent action.

Dobson drew the revolver, opened his legs and assumed the double-hand grip as the German came toward him, rage red-streaked against the weathered granite on his face.

Kursbuch had no wish to leave the world yet. The revolver stopped him—not quite in his tracks, for he was moving with speed. Dobson, still in the small passageway, kept the barrel trained on Timetable's stomach as the German put out his hands, slamming them into the walls and coming to a halt at the bedroom end of the passage.

"You are Dobson?" he said in surprise.

"Yes. We work for the same firm. I'm sorry, I only wanted a private chat. I thought you were being overcautious."

"I was just going to have a bath." He frowned, chest heaving, belly loose. "You rang me from downstairs?"

Dobson nodded.

Kursbuch smiled. "It was very good. You had me fooled. I cover myself, yes?"

"Yes."

He waited to reholster the revolver until Kursbuch had pulled on a pair of jeans. He tugged at the strap of his belt to pull in the sagging gut, then slipped a roll-neck sweater over his head.

"We talk now?"

"If you don't mind." Dobson offered him a cigarette and sat on the end of the bed while Kursbuch dropped easily into the one armchair provided by the management. He had only just settled when he remembered the bathroom and the running taps.

There was the same careful, stealthy walk Dobson had first noticed in the Charlotte Street flat.

He followed the German across the room, leaning against the bathroom door, watching as Kursbuch bent to turn off the bath taps. He straightened, and caught sight of Dobson, opaque in the steamy mirror.

"You don't trust me? No?"

"I am trying to follow your example. Being careful." He let Kursbuch pass through the door and went after him back into the bedroom, sitting on the edge of the bed only when the German was resettled in the chair.

"I have talked to Bud—to Colonel Hackstead. There is nothing," Kursbuch said. Then a glint of understanding came into the alert eyes. "Does Bud not trust me any more? I swear there's nothing else in Koblenz on *Rattengift*."

"I believe you."

"Maybe. But Bud? Bud was always a disbelieving sonofabitch."

"Bud didn't send me. Call him and ask if you like."

Kursbuch shrugged. "And where would I telephone him? He calls me. He is not in London. I ask him where I can get him and he says, 'In Hell.' Is something wrong with him? He usually makes a fallback number or something. This time all he says is that he is in hell. Strange."

"He's under pressure. I simply want to ask you a few questions which you might find distasteful."

"I find a lot of life distasteful, my friend. I am used to it."

"You couldn't get used to it in the forties. You found it too distasteful."

"Meaning?"

"Meaning, Peter, that I think you are a brave and honest man. But, like most men, you perform feats of mental dishonesty by trying to forget some things; to cancel them out by acts which you find more moral."

"A man can expunge his sins."

"Yes, but that doesn't give him the right to forget them."

"Tell me, Dobson my friend, what you want?"

"A guess. I could be wrong. If so then I'll ask no more. If I am right, you can still deny it and I'll still go."

"Guess? Deny?"

"When we met in my flat, you told me, quite proudly I

thought, that you were a member of the SS and that you refused to accept a posting to Auschwitz."

"True."

"And they sent you to the Russian front."

"Also true."

"What you really mean, Peter, is that you were transferred at your own request. That you were moved from one branch of the SS to another."

"I can't deny that."

"You were moved from concentration camp administration to the Waffen SS."

The silence lasted only a few seconds, then Kursbuch nodded. "Yes," he said simply. "At my own request. I had seen enough. Done enough. They were understanding. They simply sent me off to get killed. I was with the WVHA—you understand? The camp administration. I went to the Waffen SS—to the fighting."

"You'd had enough of the death camps? Enough of the slaughter of women and children, old men?"

He nodded again, not looking at Dobson.

"Peter, it's a shot in the dark. I need to know the kind of things that went on in those camps."

"Read about it. It's in the books."

"Not all of it, and I haven't got the time. Too much evidence was destroyed. Too many people, like yourself, are afraid to tell some things. Peter, where did you serve before you refused the posting to Auschwitz?"

"I served at several places. Nameless things..."

"Don't distress yourself. I told you it was a guess; a hope that you could open some locked doors. Where did you serve?"

"Bud Hackstead knows, so why not you? Natzweiler-Struthof; then Birkenau—the Auschwitz satellite camp: that's why I wouldn't go back to Auschwitz. Last of all Sachsenhausen."

Dobson could hardly believe it. More than he had hoped for.

"What went on?"

"For Christ's sake, you know what went on. The story's been told—the gas chambers, the experiments..."

"The experiments. You saw..."

"My work. I was in the medical sections at all three camps."

"What went on?"

"You know it all. Just leave it alone."

"There are things missing in the records. You might just be able ..."

"I want to forget."

"Six million Jews and God knows how many more—Russians, Poles, Slavs ..."

"Okay," belligerent. "Okay, you haven't got time to read the books—sterilization for one, carried out unhygienically and without anesthetics; the altitude tests, men and women put under pressure until their brains burst; the gas tests; the biological tests. They would take people—children—and inject mustard gas into their arms. They took days to die, in great pain."

"Epidemic diseases?"

"Yes, of course epidemic diseases."

"The records don't show much on epidemic diseases."

For the first time since Dobson had begun the questioning, Kursbuch relaxed. He even smiled. "You said it yourself. There's a lot not mentioned. There was much work done on epidemic diseases."

"Peter, truly I did not know that you were ... that you had to do work in the medical research sections. I was pretty sure you had worked in the camps. It's true what I said, I merely wanted to talk with someone who might know of what went on; the things not in the books. I don't think there's much about the epidemics in the books."

"At Birkenau the epidemics were always getting out of control. They had many Russians there. Always the epidemics were spreading. We had special inoculations; shots to make us immune."

"And at Sachsenhausen?"

"More careful there. I think they were more dangerous—the diseases. There was a special wing—right up at the top—at the top of the triangle where they kept the Group One prisoners. The cemetery was straight ahead and the crematorium on the left-hand side. The wing was kept near to the crematorium so that bodies could be disposed of with speed. I think they did awful experiments with epidemic diseases there."

It was pure luck. He had gone to see Kursbuch hoping for a hint. Given time he would probably have probed it from the books, dossiers, files. Now he had it from one with personal experience.

He thought of the document—Kaltenbrunner to Anton Kaindl, Kommandant of Sachsenhausen. *You will proceed with my instructions regarding the chosen prisoners. The medical staff will, of course, accompany the prisoners and deal with the last things at the airfield designated.*

The chosen prisoners? The bodies with ID tags in the names of Potts, Goldberg, Wilcox Pride, Flax, Sailby, Free. Chosen for the epidemics they carried? The epidemics manufactured in that wing near the crematorium at Sachsenhausen. Did the other stuff—the RVF and cholera—get packed, under pressure, into the aerosols at Sachsenhausen also? Whatever was in the circular container—did that emanate from the same source?

Too dangerous to use the rockets in case of a breakup over occupied Europe. An aircraft, under cover of Allied type and markings, aimed with an epidemic of death, possibly at the heart, or at least the outskirts, of London. Kursbuch looked an old man when Dobson left.

In the dark, back in Charlotte Street, he salved his wounds and pushed away the vision of the apocalypse, with Ann, in spite of the plaster cast—just as she wanted. But he felt unclean nevertheless. In the morning he spent more time than usual scrubbing his body.

Before they left for the airport—Ann excited at the prospect of the day and a mystery solved (she had no hint of the horror)—Dobson phoned Sugden.

"I think you should speak to the groupie. He's back." Sugden was on edge.

"I haven't time. I'm in the field. Remember? I'll say this once, Sugden, and it comes with Colonel Hackstead's blessing." He gave his instructions simply, almost in words of one syllable.

"I'll do my best," said Sugden when he had finished.

"Not good enough." Dobson slammed down the telephone and prayed.

34

They announced the arrival of Flight BE-005 on the screens and the loudspeaker system.

"They're here." Dobson smiled at Ann. "Better have a word with our smooth Charles."

He squeezed her hand and went over to where Charles was standing with the photographer. A uniformed chauffeur had joined them carrying a board on which was written COLONEL POTTS AND PARTY.

"On time then." Dobson always felt vulnerable when he talked with Charles. The journalist made him too aware of his lack of sophistication.

"Bet they're a damn half hour getting through customs and that lot."

"I think Bud Hackstead's put the hurry on it." He did not think, he knew. He had checked and done it himself in Bud Hackstead's name. "If we run to time, can I give Bud a zero hour for Fenwell Manor?"

Charles ran a hand lightly over his hair. "I'll have them there no later than eight-thirty, that suit you?"

"I'll check with you before I leave the Hilton. We *are* having drinks at the Hilton?"

"Yes." Charles sounded weary. "Yes, there'll be drinks at the Hilton."

"Are you the party waiting for Captain Potts and his crew—I mean Colonel Potts?" A soft American voice came from behind them.

Dobson turned. The man asking was tall, thickening around the middle, but not yet paunchy. He still had a good head of hair, distinguished gray flecks among the dark thick neat thatch. His face was tanned, eyes clear and nose a little too large for the face. Dobson would have put him in his mid-fifties, maybe a trifle younger.

"Yes," said Charles, disenchanted. Probably taking him for an American journalist.

"Great," said the newcomer, holding out his hand. "My name's Goldberg. Daniel Goldberg. I'm one of the crew."

"Where'd you spring from?" Charles looked around, as though expecting the rest of the party to appear. "Your aircraft's only just landed."

Goldberg laughed. A really humorous laugh, infectious even. "Hell, no. I thought the message had been passed on. I've been over for almost three weeks now. Bill Potts knows I'm meeting everyone here, and I spoke to another old friend. I thought he'd be here but I can't see him around. Bud Hackstead."

"You'll see Bud later." Dobson spoke automatically, not really certain that it was his own voice. Hackstead had told him that he would know within ten minutes' conversation why Goldberg figured in the situation. He knew in a matter of twenty seconds. Daniel Goldberg, co-pilot of *Dancing Dodo*, had been in the country during the last, hectic and dangerous days of the investigation.

"Here on business?" Dobson still spoke like a robot.

"Bit of business." Goldberg reached inside his coat pocket, extracting a leather cigar case. "Care for one of these?"

Charles, who was now looking around frantically, expecting the imminent arrival of Potts and the remaining members of *Dodo*'s crew, declined. ("I'll be with you in a moment, Mr. Goldberg, nice to see you, but I want you all together." He introduced himself and made it plain that he was in control on behalf of the newspaper.)

Goldberg did not even ask who Dobson was.

"Business?" asked Dobson again.

Goldberg pierced his cigar and lit it. "Bit of business; bit of pleasure. Spent some time along your south coast. You know us

Americans, the eternal tourists. I didn't get to see nearly enough when I was over during the war. Been making up for lost time ever since."

"You come over often?"

"Once a year—two years sometimes. Been over five times in the past six years anyhow. Hey, where's old Potts got to?" The cigar smoke wreathed around his head. "You know there's so much to see in this country, even though it's changed out of all recognition since the war. I'd never seen Canterbury Cathedral or Dover Castle till this trip."

Dobson could not take his eyes from the American's face. No wonder Hackstead wanted him watched; no surprise that he had to have Goldberg down at Fenwell Manor. Dobson wondered if it was Goldberg or Free who had crushed Ann's shoulder, and which one of them had dented the side of his face; whether it was Goldberg who had set up his old buddie, Herbie Flax, and pumped three nine-millimeter bullets into him.

More, he wondered whether they both knew where the real body was buried—the canister—and how lethal it was.

"Potts—Skipper—Bill Potts," Goldberg was shouting. A tall, very military figure came through the gates, a short dark woman with dyed hair and an overabundance of jewelry clinging to his arm. Though thirty-three years had passed, even Dobson could recognize him as the man who smiled from the photograph of *Dancing Dodo* and her crew, the man with his officer's cap, tilted jauntily on his head.

"Back in a minute," he muttered to Charles. "No later than eight-thirty, can I tell Hackstead that for sure?"

"Right, okay. Don't go off without meeting them, though."

"Back in a moment." He paused by Ann, who sat, a smile of half-amusement on her face, her body leaning at an awkward angle.

"Is that Captain Potts?" she asked.

"Colonel now."

"He's a dish, but who's the woman?"

"His wife, sweetheart."

"Christ, she looks like a barmaid."

Dobson flicked his smile on and off. "She was."

On his way to the phone booths he passed close to Trotter, who was picking up paperbacks and putting them down. Dobson leaned forward from behind and picked up a copy of Evelyn Waugh's *Black Mischief*.

"Buy it, read it and digest it. A laugh a line," thrusting it into

Trotter's hand. "And please, Claud, give me air. Don't stick like a leech, we'll have it sorted by tonight."

Hackstead answered the telephone as though he had been poised over it. "They're here?" he asked.

"The lot, but I've only met one of them."

"Let me guess?"

"You did already. How Goldberg, Bud? How him? Free I can understand, being in Germany, at Stalag Luft III. I could understand Sharp or Klein, they were POWs, they could've been got at. But Dan Goldberg was with Potts to the end."

"In the fullness of time," Hackstead intoned. "And talking of the fullness of time, when're they due down here?"

"Eight-thirty. Any change I'll call you."

"Good. I'll expect you around seven-fifteen, seven-thirty, then."

"It's fixed. Trotter'll be lost as well."

"Glad to hear it."

"How's it going with Free?"

"He'll be ready, willing and able by the time everyone gets here. Now go see them off, Dave. Look forward to tonight."

Dobson turned away from the telephone booth. Trotter was walking from the bookstall, the copy of *Black Mischief* tucked under his arm.

"Good choice," Dobson grinned.

"If you say so."

"I asked you not to crowd me, Trotter. Your presence here is not requested."

"Doing a job. Just doing a job."

"Well, go do it somewhere else. I presume you have an itinerary?"

"Of this caper? With the boys from the wild blue yonder?"

"Uh-huh."

"Sort of."

"Well, if you promise me not to stay too close, I'll give you my personal itinerary."

"Be obliged, boss." Trotter's eyes did not smile and the mocking look deep within them held little humor.

"That lot," Dobson inclined his head toward the former crew of *Dancing Dodo*, "will be riding in big limousines to the Hilton Hotel, where they will check in and be immediately entertained to drinks. Miss West and myself will be going there by cab. We shall be leaving around one-thirty to lunch at a well-known, and very good, Indian restaurant in Rupert Street.

After that we shall join our American cousins again and go with them on their little outing. Just thought I'd save you the sweat of wondering who was doing what to whom and when."

"Much obliged."

"I am a man of honor," lied Dobson, pushing Trotter lightly on the shoulder with the ball of his right palm. "See you at a great distance, Trotter, a distance of many miles, otherwise I shall personally arrange for you to be back pounding the beat, in uniform and preferably in Notting Hill."

He turned and walked toward the crooked figure of Ann, who watched the cavortings of *Dancing Dodo*'s former crew with a look of complete disbelief.

35

The room they had hired for the reception, at the Hilton Hotel, looked out across Park Lane and Hyde Park, the grass browning through lack of rain, but the park looking its mid-summer best.

The whole of the far wall was covered by a huge blowup of *Dodo*'s crew standing in front of the aircraft's nose (the picture used widely by the press when the fragmented machine had been pulled from the marsh).

There was a well-stocked bar, behind which hung a large color replica of the top-hatted, strutting *Dodo* cartoon figure, the emblem of these men who now circulated among the few chosen guests, mostly *Express* executives, the journalists from Features who would be working on the series, some senior people from the U.S. Embassy, a sprinkling of RAF top brass, and some faces he knew from photographs, men who had proved themselves.

There was background music: Glenn Miller and his orchestra; the real thing, the original recordings. The forties were being piped back into the present, through the work of one phenomenally successful popular musician who, with his distinctive style, captured that whole era in a blast of brass.

Dorothy Claire and the Modernaires sang "Stairway to the Stars," Tex Beneke and the Modernaires boarded the "Chattanooga Choo-Choo," Ray Eberle sang of his "Serenade in Blue," and the whole of the orchestra came in on time with Miller's first telephone number—"Pensylvania Six-Five Oh-Oh-Oh."

Waiters moved among the guests with trays of champagne.

"It's years since I've had champagne," Ann said.

"Make the most of it," Dobson spoke low; "we're not staying long."

The music was changing to a new number, the soft rhythm building and then reaching out into solid brass blare, the clarinet, then the trumpet solo, piano, brass again and a dialogue between trombone and clarinet. Dobson, who knew his forties music, paused, then recognized it. "String of Pearls." He looked across the room toward the tall figure, ramrod-backed, gray, yet with a young smile and eyes which had remained clear, seen death in the skies and reached up again and again into what had been his only real element. Bill Potts did not look his fifty-eight years. Perhaps it was the mark of a good aviator?

Thirty-three years ago, Glenn Miller had been playing "String of Pearls" on the radio while Potts and his crew climbed out of their flight jackets and gear after a routine flight test. Potts had told that to Hackstead.

Wilcox Pride had joined Potts and Goldberg, who had a fair number of people around them including Wilson Sharp. Sharp was one of those Dobson knew least about. Sharp, who had left the *Dodo* crew and sat out the last part of the war in the South Compound at Sagan. He was pressing himself through to Bill Potts, trying to say something. Finally he caught his former captain's attention.

Dobson turned to Ann, still standing next to him, her good hand resting lightly on his arm, the fingers curled around a second glass of champagne.

"You okay?" he asked.

She nodded. "Another of these and I really won't feel a thing."

"We'll be making our move in a minute or two." His watch showed one-forty and he prayed Terry Makepiece was in place as he had directed Sugden. The next phase would be crucial.

Potts was nodding to Sharp and trying to get the rest of his old crew to stay quiet while he said something. He turned and spoke to Charles, who hovered near the center of things. Sheep dog-sleek Charles.

They began calling for quiet down at the far end of the room.

"Colonel Potts wants to say a few words," Charles' voice,

rose, shouting above the babble. "Can someone turn the music off?" Glenn Miller faded and disappeared, just as he had vanished somewhere between Twinwood and Paris, a passenger in a light aircraft. December 1944. Requiescat in pace.

Potts had a crisp voice, the voice of a man used to giving orders, making quick and accurate decisions. There was nothing lethargic about Colonel Potts.

"I just want to thank you all for being here." He spoke without any depth of feeling, the complete senior officer. "And I want to say thank you from all of us for providing this unique opportunity to come home as a group. I mean that, because England was home to us for a while. I think all my old crew would agree with me." He gave a shy smile and looked, in turn, at the men lined up around him. They each gave a brief nod.

"There are two of the original crew of old *Dancing Dodo* who will not be making this pilgrimage with us. One, I'm afraid," a shy grin, "is otherwise engaged in government duties."

There were chuckles from the few present who knew about Klein.

"The last member of our team, as I think most of you are aware, has gone—in tragic circumstances—only a few days ago."

He paused, not emotion but more of a silent mark of respect. "We'll miss him. But—and I'm not getting maudlin—I guess a lot of us have been living on borrowed time for a long while now."

Dobson's eyes did not leave Goldberg's face. Goldberg? How had Potts described him to Hackstead? Dark and serious? Goldberg was dark all right. Goldberg and Free both.

Potts was still speaking. "...but while you've been the prime movers in this reunion and visit, there is one thing that has really brought us back—our old ship, *Dancing Dodo*. This may seem a bit mushy to some of you. Those of us here did not fly in *Dodo* for long. I think we only logged some twenty missions, but she was a special machine. She was different. Those of you who are, or have been, fliers will know what I mean. We were kids then." He looked around the faces of his crew, taking each one individually. "From what my eyes tell me, we're not kids any more. But those kids we were then had a kind of ritual, a talisman of words, a..." he faltered, "a sort of liturgy—litany. It applies today of all days, as much as it did every time we came back from a trip in *Dancing Dodo*. I ask the crew to raise their glasses and see if they can remember, as clearly as I can, what we used to do every time we touched down in *Dodo*."

He turned to face the bar, looking directly toward the

replica of the cartoon *Dodo*, the dancing extinct bird with hat and cane, legs set as if about to go into an Astaire routine.

Colonel William E. Potts, transformed for a moment into young Captain Potts, lifted his glass toward the painting of the insignia.

"*Dodo* brought you back," he intoned.

The other four voices—Goldberg, Sailby, Pride and Sharp joined in, loud and very clear.

"Honor to the mighty *Dodo*."

They held their glasses for a second and then tipped back the champagne as though it was water.

There was some shuffling. Beryl Potts, Dobson noticed, was getting emotional, and Edward Sailby's wife appeared to be forgiving him all his misdemeanors—past, present and to come. A few of the Royal Air Force and Embassy people looked embarrassed.

"I think it's time for our exit." Dobson put his hand on Ann's.

She said nothing, just the smallest nod of understanding.

"Tired?"

"It's not easy. Standing for a long time's not easy."

"You think you can make it as far as Curzon Street?"

"Lord, yes. If you can put up with my go-slow."

"Slower the better. You just do exactly what I tell you."

"Every time."

"Get your things together. I want a quick word with cheerful Charles."

He weaved his way through the small groups, tracking in on Charles, who still hung around Potts and the crew.

"A word," he said, leaning over Charles' shoulder.

The journalist turned his head. "In a moment. I'm a bit tied up."

"Now. This minute; or you'll never work in the Street again. I know I'm not Hackstead, but the word I want is on his behalf."

Charles made a petulant noise and moved to one side. Dobson spoke softly; not that it mattered, for the crew, their wives and those around them were all talking at the tops of their voices.

"Eight-thirty sharp. Fenwell Manor," said Dobson.

"We've been through all that. I told you. We've plenty of time, as long as they don't go wandering off."

"Bud's going to be very unpleasant, even to old friends, if any of them wander off."

"Okay, then let me get on with it."

"There's one in particular who mustn't go missing."

"Hey, Charles," called Potts over the noise. "Charles?"

"One second, sir," the journalist shouted back. "Which one?" he asked, dropping his voice again.

"Daniel Goldberg. We're really looking forward to seeing him down at Fenwell, and you're carrying the can if he doesn't make it."

Charles pulled at his jacket lapel nervously. "I'll get them all down, don't worry."

"Charles," Potts called again.

"Yes, Colonel?"

Dobson turned away, heading back toward Ann standing ready near the door. She looked tired, he thought. Tired and lopsided, ungainly with the heavy plaster bulging around her left side.

His way was blocked, so that he was forced to make a detour bringing him back to the fringe of Potts and his party.

"... really looking forward to seeing him," Potts was saying to Charles. "The old devil taught me to fly Marauders, you know. I always reckoned him ..." The rest was lost as Dobson passed out of earshot.

Dobson and Ann rode down to the ground floor, stepping out into the big, sumptuous foyer.

"Just do as I tell you," he said again. "Even if it sounds crazy, do as I tell you."

"Don't worry."

He did not even try to spot Trotter or any of his men. They were there. He knew it; accepted it. With luck, they would shake them. Taking hold of Ann's arm, he guided her through the foyer, past the glass tables and deep armchairs, the soigné women and immaculate men, the people who could afford places like the Hilton.

A uniformed commissionaire asked if they needed a cab. Dobson shook his head. "Not going far," he said, and the commissionaire touched his hat and looked away. There was no profit in people who did not want cabs.

"We're moving right," Dobson told her. "Up Park Lane and turn right again into Curzon Street. It depends what I see when we get to the top end on what happens after that. Just act normal and talk to me."

He thought Trotter was in a car parked across the forecourt with the taxis. He could have been in the other car he noticed on the right, down the cul-de-sac as they crossed toward the pavement of Park Lane. He could feel the eyes there, but was determined not to look for them. By the tobacconist and souvenir shop they paused to buy a paper. Even if the cars were not moving as yet, Trotter would have a marker onto them. On foot and at a distance.

"There was a young plumber of Leigh . . ." Ann began.

"What?"

"You told me to talk to you."

Dobson looked at her, feeling her arm close in his and the weight of her body leaning against him. He tried to take up as much of her weight as possible.

"We're being watched, and we're going to lose them." He hoped, realizing that, like a small boy lying or wishing for luck, he had his fingers crossed. "Go on then, talk."

The corner of Curzon Street was coming up. They could see the dark glossy pile of the Playboy Club at the corner, and he still knew there were eyes.

"Who was plumbing a girl by the sea."

"Is this rude?"

"It's reputed to have been Arnold Bennett's favorite limerick. Of course, if you don't want to hear it."

"Go on."

Nearly at the corner, and a light blue Rover was turning into Curzon Street. Terry Makepiece at the wheel. Been cruising around, thank God. Dobson hoped he had spotted them.

"Said the girl, 'Stop your plumbing . . .'"

They reached the corner. Makepiece had pulled up just past the Playboy Club. He had his reversing lights on, but was not moving.

"'There's somebody coming . . .'"

"We're going to cross over as if we're heading straight up Park Lane." Dobson tightened the grip on her arm. "Then we're going to turn and walk slowly down Curzon Street on the Playboy Club side."

"Right."

They had to wait a few moments for the traffic before they crossed.

"You see the blue Rover 2000?" Dobson said as they reached the pavement.

"Yes."

"When we get past it—just by the hood—you're going to have trouble with the heel of your shoe. I'm going to help you with it. Only take a second, and for Chrissake, don't look at that car if I start talking to it. Terry's driving. I only hope he doesn't muck it up."

The marker was probably at the Park Lane end of Curzon Street now. They were almost abreast of the car.

"Now," said Dobson. "Now. Your heel."

"Oh dear," Ann said brightly. "I've got some trouble with the heel of my shoe."

"It's not a game. Twist yourself round. Stop and look at it."

"Of course it's a bloody game. You're all playing cowboys and Indians." She turned and tried to reach down to her shoe, bending her leg back. It was a good performance.

"They were cowboys and Indians who did your shoulder then." He knelt down and fiddled with the shoe. Terry Makepiece had the passenger side window open.

"Now?" he asked. "Do you want to switch now?"

"Start to back up to the Playboy. Ask the commissionaire if you can leave your car outside. He'll say no, so drive off again—whatever he says. Come on down and turn left into South Audley Street. We'll be just round the corner there. We do the switch then. Damn fast."

He straightened up. "Test the heel," he said to Ann. "That's it, now we go on walking."

Makepiece was back toward the main doors of the Playboy Club.

"If we can manage a bit more speed."

"Sorry. Of course. Sorry about the cowboys and Indians as well. You're quite right."

"Okay."

South Audley Street was twenty yards ahead sharp to the left. They reached it, turned in and went on about ten paces. If Terry was quick enough they would do the switch and be away long before any marker got to them. Even if they had a car on the go. Trotter just would not have that large a team working for him.

The Rover came round the corner and pulled over. Makepiece was out almost before he had the hand brake on. Dobson yanked the door open. "In," he said sharply to Ann. "Quick as you can manage. Get her in, Terry." Then: "Manual or auto?"

"Manual," said Makepiece, slamming the door as Ann made a cumbersome job of shifting her damaged body into the seat.

"Good luck," Makepiece said quietly, turning away and

walking off back toward Curzon Street.

"Get your seat belt on as fast as you can and hang on to your knickers."

Dobson shoved the Rover into gear, held the clutch down, took off the hand brake and let his toe press gently onto the accelerator. They had taught him this one when I3 (Air) had sent him to do the course at Hendon. The driving course. "It's a stoppo man's take-off," the instructor said.

The accelerator was three quarters of the way to the floor when he smartly took his foot off the clutch. Nothing showed in the rearview mirror: luckily, for the tail swung hard left as the wheels burned a lot of rubber. Then he held her straight and they were away.

"Not bad," he muttered aloud.

"Where're we going?" Ann asked, patient and showing no signs of nerves.

"Charing Cross. Train to Dover or Folkestone. Anywhere along there."

"They'll expect us to go by car?"

"Got it. We'll ditch the car at Charing Cross."

"Won't Trotter have thought of that?"

"Doubt it. He has an *idée fixe* that people like us shun public transport."

There was a taxi passing them, and the usual traffic, but nothing looking suspicious. No tail.

"From Dover or Folkestone to Fenwell Manor?" she asked.

"Hire a car. Stop off for a bite."

"Thank God."

"We're well ahead of schedule. I think there's a train about three." He had slowed down to normal speed, making good headway.

"The last line. You didn't give me the last line."

"I love you."

"It doesn't rhyme."

"I know, but I do."

"And I do."

"Good." She gave a single, one-note laugh. "Said the girl, 'Stop your plumbing, there's somebody coming.' 'I know,' said the plumber, 'it's me.'"

36

Luck stayed with them. There was no sign of a tail during the drive around the back-doubles down to the Strand and Charing Cross.

Their timing was right. There was a train at three o'clock which got them into Folkestone Central at seventeen minutes past four.

They had words on the journey.

Dobson was adamant that she should not come with him to Fenwell. She protested—at length. He remained firm. With her shoulder as it was Ann could be a liability.

She thought about it for a long time. Not speaking, staring moodily out of the window watching Kent roll past. Reluctantly she capitulated.

"The hell of it is that you're bloody right," she smiled. "I might get in the way. I'm also tired and hungry. If the situation was reversed, I'd feel the same way about you."

They got into Folkestone on time, hired a car, bought a suitcase and one or two things which Ann described as "personal"; then fish and chips at a cafe supported on one side by an arty-crafty shop and on the other by an amusement arcade.

Dobson booked her into a great granite bunker built on the

site of a hotel which had once known better things. She reported that the rooms were clean and good, that she had a television and would stay put waiting for his call.

They kissed goodbye in the foyer and she held her good arm around his neck tightly.

"When it's over," Dobson began.

"Yes." She was firm and convincing, her eyes very clear behind the big goggle-like spectacles.

"I'm talking apple blossom and legal certificates."

"I wasn't exactly thinking about some walk-down basement and unmarried bliss."

Dobson grinned. "Good. You're on."

She put a hand against his chest, feeling the hard bulge of the revolver. "For Chrissake, take care."

"I've got old Hackstead. He's a tough man. He'll take care. The shooter's only for show. Anyway, Free is under guard."

She nodded. "The shooter's only for show. Like the night the ghouls jumped us."

It was when he was actually on the road, heading along the coast toward New Romney, that Dobson began to feel his stomach churn, fluttering both with anxiety and the need, the deep almost consuming necessity, to know the truth: to be in at the kill and discover what no expert from the Accident Investigation Branch or Division could ever detect with all his specialized and technical knowledge. So much for the shufti-scope, he smiled to himself as he turned off the main roads onto the smaller A and B roads which skirt Romney Marsh. He knew that he was driving too fast, but it somehow did not seem to matter.

The smaller roads over the marsh can be very bad, sometimes intersected by even worse tracks and pathways. Inside the triangle of the marsh you can be in the bustle of a small town one minute and, within fifteen, by car, out into what appear to be bleak and remote villages.

The village of Fenwell is just such a remote spot. It lies only six miles from a comparatively good road which cuts diagonally inland from New Romney, and even in the flat landscape you come upon it with a startling suddenness, for the plateau effect of the marsh at that point produces an optical illusion.

Fenwell, in fact, lies at the foot of a gentle slope, the ground farther on rising once more to the horizontal plane so that when you reach it by car the village surprises you by its sudden presence.

Not that there is really much to jolt you into amazement: merely a huddle of cottages built in a circle, like some ancient ring of stones, around a church of Norman origin, with a short stubby and solid tower.

It was around seven o'clock when Dobson arrived in the village. It would take him another five minutes, he reckoned, to get to the Manor. The map showed it standing back from the road some two miles past the church. He checked, however, at the public house, feeling uncomfortable at the silence which descended among the elderly drinkers as he entered, sank a very quick half pint of ale, asked directions and received the curt reply from the landlord that he couldn't very well miss it if he kept going straight on.

The locals, obviously remembering better days, probably did not approve of the new ownership.

The landlord of the pub was right. It would be hard to miss Fenwell Manor. Like the village, you came upon it suddenly, yet no person could surprise it. The gentle slope up from the village flattened unexpectedly, revealing, at the edge of the marsh, a wide green parkland, dotted with clumps of trees.

There must have been twelve acres in all, surrounded by a gray stone wall which differed in heights, as though parts had been knocked away and rebuilt at lower levels from the rest. It gave the boundary an odd unsymmetrically serrated look.

Bordering on the road from the village, set clean into the highest part of the wall, were a pair of iron gates, from which the drive snaked like a dun-colored river toward the house: a long, gray stone building—immediately recognizable as early Tudor—with a barn separated from the house and built to a higher level.

The setting, like the house itself, was breathtaking, for no hedges, trees or bushes lined the drive, which curved up and around the building in a long regular oval.

For a moment, as he turned the hired car in through the gates, Dobson paused and just sat, balancing the clutch, so that he could look across at the Manor with its trim lawns dividing the buildings from the drive—a small rockery, chunky, to the right of what was undoubtedly a small jutting porch.

The sun was changing from its high globe of heat into the first faint tinge of pink that, in a few hours, would become a ball of scarlet; and the light caught the front of the rough gray stone, proclaiming its texture in a manner which neither artist nor photographer could ever capture.

Hackstead has friends with money, thought Dobson. The idea took on a more concrete shape for a second. Could Hackstead, perhaps, talk his friends into letting this place to him for the honeymoon with Ann?

Then the dream was banished, for something caught his eye.

The Manor had two stories. Along the upper line were four beautifully carved stone oriel windows, the glasswork latticed with diamond leads. There seemed to be a flash, like a brief movement: the second window from the gable end which faced him down the drive. Instinct? Someone watching for his arrival? Bud himself?

Dobson kept his eyes on the spot. Nothing else moved. A glint of sunlight perhaps? Automatically, he dropped his head, craning to see the position of the sun and the state of the sky. No cloud in sight. A mirror? A car passing on the road below the far end of the parkland?

Nothing. But his senses were inexplicably on edge. A new kind of anxiety. Gut reaction.

He let out the clutch and moved through the gates, feeling the change of surface under his wheels, hearing the crunch of good, thick, well-weeded gravel.

Gravel under rubber had about it a particular opulence. He put on a little speed, juggling the steering against the unstable surface, and brought the car to a halt in front of the main porch.

From the driving seat he could see into the darkness of the porch, even pick out the wooden plank seats—like those in a lych-gate—and the heavy carved door beyond. The door was open, half back on its hinges, but nobody came out to meet him. Looking forward, Dobson could see the rear of a black official-looking car parked between the far end of the house and the big barn.

Slowly he unclipped his seat belt and opened the car door, stepping firmly and quickly onto the gravel. Silence, but for the solid clunk of the door slamming as he gave it a swipe.

Silence. No movement. The feeling that all was not as it should be. Bud was there with the pair of confessors and Free. Someone should have seen, or heard his arrival.

He bent his knees slightly and performed a quick parabola, at the same moment slipping his jacket button for easy access to the revolver.

Nothing.

He began to move around the front of the car, heading for the porch, when he saw it, behind the rockery which sprawled, a mass of color, to the right of the porch under the ground floor stone mullioned windows with oblong leads. A crumpled mound, legs just visible.

The man was undoubtedly dead. In life he had been a neat dresser, the light gray suit was of good quality. A tall man, broad, muscular.

You could not tell what his face had looked like. A bullet, maybe two, had taken away the cheekbones and nose, splitting the head almost in two.

Tall, heavy, broad, muscular, well dressed. One of Bud's confessors. Christ. Sweet Jesus. Dobson felt a fraction of panic: Free, he was certain, had got loose. The revolver was out and in his hand without his really thinking about it; back automatically against the wall, eyes moving, scanning a half circle, ears strained.

Silence. Nothing. No sound, not even a bird stirring. If Free had a gun . . . ? Free would have a gun, what in God's name was he dawdling for. Slowly, as softly as possible, Dobson eased his way along the wall behind the rockery, toward the porch. Once inside he stood still, revolver up, blinking, allowing time for his eyes to adjust to the half-light.

Still silence.

Slowly, Dobson put out a foot and pushed with his toe against the part-open door, trying to swing it inward. It moved a few inches, then hit something solid and heavy. Stepping forward he tried to push again, using the ball of his foot, constantly glancing back, out into the empty sunlit grounds.

The door would not yield, and was not open quite wide enough for him to squeeze through. The warning vibrations were going on in his head—like something not right on take-off or approach in a jet fighter: the rapid ding-dong-ding-dong resounding through the headset, alarm lights coming up on the panel. But they were airman's thoughts. This was on the ground. It was now, and he could smell the danger.

One confessor—it could only be one of Hackstead's men—shot dead. Something heavy blocking the door. The screaming silence. Decision. Abort fast, punch out and drive away? Get the police? Or go in and possibly find himself face to face with Free. Free armed, having killed once and ready to kill again.

The decision was quick and almost entirely emotional: a rapid succession of pictures in his head. The thing on his landing could have been Free; one of those who had attacked Ann could have been Free—Ann in plaster and possibly never again being able to move her shoulder properly; the responsibility of *Dodo*'s last flight? Could that have been Free? Maybe. Rift Valley fever, cholera, the nameless disease in the missing canister. Free? Free in Mrs. Lambert's garden? Free killing Mrs. Lambert?

Now, one of Bud Hackstead's men with his face half shot away. Free? Silence. Bud had signified that he had two men with him. Two confessors and Free. What of the other? What of Bud himself?

Dobson threw all his weight against the door. Impact of shoulder against the old oak. It gave, pushing back whatever was blocking it, and he moved inside, fast, jumping left in a weave, the revolver clutched ready in both hands.

Such was his knife-edge anxiety and readiness that, he knew later, anything that moved as he jumped into the hallway would have had a couple of .38 bullets hurtling at it.

But there was nothing.

Silence.

He stood, stiff against the wall, hands raised with the weapon held as in a vice, then, flexing his knees in a crouch, Dobson circled, first left and then back arcing right, eyes adjusting to the dimness after the sunlight outside. It was like coming through a grayout; a rate-five turn in a light aircraft without wearing a G-suit.

The main door opened straight into a great hall, huge, paneled. Dimly he could see paintings lining the walls, and a long highly polished floor, oak again, he thought.

There was furniture; heavy, leather, large and deep armchairs, a buttoned settee, occasional tables. At the far end a wide flight of stairs—still polished wood, uncarpeted—mounted to a gallery. There were doors leading off, and an archway directly ahead from where the stairs ended.

As he turned, Dobson could now see that the gallery ran right around all four sides of the hall, and on either side of the staircase there were doors leading deeper into the house.

He swung back from his slow left track, circling again, right round to the door—and to what had blocked it.

This one was also well dressed; a dark, conservatively cut suit: an older man, probably the senior of the two confessors. In pushing open the door, Dobson had turned the body onto its back so that it lay, not spread-eagled, but in a twisted heap, the eyes open, staring upward, misted as they looked across the Styx for Charon, the head turned slightly as though listening for the ghostly oars.

He had taken two bullets in the chest. The shirt was white no more, pressed in rags inward, the scraps of cloth inserted into the torn wounds.

So Free was probably away. Gone on his toes; maybe, at this very moment, making a desperate attempt to get to a telephone and warn Goldberg.

Dobson took two paces into the hall, stopped, listened and could still hear no sound from outside nor in. He strained his ears, expecting movement.

Nothing.

Starting toward the staircase he called, softly at first:

"Bud? Bud, are you okay? If you've any life in you, try and call," knowing that if Free had got his hands on a gun and killed the pair of confessors, then he would make sure of Hackstead also.

Almost in the center of the large hall now. Then the first sound. A scraping noise. Bud? Bud Hackstead injured, dying, trying to attract his attention?

Then the ice slithered down his spine, nausea rising, sheer panic mingled with fear enveloping him like a shroud. The noise of scraping came from the door in the porch behind him. Now another, more familiar noise, coming in regular gasps, as though the thing which made the noise was having to exert itself. The gasps were hissing, groaning, like the sound of a snake, recorded and then put onto tape as a series of pulses.

Then the words, clear, clipped and steady, as though the taped hissing had been suddenly switched off.

"Drop the gun or you will be dead before you even start to move. Now; drop it now or you're dead."

There was something familiar about the voice. It also sounded too businesslike to be bluffing. Dobson exhaled and allowed the revolver to fall from his hand. The noise as it hit the wood seemed deafening.

"Good. Now put your hands on your head and turn around. Slowly."

This time there was no putrid stench, but it was there dressed in the leather flight jacket, ragged U.S. Air Force pants and torn shirt, the face half eaten away and suppurating, the hideous gash of mouth and a cheekbone showing through below empty eye sockets.

One claw hand, frayed with eaten flesh, held an automatic pistol, while the finger bones of the other hand clutched at a walking stick upon which the gross thing leaned heavily. The hissing noises had been partly a matter of effort, for as it moved toward him, Dobson saw the creature was dragging its leg. This was the one he had winged in the hallway at Charlotte Street.

"Well done, Franz." Another voice now, from the stairs behind him.

The eeriness of the place and time, the make-up of death and decomposition, his own tension mingled with anger, all combined to present a sense of unreality, as though this was a dream in slow motion.

Now the voice from behind increased the feeling of insubstantiality. It even crossed his mind that he was, perhaps, hallucinating.

Then the terror passed and, disregarding the automatic pointing at his stomach, Dobson turned back again to face the dead, or undead, there.

It stood at the foot of the stairs, its peaked cap set at a rakish angle, the face a matted tangle of bone and blood, wet, putrefied. The right hand held an automatic pistol—a Lüger. It was the first thing that Dobson accepted as reality, for the rest of what he was looking at was far out into the extremities of sanity.

There was a difference about this figure. Not in the disguise of physical death, but in the clothing. This one did not wear the tattered, disintegrating uniform of a United States Air Force officer of the 1940s.

Instead, he was turned out immaculately, the uniform razor-pressed and clean, arrogant and tailored. The black tunic and breeches; highly polished gleaming jackboots; Sam Browne belt, the leather holster for the Lüger, unbuttoned; white shirt with black tie and a small enamel stickpin badge.

The lapels of the jacket carried gold thread symbols of rank, and the unmistakable lightning-flash runes, while on the center of the peaked cap a badge gleamed, polished, immediately recognizable—the silver death's-head, symbol of the greatest dread of this century, perhaps of any century since the hordes of Attila the Hun, Scourge of God, swept through the Roman Empire.

The uniform was that of a Schutzstaffel officer: a member of the Nazi elite. The SS.

"For Chrissake. Fancy dress?" Dobson blurted out.

"I'm sorry about the dramatics," the creature said coldly. "There is not much time before our friends arrive. I regret them because they were forced on me, but their coming does give us a link with the media. We have a little under an hour."

"Take it off," said Dobson, cold and calm now.

"My uniform? I'm sorry. It is my right to wear it, and I am a proud man. I suggest you move over to the settee. There is a table there. You will move over and place your hands where we can see them, on the table."

"The mask," Dobson said. "The make-up. Take it off."

"Move first."

From the ghoul behind him, the one with the stick: "*Schnell . . . schnell.*" Rapped out like a double drum beat.

Dobson, trying to move carefully and with an outward show of calm, walked to the settee, sat down and placed his hands on the table.

"Now take off that bloody stupid mask," he said.

"Oh yes." The one in SS uniform came forward, standing by an armchair across the table, well out of reach. "It will be more comfortable, and I suppose we have to talk. You, of all people, have a right to know before the wretched living crew of *Dancing Dodo* arrive. I really could have done without that lot, but we couldn't figure a way of getting the media into the act without involving them. Hostages are the last thing we want—or need." He made a movement toward his companion. "I think we can do without the skull faces and the other muck. Can you manage to pick up Wing Commander Dobson's gun?"

The one with the stick dragged himself forward. It was not going to be an easy job.

"Kick it with your good foot," said the SS corpse. "Kick it to me." Then he added something in German.

The limping one laughed and kicked the revolver in the direction of the table.

Dobson did not even think of making a possible dive for the weapon. The SS officer picked it up and placed it on another, smaller table standing at the far side of the armchair.

"Keep him covered," he added to his companion cadaver, putting the Lüger on the table next to Dobson's .38, then completing the pile by removing his uniform cap.

"I should warn you here and now," he said through the empty black gap of a mouth, "that any tricks on your part at this stage could be the cause of considerable catastrophe."

"The circular canister?" Dobson felt the nausea rise in his gullet. "What is it? Botulinus toxin?"

"Oh no," a sharp laugh. A laugh with a cutting edge. "Not quite as quick or as lethal. Lethal enough though." His hand dipped into the right pocket of his breeches and came out holding a small glass scent spray. "You'll have already noticed that we've spared you the nasal effects this time. The smellies." As he said it, his hand moved upward, away from both his companion and Dobson. A small cloud of vapor disgorged from the spray.

Dobson smelt it at once, the vile stench of putrefaction. He gagged and retched, drawing back deeper into the settee.

"Takes some getting used to." The SS officer placed the glass bottle next to his cap. "The stink will go in a moment. It evaporates quickly and, happily, is soluble in water. Clever though; we were pleased with it. For your record, should you live, it is called pentamethylenediamine, better known, and available at all the best forensic laboratories, as cadaverine. Sick, yes? But true. They also keep putrescene. For comparison tests. It was not easy to come by."

The one with the wounded leg laughed again, leaning on his stick. The pistol in his claw remained steady.

"Now, excuse me." The SS officer nodded. "These masks are well made and effective, but uncomfortable; not easy to get on or off." He eased his fingers down under the collar of the spotless white shirt. Fingers, then thumbs, inserted and prising upward.

Dobson felt he was looking at someone performing an action in slow motion, looking from a long way off—detached.

The mask of the decomposing face appeared, at close quarters, to be made of latex, overlaid with foam rubber, skillfully designed, even down to the details of wetness and bone.

With great care the SS-uniformed figure began to peel the mask upward. It stuck slightly on reaching the nose, and he had to ease the bone fingers round to the back of his neck. Then, in one upward effort, the thing peeled away.

"Hi, Dave. Sorry about all this, but I guessed you were getting pretty close to the truth. I was kind of busy dealing with my plans. We tried to scare the bejasus outa you. I like you, but it's all too late now," said Bud Hackstead.

Even though he had recognized the voice before the mask came fully away, the shock numbed Dobson. The only outward sensation came from a quivering of the hands, uncontrollable on the table.

Hackstead wiped his brow with a clean handkerchief, picked up his cap and replaced it carefully on his ruffled hair.

"Allow me to, finally, introduce myself—God, that sounds like something from a soap opera. Sorry." He picked up his

Lüger from the table, holding it loosely in Dobson's direction and nodding toward the other figure, giving him the go-ahead. "I am, alas, SS Oberführer Bernhard Hackensteiner, Ausland SD." He glanced in the direction of the other figure, who had now almost removed his mask. "This is SS Sturmbannführer Franz Ebenskrumm. A good actor, yes? He even stayed in character after you wounded his leg in Charlotte Street. You remember? He kept calling me Goldberg. Poor, grave, serious, innocent Goldberg."

Hackstead even clicked his heels, still holding the Lüger, but pointing it down slightly as he peeled off the tight disguise rubber gloves which transformed his hands into ragged bones and eaten flesh. As the true right hand came into view, Dobson saw that he wore, on the middle finger, the coveted death's-head silver ring.

The one with the wounded leg had his mask off now. SS Sturmbannführer Ebenskrumm was the man Dobson knew as former Flight Lieutenant Frederick Free, Royal Air Force.

"It's a long story," said Hackstead. "But I'll be brief, because this operation really concerns the media coverage which Charles—though he does not yet know it—is going to handle. You see, Dave, I am probably what you might call the Kim Philby of the CIA. Only my position is not like his. I am an anti-Communist, an anti-Socialist—except of a certain kind; national socialism. I cannot run to Moscow, but—among other things—I want out; and the finds from *Dancing Dodo* can get me out. They can also restore the Führer's dream of Europe."

"There's nowhere to run. Not for men like you. Traitors from the far left can cross the iron curtain. Traitors from way back have nowhere to go. I presume all the gear is real." Dobson heard his own voice but it sounded far away, as if he was speaking a great distance from himself.

"The gear from *Dodo?* Oh yes, it's only too real. And who talked about running and hiding? I need bread, for a little comfort far away from Europe while the final struggle takes place, the final shaping of the true way. Then I shall come back to a land that has been cleansed. After Europe, perhaps America. The Führer prophesied what would happen and he has been proved correct." He began to sound like some demented preacher. "He said, 'Those who are our enemies stand at the furthest extremes: ultra-capitalist states on one side and ultra-Marxist states on the other.' He foresaw the collapse of the British Empire and its slow sinking into the murk of that most evil ideology, communism. Can't *you* see it? *Now* can't you see it?"

"Oh for Chrissake," Dobson groaned.

Hackstead laughed. "*Dodo* almost killed me when Ebenskrumm and I did *Rattengift*. But now she is going to bring the dreams to reality. Now, I really have to be brief." He glanced at his watch. "I warn you, as I am going to warn your establishment and your government, that the canister is in position and the time clock is running. At this moment it has a little less than twenty-four hours to go. Unless, of course, I stop it—and only Ebenskrumm and myself know how to stop it or where it is. And if the clock isn't stopped, if our demands—our terms—are not met, there will be a disaster—an appalling disaster. The pestilence which was meant for this country in 1944. The real miracle weapon."

"Your terms?"

"Later." Hackstead waved the question aside with the Lüger. "Simply, let me say that they concern, naturally, a little finance, but, more important, the political situation and status of this country and the key to its future greatness."

He leaned back, settling himself into the deep armchair, confident and quite at ease; the Hackstead whom Dobson knew, overlaid with another personality which reached out, taking over from the distant past.

"This," he said, "is the truth about Ebenskrumm, myself, *Rattengift*, *Dancing Dodo* and the things that have been happening to you in these last days. After that, I will give the final orders." He looked at his watch again. "We have a little over forty-five minutes."

He began back at the start of it all: in 1936, eight years before *Operation Rattengift* began and remained unfinished.

37

"In 1936 I fulfilled a family ambition," Hackstead said, his right hand brushing a piece of dust from the knee of his black breeches as a man might flick or swat a fly.

Dobson thought, he would do that to any human being who got in his way. Clap him, squash him, like an insect. There would be no remorse, no sense of guilt.

The facts were simple, emotional maybe; certainly chauvinistic. Hackstead's grandfather died a very old man—ninety-two years of age. He had come to America, with a large portion of his village, in 1856, at the age of nineteen. His name was Joseph Hackensteiner and he came from Bavaria, from a small village near Nuremberg, an apprentice toymaker. His employer was also among those who emigrated.

They came mainly because they felt the Fatherland was the Fatherland no more. The revolution of the late 1840s had been the last straw.

"My grandfather's brother stayed in Germany," Hackstead said at one point, "and I have seen many of my grandfather's first letters written from America. He regarded the change of domicile—the change of country—as a temporary matter. He wrote constantly that he would prefer to live in Germany, for he

271

regarded Germany as the most civilized and cultured country in the world. However, the former orderly conditions had disappeared; there were threats to both religion and politics. However civilized and cultured, compared with America, he would not return to Germany until order also returned. But he firmly believed that order and discipline would return. It did not do so in his lifetime. It did in mine."

Young Joseph Hackensteiner lived in Cincinnati's "Over the Rhine" community. Hard-working, and the life very little different to that he had known in Germany. There were German newspapers—Cincinnati *Volksblatt* and Cincinnati *Freie Presse;* German bands played, there were shops with German inscriptions over their doors; German restaurants, beer gardens, churches and theaters.

The man who had run his little village toymaking shop, with the help of the teen-age Joseph Hackensteiner, prospered. Soon he had a small factory, making toys which were both attractive and ingenious. In 1876 Joseph, already a partner in this thriving business which supplied many shops throughout the United States, suddenly found things changed dramatically. His employer—the director of the firm, now a wealthy man—died, and Joseph Hackensteiner became the sole owner of the factory, the wealth and all that went with it. The boy who had come, almost penniless and dependent on an employer who carved wooden dolls and little moving figures, was now a businessman to be reckoned with. For twenty years he had labored. Now came his reward.

Joseph was prudent. He did not marry until he was almost forty-five years old—and then to a woman twenty years his junior. There were three children, only one of whom survived: Ernst, born in 1891 when Joseph was already fifty-four.

Ernst grew, and with him the same ideals which so obsessed his father. In 1914 the First World War broke out and Ernst dearly wished to go *home*—they still referred to Germany as *home*—and fight. Old Joseph, however, said no. The Fatherland had to prove itself before any of them went back. Besides, a new interest had come into the life of Ernst Hackensteiner: a blond-haired beauty, the granddaughter of another immigrant family—from Munich. Her name was Emma Arnholdt and they met with friends one evening at one of the *Männerchöre*—singing societies—to which they both belonged. Within a week they were seeing one another almost every day.

They were married in December 1914 and produced three

children in quick succession—Joseph (named after his grandfather), Hanna and, in 1918, Bernhard.

"You know what happened when America entered the war," said Hackstead. "The German communities were shunned, even persecuted: a fact which enraged both my father and grandfather. Grandfather Joseph was an old man by this time and he saw, in the attitude of many Americans, the same cracks and fissures from which he had run all those years before. The defeat of Germany was the last straw, and you know what happened in America then. It was bad enough when America entered the war—I was a baby, but the history books do not lie. Even German dishes were banned from menus in the restaurants; sauerkraut was renamed 'liberty cabbage.' Once Germany had lost, the great wave built up and we were swamped with 100 Per Cent Americanism. We had to be, not German-Americans, but Americans with a capital A.

"My schooling, and that of my brother and sister, was aimed to that end." He smiled, not the old crinkled smile of the Bud Hackstead whom Dobson had come to know and respect, but a hard-line smile, the smile of the victor, ruthless to those whom he had conquered.

"At home, though, it remained the same. My father was as convinced as my grandfather had been that one day Germany would rise from its ashes and prove, for all time, that it was master of its destiny, the race apart, the greatest nation of nations."

There was no wild look in Hackstead's eye, but the words had a strange and familiar ring: the sound of Hitler's oratory during the years in which he was welding the German people, bending them to his totalitarian dream.

"At home," Hackstead continued, "we spoke only German, and my father constantly preached the gospel which his father had instilled into him. Unhappily, my brother and sister were seduced by this American dream. They did not wish to know about the homeland. It made my father sick with rage. Particularly when things began to happen in Germany that seemed to point, at last, toward recovery."

He shrugged. "Outwardly, of course, we had to conform. For instance, when my grandfather died in 1929, we changed our name. That was when Bernhard Hackensteiner became the all-American boy, Bernard, 'Bud,' Hackstead. My brother left home when he was seventeen and my sister shortly afterward. I stayed and listened, and worried. Because my poor old pop was a sick man." He patted his chest. "The big C." He reached for the table to pick up his Lüger and spoke a few words in German to "Free." "He's just going to take a look-see," Hackstead explained before taking up the narrative again.

The figure in the torn, ragged and bloodstained flight gear hobbled out, dragging his leg, the stick clumping hard on the bare wood.

"In 1936 my father sent for me. I was eighteen years old. He told me that he did not think there was much time left for him, and he was not well enough to travel—actually he did not die until the forties, when I was over here serving my country."

"Which country?" Dobson sneered.

"*Ein Reich; ein Volk; ein Führer.* What do you think? Dave, there's not much time, and you want the truth before I brief you about what's going to happen, so keep your goddamned mouth closed. Got it?"

Dobson felt disorientated. If, at that moment, he'd had time to look back over his life, he would have known that in truth there were few people he could call real friends. The relationship he had built with Hackstead . . . that had the makings of a lasting friendship. He recalled thinking it right at the start, when they first met, and he imagined they would be engaged in what he had called a paper chase, a routine rout through documents and files.

"My father sent for me," Hackstead repeated. "He spoke to me in our proper tongue, as we always did when we were alone. He said that things were happening in the home country which pointed toward the final greatness. I was aware of it, of course. He gave me money, made the arrangements, and sent me *home* for two months.

"I saw the Führer for the first time and I knew that if anyone could place our country on the right course it was him. There was order from chaos, there was discipline, strength, joy. It came at you like a great revelation, like St. Paul on the road to Damascus, like scales falling from the eyes. Here was the orderly country my grandfather and my father had hoped for through all those years. It was time to come home."

SS Sturmbannführer Ebenskrumm—Free—came back through the main door. He did not even glance at the corpse, which still slept eternally, twisted on its back.

There was a quick exchange in German.

"He says there's no sign of movement." Hackstead lowered the Lüger, looking at his watch. "We've half an hour or so yet anyway. I can't imagine Charles getting them here on time, but I want to play it safe."

Strange, Dobson worried. Strange how Hackstead seemed to take on this double personality, at times speaking in the distinct American vernacular, then changing to a stilted, precise form of speech.

"During my last week in Berlin," Hackstead continued, "I went to the authorities and said I wished to return to the Fatherland. To reclaim my citizenship. To serve my Führer." He nodded. "I know what you're thinking, and you're right. They were very suspicious. They tried to be casual about it and said it would be considered, but they asked me a lot of questions—my real name, for instance, didn't seem to please them. They wanted to know a great deal about my parentage, my background, my grandfather and his family. That's obvious now. In the end they were polite, said that my request would be considered and the American authorities would be consulted." The humorless un-Hackstead smile again. "I thought that would be the end. I left Germany a sad young man, because I so desperately wanted to do the thing my grandfather and father would have wished."

He sighed heavily. "I heard no more for three, four months. Then I had a visitor. He wished to see me alone. Very American. Almost what you'd call Ivy League. He said he'd been asked to see me about my application to return to the Reich and resume German citizenship. I thought, immediately, that he was from the FBI, or one of the government agencies. Then he started asking really difficult questions. Tricky questions if he was an FBI man. I hedged and then he said, 'Herr Hackensteiner.' I'll never forget that. 'Herr Hackensteiner, your request has been granted. The Führer has work for you.' Me? Eighteen years old, and the Führer had work for me. I said my father was ill, but I'd be ready to leave for Germany at any time. Then I got the kicker. No, he said, the work was not in Germany, not yet. He gave me an address in New York. I was to go there on such and such a day, at such and such an hour."

"And there you became a traitor to the country that had taken you as one of her own." Dobson said it with the disgust he felt clear in his voice.

"That would be one view, yes. It depends on one's perspective. I would put it another way."

"I'll bet."

"You want to know the truth, or not?"

"Go on."

"I was to be a true-blue American. A 100 per center. In any way I chose—preferably military. Just go do the job. When they had need of me they'd be in touch."

"A sleeper?"

Hackstead laughed. "That's the modern term. You had them. We had them. I was one of them."

"So?"

"So I joined the Army Air Corps as soon as they'd take me. I learned flying and ended up training Marauder crews at MacDill Field until I pulled myself a better job. The job with the OSS."

Christ. Dobson saw himself lying on the lounger at Herbie Flax's pool, and Flax telling him that Bill Potts and Dan Goldberg were the best pair of Marauder pilots in the business—bar one. What was it he had said? *A guy out at MacDill Field . . . this guy could do anything with that airplane. The only man I ever met who really liked the Marauder.*

"You took Bill Potts and Dan Goldberg through their conversion," he said aloud.

"Guilty. I took a lot of guys through. Potts and Goldberg were, I must admit, two of my better pupils. How did you know?"

"Herbie Flax."

"Figures. That's why you had to see Herbie, not me. He'd have asked difficult questions and recognized me. He'd never seen Franz so he couldn't recognize him when he saw him in the layby. I made the call, of course. Arranged the meet, as you might say."

"I should've guessed."

"You did very well as it was. Too well. That's why we tried to scare you off. Sorry about that. Nothing personal about the second time, when your girl's shoulder got done up. Nothing personal, but you were getting too close for our comfort. We only wanted to put you away as quietly as possible. In a nuthouse or a hospital. As it was, everybody had gotten a little too smart. Peter Kursbuch got too smart. I figured he was over the hill anyway—and I didn't think there was anything left on paper concerning *Rattengift*. Old Timetable had me rattled when he turned up the stuff in Koblenz."

"Herbie said you actually liked flying the Marauder." Dobson felt cold, as though he was sitting in a mausoleum.

"She was a bitch, but I'm partial to bitches. I had to master her. I did. If you work at it you can master any bitch in the book.

That's really why I asked for a Marauder for *Overshoot*. Coincidence has a bloody long arm, though. I'd no idea we'd end up with Potts' airplane."

"You set up *Overshoot*." He was not asking but stating.

"Of course. When I really got into the act. When the ball started bouncing—after Pearl Harbor—I went to my CO, told him I was a German-speaker and asked if they had anything going in among the hush-hush boys. It took four interviews, six tests, and I was in."

"OSS."

"Technically, yes. By the time I arrived in London they had virtually amalgamated SOE and OSS. There were some wonderful opportunities, and about a month after I got over here, the boys from Berlin woke me up."

"Another anonymous visitor?"

"Something like that. One day they'll write the true story about our secret operations in England. Maybe I'll do it from my last redoubt. Make some spare money doing that. Our job wasn't quite the same as SOE, but we monitored, and we brought people in and took them out."

"Okay, I'm interested. The Nazis had a network or two going. In and out stuff by air ..."

"And radio, of course. I really do have to write that book."

"You've got to the chapter where they woke you up. I thought you were in a hurry?"

"Orders. They needed delivery of one American or British airplane, intact. With me." The grin this time was more like the old Hackstead. "So we worked out *Overshoot*. The information was fed in from France, Germany, Belgium, and I came up with this crazy scheme to shoot up Kammhuber and all his technical staff on the ground at St. Trond. I really didn't think they'd buy it, but they bit like stupid fish. It was a dream."

"So you were the pilot on *Overshoot*?"

"Sure. Denis would've recognized me. That's why he had to go."

"And my other source?"

Hackstead frowned. "He's a bit of a thorn. We haven't been able to get near him. It's been a worry."

"Good." Dobson smiled broadly. "I'm glad about that. What about the rest of your crew—on *Overshoot*?"

"Wartime," Hackstead said flatly. "I don't know what happened to them after we got them out of the aircraft. The Gestapo took them away. That wasn't my business."

"You shit."

"SOE didn't bother overmuch about the people they sent in after networks were blown. Wartime, Dave. It happens. The cross and the double cross. Part of the game of nations—that would make a good title for a book."

"Already been used by someone you might know. *The Game of Nations:* Miles Copeland."

"Good old Miles, yes. He'd understand."

"He'd more than understand, I'm sure. He'd see you under."

"Possibly."

"Time? I'm jogging you along, Hackstead, or Hackensteiner, or whatever you want to call yourself. Pushing you because I want to hear the crunch. I need to know what's going to happen." It occurred to Dobson that he was unconsciously trying to take over the initiative of the conversation.

"Okay, Dave. We did *Overshoot.* No trouble, because it was laid on from the other side. Nobody bothered us. We went through all the dramatics; landed, and I simply pulled her off the runway, pointing in the wrong direction. There was a reception committee. The rest of the crew were taken off. I think a couple of shots were fired, and then I was taken to lunch, where I met my controller for the first time. We flew the aircraft into Germany and I cooled my heels there for some time. All they told me was that I was to stand by for a dangerous mission which might, or might not, take place. It was a backup job. They were ecstatic with the aircraft. Very excited."

"So now I know," said Dobson. "One Marauder stuffed full of biological devices, set on a glide slope and then left to go in. You going to tell me about the operation? About *Rattengift?*"

"You know it all, Dave. You must have worked it out."

"Most of it. The Allies were massing for the invasion of Europe. Hitler's miracle weapons were suffering setbacks. The great V-offensive was running behind schedule. The main operation was that England should be bombarded with the long-range V-1s and V-2s, plus the coastal batteries. They'd had problems. The V-1s, though effective, had supply difficulties, and the big fellows, the rockets, just could not be ready on time. I should imagine that the original operation included biological warheads on the first firings."

"Correct. The scientists had ruled out the flying bomb as a delivery system. The V-2 rockets were the answer, and warheads were already past the design stage. But the rockets just would not do the job with any safety. In the spring of '44 when they were most needed to perform the miracle, they still had guidance system problems and a nasty disintegration habit. The SS were pressing for control of the whole business. Eventually they got it."

"You were going to drop the bugs—germs—a week or so before the main offensive, to give them time to work? Then the high explosive would rocket in?"

"Nutshell. Biological devices to start up large-scale epidemics. Once they were raging, the big bangs from the sky. The Führer, and one or two of his staff, had made up their minds. The only way to bring a quick end to the war—to stop the invasion—was to use the whole plan in its entirety. Now it had gone wrong, time was running out, but we of the SS had a substitute." Hackstead's head inclined toward Ebenskrumm. "Franz was an English-speaker and a very experienced pilot. We worked well together."

"Wouldn't it have been more simple for a couple of Luftwaffe aircraft to go in and drop the things?"

"The Luftwaffe refused. In any case, accuracy was essential. They were forced into allowing us airfield facilities, but they refused to perform the operation. I was given to understand that, even with Göring threatening the execution of large numbers of senior officers, they still refused." He chuckled. "Mind you, the Luftwaffe had everyone over a barrel. Even Big Hermann could see that."

"So you took it on?"

"Why not? I wanted victory for the Führer. There were others who did not. Both Franz and myself agreed."

"The thinking behind it, though, Bud," he pushed, ignoring the fancy dress, trying to put up a pretense of their old relationship. "I mean why an American aircraft."

"Because I was available and exceptional with that airplane. We were to go from Beauvais."

Dobson recalled backtracking the Marauder's compass course. The line had gone straight over Beauvais.

"We had facilities there," Hackstead continued, "Luftflotte III, IX Air Corps. They were flying the heavy stuff out. We were to go at dawn on May 21. The team assured us that we would have all the necessary call signs for ingoing missions returning to RAF and USAAF bases. All the identification we needed to avoid attack. Full war paint and U.S. markings. We would be carrying three devices. You know about two of them. The third was the nasty one—is still the nasty one. Time fuses. We both had protective clothing and were supplied with documentation—papers. The let-down would be a clearance into Manston on a mayday, crossing the coast at about six to seven thousand. We were then to give them another mayday and cut all radios, put her onto what would nowadays be called a glide slope—very gentle. Lock and trim, set the time fuses and leave the aircraft."

"So that it would continue the glide and hit where?"

"Just this side of London. Outskirts. Greenwich. Fuel was at minimun and the extinguishers were to be activated as soon as we cut the engines and feathered. All fuel cocks off. A straight glide in. Crump on the outskirts of the capital. No fire. People rushing in to drag out the gallant fliers. Immediate infection for a lot of the rescue party, and impregnation over some four square miles. Within a couple of weeks, England would have at least three epidemics on its hands—maybe four, plus combinations, cross-infections."

"And you'd be in the middle of it?"

Hackstead shook his head. "No way. We had our exit neatly worked out. Most of your south coast was sealed off because of D-day build-up, but there were gaps. We were to go out, in one of the old Fiesler Storks, the following evening."

"But there was a crew. Papers, documents, a flight plan. When we pulled the aircraft out of the marsh there was a real flight plan, one from Potts' log."

"The papers and flight plan? Yes. An added refinement. We didn't discover that until the briefing. Flight Lieutenant Frederick Free, rest his soul, talked a great deal. He didn't know it, but he talked. That's why everyone got so excited at St. Trond when they discovered the Marauder I delivered was *Dancing Dodo*. They had a lot on that aircraft. It was thought that the documents might cause initial confusion. Don't forget that people were going to become very ill in a short space of time. Confusion is one of the arts of war."

"There was a crew, though," repeated Dobson. "A crew apart from Pegleg Pete here."

Ebenskrumm swore in German and took a step toward the settee.

"Hold it, Franz. No scenes. We need him." For a fraction, the Lüger changed direction, then back again, held loosely toward Dobson.

"You had a crew," Dobson said again.

Hackstead remained silent for the best part of half a minute. "Inmates from one of the remand homes."

"The camps?"

"Okay, the camps. Inmates from Sachsenhausen—the documentation was all forged at Sachsenhausen also. Confusion, that was mainly the reason for the crew and documents— additional contamination and confusion."

"What went wrong?" asked Dobson, holding Hackstead's eyes with his.

"I'll tell you. As simply as I can."

38

They had not seen their "crew" put on board, but they must have known what was happening. They were elderly Russian Jews, brought to Sachsenhausen for experiments in ricketsial diseases. Sick, bewildered, dying, not able to walk, in fever and terrible pain.

The SS men who brought them from Sachsenhausen were all part of the medical team. So that the victims were not frightened too much, they were told that at last they were being flown home. They would have warm clothing and good food. Hackstead seemed to think they were given some decent soup before being put into the American flight kit—one of them in RAF gear—and had the dog tags hung around their necks.

They were carried into the aircraft and strapped into their various seats and positions. They even put one in the right-hand pilot's seat—Hackstead, as captain, would be in the left-hand seat. Ebenskrumm's work would keep him moving about the aircraft, apart from the crucial times of take-off and the let-down into the glide slope, when he would have to assist with trimming, feathering the propellers, cutting off the fuel cocks and checking flap settings. His main job was activating the three devices and starting the time clocks.

When the now calmed prisoners were strapped in, the doctors performed the last rites. It would be a long flight, they said. There would be injections to ensure that the men would be able to sleep.

They were all dead, Hackstead told him, by the time he went on board with Ebenskrumm. They had been briefed and the Met report was in their favor—sticky over France, clear across the Channel and a very light drifting ground over most of southern England. Cloud base around two thousand feet.

Hackstead remembered going out of the briefing room to cross the few hundred yards to the hut they were to use as their crew room. They stood and watched as six Dornier 217s took off, the red-blue streaks from the exhausts reaching back as though the engines were on fire.

Ebenskrumm climbed into a Royal Air Force battledress with flight lieutenant's bands on the shoulders. Then the white coverall protective clothing with a hood which came up over his helmet, and the strange tight-fitting, Perspex-visored helmet on top. The visors, they had both been instructed, were only to be raised when oxygen masks were operating. On top of this bulky outfit, there was harness and parachute—the chute carried, ready to be clipped to the front of the harness: the RAF setup as used by bomber crews.

Hackstead wore a regulation U.S. captain's uniform, covered by a flight jacket and boots, then the protective clothing and a seat parachute, strapped from shoulders and between his legs, the parachute pack itself tight to the lower part of his back and buttocks, used as a cushion in flight.

Two scientists came into the crew room and, for the last time, went through the drill with the canisters—the gray and blue boxes—which were straightforward—and the big round drum, which, for protection in case of accident over German-occupied territory, was sealed into a lead-lined strengthened casing. To activate that one, Ebenskrumm would have to remove the seals and lift the drum clear before setting the timer.

The scientists went out to the aircraft with them and made certain the devices were stowed in the correct places. They then stood by *Dancing Dodo* and gravely shook hands. Two of the Ausland SD conducting officers were with them as well as a senior Luftwaffe officer. When the handshaking was over, they stood to attention and raised their arms in salute:

"Heil Hitler."

"We'd been over that crate a million times," Hackstead

said. "*Dodo* was just as though she'd come straight from Mr. Martin's plant. We started up the engines; did the run-up, checked on the time and got clearance. I still remember, after the gear went up, Franz leaned forward and gave me a time check—oh-four-twenty. Then the course."

"Three-four-two magnetic," said Dobson.

Hackstead raised an eyebrow. "Yes. The final turn was to come after we had crossed the English coast. She hardly deviated."

The trip from Beauvais to the coast was uneventful. They crossed near St. Valéry. Five minutes later things started to go wrong.

"Franz had gone back to get things ready for the let-down, because once we reached the coastline near Dymchurch there was going to be a lot of work to do. The mayday calls, simulated radio malfunction, trimming, settling her at the right angle, locking the controls. Then the final bits and pieces—fuel cocks, fire extinguishers and the time fuses. All those had to be done fast, and it wasn't going to be easy. The gear we had on was cumbersome enough, and once the time fuses were running we had to get out, but quick."

Franz went back to remove the large canister from its protective drum. He had just got the seals off when the port engine faltered.

Hackstead juggled the mixture controls, but she had started to run rough, shaking the aircraft so that he was almost fighting her.

"I had the cockpit lights on low, and I saw straightaway that the port engine was overheating badly, the temperature rising fast. I reduced speed on both, and of course we started to lose height."

The temperature was still rising and they had only some eight miles to run before crossing the coast near Dymchurch.

"We were losing altitude badly, because I had to pull back on both engines. You know what can happen if one engine goes on a Marauder?"

"You weren't in a landing configuration, though. No gear down. You could have feathered and used the one."

"And lost our glide slope? I was trying to figure out a fresh angle from, say, two thousand feet. One that might just bring her down gently on target. I was in the middle of that when the fire warning went and I saw the port motor start to burn. Flames coming out through the gills. Franz tried to get forward, and eventually made it by the time I had the extinguisher on and the prop feathered. She was flying like a brick, and we were down to just above fifteen hundred, so I told Franz to cut the fuel cocks in the navigator's position, then go aft, set the clocks and get out."

By himself, Hackstead trimmed the aircraft to the safest gentle glide slope, turned off the master fuel cock, cut the starboard motor, feathered that propeller, activated the starboard fire extinguisher, trimmed her, put on some ten degrees of flap, then opened the canopy above his head and, as he put it, "went out like a flying fart."

"I had no idea where we were. All I heard was this whooshing noise, like a glider. Just for a second or two after my chute opened. Then it was peace and calm—just like they all describe it in the books."

He landed by a road and did the only thing possible: buried everything—protective clothing, parachute, flight gear. Then, wearing standard number-two uniform, Captain Bud Hackstead, SS Oberführer Hackensteiner, started to walk up the road.

"I had no idea of what had happened to Franz; whether he'd set the time clocks, or even got out. I figured that he hadn't had time to do either. At six in the morning I found myself in Rye. I was in a restricted zone, but I did have passes and documents. I knew it was going to be tough trying to work my way back through the zone—the place was crawling with troops—and then round for the rendezvous that night with the Stork. But I had a go."

Hackstead got to the rendezvous. One hour late.

"I waited for another hour, just in case, then gave up."

"How . . . ?"

"Franz did make it. He made it with the big canister—out of its container. Landed almost in old Mrs. Lambert's garden. He used great common sense, didn't you, Franz?"

"I tried." The accent was wholly English. Dobson wondered about Franz's real history. Where had he come from? What was his background? "I left the blue and gray timers until last. Started on the drum. I'd already got it out of the protective casing and was holding it, clumsily, in the crook of my left arm, just putting my hand out to set the timer, when I felt the aircraft begin to go. I don't know why, but there it was, like a baby in my arms. I went out fast, through the rear exit—the camera hatch—and it wasn't until my parachute opened that I realized I was still carrying the thing. Unfused, thank heaven. He's already told you, I landed almost in Mrs. Lambert's garden. I checked that the safety catch was on the timer, wrapped the drum in my parachute and buried it. I'd just finished when the front door opened and there she was, standing looking at me. So I did the ghostly bit and walked away. She was a funny old bird. I gather she regarded me as a friend."

"It *was* you who went back?"

"Of course. I buried the protective gear in a field not far away. When I finally got back to England it seemed the only sensible thing to do—check that the canister was okay. I cleaned and oiled it regularly. You see, the experts from Sachsenhausen said the stuff inside would remain active for maybe fifty years as long as none of the casing corroded."

"So you came back to England, home, beauty and a bucket full of death."

"What else could I do? I made the Stork pickup and put in a report. They took forever working out what was for the best. They wanted to fly me in—drop me and let me activate the monster. But by the time they got that far there was too much going on: invasion, the Caen breakout, the dash for the Rhine. I hung on to my RAF uniform and some of the papers, then sat around waiting. Everyone was fighting except me, and I had Free's papers. I knew he had been in Stalag Luft III. They sent me back to Berlin and I sat behind a desk for a while, trying to organize bits and pieces of the resistance. The old men and the children. Then, when the Russian winter offensive started, I just pinched a staff car and headed in the general direction of the Elbe, changed into the RAF gear and walked toward the British advance—I wanted nothing to do with the Russians."

"You weren't with the people from Stalag Luft III when they were found?"

"Lord, no. Mind you, that was the story I told when they got around to the final debriefing. Just said I'd come out of Sagan and they believed me. Put me down on the list with the other boys—they were probably still fifty miles to the east when I got myself out and into British hands. They gave me all Free's back pay and his demobilization grant. So I became Free—in every sense."

"And you?" To Hackstead.

Hackstead grinned. "I had a great big leave pass and plenty of cash from the survival kit. I just headed for London, bought a new uniform, checked in at the Officers' Club and had a ball; moved around a lot—different hotels, other cities. Mind you, when I was sober I prayed a lot that Franz hadn't set the canisters going. But I had no idea that he was even alive until the *Dodo* report landed on my desk."

"That's why you were so frightened when people started getting ill?"

"Yep. Thought it might be cholera. Then I got to Franz and knew what he was sitting on. Silly bastard just didn't know what to do with it. So I told him."

Ebenskrumm smiled. Unpleasant. "I was doing certain things. Got the jitters when they found the wreckage. The black container for the drum would still be up there among the bits and pieces. At least I knew that, so I went up and tried to find it, get it away before anybody started wondering what it was."

"You were the phantom figure flitting around the crash site at night?"

He nodded. "Dead loss," laughing as though it was a good joke. Then, turning to Hackstead, he muttered something in German and hobbled away toward the door.

"Mrs. Lambert?" asked Dobson, pointing toward the retreating limping figure.

"I'm afraid so." Another look at his watch. "It's almost time for Potts, Charles and company to arrive—damn it, I wish it was only Charles and a TV crew. Potts and his lot'll have to be locked into some basement." He frowned. "Okay. Down to the nitty."

"After the war . . . ?" Dobson began.

"Oh, don't be so naïve. I hitched into Germany and then reported that *Overshoot* had been a disaster. I was the only survivor. I had plenty of friends in moderately high places. Nobody queried. When they disbanded OSS, Mr. Dulles and his team kindly took me onto his other payroll. I've been feeding CIA info to fascist organizations for years."

"They'll have you yet, Bud. Trotter and his gang'll turn up. Eventually. They were watching me like hawks. They know about the Fenwell visit. They may take time, but they'll get here."

"I doubt it. They'll check with my people first and, as far as they're concerned, I'm down here helping Mr. Free to cough—with the two poor dead gentlemen who were once close colleagues. I'm clean. That is, until Charles arrives. Then we deliver the ultimatum."

"Which is? Couple of million and a safe journey to South America?"

Hackstead sighed. "The hijack, skyjack and terrorist trade has petrified people's imaginations, David. A couple of million? Is that all you can think of? Release of political prisoners or we blow up the hostages? Let me make it plain, there are no hostages. Not you, Potts or his crew. If anything, the whole country are hostages. But they're hostages already—hostages of a crumbling economy and weak, uninspired leadership since the forties."

"Then?"

"Our ultimatum concerns the whole of England being at grave risk—maybe the whole of Europe: the world."

"You're crazy."

"Maybe a little, but I have a mission and a destiny like the Führer. No, I give the ultimatum to the press—to Charles—who will have to take it to the top; and the top is going to see that it makes very good copy. Only the government won't allow it to be printed. They will conform."

"You sure? I'm personally uncertain of the sanity of our present government."

Hackstead picked up his cap. "There you have it," he grinned. "We're after a new kind of government."

"So what've you got hanging over us, Bud—or may I call you Oberführer?" Don't show fear, he told himself. It's like with animals, you must not show fear.

"Well." Hackstead adjusted his cap to the jaunty, arrogant angle. "Well, until now I've had access to most kinds of passes and documents. The dear departed here," he waved toward the door and the corpse on the floor (obviously also meaning the corpse outside behind the rockery), "were very helpful; thought we were doing a covert job with a new piece of surveillance gear. They did me a favor and acted as laborers to set up the canister. Safe as safe houses. They were trained confessors; wouldn't know one end of a sneakie from the other. What we have done—listen carefully—is install the canister and set the time clock for around six tomorrow evening—well, nearer five-thirty really. Call it five-thirty to be on the safe side. Happily, it's a very well-made, sophisticated time clock. You may remember that as far back as the thirties we had people very experienced in delayed-trigger devices. This one can be set for a twenty-four-hour period, with a manual override up to forty-eight or seventy-two hours." He smiled, the thin, brutal smile this time. "About five-thirty tomorrow afternoon. So the deadline is short. It's in a very public place and there are going to be a lot of untraceables. By Christ, the medics'll have their work cut out trying to contain the problem. Impossible."

"Contain what?"

"Think hard, David. It's all simple, obvious. *Rattengift. Ratpoison.*What's the worst disease you can think of connected with rats?"

The dreadful fear rose, volcanic, through Dobson's body. "Oh...oh, Holy Christ."

Hackstead nodded. "Yes. Bubonic, with a couple of aerosols of pneumonic just as a makeweight. Twelve in all. Remember what happened when that guy died of pneumonic plague at Porton Down? They were able to contain it because they had all his contacts on site. When this lot goes off tomorrow evening there's going to be no way of containing it. Not for a long, long time. Unless we get what we want, it's going to be the Black Death all over again."

"To contract bubonic, you have to be bitten by a rat flea," Dobson thought out loud.

"Yes. Unless you catch it by droplet from someone who already has it. The stuff they made up in Sachsenhausen and Birkenau is in the form of droplets. All ready made, just as though you're catching it from someone else. The Black Death. Instant, ready mixed: just add people; and the stuff is still highly active."

"There're vaccines now. You can treat it."

"A whole country? Several countries, because there'll be travelers. Oh yes, eventually—with world medical aid. But a terrible lot of people are going to die. I can give you a positive guarantee of around seventy thousand people being infected tomorrow evening. Seventy thousand individual cases developing within a week. Consider the untraceable contacts of seventy thousand cases during the incubation period—eight, nine, ten...fifty? It's incalculable. The Black Death, David, is due to strike like the giant which people knew back in the fourteenth century."

"Unless?"

"Unless the government resigns and sets up a new national coalition government led and headed by five people whom I nominate. I've got the list—two active politicians, a prominent industrialist and two high-ranking military figures." He looked at his watch again. "Think of the panic when Charles' people take that into Downing Street in an hour or so. There's no choice; and, to be honest with you, I think there will be some people in government who will be most relieved."

"And you?"

"I think it best if we're out of the way for a while. Unhappily we have to resort to the terrorist demands. Fifty million, in dollars naturally, and a jet clearance to the place of our choice. You can come, David. In fact I think I'll insist on that. You and your young woman."

"South America?"

"Possibly. Really, Dave, I'm more concerned with getting this country and Europe whipped into line. But I am a survivor. I want to live to see it all happen as it was originally planned."

"Nobody's going to play, you know, Bud. You're doing a kind of terrorist skyjack—on a huge and mad tapestry. They don't play that game any more."

Hackstead laughed, a beer-cellar guffaw. "I'm doing a blackjack, David. If they don't play, then the four horsemen of the Apocalypse will ride roughshod over Europe."

"You're crazy, Bud. You're pissing at the moon."

"It can't miss."

"Oh yes it can. We'll all get very wet—including you and your chum. My old man was a clergyman. He had a favorite saying: 'While there's death there's hope.' I used to think it stupid. Now I'm not so sure."

Ebenskrumm was in the doorway, calling out something in German.

"The coach is here," said Hackstead, his voice terrible in its cold, clear, single calm. "You, Dobson, are going to stand in the porch and greet them; and if you don't do it right you get bullets. It's no time for heroism. Now, go and see them in."

Dobson's mind was blank. There would be men and women coming through that porch. Maybe—just maybe—he could turn it to his advantage.

"Anything for you."

He started toward the door and was halfway across the hall when Ebenskrumm suddenly turned back and began to shout.

"They've got two cars with them."

"Charles'll be in one of them. Don't worry . . ." Hackstead started to reply.

He was cut short by another voice which seemed to come out of space, from the air above.

"He's not, you know, Hackstead. The coach is full of our people. Arthur and I came in the back way, and if you don't drop that bloody Kraut pistol I'm going to blow your head off."

Trotter stood at the top of the stairs. On the far side of the gallery was another figure. He stood stock-still, both hands raised gripping a revolver pointing straight at the main door.

Hackstead whirled around, and, as he did so, Ebenskrumm turned in the doorway, his hand coming up with the pistol rising in the direction of the figure on the gallery.

Arthur—Richard Martin Lewis—pulled the trigger twice, and Ebenskrumm went tottering backward, in funny little steps, his hands thrown up, his automatic pistol spinning through the air.

Eventually he tripped back over the body of the dead confessor, and lay still; but by this time, Dobson had also moved, locking his right arm around Hackstead's throat. His hand clutched his own left triceps and the left hand pushed hard onto the back of Hackstead's head.

"Drop that gun, you bastard, or I'll break your neck," he muttered. Then, loudly, to Trotter. "Don't kill him, Trotter, he's holding the aces and they're nasty. But I'm personally going to beat the truth out of him."

The Lüger fell to the floor with a dull clunk and SS Oberführer Bernhard Hackensteiner's cap slewed from his head.

"There's no way," he croaked. "No way that disaster can be averted now."

Suddenly the hall was full of people.

39

It took three large plain-clothes policemen to pull Dobson from Hackstead's neck. Later, he realized they were right. In spite of his call to Trotter, he had almost killed the last captain of *Dancing Dodo*.

Now, he stood there in the hall, lost, his body in a bad state of disorder, his mind in chaos. Through this disharmony he was conscious of the activity: of Hackstead screaming something about *Rattengift* now being completed unless his demands were met, and Trotter, very cool, ordering a pair of heavies to get him out of it. They dragged the shouting Hackstead away through the door to the left of the stairs. You could still hear him for a few minutes, then the abuse and hysterical yelling faded.

Nobody appeared to be bothered about Dobson. His hands were shaking badly. He became very conscious of that as he dropped onto the settee and tried to light a cigarette. God help us. The prayer, a real prayer, running through his mind, tracking in a circle. Through the disarray he was focusing on one thing. Somewhere, most probably in London, there was a canister containing ten aerosols of active droplet-form bubonic plague bacilli, and two of pneumonic plague. At around five-thirty tomorrow afternoon the aerosols would be activated unless ... But who would really believe? Who could, or would, move fast enough?

There were a lot of people around, some uniformed police, many men and some women in plain clothes. Ambulance men were taking care of the bodies by the door—the confessor and Ebenskrumm.

Automatically Dobson looked at his watch. Time seemed to have stood still, for it was already nine-fifteen. He reckoned that he could have walked out and driven away without anyone bothering.

Then he thought of Ann, and knew that he must do just that: leave, go to her and take things from there. He was about to stand up when Trotter appeared behind him, putting a huge black hand on his shoulder.

"You're a stupid bastard, Dobson." Trotter sounded as if he meant it.

"I know now, don't I? Ann. I've got to get to her."

"She's okay, Dobson. They're looking after her."

"Looking after her? Where?"

"Last I heard in Folkestone jail, but some doctor was on his way down to check her out."

"In jail?"

"Well, we put out a general for both of you along the coast. Didn't do much good with you. It was you we wanted to stop. But the manager of the hotel reacted kindly to Miss West's description."

"I want to see her."

"I'll do what I can to fix a quick reunion." Trotter came around the settee and sat down. It was like being on the wrong end of a seesaw; the big policeman's bulk even affected the craftsman-made piece of furniture. "Look, man," he said, "why didn't you take heed? I told you I was watchin' out for you. Gave you protection, and all you did was give us the runaround. We even provided you with a shooter, and that saved your life. Yours and your girl's."

"I thought he was straight. Hackstead. I thought the bastard was leveling with me."

"We wanted you to think so. We needed you as cover to get in here. It's a bitch, this place. Nowhere to hide or watch, no dead ground. Getting up to the back of the house was like walking naked through a nunnery." He gave a big shrug which shook the settee. "We didn't really know how many men he had here. The two guys from his own people: we thought they could have been watchers. Arthur and I squirmed up from the far road on our bellies using anything possible, tufts of grass, stones. We nearly dug a trench in the ground to make the back of the place."

"You did it, though."

"Only 'cos you distracted them."

"Ann?" He almost pleaded.

"All in good time. There's people here that'll want words." Dobson sighed.

"Here they go," muttered Trotter. "The two in front are the best, most senior, confessors in the trade."

A knot of three men were progressing fast across the hall, from the direction of the porch, shepherded by a uniformed officer. The two to whom Trotter referred would be in their mid-fifties, Dobson thought. They looked like high-ranking tax men, or bank managers who never allowed overdrafts. The third, walking a few paces behind, was younger. A big lad: the heavy, in case it came to that stage of play.

The group passed through the door by the stairs. They would be with Hackstead in a matter of minutes.

"They'll want words." Trotter made his point again. "I'll do what I can about getting Miss West up here. They may want words with her as well."

"Arthur?" asked Dobson. "If you can't do anything about Ann yet, then at least you can tell me about Arthur."

"Arthur? Yes. Mr. Lewis really. What about him?"

"I don't follow. You were interested. Marking him."

"Only to put you off. He's Department, if you know what I mean."

Dobson knew. "Five?"

"Sort of between the two. Five and Six. Yes, and even the Department can't be everywhere at once. They dropped him out about ten years ago. The old heave-ho cover game. Mr. Lewis keeps an eye on the unofficial activities of foreign agencies operating in this country with government sanction. He deals mainly with the air side."

"He would. In the war . . ."

"Yes, we know what he did; and the evidence regarding *Overshoot*."

"What you really mean is that he's a CIA-watcher?"

"The CIA among others. The departments, between them, keep tabs on most of the NATO security agencies who have operating facilities over here."

"So what happened?"

"With Mr. Lewis?"

"Of course."

"He'd been working a different area, then your snappy, hair-triggered Sugden put out feelers for old Tempsfordians. The first one, Denis, got put away, so they brought in Arthur and gave him to Sugden. We carried Arthur."

"You would, being the executive arm of Five."

"We carried him. The night I gave you the shooter, he thought he recognized somebody. Not a positive, but it worried him, having just been asked to do the *Overshoot* recall. He applied for access to make a positive ID. He got one. There were two Department men down on the Farnborough thing."

"We marked them all right. Stuck out like ... Well, I wouldn't like to say what they stuck out like."

"Yeah, Dobson. You were being marked by another one as well. Your Arthur—at a distance. He got his positive ID at some ungodly hour in the morning."

"Hackstead?"

"Of course. He made a positive that Hackstead was the pilot on *Overshoot*. That made people jump."

"I can imagine."

"We were covering you and we put an immediate tail on him. We knew he'd eventually end up at Fenwell, but it's not the most ideal place for a permanent surveillance. Unhappily our marker lost Buddy Boy a couple of times. We've got a lot of blank spaces in his schedule. It didn't worry me overmuch because I thought we had you. Why did you start playing games? Hackstead set you off?"

"I told you. I thought he was straight. Come to that, why didn't you let me into the secret society?"

"The initiation rites last too long. Besides, we're running out of virgins." He raised his voice. "Because we wanted you to believe: to come in here happy and contented with the rest of the party—only you would have been in one of the cars, away from the coach which would have been full of our people, dummies. Potts and his crew were to be kept at the Hilton. We might have got in nice and quiet. Instead we had the bloody storm troopers."

"You'd have had them anyway. Hackstead and his mate did for their own boys before I arrived."

"I wonder," mused Trotter, "how our confessor friends are doing with him. They're here to take him apart, and I don't think they're too worried about putting him back together again. You talked to him?"

"Yes."

"So you know what he's on about."

"I know what he says he's done and what he wants."

"From the way he was shouting I gather he thinks he has the lot of us stitched up."

"He has."

Trotter looked at him. "Bad?"

"Horrific."

"You want to talk to me..." He was stopped in mid-flow. The big younger man who had gone down with the senior confessors emerged from the door to the right of the stairs and beckoned Trotter.

"They want to talk with you," the Special Branch man said, returning to the settee. "They also sound worried."

The big lad led the way. They went down a long passage, then farther into the bowels of Fenwell Manor via a short flight of stairs and into another passage.

The heavy tapped at the second door on the left and opened it immediately.

The two older men were seated in armchairs. Trotter did the introductions. No names, just, "Wing Commander Dobson, I3 (Air)."

They gave him quiet nods. The young tough took no notice.

One of the men wore a dark, conservative pinstripe and an old Etonian tie. The other was dressed in light gray, which proved he had reasonable taste but gave no hint of his background. Jack the Lad was in a sharp light suit. He did not wear a tie.

"The subject's in the kitchen," one of the men said to nobody in particular. "That's very good, Trotter. I like the bars on the window, and the locks. We've left a couple of your people there, but, if I were you, I'd keep checking them while we're having words with the wing commander."

Trotter left quickly.

"I don't think there's any time to waste..." Dobson began.

"Then we won't waste any." The old Etonian managed a smile. The only trouble was that the smile did not touch his eyes, which had irises like small-caliber bullet holes: entry holes which had been left for the blood to blacken.

The door opened without any preliminary knock. Trotter ducked his head in for a moment. "We've got the heavy brass from the Home Office with us." He lowered his voice and the reason became apparent a few seconds later.

"Oh Christ," muttered the old Etonian.

A new figure appeared in the doorway. The garb was Whitehall exclusive, the well-groomed-at-any-time-of-day look.

"Sir Robert," the old Etonian acknowledged.

"Just here to sit in." The newcomer had the languid manner of his particular class and calling. "I'm just here to sit in. I gather there's some kind of emergency and I'm to oil the wheels, if they need oiling."

"As long as you can keep the press off our backs, sir." Gray suit sounded an obsequious bastard.

"I can if it's done with haste." Sir Robert, whoever he was, had the natural gift of authority. "The Farnborough fiasco was difficult enough. I gather there's something a little more dangerous floating around."

The old Etonian sprayed out the facts. A near résumé which left nothing to the imagination. "We've only had the one go at him," he said at the end. "He's either a loony or in dead earnest. Probably both. I gather that he's unburdened himself quite fully to Wing Commander Dobson. We were just going to talk to Dobson and get his views."

"Get them then." Sir Robert remained outwardly unperturbed by the story he had just been told.

"Dobson?" queried the old Etonian.

"For my money, we're in deep trouble. You know my involvement?"

"Naturally. That's why we regard you as the oracle."

"He means every word. The canister exists. It has been planted. It will activate on time. We have until five-thirty tomorrow afternoon."

"That is your earnest and considered professional opinion?"

Dobson told them it was, and why. He also quoted long passages of what Hackstead had said to him.

"That's all?" Gray suit raised his eyebrows. He sounded flippant and even sarcastic.

"Isn't it enough? He's off his rocker, yes. But he will not back down."

"Want a quack?" gray suit asked the old Etonian. "Spot of the old talkie-talkie serum?"

"I think we'll have another word with him first before resorting to those methods. So unpleasant, that kind of thing." The old Etonian had immense cool. "Doubt if it would work with a man like Hackstead. He knows it all. CIA. Kim Philby of the fascists, eh? It's a challenge."

"They were his words," nodded Dobson.

"Poor old Kim," Sir Robert whispered, then looked up quickly, as if to see if anyone had noticed. Slowly, he pulled himself from his chair; there was no hint of diplomatic stress. "I think I should talk with Reeves from Porton Down. Then the bomb people at the Yard, and, last but far from least, our beloved Premier and the Minister of Health." The ghost of a smile passed over his lips. "Both of their jobs appear to be in danger."

Dobson had heard about the way these people worked, but until now he had never really believed the stories.

"Might be worthwhile, sir." The old Etonian was busy with a silver cigarette case. "Might I suggest that while we're going over—I mean, while we're interrogating—Oberführer Hackensteiner, Wing Commander Dobson takes charge of drawing up a list of possible planting points for the device. The planter, in this case, had access to a very large number of official passes and authorities. A man with Hackensteiner's cover could probably plant in the main loo at Buck House if he so had a mind."

For the first time, Sir Robert's face changed from its impassivity to the edge of worry, as though the terrible truth was just dawning. Dobson wondered if Sir Robert's journey had been really necessary.

"Dobson has worked very closely with Hackensteiner. That's a point of psychological advantage," added gray suit.

"Very well." The Home Office man gave a quick nod. He was at the door, obviously in a hurry to be off.

"If I take that on," Dobson said sharply, "I'll need assistance and authority."

"You can have Trotter, he's the law." Old Etonian glanced toward the Home Office man. "And authority?"

Sir Robert nodded, then hesitated. "Before I leave; you have given me to understand that this is not an idle threat?"

"I would say that it's a greater threat than a planted nuclear device. It's immediate and urgent." Old Etonian, despite his relaxed and cool manner, was firm and serious.

"The terms," Sir Robert continued, "concern money and an unrestricted flight out of the country to destination of choice?"

"Just as we've told you, but that is the minor part. The main demand is the political one."

"That's ridiculous as well as being unconstitutional."

"He's got it worked out in great detail." Old Etonian exhaled a plume of smoke. "The government is to announce its resignation by ten-thirty tomorrow morning. The leader of the opposition will, naturally, stand by to be summoned to the palace. At one o'clock the national shock will come. Five people will be summoned by the Queen and asked if they can form a government."

"You said two active politicians, an industrialist and a pair of well-known military figures. What about names?"

"I have them." Old Etonian tapped his pocket. "All typed out. Addresses, telephone contacts, the lot."

Sir Robert stretched out a hand. "Then I think I'd better . . ."

Old Etonian shook his head. "I'm sorry, sir. No. This is no reflection on yourself, but we wouldn't want the Home Office botching it; dawn raids; arrests. In the final gambit, we might have to bluff it out and go along with him. Renege afterward, of course. If there's no other way." Another plume of smoke. "We'll try to find another way, here with the subject. Dobson, Trotter and the might of the police and armed forces," he allowed himself a grim smile, "will attempt to find the wretched thing. Agreed?"

The Home Office brass thought about it, then nodded and left. He looked a most unhappy man.

"You're not trying to pass the buck by any chance?" Dobson's mind was becoming increasingly sneaky.

"What *do* you mean?" Old Etonian reminded him a little of the late Sir Noël Coward.

"I mean that, if the canister is not found and deactivated, it all goes down to me and Trotter."

"Don't be a fool," snapped gray suit. "You'll have all the backing you want. Trotter'll be with you in a few minutes. I think we . . . ?" He turned toward old Etonian.

"Yes, I think we should start pulling the aces out of the gallant Oberführer's sleeves. Good luck."

The confessors went off in the direction of the kitchen, leaving Dobson on his own. By the time Trotter returned he was already seated at the table, notebook open, making his first list of plant points.

"I hear we're a team," Trotter said gloomily.

"I hear we have authority, which means we can call up what we need." He paused, pen over the notebook. "Ann?"

"On her way here with the doctor. She's okay."

"The doctor? Marsh?"

"Yep. There's a WDS with her as well. Just protection while we're doing the job."

Dobson nodded. Again he was surprised by the fast passage of time. His watch showed nearly ten-thirty. Trotter sat at the other side of the table. "Down to cases then?"

"Due to activate around five-thirty," sighed Dobson. "Five-thirty tomorrow evening. We have around nineteen hours to locate. He also claimed, to me, that at least seventy thousand people would get the first dose."

"Narrows it down a bit. You scared?"

"Witless."

"If it's true, they'll never contain it. It would mean vaccination of every man, woman and child in the country. Seventy thousand for starters."

"Let's do the logic. Five-thirty in the afternoon. Seventy thousand with one blow. It *does* narrow it down. It has to be a fairly enclosed public place through which around seventy thousand people pass between, say, five-thirty and seven. The stuff vaporizes. Nobody would know what they were getting— like catching the flu from someone sitting next to you on a train."

"That's it. Commuter time. High-commuter railway stations. Reasonably enclosed places. You got it, Dobson."

"Or airports. Heathrow. Gatwick."

"Yes, but..."

"And we don't really know if it's in London. There are other big commuter centers as well—Birmingham, Liverpool, Glasgow..."

"Hey, man, we have to make a decision. When the time runs out our decision is all that counts. I say London, and I say it could be one of the main railway stations, or Heathrow. In fact, I'd put Heathrow down as first choice."

"Yes, sir, Mr. Trotter."

"Oh shit, don't pull rank on me. We have to look as if we're doing something—and who knows?"

"Okay. We got a car?"

"We have the works."

"How long to get us into London?"

"Couple of hours. Hour and a half if we hustle."

Dobson went through the timing in his head. Heathrow, Gatwick, the main commuter railway termini. If the search and bomb people went in now—within the next hour or so—and combed the places, it would cause less fuss. The traffic flow would be minimal during the night—after midnight. No need to cause panic. If the search boys were really hot and came up quickly ... Well? If not, they would have to start thinking again. Museums, other public places. They would have to do that in the morning if nothing came up during the early hours.

He passed on his thoughts to Trotter. "Search boys, bomb squads, military, and the Porton Down people standing by in some central position so that we can move them in," he ended. "It wouldn't be a bad idea to get the statistics of commuter flow as well. Can the Yard do that?"

"I'll try. Sit tight and I'll see. Do I get the other boys in action now?"

"Check on statistics quickly, then we'll alert the others. There may be a clue regarding statistics. Direction might be faster that way."

"Okay, Dobson. Nice to have you on the team at last."

"Get on with it."

Trotter disappeared in search of a telephone. He seemed to be away a long time. Dobson carried on going through his list.

"Bloody Home Office burk." Trotter was breathless when he got back. "Talkin' to Downing Street. I had to wait, there's a shortage of telephonic communication. Talkin' to the PM."

"Why not the police radio?" Dobson stayed as calm and light as he could muster.

"Oh shit." Trotter cursed with feeling.

"They got the statistics at the Yard?"

"Traffic flow; CRO. The rest you have to get from the Department of the Environment. At this moment there's a car dashing through Wimbledon heading for the home of the man in charge of statistics there. They're going to relay his answers to us as soon as possible."

"This is how I read it." Dobson turned his notebook around for Trotter to see.

The Special Branch man went through it aloud. "Heathrow, Gatwick, King's Cross, Paddington, Charing Cross, Waterloo, Euston, Piccadilly underground, St. Paul's, Bank ..." He went on, the voice dropping to a mutter. "The Yard and all local areas'll have to pull boys out of bed."

"It's been done before. I want those statistics, though. Hackstead's a former Nazi and he's dead methodical. If he says seventy thousand he's got access to statistics. He knows what he's doing. We cover everywhere; then we put more people into the one that shows up nearest to seventy thousand on the commuter flow from five o'clock onward. Right?"

"Putting all the eggs in one omelet, Dobson."

"We have no other options. But *all* those locations have to be combed."

Trotter nodded just as the door opened.

It was the young heavy from the confession team. He carried a tray with two cups and a pot of tea.

"Bleedin' tea boy. Been relegated to bloody tea boy." He put the tray down heavily.

Trotter laughed. "How's it going in there?"

Dobson cut in. "Inspector Trotter hasn't time for tea." He tried to look sympathetic. "Claud, time does not hang heavy. There are things to be done. Get those lads cracking, will you? Tell them we'll come straight in to Heathrow first. But get them moving."

Trotter said nothing, just got up and left quickly. Jack the Lad turned to follow him.

"Just a minute." Dobson felt no flutter, suddenly as calm as a lake with no breeze.

"Yeah?"

"Inspector Trotter asked you a question. Give the answer to me. How's it going in there?"

"Not a chance in hell. He's off his chump. Last territorial demands and all that. Been spouting Kraut at them for the past ten minutes. Giving them a lecture on how Hitler was the greatest. I always thought it was Muhammad Ali."

"Seriously, no chance?"

"No way. I've seen those two extractors at it before now. They're amazing. But this one won't crack. He wants the government out; his people in; the cash, and out. Otherwise the balloon goes up. Prime Minister and Home Secretary say no. He won't see reason. Last I heard was that he's prepared to perish with everyone else. You'd better come up with something because I, for one, believe him."

"So do I." Dobson knew Hackstead well enough for that. "I think I'd better speak with your guv'nor if he can spare a minute."

"I'll try."

"I haven't got long. We're off as soon as the DI has things under way."

He poured two cups of tea. Trotter might just have time to drink one when he got back. Etonian tie came in.

"You wanted to see me?"

"I gather you're getting nowhere at the speed of light."

"Hard case."

"In truth: are you going to break him?"

The confessor looked away and sighed. It was not weariness. "Haven't lost many in my time, but I think we're going to cop out on this one. The time element's against us. He's been well trained and knows how long he has to hold on. Five-thirty tomorrow afternoon. I'm seriously thinking of calling the medics in, but that could be messy and they can foul up as easily as anyone else."

Dobson told him what they were doing, and handed over a duplicate list of principal plant points.

"Good." Etonian tie's face cleared a fraction. "I'll put some pressure on, using some of these names. Might get some clue or reaction. Sounds very logical. What time're you moving in?"

"They should be starting now. Trotter's radioing instructions, then we're leaving. Can you see that we're kept up-to-date, through whatever radio channel we're using?"

"If we get anywhere you'll be the first to know."

They wished each other good luck, and the confessor went back to his job with a touch more spring in his walk.

When Trotter returned, Ann was with him. As though by mutual consent they were restrained. There was a plain-clothes policewoman by the door, and Dr. Marsh stood in the passageway outside.

"They're hanging onto you down here for safety only," Dobson told her.

"I know." Behind the big lenses of her glasses, her eyes seemed to be searching his face. "You all right?"

"Fine. A lot to do."

"It's a mess, I hear."

"Most messes are cleanable. That's what Claud Trotter and I are about to do. Clean it up."

"You have to go now?"

He glanced toward Trotter, who nodded, signifying that the operation was in progress. In London police and the military would already be converging on the main-line railway stations and underground junctions, as well as at Heathrow and Gatwick. He could only pray that they were playing it as gently as possible.

"Yes, I have to go now," he answered. "How's the shoulder?"

She tried to grin. "You were right about me not coming on up here. There's a bit of pain. Dr. Marsh's going to give me a shot. I just wanted to see you first."

"I'm glad."

"Still apple blossom?"

"Of course."

He hoped there would be apple blossom next year for everyone.

They embraced, and he left quickly, nodding to Marsh as he followed Trotter along the passage and up the stairs.

The hall was full of activity. As they crossed to the porch, Dobson saw, to his relief, that a radio transmitter was being set up.

"It's only for patch-through jobs," Trotter said. "There's no coding yet, and our orders are to play it down for the next few hours. No panics."

"And they're on in London?"

"Search and bomb squads; military; Porton Down team on their way in. All plant points we've given them. I've said you want everything counted including the light bulbs."

"Dimensions? They know the dimensions of what they're looking for?"

"Taken care of."

It was chill in the air outside, and the police Rover had its engine running, the driver at the wheel.

Dobson looked at his watch as he reached for the door handle. It was nearly twenty minutes past eleven.

"Plenty of time," Trotter said as they went up the drive. He sat in front, next to his own man. Dobson stretched back, alone in the rear, and closed his eyes.

"Five-thirty tomorrow night will soon be five-thirty tonight," he said, knowing that there really was very little time to spare.

"I meant we had plenty of time to get into London. Let the search people get on with it."

Dobson suddenly felt very tired. He kept his eyes closed and started to drift away from reality.

He must have been asleep for the best part of half an hour when the sound of the radio brought him round.

Trotter was answering a call. "Sierra Bravo Six I read you."

The message crackled from the speaker set into the dash. Sierra Bravo Six was requested to use the nearest telephone and call a number. Dobson recognized the number immediately. Hackstead had first given it to him. They were to call Fenwell Manor.

"Has to be high-risk. Where are we?" he asked, blinking the sleep from his eyes.

Trotter was returning the handset to its rest. "Just coming onto the M2 at Exit 5." A straight run into London.

"There's a service area about six miles on," said the driver.

"Siren and lights then," Trotter ordered. The siren started almost before he finished the sentence, and Dobson felt himself being pushed back by the acceleration.

"You heard that?" Trotter shouted.

"The radio? They want us to call into Fenwell Manor." His watch showed two minutes past midnight. "We've got till five-thirty tonight." By this time they were over in the fast lane going like a jet.

They made the service area in under six minutes and Trotter was out of the car and running before Dobson even had the door open. He caught up with him just inside the complex, which seemed to be full of long-haired truck drivers and pinball machines. It stank of stale fat, from the french fries, mixed with sweat and urine.

"Perhaps he's cracked," Dobson panted.

"I sure as hell hope so."

Trotter dialed and identified himself. There was a pause and then a voice speaking. Dobson could not hear, but it sounded urgent.

"Jesus Christ," Trotter shouted into the phone. "Okay." He listened tensely for a moment and then hung up.

"Hackstead's cracked up," he said flatly. Dobson had never seen a man with black skin go almost white, but certainly the blood was drained from Trotter's cheeks.

"Great," he said. "So where's the germ drum?"

"Cracked up, not cracked. He's cracked up and boobed on us, and on himself." He paused, his hand moving shakily over his brow. "The car." He was already on his way.

"For Chrissake, tell me," shouted Dobson.

Trotter was walking fast. "They gave him a break and left him alone for half an hour. After ten minutes they heard him screaming. When they got to him he turned off the screams and started to laugh and burble about irony. Then he told them."

"Well, where is it?"

"He didn't tell them where it is. He told them he'd suddenly realized that he and that dead mate of his had come unstuck."

"How unstuck?"

"Unstuck with the timing device. Fucked up the setting on the clock."

"What?" Dobson was shouting.

"We've got one piece of vital info. They set it in the early hours of Monday morning—yesterday, between one and two—and set the time clock for it to blow between five-thirty and five forty-five Tuesday evening. Tonight. With the override switch on the timer that means at least a thirty-six- or thirty-eight-hour delay. They got it wrong and Hackstead's only just tumbled. In their hurry to get out they've underdelayed the setting by twelve hours. The bloody thing's going to spray plague bacilli out at five-thirty all right. This five-thirty. Five-thirty Tuesday morning. Now." His watch came up, the glass glinting. "We've got around five and a half hours to find it."

40

"Still Heathrow, Guv'?" the driver asked, unaware of the sudden shrinkage of life.

"Like a time machine. I want us there yesterday. Through the barrier."

The Rover squealed around the parking area, headed for the entrance road, flashed onto the highway and crossed diagonally into the fast lane.

"Who's doing what?" snapped Dobson.

"You are. They say it's down to you now. Those were the words: not *up* to you but *down* to you."

Dobson knew what he had to do. "Okay. Standard radio procedure, to hell with anyone picking up calls, we haven't got time to worry about the press and panic. Lots of work for everyone. Check the plant points to make sure nobody's come up with anything. Then they've got to move. I want interrogation centers set up now—within the half hour—close by every plant point, but not in them. The plant points are to be cleared once searched, then searched again. I want every available copper or soldier working, hauling in each and every man, woman or child who was on duty, in whatever capacity, at each of the plant points between eleven o'clock on Sunday night and six on

Monday morning. Make that eight on Monday morning. People who were on duty during those periods—porters, bar staff, aircrew, engine drivers, tea ladies, whatever—are to be interrogated individually. Pumped dry, questioned about everything, no matter how trivial."

"Done." Trotter began talking into his transmitter: precise, brief, lucid; giving instructions with great clarity.

After a while the calls began to come back.

"Jesus, they want to know exactly where to set up interrogation centers," he shouted at Dobson.

"Tell them to use their bloody initiative. Heathrow can take over the foyer of that hotel—the, what's its name?"

"The Holiday Inn's close."

"There if they have to, only they've got to let us know. Piccadilly underground can commandeer the foyer of the Regent Palace; Charing Cross has its own hotel on the doorstep. If they want authority with difficult customers tell them to get it from the local police. No need to pussyfoot or be polite, it's too urgent."

They came in through the Dartford Tunnel before one o'clock, and by that time, heading for the city, they had a rough idea of where the interrogation centers had been set up and which ones were operating.

The radio crackled into action again.

"Statistics' man Department of the Environment has been located and a car is going for him now. Should be at his office within the hour."

"Sierra Bravo." Talk button off. "My God, a lot of use he's going to be."

It was almost a quarter to two in the morning by the time they reached Heathrow and the hotel. It took them only a few seconds to get into the jammed and crowded foyer, where the atmosphere was tense, restless, yet politely efficient.

There were four tables, each with two officers, one plain-clothes and one uniformed. Queues of men and women were formed in front of each table.

As they passed down the lines Dobson and Trotter heard nothing but grumbling. A group of men by the entrance door were arguing with four helmeted policemen.

"Who said the British weren't an orderly race?" Dobson grinned.

Behind the four main tables were two others, occupied by a pair of uniformed inspectors. Right at the rear of the foyer a clutch of army officers and NCOs stood talking and smoking.

Occasionally one of the men at the interrogation tables would raise his hand and a uniformed inspector would hurry across and take note of what was being said.

Trotter had passed ahead of Dobson and was talking to one of the uniformed inspectors. He shook his head as Dobson approached.

"They're still in there searching. Nothing. Nothing that's proved any use."

Dobson turned away. The place was starting to smell of human odors and he felt suddenly sick. "I'll have to go outside..." he started, then spotted their police constable driver pushing his way through the queues, gesticulating. "Something's up."

They both shouldered through the lines of waiting people.

"Call for you, sir. They think they've got something at Charing Cross. Will you call in, please."

They ran.

The news from Charing Cross was that some work had gone on, high up in the girders of the giant roof, during Sunday night and the early hours of Monday morning. Nobody had, as yet, accounted for it, and a team of commandos with bomb disposal units were going up.

"Sounds promising. Charing Cross then." The car moved away and onto the M4, heading back into London.

Dobson's watch showed two-fifteen.

All three of them could feel the tension in the car. As it swept up the Hammersmith overpass the radio sparkled again. The statistics man had some of the commuter flow figures to hand.

"Get us the Charing Cross figures." Dobson's throat was getting sore.

"Message timed at zero-two-twenty-nine," came the response from Trotter's call. "Commuter flow between seventeen hundred hours and nineteen hundred hours, during weekdays at Charing Cross Station, as follows. Four-five-zero-zero-zero."

"Fall short of twenty-five thousand," Dobson frowned.

"So what's twenty-five grand between plague bacilli?"

"I told you before. Hackstead was an efficient Nazi. When he talked of seventy thousand, he meant seventy thousand; or near enough."

"Ask them what the next highest figure is on the sheet; just in case Charing Cross is a blank."

Trotter called up again. There was a pause.

"Sierra Bravo. Next figures read Victoria Station: six-zero-zero-zero-zero."

Trotter turned in his seat. "That suit you? Only ten thousand short."

"We'll try Victoria next if Charing Cross clears." Dobson was not quite convinced. Hackstead had been most specific: *I can give you a positive guarantee of around seventy thousand* . . .

"Call up Charing Cross. See what progress."

Trotter complied. The response was negative.

"Commando and disposal team still searching roof. No positives."

"You make it nearly quarter to three?" Dobson squinted at his watch, turning his wrist so that what light there was from outside caught the dial.

"Just gone. Around—no, exactly two-forty-seven."

Through Admiralty Arch and around in front of the National Gallery. They were almost home now. Charing Cross and the Strand lay ahead.

Charing Cross Station. Cars. Three large coaches. An armored car. More police and troops than he liked to think about, all of them jumbled around that famous cross in front of the station.

As they turned into the station yard, the radio crackled again:

"Control. Sierra Bravo."

Trotter grunted.

"Charing Cross confirms negative. Repeat negative. Work on roof authorized. Team has not—repeat not—made any positives."

"Guv'nor?" The driver uncertain.

"Victoria." Dobson decisive for a moment, then, "Hang on. Call up for the nearest statistic to seventy thousand peak period."

"Really bugging you, that Kraut." Trotter grumbled and began to make the call.

Control identified, patched through, and whoever was with the Department of the Environment man asked for a hold.

Two uniformed policemen were approaching the car. Trotter wound the window down and shouted at them. "We are Sierra Bravo Six, if you understand. If you don't, go ask your senior officer."

"Sierra Bravo Six. I have figures. Nearest at peak period to seven-zero-zero-zero-zero is figure seven-five-zero-zero-zero. Waterloo Station."

"The hell and back to Waterloo," Dobson said, cold and still. He had a gut reaction. Pure instinct. Somehow he knew. Perhaps because he had known Bud Hackstead—SS Oberführer Hackensteiner. "Where're they doing their interrogations?"

"Would you believe the Festival Hall?" Trotter shifted round. He was grinning. "I can see your face, Dobson. You believe it, yes?"

"Call them. Ask what progress."

The progress from Waterloo was negative. One thorough search had been carried out. The station was now cleared and the second search still in progress. Up to three hundred employees were being interrogated—in an orderly manner, they stressed—at the Royal Festival Hall.

The gray squat and sharp-lined Festival Hall, overlooking the river across from the Royal Palace of Westminster, was fully lit, and in the foyer they were right about the orderliness of the interrogation. Festival Hall staff had turned out to assist the police and military. There was a total lack of confusion or unrest. The same orderly lines snaked up to three tables, and, as at Heathrow, uniformed inspectors stood by to examine possible contacts. There was also an operations table, a long bare oblong, at which three other officers sat, interspersed with two girls. It was immediately obvious that they were cross-referencing dubious statements.

Behind the uniformed inspectors there was one Army major wearing a flack jacket, and a sergeant similarly dressed. The sergeant carried a walkie-talkie.

They were taken straight through to a superintendent of the uniformed branch who was in over-all control. He shook hands gravely—a tall, gaunt man—with Dobson, but barely acknowledged Trotter's presence.

"We've checked out a couple of possibles," he told them. "The first search drew a blank, but we've got teams all over the complex again now—even in that bloody great roof—and there's a disposal team standing by. Their controller's over there." He indicated the Army major, who looked very young and bored.

"Wing Commander Dobson's convinced this is the plant point," Trotter said, a burn of acid in his voice.

"Not convinced. I think it likely, but I could be more than wrong." Dobson felt the twinging taste of confusion in his thoughts. He could be so wrong. Then: "Would you spur them on? Tell them it's here..."

"Dobson...?" shocked from Trotter. "You've no..."

"Tell them it's here. All of them. The searchers and the interrogators." He turned his back on the superintendent and muttered, "Positive thinking, Trotter. We've ended up here. It's past three, we've less than two and a half hours and nowhere else to go. Unless a positive shows at one of the other points. Can you go down to the car and check where the Porton Down team are? How near?"

"You've flipped."

"Check again on the figures while you're at it. See if they've missed anything. One that comes exactly on seventy thousand commuters. If not, providing the bloody thing's in London, I figure this is the best bet."

A smile spread slowly over Trotter's face. "There's really nothing to lose either way, is there?"

"Not a thing." Except Ann, he thought. "I'm not giving up on it, Claud. It's here." He punched at his stomach. "Here in the gut, and here, in the brain. I see no point in charging around London when I feel this is the most logical place. If you come up with a statistic that's on the mark, then I'll change my mind."

He excused himself from the superintendent, and walked with Trotter to the big doors, then out onto the terrace which fronts the Festival Hall.

Trotter went off on his errand, and Dobson stood there, looking out over the river: gentle, calm, unruffled water. Across and downstream he could see the lights of the Embankment, like pearls strung out between the standards.

"String of Pearls." Dobson could hear it in his head. Glenn Miller. This is where we came in. Maybe it's the best place to go out.

He sniffed at the air, reflected, for only a second, upon Ann—her face, mind and the feelings he held for her—then turned and went back into the gleaming foyer.

"You fancy some tea? Coffee, or something?" the superintendent asked him. The police officer had followed and now stood just inside the door.

"Love some coffee." What else was there to do but sound perky?

"Some of the kind ladies have provided in the bar," smiled the super. "Might as well get Major Addenbrooke in with us."

Major Addenbrooke was CO of the Army bomb disposal team: the man Dobson had seen in the foyer. He had a firm handshake, but looked almost boyish. Accepting the coffee, he asked if his sergeant could join them.

"After all, he's got the radio." He spoke in the matter-of-fact manner of a tough, Sandhurst-trained man who had seen a fair bit of service and knew the score about life, death, love and the pursuit of peace.

The sergeant was friendly, sitting just a little apart: with them but not of them. A woman with gray hair showing in small streaks through its jet dye served the coffee, and they began to talk. Major Addenbrooke and his sergeant had served together in Ireland, though Dobson was surprised they had not been briefed on the type of device they might have to deal with. He sprang it on them, uncertain if he was being wise.

Nobody showed any visible sign of alarm. "Well, at least it's something different," the major said. "Bio-device. They did tell us not to tamper except in the desperate emergency period from five o'clock onward. Five-thirty, five forty-five's the clock setting?"

"That's what we're told." Dobson sipped his coffee and wondered if he should say more.

The major muttered, "Respirators," to his sergeant, who went away into a corner and began to talk into his handset.

Dobson did not disillusion them. Respirators might not be much help.

Then Trotter came back. The super got himself introduced this time, the major was pleasant and more coffee arrived.

"This is the nearest to your seventy thousand," Trotter said, speaking low. "And the Porton Down team're sitting in one of their vans at the Yard. There's been one small, abortive panic at Piccadilly. Apart from that, nothing."

"Drink your coffee and stay with me."

Later, during the spasmodic conversation, Trotter leaned over and muttered, "You're right. What you're doing, I mean."

Dobson acknowledged with a smile.

After four o'clock things began to tense up. Then the first real hint came a couple of minutes before the half hour. One of the inspectors from the foyer came in, moving fast, looking for the super.

"I think we have something." He dithered, not knowing whether to speak in front of everyone.

"Come on, man." The superintendent was on his feet. They all were, except Dobson, who just sat, waiting, feeling a spring coil inside him.

"Small, sir, but useful. A Post Office van driver—I've got him outside..."

"Just tell us," Dobson cut through.

"Delivering a van-load of mail at around two o'clock on Monday morning, from Mount Pleasant. Says he parked in the usual area and noticed a small black Commer van in among the Post Office vehicles. There were four men coming back to the van from along the main concourse..."

"Descriptions?" Dobson was on his feet now.

"Not very clear."

"Carrying gear?"

"They were dressed in British Rail overalls and carrying toolboxes. You want him in?"

"Now." Dobson knew he was speaking too loudly. Shouting almost.

Trotter gripped his arm, for a second, as though holding him back.

The Post Office van driver was in his late twenties; intelligent, not overawed by authority.

"I didn't think nothing about it until they hauled me in here tonight," he began. "There were four of them. One carried a large metal toolbox, and one of the others had some kind of big metal case. I took them to be maintenance. Lot of them around at night."

"They probably were," Dobson tried to reassure him.

"It was the van, though, that made me first think. It wasn't an official vehicle. Didn't even connect till the man asked me, out there."

"Definitely four."

"I been counting since I was two years old, guv'nor. One of them even said, 'Good night, mate.' Four—like two from six."

"We should've had photographs." Dobson turned to Trotter, who stepped forward.

"Listen, man, I'm the law and I'm not bein' heavy..."

"Oh yeah?"

"And I'm not goin' to put words in your mouth, but listen very carefully. I'm going to describe a fella." He did so, giving a word picture of Hackstead that Dobson could never have matched in a million years, it was so perfect.

The Post Office van driver nodded. "That was the one what spoke to me. Him to a T."

Yes, Dobson considered, it would be like Hackstead to speak—"Good night, mate," using his English voice.

Trotter asked the inspector to get a statement from the van driver.

"Sure."

"They got into the van and drove off?" Dobson asked the driver.

"Two in the back. Two in the front. Irish caper, is it?"

"Quite possibly." He turned to the young major. "I'm going down onto that main concourse. Your people there already?"

The major nodded.

"You can come down in our car then." To the super he said, "Get some kind of permanent patch-through with our car and start asking everyone again. The same question—four British Rail maintenance men. Right?"

"Will do."

Trotter went hurrying after him, to talk about the radio link and then get down to the car.

"We'll have to do it through control," he told Dobson as they hurried round the terrace and down the steps to where the car was parked.

It was now almost quarter to five.

"I'll have them tear the place to pieces," Dobson snarled, the major and his sergeant at his side. To Trotter: "As soon as we're in the car I want you to call in the lot. Porton Down, troops, even the Foreign Legion. The plague is on that bloody station."

The pair of Army men crammed into the back with Dobson; Trotter was speaking before they even started to roll.

They circled the station, coming in down the long drive slope, police and military moving out of their way—straight onto the main concourse.

It was an eerie sight—the station divested of its normal bustle of travelers, or the nighttime peace of a few tired, waiting or stranded people. Now there were just uniforms—police and military—everywhere. Wherever you looked doors were ajar, the bookstalls, usually tightly shuttered during the night hours, wide open; men searching everywhere.

Two Army colonels with some high-ranker from the Metropolitan Police were at the car within seconds, obviously briefed that they were coming. They showed extraordinary deference to Dobson, who found it both amusing and disconcerting. Then his stomach started to turn over again. Looking up, he saw the big station clock that he had known since childhood. The large hand moved as he looked at it. Three minutes to five.

"Up there?" asked one of the colonels.

"Could be." Dobson knew it could not be. Nobody would

have missed people working on the clock. "I've called up reinforcements. Just take the place apart. You know what we're after. A canister about..."

"Everyone has the description," the other colonel said. "It's definitely here?"

"Absolutely. If we haven't located in twenty-five minutes I'm asking you to evacuate."

"Almost doin' so already," Trotter murmured in his ear.

"Then we'll see if the squad from Porton Down can do anything," Dobson went on. "Just dismantle anything that moves or can be dismantled."

The car radio started to crackle. Trotter was there in a second, acknowledging, Dobson leaning at the open door as the big policeman sat, half in, half out, of the car.

"Sierra Bravo Six I read."

"Sierra Bravo Six we have a patch-through to Waterloo Control. They have vital information."

The radio crackled as Trotter acknowledged.

The spring within Dobson tightened. He could feel the bomb disposal major and his sergeant just behind him, listening.

"Sierra Bravo Six. Waterloo Control. We have a positive. Railway Police officer, questioned for the second time, now refers us to four BR maintenance workers carrying out repairs on top—repeat top—of train departures indicator board. Says he queried and their papers in order, including work sheets, but four men match earlier description."

Trotter acknowledged, swinging himself out of the car. "Over there," he pointed up the platform. The big indicator board stood almost immediately in front of the main bookstall. "On the top somewhere."

"One of my lads has been along the top already," the second colonel said, sounding quite shocked.

"Right, lads. Into the station." The sergeant was talking into his handset. "Main concourse. Departure indicator board. Ladders. All usual equipment."

Dobson began to run, slithering to a halt in front of the big wood and metal structure with its little black metal oblongs which ran, in columns, down the front. The oblongs, as he remembered them, constantly changed, so that you could read off the station names against times and platform numbers which ran along the top of the board. He had never realized before what a thick and solid structure it was.

The military bomb disposal team was breaking through

onto the concourse now. They had obviously been kept on
standby in the parking area running along the side of the station.
Three teams of men were carrying ladders.

"To hell with the ladders," the major said. "That's going to
take too bloody long." He began to run, mounting the barrier in
front of the board, his sergeant following him while their men
plodded on, setting up ladders.

Dobson was vaguely aware of other people coming
through onto the concourse now, and of vehicles and the sound
of police sirens.

The big clock was just behind him, suspended above the
entrance to the underground station.

It was six minutes past five.

Dobson turned on the little group of officers. "I want
everyone off, except those immediately engaged in trying to
locate. That means everyone except the team now in operation,
and the Porton Down people when they arrive."

"Just arriving now," somebody said. There seemed to be
general confusion, and the bomb team were not doing their best
with the collapsible ladders.

The major and his sergeant were making progress, though,
scaling the board from the front, smashing their boots through
the oblong revolving signs, hauling themselves up from the place
names so well known to London commuters—through Bentley
and Alton, Farnham and Aldershot, Woking, Surbiton and
Southhampton—their boots sliding, hands grasping and gripping, slipping, when a sign would not give way.

The major made it first. Crawling along the top of the
wooden framework.

Dobson looked around to find Professor Reeves from
Porton Down standing next to him, hands cupped to his mouth.

"It's a drum. Old with a clockwork timer."

"I bloody know that," the major shouted back. "There's
nothing here... Hang on..."

The sergeant made the top and was crawling, on hands and
knees, toward the major, who now knelt as though examining the
wooden framework. Then he shouted again.

"There's a panel here... Been tampered with... Screws
loose..."

The two men were kneeling opposite each other working
with screwdrivers. A clatter, then a piece of wood coming away,
as they lifted a section out and then slung it down onto the
platform, where it splintered, cut in two as if with a saw.

"It's here," the major shouted down. "They've bolted it inside the framework. No...they've bolted a shelf inside...It's sitting on the shelf. I can see the timer...Christ, it's close..."

"Get those bloody ladders up, for God's sake," Reeves was yelling. "If we can get it out and lower it...We've got a sealed van outside..."

"I think I can stop the clock."

"Don't take any chances, man. There may be a trigger if you try to stop it."

The voices echoed in the concourse, and Dobson turned, momentarily, as though to look for somewhere to hide.

The major's voice floated down. "No traps on this: it's as old as Hades."

"For pity's sake," from Reeves.

"Spot on," the major shouted back. "I can do it from here."

A fragment of time seemed to reach out into eternity.

"The clock has stopped." The major's voice drifted down loud. "All safe and sound now. Let's have some ropes and tackle. I'll putty up the timer and we can defuse in your van, sir—that is, if you're one of the Porton Down team."

Reeves looked a little shocked and hurt.

"No way she can blow now." The major was standing upright.

Dobson clapped his hands together.

The major acknowledged with a small bow, then turned back to his sergeant.

The news spread. Police and military were filtering back onto the station concourse, starting to clear up, pack away gear, put things back together again. It was almost five-thirty and the trains should be running.

Dobson leaned back against the bookstall and felt for his cigarettes. As he put one between his lips, a large black paw came up clutching a lighter.

"I've just done one of the most stupid things of my life," Trotter said, shaking with laughter. "I got myself so shit scared I tried to hide."

"Stupid?" queried Dobson.

"Come see where I was hiding." He took hold of Dobson's arm and led him around the bookstall. Toward the back of the concourse, in front of the restaurant areas, was a display platform set up by a firm advertising their particular brand of double-glazing. The center of the display was a flimsy little house—like a child's doll house—with one wall made up of double-glazing. A large banner said, *Wild's Double-Glazing Keeps Out Anything.*

"That's where I hid." Trotter's chuckle became infectious.

Slowly Dobson began to laugh, not knowing if it was because of Trotter or the overwhelming relief giving vent to a kind of hysteria.

The radio stations around the country were already starting to warn people that Waterloo would not be running its normal schedule until later in the day, owing to the successful defusing of a bomb in the early hours. Someone, somewhere, suggested that it was the IRA's work.

Dobson walked back toward the indicator board, where they were lowering the canister with great care. It looked, as he imagined, like an oversized biscuit tin.

He wanted nothing more to do with it now. What he wanted was the fresh early morning air on his face. He turned and went down the subway, following the signs to Waterloo Bridge. It was light, and the string of pearls across on the Embankment had gone out in favor of a pearly morning.

It's what people must have felt like at the height of the London blitz in the forties, he considered. A headiness, relief that you were still alive and that the city was still there.

As he reached the middle of the bridge the hands of Big Ben moved, the minute hand springing onto six. Suddenly he wanted Ann very badly.

41

They were married the following summer. It took that time for Ann's shoulder to mend. It also took concentration, sheer guts and determination. Days when she would weep and feel she was never going to use the shoulder again. But with the daily sessions of physiotherapy, and the nightly exercises, the afternoons in the swimming pool working with one of the best specialists in that field, the muscles began to gather strength and the nerves, like the bones, knitted together.

It was a tough year for Ann, and difficult also for Dobson. There were the nightmares and sudden bouts of nervous fear—anxiety states, the doctor told him.

He never found out what happened to Hackstead. He was certainly never brought into court. Dobson wondered how they arranged these things. Had they given him a few thousand pounds to forget and purge himself, then put him on a flight for South America? He thought not. There were other ways, far more effective.

In an attempt to erase the fear within himself, Dobson resorted to many things. They included reading every book he could find about the plague: the Black Death. Surprisingly it helped, for he knew that he, David Dobson, was partly responsible for saving England, at least, from a revisitation of the *Pestisatra*.

Yet when he read he always thought of Hackstead and that strange, ghostly, eerie flight which had ended in a kind of disaster, though much smaller than it might have been. There were questions he dearly wanted to ask Bud Hackstead— Bernhard Hackensteiner. What, for instance, was it really like to sit in the shrouded part-lit cockpit with a dead Russian Jew swaying about in the seat harness next to him? Did he know or feel anything about the load he carried? Probably not. Did the boys from Bomber Command feel for the people of Hamburg, Cologne, Berlin? It was war.

So he and Ann were married, and he chose the date carefully: June 5. Claud Trotter was his best man, Sugden and Terry Makepiece came to the reception. The groupie did not. They had put him out to grass properly at the end of the year. He had gone to live in Spain.

They spent their first night, lavishly, in an inordinately expensive London hotel. Rose early the next morning and drove down to Dover. The honeymoon was to be spent motoring across France down to the waterholes of the Mediterranean around Cannes, Nice, Monte Carlo.

They rose early and drove down, even though they were not crossing until the late afternoon boat. They had both decided there was something that had to be done first, and before leaving the opulent London hotel, Dobson picked up the box he had ordered from the florist.

They turned off the Dover road and headed along the coast to New Romney, then went inland, through the lanes and out onto the track where Dead Clump had once been.

The ground was quite flat now and there were no traces of any unusual happening. They stood, hand in hand, on the exact spot where *Dancing Dodo* had been found a year ago. Today was June 6.

Dobson went to the car, opened the box and took out the small posy of flowers. Okay, he thought, maybe it is sentimental. Maybe there were people who would not understand, but it was important to him.

Gently he laid the posy on where the wreckage of *Dodo*'s fuselage had lain for so many years, undisturbed and undiscovered.

There was a card attached to the posy. Some of the words on it were written by one of the greatest war poets who ever died in battle.

The card said:

In memory of six unknown Russian Jews; Herbert J. Flax, USAAF; Doris Lambert; SS Sturmbannführer Franz Ebenskrumm and SS Oberführer Bernhard Hackensteiner, who died for their various countries and ideals.

> *"I am the enemy you killed, my friend. Let us sleep now."*

As they stood there, a chill gust of wind came in over the marsh from the Channel. Dobson shivered. Someone walking over his grave? Perhaps he had seen a ghost here: or even a world full of ghosts.

ABOUT THE AUTHOR

JOHN GARDNER lives in Surrey, England. Mr. Gardner's life has encompassed many experiences and occupations, including Royal Marine Commando officer, magician, theater critic, and writer. His writings, which include the famous Boysie Oates stories, are tough and compelling novels of superb background detail. Those books include THE DANCING DODO and THE WEREWOLF TRACE.

Currently Gardner is on all bestseller lists with his James Bond novels including ROLE OF HONOR, FOR SPECIAL SERVICES, and ICEBREAKER.

The terrifying new bestseller
by the author of
NATHANIEL and SUFFER THE CHILDREN

JOHN SAUL
BRAINCHILD

La Paloma—once home to a proud Spanish heritage, now a thriving modern community high in the California hills.

And home to a boy named Alex Lonsdale . . . who is about to become the instrument of a terrible, undying evil. An evil that cries out for vengeance for a terrible deed done long ago.

An evil that now waits in the dark and secret places of La Paloma . . . for Alex Lonsdale.

Don't miss John Saul's BRAINCHILD, coming in August 1985 from Bantam Books.